**Durham** County Council   Adults, Wellbeing and Health
Libraries, Learning and Culture

Please return or renew this item by the last date shown.
Fines will be charged if the book is kept after this date.
Thank you for using your library.

Renew online at www.durham.gov.uk/libraryonline

ALSO BY ANNEMARIE BREAR

<u>Historical</u>

Kitty McKenzie

Kitty McKenzie's Land

Southern Sons

To Gain What's Lost

Isabelle's Choice

Nicola's Virtue

Aurora's Pride

Grace's Courage

Eden's Conflict

Catrina's Return

Where Rainbow's End

Broken Hero

The Promise of Tomorrow

The Slum Angel

Beneath a Stormy Sky

The Market Stall Girl

The Tobacconist's Wife

<u>Marsh Saga Series</u>

Millie

Christmas at the Chateau

Prue

Cece

* * *

Nicola's Virtue

ANNEMARIE BREAR

CHAPTER 1

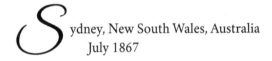
ydney, New South Wales, Australia
July 1867

NICOLA STOOD on the worn deck, one hand holding the rail, the other raised to shield her eyes from the sun's harshness reflecting off the dark water. A cool breeze rippled over her, reminding her that July in this part of the world was winter. Not much else seemed different for she was used to the strange looking trees now, as they'd been hugging the coastline for a few weeks. At first, the sharp smell of the eucalypt trees, with their thin grey-green leaves and the piercing squawks of unfamiliar birds had been a novelty after weeks of ocean. She had filled a sketchbook of the new land in the glimpses she'd been afforded from the ship's deck. Once settled, she'd do many more and try to sell them. Lord knows she needed any income available.

Shaking her head, she pulled her black shawl tighter around her shoulders, closing her eyes for a moment. She had to think positive thoughts. But, try as she might, the confidence, which had made her tempt such a drastic alteration to her life, began to ebb as easily as the tide beneath the ship. The excitement that gripped her on the wharves at Liverpool had vanished on waking this morning and realising that today they would dock, her ocean journey would end and a new life in a new country would start.

Behind her the ship's crew urgently jostled each other as they prepared to disembark. Amongst the flotilla of the vast harbour, a small white boat sailed towards the Lady Fair, the ship that had cradled her for seventy-one days. An easy voyage the crew stated, but she was simply relieved to have reached the other side of the world without mishap.

A weather worn deckhand paused by her side. 'Ere, Miss, yer off on't first boat?'

She turned to him, unable to smile for the nervousness that coiled her insides like the rope loops the sailors twisted. 'Yes, if I am able. Is that it there?'

He looked to the small boat coming close to rub alongside the hull. 'No, that's the pilot's boat, taking him back ashore. He's done his job and got us safely through the harbour.'

'Oh, I see.'

'Yer passed all clear?'

'Yes, Mr Gyngell, the surgeon, signed my papers. I'm in excellent health.' She glanced away as a line of rowboats headed towards them. The first one bumped alongside the ship's bulk. The flurry of activity in securing the small boat kept her speechless for a moment. She gazed over at the busy wharves and nibbled her upper lip in apprehension. She would need all her strength and well being to cope with what was ahead.

A vista of sailing ships, timber warehouses, pale stone buildings and narrow streets opened out before her. People scurried like mice found in a corn barrel. For a fleeting moment she wished one of those people were meeting her.

'How much do yer have below, Miss?' the seaman asked patiently.

'One trunk.'

He bent down to grasp her green velvet carpetbag. 'Is this going over the side with yer?'

'Yes, thank you.' She followed him to the rail where the First Mate stood giving orders. She interrupted the officer. 'Excuse me, may I go ashore now?'

The First Mate, Jones, flashed her a short smile. 'Ah, Miss Douglas. I see from my list you have been passed by the ship's doctor and your papers are correct.'

'Yes. Thank you.'

'Is there anyone coming aboard to meet you, Miss Douglas?'

'No.' She raised her chin in defiance to her plummeting heart. She would cope alone. Hadn't she been doing it for two years? Would this new place, this new town...Sydney be very different from home? The country was full of Englishmen, her people; they had the same language and customs. What did she have to worry about?

'Very well, since all is in order—'

'Thank you.' She nodded once, her gloved fingers gathering her black skirts in preparation to descend into the little boat below. With a deep breath, she climbed down the rope ladder until thick hands held her steady at the bottom.

Gripping the sides of the rowboat, she balanced herself and sat down. She was used to the gentle sway of the ship, but the rowboat's wild rocking as it filled with passengers alarmed her and she clutched her bag in mounting fear of being flung into the shadowy blue-green depths just inches away.

The crew settled themselves into the pull of the oars and the regular splash while they crept towards the wharf calmed the rocking and her. The fresh saltiness on the breeze tickled her nose. Land noise, not heard for some time, assaulted her ears as the wharf's steps loomed ahead. She tried to think clearly, to order her thoughts, only the feeling of trepidation made it difficult.

With a bump and a grind against green slime-covered stone steps, the rowboat was quickly secured and before she was aware, men handed her up the slippery steps and onto the wharf. The incessant noise, the sharp smells and the confusing sights of a busy dock area reeled her senses making her giddy. Her heart thudded. It seemed as though the wharf swayed, but she knew it didn't. How long would it take to get her land legs?

People crowded around, calling and talking, all busily going about their business. She shrank from a man who stalked by whistling loudly. Faces came and went in front of her and for a moment she couldn't take a step for the press of the crowd. Panic rose threatening to choke her. What should she do? A frightened moan escaped and she glanced around in mounting alarm. The carefully constructed plans she'd made on the voyage lay in tattered pieces floating around her mind. Nothing sensible formed and she had to fight the desperate urge not to cry. No, she must focus. She blinked rapidly, took a deep breath and fought for calm. Her sleeve was suddenly pulled. An urchin with a dirty face pushed back his cap and grinned at her. 'Want a cab, Miss? For a penny I can get your luggage to George Street. Do you have an address? Do yer want food? Drink?'

'No...' His persistent questions jabbed at her, leaving her even more unable to think clearly. 'No, thank you.'

The urchin grabbed her bag. Instinctively, she wrenched it from him. 'Get away from me!'

The boy laughed and ran off, leaving her trembling. She walked a few steps, the call of a newspaper boy filling her ears as he yelled out the latest details of the flooding disaster at Windsor. For one strange moment she thought he meant Windsor in England, but soon realised there must be another Windsor in this country.

'Miss Douglas!'

She turned and sagged in relief. First Mate Jones from the Lady Fair walked towards her, carrying her trunk over his shoulder as though it weighed no more than a bag of flour. He dumped it at her feet with a smile that showed a broken front tooth.

'You are kind.' She pushed back a stray tendril of hair that had escaped from under her hat. 'I had quite forgotten about it.'

'Not a bother, Miss. It's not hard to get muddled in a new port.' He swiped off his cap and wiped his sweating brow. 'I'll be glad to see the sun go down, that I will, for then we are ashore on leave for a week.' He smiled again, and she returned it.

'And you deserve it. It's been a long journey.'

'Are you waiting for a cab?'

'No…' She gazed around. 'I'd rather not waste money on that. Perhaps I can walk…I need accommodation…' Looking around at the hundreds of strangers filling the area, she doubted her sanity. How had she expected to cope alone in this place? She knew no one. Simply leaving the wharf would prove difficult with no clear direction of what to do. Where would she go?

'Listen, Miss, you need to get yourself up into town proper like, away from here. It's not the place to be, for a young lady like yourself, when it's dark.' His dark eyes shone with sympathy at her plight. 'Spend the money to get a hansom cab and find a decent hotel. There's plenty about the city. Hire a room for tonight so you can get your bearings and rest up a bit. Everything will seem better in the morning.'

She nodded. He talked sense. A hotel, of course. She

didn't want to be here at nightfall and a good night's sleep always made things seem better the next day. 'Thank you. I will.'

'Have you been cleared through immigration yet?'

'No.' Her spirits sank once more. She'd completely forgotten. How foolish was she? Had she lost all common sense? Her father wouldn't know her if he saw her standing in such a muddle. What was wrong with her?

'Right, then.' He heaved her trunk back up onto his shoulder. 'It's over here. Follow me.'

'You are extremely good, thank you.' The hollow ache of being alone lifted slightly and she quickened her step as he strode out amongst the teeming dockside.

The immigration building was airless and the rank odour of unwashed bodies made her breathe through her mouth. Rows of tables lined the far wall, and she spied other members from the ship in the snaking lines.

'I have to get back to the ship, Miss.' Jones deposited her trunk on the floor inside the building. 'You'll be all right now?'

'Oh yes. Thank you again.'

Jones grabbed a boy who lingered by the doorway. 'You, mind this lady's trunk until she comes back and you'll get ha'penny for your troubles. Yes?'

'Aye, mister.' The boy promptly sat on the trunk and picked at his dirty chipped fingernails.

'Here. I think you need this more than me.' Jones opened her hand and placed a half crown in her palm. 'Good luck, Miss Douglas. I hope you'll be happy.' He slipped away before she could thank him once more.

Staring at the half crown, emotion welled. There were kind people in the world. The First Mate had been particularly nice to her the whole voyage and often sought her out to chat in the evenings. He said she reminded him of his sister, whom he sorely missed back home in England. Generously, he had spent time with her and supplied information about the new country she'd be calling home.

She tucked the coin into her skirt pocket and took out a farthing from her own meagre supply in her reticule and handed it to the boy. 'You'll get another when I come back. I'll be watching, mind! So don't try anything.'

'Yes, Miss.'

As Nicola joined the queue she felt Jones's half-crown against her leg. It would be her talisman for the future. She would never spend it...unless she was desperate, but hopefully it would never come to that. The line surged forward, and she turned back to watch the boy, but he was busy scratching his head and paying no attention to anyone. Unlike the urchin on the wharf, he seemed happy to earn his money truthfully and she relaxed a little.

Around her families huddled, some complaining, some smiling in open relief to have made the voyage intact. A few foreigners talked in whispers, clutching everything they owned. A woman slipped her hand through a young man's and he gazed down at her with devotion. The feeling of being alone once more hit her. Had she been mad to make this journey, to leave England? After another glance back at the boy, she stepped forward as the line moved ahead. Eventually she stood in front of a desk and a young clerk, with a large Adam's apple bobbing above his starched white collar, asked for her papers. 'Name, Miss?'

Some of her spirit re-emerged. A new beginning. She had to be strong. Straightening her back, she raised her head with dignity. 'Miss Nicola Matilda Douglas. Spinster. Twenty-five years of age from Wakefield, Yorkshire, England.'

CHAPTER 2

*N*icola kept her head down against the cold wind. Scattered raindrops fell against her and she hurried along the street, eager to be back in the hotel. She laughed inwardly at the thought. The hotel room wasn't worth the money she spent on it but having no other choice she tolerated the peeling wallpaper and squeaking bed, the cheerful but slatternly landlady and the noise of the public house next to it. At least it was cheaper than the old Governesses Home, saving her three shillings a week.

At the end of the street she turned right and headed up the slight incline towards the shops at the top. She wished the post office was closer to the hotel to save her this walk, but still, it got her out of the oppressive room and also gave her a chance to become familiar with her surroundings. After four weeks of living in the area, she now knew all the street names between the hotel and the post office and where to buy the few supplies she needed.

Passing the small glass fronted shops, she nodded to one shopkeeper outside fixing his sign that seemed in danger of being blown down the street. 'Nasty day, isn't it, Mr Price?'

'Indeed, Miss Douglas. Not one to be out in,' he called back. 'Been to the post office again, have you?'

'Yes, I have.'

'Any luck yet?'

'No, but I'll keep trying.'

'No luck on selling your drawings so far, I'm sorry to say.'

'Thank you anyway, Mr Price.' She waved and walked on. The sale of one of her drawings displayed in Mr Price's shop would be welcome. Each day she became a little more frightened and desperate when she received no replies from the letters she sent about the 'Governess Wanted' advertisements in the newspapers. Even more alarming was the amount of advertisements from governesses wanting work. She had so many to compete with, many more than she expected.

When she had listened, totally enthralled in Miss Maria Rye's speech back home in England, she'd been led to believe that Australia was crying out for the want of decent educated young women – women who in turn would educate the children of the growing wealthy families the colony produced. She'd spent days in the local library studying up on the rise of the colony from its convict beginning to the successful and prosperous place it was today. Miss Rye's scheme to send out teachers and governesses seemed sound and Nicola had quickly spent what money she had on purchasing a ticket to Australia. At the time she felt assured she'd made the right decision. After all, what was there left for her in Wakefield? Her parents were dead and the last job she'd held as a governess had ended when the little girl she'd been instructed to teach had died of fever.

But now, she wondered how prudent she'd been. Her money pile grew shorter each day, and for the last few days she'd cut down on food to stem the amount being used. Soon, all she'd have left would be the First Mate's half crown and she was loathed to use it. She wasn't desperate yet...

Thinking of food made her stomach grumble. The slice of bread and weak cup of tea she had this morning wasn't enough to last all day, but she tried not to think about it. A bowl of warm soup this evening would be worth the wait and if her landlady took pity on her she might spare her a bit of cheese to go with it. The weight had fallen off her in the last weeks. Her poor diet resulted in the sharp jut of her bones, the lack of shine to her hair and her clothes became ill fitting.

Once at the top of the hill, she paused to catch her breath. The wind, being less encumbered by large buildings here, battered her, nearly ripping her hat from the pins securing it. Dust from the dirt road whirled in the gutters, coating everything in sandy grit. Tired and hungry, Nicola took a step, facing the gale head on. It wrapped around her, thrusting her skirts against her legs, imprisoning them. Within the time it took to walk a couple of steps, a wave of dizziness swamped her. The warmth drained from her face. She put out a hand on the shop wall to regain her balance. Strength seeped from her legs, her knees buckled, and she collapsed against the wall.

Closing her eyes, she took several deep breaths, willing herself to overcome the faint. She'd never been one to swoon and always lived a healthy active existence. Her hectic life before never gave her the chance to be ill or suffer a delicate disposition like her mother...

Nicola tried to regain her feet, but the effort took strength she didn't feel she had.

A black carriage pulled up further along the road. A stout gentleman climbed down the carriage steps and after donning his tall hat hurriedly walked towards her. 'Miss? May I be of assistance?'

She turned to him like a child seeking its mother. 'Oh, y-yes...'

'Are you ill or have you been attacked?' He looked about for an assailant.

'Not attacked. I-I felt faint.'

'Come, lean on my arm.' He took her elbow, supporting her weight easily. His large grey side-whiskers and friendly blue eyes helped to calm her. He reminded her of her grandfather long buried in a small graveyard in Wakefield, Yorkshire.

'Thank you.' She managed a quick shaky smile.

'Do you wait for family?' He scanned the area as if expecting someone to come and claim her.

'No. No one at all.' She blinked back the tears that blurred his round profile. In all her life she'd never been as emotional as she'd been in the last weeks; even saying goodbye to her homeland hadn't wrenched the tears as quickly as they formed now.

'Do you live close by? I can take you.'

She swallowed past the tightness in her throat. 'I shall be quite all right in a minute. Silly of me to not eat properly this morning.'

'Come to my carriage, I shall escort you home.'

'Thank you, but there is no need.' She straightened, ignoring the dizziness and forced her shoulders back and held her chin high. 'I'm much better already.'

'Where do you live?'

She smiled at his friendly persistence. 'I lodge at Cordell's Hotel.'

'Cordell's Hotel.' He frowned. 'You lodge, did you say?'

'Yes, until I can find work.'

'You are newly arrived in the city?'

She sighed. 'Is it obvious?'

'To me, yes, but that is because of my experience.' He gently guided her back to his carriage, his gold-topped cane tapping with every step. 'I am Frederick Belfroy.'

'Nicola Douglas. I thank you for your help.' She stopped and gave him a brief smile. Slight dizziness remained, but she grew stronger each minute.

'What is your trade, Miss Douglas?' Mr Belfroy asked, opening the carriage door.

'Governess, sir, but I can work as a teacher or child's nurse. I have-I have experience in both.'

'Do you have a letter of introduction?'

'Indeed, yes. In my room.' She gestured towards the distant hotel, where, in between the pages of her diary, lay her most important papers. 'Do you need a governess or perhaps might know of someone who might?'

'No, not myself, but I may be able to help you.'

Hope flooded her and she swayed again. 'I can show you my references. I'm honest and loyal and very punctual. I can teach piano and—'

'Come, come, my dear.' Belfroy gently stayed her urgency. 'First things first. Let us find an establishment that offers a refreshing cup of tea. Yes?'

In a daze she followed, not asking why he helped her and not really caring at the moment.

'Douglas... A Scot?' He helped her into the carriage before climbing in himself and giving instructions to his driver.

Nicola relaxed against the dark leather seat. 'My grandfather was, yes.'

'Splendid. The Scottish are fine people. Very hard working. And inventive. I met a man once…'

His words grew dim as Nicola swayed, blackness threatening to swallow her.

'Oh I say, Miss Douglas!'

Her last thought was of Mr Belfroy's alarmed expression.

* * *

NICOLA SAT STIFFLY on the iron bed, its white sheets and grey-green blanket pulled so tight, she was worried she might bounce right back off them. Beside her she placed the carpetbag, and at her feet, stood her large trunk. Through the small square window opposite, she looked out over a narrow yard with its own vegetable garden and line of washing at the end. She remembered little of the last hour. Only, that Mr Belfroy had collected her luggage and insisted that she be looked after in his own establishment. The rest of his conversation, of packing her things, moving to this house and being greeted by an older couple had simply gone over her head. She had been guided and led, talked to and fussed over and her mind, which felt like it was stuffed with wool, couldn't take in any of it.

Mrs Eldersley, the landlady, had brought up a jug of hot water and a freshly laundered towel before bustling back downstairs. The wash refreshed Nicola but she longed for the bath she had ordered for later. Weeks without a proper bath made her skin itch.

A knock sounded at the door and it was opened before Nicola gave admittance. Mrs Eldersley hurried in, her thick bulk instantly dwarfing the room. She smiled with motherly wholesomeness.

'Well, my dear, are you settled yet? At least your colour has returned to your cheeks.' She spoke between puffs while placing a tea tray onto the washstand.

From her earlier experience downstairs, Nicola knew the older woman didn't need an answer to her questions.

'I've got a nice pot of tea here for you and some of my pound cake. There's a good piece of mutton simmering for your dinner,' she continued, pouring the tea and adding a dollop of cream to the cup. 'Mr Eldersley is cutting some kindling for your fire, and I'll have it laid ready for when you have your bath.'

'Thank you, Mrs Eldersley, you are most kind.'

The landlady swelled at the compliment. 'Well, happen I don't want my reputation to suffer by not giving a good service.' She heaved up her heavy bosom with her arm and swept a critical glance around the plain but spotless room. 'I may not have run a boarding house for long, a mere six months, but I can keep a clean house fit for Queen Victoria herself.'

Nicola smiled. 'I am most fortunate Mr Belfroy brought me here.' The gentleman had proven to be a valuable new friend.

'Aye, Mr Belfroy is a good man. It was his idea for me to set up a boarding house once my husband's ill health made me unable to work for him any longer.'

'Does Mr Belfroy live close by?' Nicola sipped the tea handed to her. It tasted different to that of home, but it was not unpleasant, and like most things she would become used to it.

'Oh no, dear, he's on yonder side of the harbour.' Mrs Eldersley flicked at a speck of fluff on the bed's thin blanket. 'Poor man is at a loss since his lovely wife died some months back. She went to the grave taking their newborn son with her. Most tragic.' She shook her head in sadness. 'I did think Mr Belfroy would lose his head over the whole incident. She was much younger than him and not of his class, not that he cared, even if others did. Now I believe he thinks he's too old to try again. You see he saved her, his wife, I mean, saved her from a marriage to a brute of a man. Such a kind soul is Mr Belfroy.'

The distant sound of the front door bell tinkling brought Mrs Eldersley's head up with a snap. 'I do hope that's not more ladies arriving. Three left yesterday and with only you here I was hoping for a bit of quiet. Now drink that tea and eat up that cake. Mr Belfroy said you're nothing but skin and bones and he won't have it and neither will I.' With a hasty exit she left Nicola alone to the silence of her room.

After finishing her tea and a piece of cake, Nicola felt better, more able to concentrate. She gazed down at her trunk. Within its age-worn timbers rested her most treasured possessions. The last link she had to her family, her home.

Reverently, she unlocked the weighty lid and carefully pushed it back until it laid bare her life. The musty odour of the ship's hulk cloaked the contents. Nicola gently lifted out the top layer of clothes and put them on the bed. She ran her fingertips over the leather bound books stacked in the corner before taking them out and placing them on the floor rug she knelt on. Little boxes of personal items joined the books, along with a pair of supper slippers, her jewellery case, and a small hatbox containing her best black felt hat, her paints, an old sketch book and a pouch of charcoal. In another corner, she picked up her mother's blue woollen shawl and buried her face into it, trying desperately to smell her mother's faint lavender scent. Wrapped sheltered in the folds of her father's handkerchief, she took out the miniature portrait of her parents. Nicola smiled at their familiar faces.

'Mother, Father,' she whispered. 'Well, I am here, on the other side of the world. Who would have thought?' She ran her fingers tenderly over the frame. 'It has been a long journey, but I am safe and well. You would have been most interested in all that I've seen, Father.' Her gaze shifted to look out the window at the endless blue sky and she imagined her parents looking down on her with pride.

The clamour of footsteps on the wooden stairs outside her door made Nicola rise from her knees. She began picking up her items when another knock sounded before the door opened again.

'My dear, Miss Douglas,' Mrs Eldersley hustled in, 'let me

introduce Miss Robinson.' She pushed in front of her a rosy-cheeked, sparkling-eyed, curly black-haired young woman, who was already laughing at Nicola.

'Pleased to meet you, Miss Douglas,' the newcomer boomed loud enough to make Nicola take a step back in surprise.

'Likewise, er...Miss Robinson.' Nicola offered her hand and found it pumped up and down.

'Call me Meg. You just docked, have you? Fresh meat and all that, hey?' Meg laughed and picked up Nicola's sketch-book. 'You draw? I just landed in from the bush out west. The countryside here is a God-awful place that is all dust and flies and nothing, miles and miles of nothing. Can you imagine? I couldn't until I saw it for myself. And then there's the threat of Bushrangers. A gang of them held up an inn only ten miles from where I was staying. Imagine that.' She put down the sketchbook and picked up a book. 'How did you like the voyage? I've heard it's a bothersome bore. I was born here, see, never been to good ole England.'

Nicola's head swam as Meg didn't pause for breath. She turned to Mrs Eldersley for help.

At once the older woman took the signal. 'Come, come, Miss Robinson, I must show you your room.'

'Lord, yes, I'm near dying from thirst. I'm sure I have swallowed more grit than a camel in a dust storm.' Meg followed their landlady out, but at the door she quickly turned back to Nicola. 'See you downstairs for high tea, Miss Douglas.' She put her gloved finger to her lips and gave Nicola a grim look. 'What is your first name? I cannot call you Miss Douglas all the time, that would be too tiresome.'

'Nicola.'

Meg grinned and her rounded cheeks developed two identical dimples. 'That's a pretty name. It suits you.' She tossed her head and her black curls bounced. 'My mother gave me a mouthful of a name and I will never forgive her. Margaret Helen Alice Mary Robinson, can you imagine?' Meg laughed. 'She was most put out that at the age of five I insisted on plain Meg.' She sobered for a moment and looked thoughtful. 'Mother spent the vast majority of her time and mine being put out over something I had done.' Suddenly the grin returned wider than before. 'Still, parents must be disappointed in their children at one time or another, otherwise it spoils their old age, nothing to whine about see!'

Nicola closed the door on Meg's laughter. Exhaustion dragged at her bones. She slipped her belongings off the bed and then laid down without taking her ankle boots off. A sigh escaped as she relaxed and snuggled further into the mattress. Images and people fluttered behind her closed eyelids. Meg's laughter filtered through the walls. Nicola smiled. What on earth would happen to her next?

CHAPTER 3

*T*he wind gusted down the street chasing papers along the gutters. Nicola held onto her black hat with one hand and with her other struggled to hold her parcels. Unable to gather up her skirts, she staggered against the battering gale. Constant cold, windy days grew tedious. Mrs Eldersley mentioned that on this side of the world late August was known for its wind and gales. Privately, Nicola would be glad to see spring, which if she looked closely enough at the trees she could just see the hint of blossom opening.

Suddenly, she was bumped and jolted to the side as a gentleman exiting a shop knocked into her.

'Forgive me, please.' He made a small bow to her just as the wind took hold of his hat, sending it trundling off along the paved footpath.

Nicola turned to watch him chase after it and couldn't help but chuckle at the spectacle. With a smile on her lips, she continued her journey back to the Eldersley's Lodging House, which although only a few miles from Cordell's

Hotel, was in a much more influential area on the edge of Double Bay.

She hoped a letter waited for her on the small table in the hall. Since coming to Eldersley's she'd had two interviews, but no appointment as yet. For a moment her smile faltered and then disappeared altogether to be replaced by a frown. If there wasn't a governess role for her at present then she could manage for a few weeks more on the money she brought with her, as Mr Belfroy insisted she pay no rent until she had work, but after that she'd have to find alternative work. So far, she'd managed to sell three of her drawings, two to Mr Belfroy friends and one in Mr Price's shop. Mr Belfroy suggested that she should send them to England to be sold, but she had no agent and knew no one well enough to trust with such a task.

Turning up the street, she squinted against the wind to see a gig outside the lodging house. Curiosity made her hurry. Maybe someone had come about the new advertisement she put in the paper two days ago.

She opened the gate and lightly ran up the path to the front door. The blustery gale helped her to open it and nearly wrenched it out of her hands as she stepped into the hallway. A vase of flowers positioned on the cedar hall table teetered dangerously at the sudden gust and Nicola steadied it before shutting the door and then placing her parcels beside the vase. A quick glance showed no envelopes with her name on them and her spirits plummeted.

Hearing voices in the front sitting room, she quickly unpinned her hat. Taking off her gloves, she then dropped them on top of her parcels and put a hand to her hair that was beyond help in its present tangled state.

The door to the sitting room was partially open and with a gentle push Nicola stepped into the room. She paused as Mrs Eldersley stood from the settee where she had been comforting a young woman, who cried into her crumpled handkerchief. Across from them in another chair sat a pale-faced older woman.

'Oh, Miss Douglas.' Mrs Eldersley looked relieved to have another to share her worry. 'Do come in.'

'I do not wish to intrude…'

'No, you aren't. We have two more guests.' Mrs Eldersley indicated to the older woman seated. 'Miss Burstall and…' She quickly sat next to the younger one, who broke into fresh sobbing. 'And this is Miss Downing.'

Nicola inclined her head to them both. 'Is there anything I can do?'

Mrs Eldersley heaved to her feet once more, her face creasing into a frown. 'Can you sit here a minute, dear? I'll go and make some tea.'

Nicola perched by the weeping Miss Downing not knowing whether she should make conversation. One look at Miss Burstall's hard features made her decide to remain silent for the moment.

Miss Downing raised her head from her soddened hand-kerchief. She was very young and pretty with wide blue eyes like a porcelain doll. Nicola smiled.

Wiping her reddened eyes, Miss Downing shuddered. 'I am sorry.'

'There is no need to be.' Although she had no idea why the young woman cried so dreadfully. Nicola patted her hand and was surprised when the girl grasped hers tightly.

'I would never have left my home if I thought I'd end up like this.'

Nicola frowned. 'Do not take it to heart, Miss Downing. Many of us are out of work, but I am sure that sooner or later we shall all find suitable situations.'

'I thought there were plenty of positions out here. I

begged my father to let me come to this country, but it was such a mistake and now I can never go back.'

'How long have you been here?'

'Two years. I've hardly been able to find constant work as a governess, so I've worked as a children's nurse, done some teaching, been a kitchen maid and even lowered myself to-to being a barmaid...' At this, Miss Burstall snorted and pulled her skirts away from them. Miss Downing broke into heart wrenching sobs that frightened Nicola. 'And now...and now...'

'You will find a good situation I am certain.' She looked to Miss Burstall for help, but the other woman merely narrowed her eyes.

'You...I cannot...not now...Oh, I'm so ashamed.' The girl collapsed into Nicola's arms just as Mrs Eldersley came in carrying the tea tray.

'Come, my dear, enough crying.' Mrs Eldersley placed the tray on an occasional table next to Miss Burstall. She crossed to fold Miss Downing into her ample bosom. 'Shush now. Here, have some tea.'

Nicola rose and poured for them all. She glanced at Miss Burstall as she passed her a cup and saucer. The woman's clothing, a black, plain dress made in serviceable cloth denoted her station in life. 'Are you also waiting for a situation, Miss Burstall?'

The woman quickly looked up with cold brown eyes. 'Naturally. Would I be here otherwise?' She declined the cup and stood. 'Mrs Eldersley may I go up to my room?'

'Yes, of course. It's the second door on the left at the top of the stairs. Shall I bring your tea up for you?'

'No, thank you.' Miss Burstall's gaze flickered over the tea service as though it was caked in filth. Head held high, she left them without further comment.

Hiccupping, Miss Downing stared after her. 'I am not one to speak ill of others, but she is such an unbending dragon.'

Nicola sipped her tea. 'You know of her?'

'We came out together on the same boat through the Scheme. Since then we have seen each other at odd times.'

'The scheme for governesses, the FMCE Society?'

'Yes, led by Miss Rye. You did not come through them?'

'No. I journeyed out by myself, but I heard Miss Rye speak and her words encouraged me to come here.'

Miss Downing's eyes widened. 'Alone? That was brave of you.'

Nicola smiled. 'Well, others would say different.'

Mrs Eldersley hurried to the window and twitched the lace curtains aside. 'Here comes Meg.' She sighed. 'Lord, I'm too old to cope with such upheaval.'

Nicola replaced her teacup on the tray. 'Who owns the gig outside?'

'That's the good doctor's. He's across the road looking in on old Mr Palmer. He brought Miss Downing and Miss Burstall here.' Mrs Eldersley let the curtain fall as noise from the hall announced Meg.

Miss Downing stood, swaying a little. 'I had better go to my room, Mrs Eldersley. I'm not fit for company.' She hurriedly left the room and they heard Meg say good day to her in the hall.

Nicola turned to her landlady. 'Is Miss Downing ill?'

With a tired sigh, Mrs Eldersley tidied the tea tray. 'Only if you call being with child ill.'

'Oh my.'

'Indeed. Terrible luck, poor girl. Doctor Armitage is a good man and brought her here when he found her wandering the streets. He knows of Mr Belfroy's generosity.'

'Wandering the streets?'

'Yes.' Mrs Eldersley paused as Meg strolled into the room.

'Oh, Nicola, you are back, good.' Meg beamed. 'Did you get my book from the shop?'

Nicola scowled. 'Indeed, I did, but only after I paid your outstanding bill of one and six! I was mortified to be asked for money. You said I only had to collect it.'

Meg giggled. 'Oh, I am sorry, you really shouldn't have paid.'

Mrs Eldersley picked up the tray. 'No, she shouldn't. I'll thank you, Miss Robinson, to not ruin my reputation by leaving accounts all around town.' She hustled out of the room.

Flopping onto the sofa, Meg unpinned her hat. 'She didn't leave me any tea.'

Nicola shook her head. 'Really, Meg, you do stretch the boundaries of a short friendship.'

'Oh pooh.' Meg straightened. 'Are you seriously cross with me?' She pouted. 'You know I will pay you back soon.'

'With what? You have nothing left and now neither do I,' she lied. She wasn't going to let Meg know about the dwindling money she had remaining.

Meg examined her nails. 'I shall write to Aunt Eunice. It has been six months since my last hand out, surely she can spare a little more of her fortune.'

'Why does she not give you an allowance or allow you live with her?'

'Aunt Eunice hates Mother, Mother hates me, so Aunt Eunice feeds me little crumbs and delights in letting Mother know.'

Nicola walked to the window and watched the wind toss the tree branches. 'Why does your mother dislike you?'

'Because she found me rolling in the hay with a groom, because I loved father and she didn't, because I wasn't a son. The list is endless.' Meg abruptly stood. 'Who are the newcomers?'

'Two more out of work governesses. The doctor brought them.' She glanced at Meg. Rolling in the hay with a groom? She'd never met anyone as wild as Meg. Shaking the thought from her mind she caught sight of Dr Armitage climbing back into his gig. 'Why did the doctor bring the women here? Is Mrs Eldersley known as a woman's safe house or something?'

'Why do you ask?'

'Everyone who comes here seems out of work, short of money and down on their luck and female.'

Meg shrugged. 'Mr Belfroy is the benefactor, as you know. He's rich and supports the keeping of this house.' She frowned, giving Nicola one of her sly looks. 'You do know about Mr Belfroy, don't you?'

'Yes, that he lost his wife and child in childbirth.'

'She wasn't of his class. Imagine that.'

'So?'

'He saved her. You see, she escaped from a husband who battered her black and blue and she ran off to live on the streets. Old Belfroy found her one day and gave her money for food, but her husband dragged her back home. A few months later, Belfroy found her again, beaten. He fell madly in love with her. He arranged to pay the husband off and managed to have her divorced through the courts. It was a long and expensive problem for him, but he wouldn't give up until she was free, then he promptly married her. Caused a huge scandal amongst his circle.'

'He's a good man then, to go against everything for love.'

'Yes, or stupid. He lost many friends. However, he doesn't seem to care.' Meg stretched and yawned. 'After Belfroy's first experience with women living on the streets, through no fault of their own, he became their champion, and that includes us lot.' She grinned. 'He set up his former housekeeper, Mrs Eldersley, in this house and vowed to save as many women as possible.'

'How admirable.' Nicola felt awed to be rescued by such a noble man.

'He's got more money than sense if you ask me.' Meg flounced to the door. 'Fancy going to see a show tonight?' She called over her shoulder.

'You have no money.' Nicola rolled her eyes and Meg just laughed.

* * *

Rain splattered their dress hems. The puddles in the road shone in the gas lamplights like spilt ink.

'We'll not be fit to be seen,' Meg complained as they dodged a spray of water from a passing carriage.

'You suggested we walk,' Nicola muttered, shaking out her best skirt in the shade of emerald. 'I didn't even want to come out tonight and only did so to give Miss Burstall a rest from your teasing.'

'Miss Burstall is a—'

'Don't say it, Meg.'

Tossing her head, Meg sniffed. 'Well, she is. She delights in giving everyone cold looks and little sniffs of disapproval. What makes her think she is better than us?'

'I agree she lacks...compassion.'

'And most other human feelings.'

They rounded a corner and merged into a busier city street. Anxious, having never been out at night in Sydney's streets, Nicola scanned the shadows for possible threats. Her parents would have been mortified about her walking the streets of a strange city at night.

Meg brightened at the growing noise and the people gathered in the front of a red painted building. 'Hopefully, we'll meet some dashing young gentlemen who will escort us home afterwards.'

'I should hope not.' Nicola raised her eyebrow. 'I want no silliness with men, Meg Robinson.'

'There's no fun in you, Miss Douglas.' Meg pouted. She peered at Nicola. 'You should have worn more rouge, and why do you hide all your lovely chestnut hair under that net? If I had hair as lovely as yours I'd show it off!'

Nicola patted her chignon hidden in the black lace net. 'I do not like rouge. My father said painted women ask for trouble.'

Meg laughed. 'What would your father have said about me?'

Nicola covered her mouth with her gloved hand to smother a smile. She dreaded to think what her quiet, studious father would have said about her new friend. She shook her head. Meg's red and black striped dress and rouged cheeks begged for attention.

They stopped outside the red building, situated between a Chinese laundry and a grocer's shop and waited to show their tickets. As a working-class theatre, the crowd, mostly made up of young men and women, was rowdy and ready to have a good time whether the show proved to be worth it or not. Gas lamps on either side of double doors filtered a dim light over the street. The queue shuffled forward, and someone bumped into Nicola.

She stared around at the people closest to her; many dressed in rough working clothes. When Meg had said earlier that they should go out and see a show, Nicola had imagined something a little more tasteful. 'Meg, I don't think this is a suitable place...' Her words died in her throat as a gentleman stopped beside them. His quality cut suit of fine material and superior manner made him stand out amongst the crowd. He tipped his hat and smiled at them. 'Ladies.'

Behind him stood another gentleman wearing a bored expression.

Meg winked at her and then, with a coy smile, fluttered her eyelashes at him. 'Well, good evening, sir.'

Nicola jerked Meg's arm. 'I think we should leave.'

The gentleman, his silver cufflinks shining in the street-lights, beckoned his silent partner over. 'Nathaniel, come look at these two beauties I found.'

Nicola cringed at the term. She stepped back as the dark-haired man walked closer. His eyes narrowed. The lights threw his face into shadows, but she made out a strong jaw line before he spun away to mumble something to his friend.

Meg sashayed forward to the first gentleman, who had a ready smile for her. 'And what brings such fine gentlemen to a backstreet theatre? Surely you have clubs to entertain you?'

'We certainly do, but sometimes, we like to rough it.' He offered his arm to Meg and laughing, she took it. 'What is your name, pretty one?'

'Meg Robinson. What's yours?'

'Tristan Lombard. What say we skip the show and go to dinner?'

Meg leaned against his arm. 'I would say that is an excellent idea, Tristan Lombard.'

'No, Meg!' Horrified, Nicola couldn't believe Meg's forwardness. Every instinct she had balked and she took a step backwards, ready to go home. The man named Nathaniel cursed under his breath. He topped Nicola's height of five foot six by another six inches or more and glared down his straight nose at her. She turned away and tugged at Meg's arm. 'I think we should return home. Now.'

The light danced in Meg's hazel eyes. 'You may go, but I am going to dinner.'

'Meg, this is unseemly. Please, let us go home.' She

lowered her voice. 'They will think us to be nothing but strumpets.'

Meg threw her head back and laughed. 'Maybe strumpets have more fun?'

Heat flooded Nicola's face. 'Meg!'

Mr Lombard bent towards them, his expression amused. 'I shall take excellent care of her, Miss.'

Nicola sighed. How did she get into this mess? 'I would rather you left us, Mr Lombard, thank you all the same.'

He chuckled, giving her a thorough looking over. 'Have you no sense of adventure, Miss?'

Bristling, Nicola raised her chin. 'Plenty. However, I also have an excellent reputation.' She turned to Meg. 'I wish to return to the lodging house.'

'Lodging house?' Tristan's eyes widened. 'You live in lodgings?' He laughed loudly. 'Maybe you could entertain us there?'

'I think not.' Nicola clenched her fists in frustration. This was getting out of hand. 'Come, Meg.'

The other man, Nathaniel, cocked his head, studying her. 'What is your name?'

She rounded on him. 'It is none of your business.'

He shrugged. 'If your friend insists on going to dinner with us, then maybe you should keep an eye on her?'

Meg clapped her hands. 'Hail a hansom, Mr Lombard, and dine me!'

Furious, Nicola glared at Meg as Lombard hailed a passing cab and they bundled into it. She refused to speak as they travelled through the dark streets, not that she was required to for Meg monopolised the conversation with Mr Lombard.

On alighting at the front of an elegant building, Nicola tried to capture Meg's attention only to find her elbow being taken by the man named Nathaniel. Glaring at him, she wrenched her elbow free and stared around. She didn't even know where they were.

'You will come to no harm, Miss,' the fellow said. 'I am a gentleman.'

She moved away from him as they entered the foyer and took a plush red-carpeted staircase up to the next level. Music drifted out from open double doors leading off the landing. A delicious aroma filled Nicola's nose as she hung back in the doorway. Before her, lay the first class of Sydney's population. Women's jewels sparkled in the golden lamp light and the soft clink of crystal mixed with the chords of a violin player performing a solo.

'What is your name?' Nathaniel whispered in her ear. She shivered at the unexpected intimacy.

Turning her head slightly, she lowered her lashes. 'What is yours?'

'Nathaniel,' he murmured with mischief. His deep sensual voice played with her good sense.

She swallowed. 'I am aware of that. If you wish to engage in childish games, then find another fool.' Nicola turned her shoulder to him, but he took her arm and edged closer.

'Nathaniel West.' His soft breath teased the fine hair at her nape.

The waiter took their outdoor clothing and ushered them to a table in the corner. Nicola ignored the curious looks she and Meg received as they took their seats. Thankfully a large palm grew in a wide pot near her chair and she sheltered behind it.

Nathaniel West sat opposite, lazy in his chair, completely at ease. His cool gaze surveyed her, and she concentrated on her hands folded in her lap, but an inner voice told her to hold her head up and meet his gaze. He possessed thick dark brown hair, eyes of violet, and a splendid lithe body dressed in expensively tailored clothes. A muscle pulsed along his jaw. He was handsome in a cold calculating way and she wondered what would make him smile and relax. She noticed women peeking at him. He moved with the grace of a big cat as though every decision and thought was calculated. She shivered again. He raised an inquiring dark eyebrow. 'Well?'

Nicola blinked. 'Pardon?' She glanced away at Meg, who laughed loudly at the patronising Mr Lombard.

A waiter came with an offer of wine. Nathaniel nodded without taking his gaze off her. 'Miss?'

She straightened in her chair. 'I am not what you think I am, nor is Meg, despite her behaviour tonight.' She rubbed her bare arms, naked without her shawl. 'She is young and-'

'You are not?' he mocked her. The corner of his lips moved slightly as if a smile was something new to him.

'Meg is merely twenty-'

'You live in a lodging house. Have you no family?'

'That is my own affair and I will thank-'

'Are you newly arrived or were you born in this accursed country or, perhaps, you came in chains as a youngster?'

Nicola shot to her feet, scraping back her chair. Her action drew stares, but she cared little. Placing her hands flat on the table, she leaned towards the horrid man. 'You, sir, are no gentleman.' She squashed the intense desire to scratch his eyes out. Her ferocious look must have jerked some sense into Meg, as the younger woman hurriedly got to her feet, her laughter dying. Nicola pulled her away from the table and out of the room. Not once did she look back. Out on the street they drew whistles from drunk sailors loitering under a lamppost. Nicola jerked Meg closer to her side. 'I should never have come to this damnable uncouth country! What does it have to offer me!'

CHAPTER 4

*S*ullen, Meg slouched on the sofa, picking at the cushions. Nicola ignored her and read the newspaper. Rain lashed the windows and the fire did little to warm the main sitting room. The door opened, and the draught made smoke billow out from the fireplace.

Mrs Eldersley bustled in, giving Nicola the thought that the woman never did anything slow, and frowned at the wispy cloud. 'I'll need the chimney sweep brought in shortly.' She paused to look at Meg. 'What's up with you, Miss Robinson, have you not heard from your last advertisement?'

'No, I haven't.' Meg tidied her skirts and glanced at Nicola. 'Although, I am certain Miss Douglas thinks I have advertised for the wrong position.'

'Oh?' Mrs Eldersley smiled at Nicola. 'Whatever does she mean, Miss Douglas?'

'I have no idea, Mrs Eldersley.' She folded the newspaper and raised her eyebrow at Meg. Since their unfortunate outing the previous week, they had quarrelled incessantly about the foolishness of Meg accepting the gentleman's offer.

Donald Eldersley, a quiet man who hardly spoke, entered,

carrying a crate of chopped firewood. He nodded to them as he crossed the room and set the crate down. His barking cough made him the centre of attention as his wife hurried to attend him.

'Nay, husband, tell me you haven't been out in the rain?' Mrs Eldersley threw her hands up in despair. 'I told you we have enough wood down in the cellar to last the day, without you needing to venture out in this weather.'

He wiped his mouth with his handkerchief and then slowly smiled. 'Don't fuss, woman.' He coughed again and, hunched over, stumbled out of the room.

'What am I to do with him?' Mrs Eldersley cried before running after him.

Meg rose and sidled over to Nicola. 'Promise me you won't stay mad forever.' She ran her fingers over the sofa's material, drawing an invisible pattern. 'It's no fun only talking to Miss Downing for she is always crying and Miss Burstall is a hard faced-'

Nicola held up her hand, stopping her. 'I promise not to stay mad forever, if you promise not to behave in such a way again.'

Meg flounced away to the hearth. 'Oh, all right, I promise, but really, it was all harmless.'

'To start with, perhaps, but I am certain Mr Lombard thought of you as some sort of sport.'

'He was fun though.' Meg shrugged. 'And far more entertaining than his sour friend who did nothing but glare the entire time.'

A tingle ran down Nicola's back as she thought of those violet-blue eyes assessing her. Nathaniel West's arrogant image had stayed with her and at odd times she found her thoughts straying to ponder him.

'I was stuck out in the bush for a whole year with no one to associate with.' Meg sighed. 'You have no idea what it is like out there. The family stayed aloof from me and in my free time I had only the workmen to talk to.'

'Perhaps your behaviour with the workmen caused the family to remain aloof from you? Is that why you were sent back to Sydney, because of your association with labourers?'

Meg grinned. 'At least they were fun.'

'Perhaps the wrong sort of fun though, hmm?' Nicola shook her head. She was only five years older than Meg, but, at times, it felt thirty years instead.

Strolling over to the window, Meg fiddled with the curtain as the rain splattered against the glass. 'What made you come out here, Nicola? Can you tell me, or must you have your secrets?'

'I have no secrets. My parents died two years ago, within six months of each other. The schoolhouse was needed for the new teacher, who replaced my father. I had nowhere to go. For a while I lodged with some neighbours before I found a position as a governess of sorts with a family, but they weren't nice people. Their boys were rather horrid actually.' She shuddered at the memory of sly, wicked little boys intent on causing her harm.

'Were you with them long?'

'About four months. I could stand it no longer. After that family I obtained work in a house of a mill owner, but the child, a little girl, was ill and weak a great deal of the time. She died... Then, I saw an article in the newspaper about Miss Maria Rye's scheme of sending educated women and high-class servants out to the colonies. I remembered my father speaking about her. He'd read all her letters she'd sent to *The Times*. He thought she was doing a grand thing, helping others.'

'Oh yes, that Society. Miss Rye was touring here not so long ago.'

'Yes, she returned to England last year. I saw her give a

speech on her return. It prompted me to come out here. She does very good work, bringing the plights of the unfortunates to the public's awareness.'

'I once heard my mother denouncing the fact that the FMCE Scheme was meant to send out governesses, when in actual fact we didn't need them. What is needed here are good lower servants, or so mother says.'

Nicola went to the fire and prodded a log with the iron poker. 'There is more than one scheme, too. Miss Rye herself assists housemaids to emigrate, for in England we were told the colonies were crying out for good servants and then, there is the governess scheme.'

Meg shrugged. 'All I know is that many educated women are landing in Sydney and have no positions to go to. Australian born women, who are educated should be allowed the first choice of any situation before 'new comers.''

'Like you, you mean.' Nicola frowned. 'Do you really believe that?'

'Of course. Mother is on some church committee and she has told me herself about the dire circumstances that have reduced women to living on credit and appealing for help to ease their debt. I have heard many tales of women thinking they can walk straight into employment when they land but find there is no one to meet them. Do women in England honestly think there is such an abundance of positions here that they can pick and choose?'

'Some do, yes. I did. You've no idea how desperate the situation is for women back home.' Deeply interested, Nicola placed the poker back in its stand. 'Where do they go, these women with no contacts?'

'Lodging houses or hotels, like you did. The last resort is the Governess' and Servants' Home, though many look down their nose at it, believing they are a much better person than to stay in such a place. However, I have stayed there and find it very suitable.' Meg wandered around the room. 'Soon enough, their money runs out and they have to pick up whatever work is available. Teaching, nursing, and if they are lucky perhaps become a companion. But mostly they suffer such tragedies like Miss Downing and have to rely on bar work, being a kitchen maid and even...prostitution.'

Nicola shivered. Her own experience of aloneness on arriving not so long ago still haunted her. What if Mr Belfroy had not helped her? She had some money, but not enough to last for months of unemployment. She looked at her new friend, amazed at her knowledge and concern. For the first time Meg had shown a completely different side of herself. 'What will you do, Meg, if another position doesn't come along?'

Meg shrugged. 'I could go home, although mother would make my life a misery.' She grimaced dramatically.

'If you come from a wealthy family why is it you live here and work as a governess?'

'I would do anything to displease my mother. Besides, our wealth has diminished somewhat since my father's death and I refuse to go back to Melbourne and be paraded before suitable gentlemen with marriage on their minds. Mother believes that is all I'm good for. I will never marry a man because he has money and position. I've seen what it can do a person. The tedious boredom would drive me quite insane.'

'All women desire marriage, a family, a home of their own.'

'I've yet to see a happy married woman. My mother was completely miserable with my father and took out her frustrations on me.' Meg came and held her hands out to the fire, a cheeky smile playing on her lips. 'What about you? Did you land here thinking you could obtain a position within the first hour?'

'No. Of course, I didn't expect to have nothing for weeks

though. I had read much about Miss Rye's Scheme. You have no idea how hard it is to find work at home, most governesses work until they are in their seventies. I had enough money to pay my way here. All I received from the scheme was a letter of introduction. I never met any of the women concerned with the Scheme, merely wrote to them for advice and then came out unassisted.' Nicola bit the inside of her lip. 'When I said I had no secrets, I lied. I do. Just one.'

Meg's eyes widened, and she clapped her hands. 'Oh, wonderful! Do tell.'

'I am not a true governess in respect of having worked for wealthy families. I am educated because my father taught me alongside his class of boys. When I was older, I helped my father run his small school and I taught piano in the evenings. I told Mr Belfroy I had nursery experience, but honestly, my skills are limited, and sadly, I have no references from influential people, only the merchants and traders of the town where we lived and the two employers I worked for before I sailed.'

'Is that it?' Meg's shoulders sagged. 'That's your secret?'

Nicola frowned. 'Yes, what did you expect?'

'That you've run away from a torrid love affair or something.'

'Don't be ridiculous,' she scoffed, appalled at the thought. 'Really, Meg, you do go on sometimes.'

'Well, I am not a true governess either, I can't teach Latin or French, but that hasn't stopped me. Some not-so-wealthier families aren't too choosy, thankfully. They are happy to just have someone to teach their children the basics and pay accordingly. Believe me, some children are positively wild.'

'I may not be able to expect a position in a good family.' Nicola rubbed her forehead. The worry of finding work forever in her mind. 'I need employment and so I shall have to take whatever I am offered now.'

'Prostitution?' Meg laughed.

'Don't be absurd.' Nicola stared at her. 'You are outrageous.'

The door opened, and Miss Downing entered with a book under her arm. She inclined her head to them and scurried over to a chair on the far side of the room. Her nose and eyes were red from weeping.

'Do you feel better today, Miss Downing?' Nicola smiled at her.

Miss Downing nodded. 'A little, thank you.' She laid her book in her lap, opened it and took out a folded sheet of paper. 'I have written to my former employer.' She raised her guilt-ridden gaze to Nicola and Meg. 'Miss Burstall says I shouldn't. It is wrong for me to ask for...' Quietly, she cried into her handkerchief.

Meg crossed to her and put her arm around the bent shoulders. 'Don't listen to Miss Iron Drawers.'

'Meg.' Nicola shook her head in exasperation and knelt before Miss Downing. 'Why do you write to your employer?'

'Mrs Eldersley says I should ask for money.'

'He owes you wages?' Meg tossed her head. 'Why, the slimy toad.'

Nicola glared at Meg. 'Go and arrange for some tea.' She waited until her impossible friend had left the room and then guided Miss Downing over to the sofa nearer to the fire.

Miss Downing wiped her eyes. 'It isn't wages I am asking for. It's for the ch-child.'

'What is your first name? If we are to be friends, then calling you Miss Downing all the time will not do.' Nicola smiled.

'Emily is my name.' Her deep sigh shuddered her small

frame. 'I need money to live. Mrs Eldersley will not let me stay here for much longer without payment.'

'I understand your need for money, but I do not think Mrs Eldersley will turn you out onto the streets. Do you think your former employer will send you something?'

'No. He is a rude beast, but I must try something. I owe five pounds to the Society and my lodgings to Mrs Eldersley.'

'Mrs Eldersley will not demand money from you, I promise you. She has a benefactor to help run this house.'

Emily's eyes filled with fresh tears. 'When the child comes, what will I do then?'

Nicola blinked, trying to think of something helpful to say, but knew Emily's crisis would only deepen. 'What about your family?'

Emily shook her head. 'My father died a few months ago. All I have is a brother in England, but his wife rules their roost. He is of no use to me.'

'You aren't without friends here. We'll help you.'

'Thank you, Nicola, but can you secure me employment or rid me of this child?' Emily stood, her chin wobbling. 'I have no future now. Excuse me, please. I wish to return to my room.'

After Emily had left the room, Nicola sat contemplating her words. She was right, of course. What could anyone do for Emily, or the hundreds of other women who'd come out here to a strange land believing there was work to be found but instead ended up being used and abused, or dying from starvation and ruinously deep in debt?

Scowling at the injustice of it all, Nicola stepped to the window and looked out onto the street. She hated this feeling of helplessness.

* * *

THE SHOUTS and jeers could be heard long before Nicola turned into Clarence Street. She paused at the corner and watched in fascination as the crowd jostled one another to get closer to the action further down. Standing on tiptoes, she craned her neck to look past a taller gentleman, when again a roar went up from the crowd. A scruffy young boy dodged through the people towards her and she instinctively held her purse tighter. Beside her, an elderly woman grabbed the lad's collar as he passed and hauled him to a stop.

'What's going on down there, boy?'

He wriggled like a worm on a hook. 'Let me go.'

The wizened old women pushed her face before his. 'Answer me question.'

'I dunno. Some women wavin' and shoutin' about rights or summick.'

Intrigued the old woman straightened the best she could with her bent back and released the boy, who quickly scarpered. 'Rights, hey?' she murmured to no one in particular, and then she laughed. 'Good luck to 'em. They'll need it.'

Nicola switched her gaze from the woman to the crowd that was dispersing now the speeches were over. The idea of rights for women had interested her ever since she read Mary Wollstonecraft's book. In the past, she'd endured many arguments with her mother about it. Her father cared little, though she believed he wasn't against such thinking, but her mother refused to consider that women's rights held the interests of benefiting women, but instead wanted to pit women against men, belittle men.

Walking closer to the central hubbub of the protest, Nicola read the placards held aloft by the protesting women. A group of young men, muttering angrily about the worth of such women, pushed past her and she jumped out of the way.

One of the young men slapped at a volunteer's box and

sent pamphlets flying. 'Go home, you bunch of scum in skirts!'

Red-faced, the affected member lunged for the man and they tussled until the man knocked her to the ground.

'That's enough!' Nicola didn't realise she'd spoken the words out loud and the fighting cock-sure spun to sneer in her face.

'I'll not stand by and let you lot preach to me. You should all know your place and that's being under your husbands!'

Nicola raised her chin and gave him a condescending glare. 'Spoken like a true ignorant.'

The fellow towered over her, fist raised, but his silent companions hauled him away.

'They've no manners and no brains.'

Nicola turned to the fallen woman who'd spoken. 'I agree with you.' Her step faltered as she stared down at the angry grey eyes.

The woman sat in the gutter and glared after the men a moment more before switching her gaze to Nicola. 'Care for a pamphlet?'

A piece of paper was thrust into her hand. Nicola glanced at it, but couldn't stop staring at the woman. At least she thought it was a woman. She'd never seen a woman dressed as a man.

'Thank you for helping. I'm Frances.' She stood, dusted off her bottom and stuck her hand out. When Nicola took it, she found it pumped hard.

'I'm Nicola Douglas.' She blinked and studied the angular lines of Frances's face. No beard stubble grew on the chin or cheeks. She had to be a woman. The green shirt she wore showed a slight outline of small breasts. Her hair was cut short to collar length and she wore trousers with a black belt and dusty black boots. But it was her large grey eyes that held Nicola's gaze, for they were beautiful with long lashes, and looking at them no one would doubt that Frances was a woman, if perhaps a strange one.

The crowd had thinned, and other members of the group were packing away their table and literature.

'Are you interested in rights for women, for the poor, for the children?' Frances asked, while together they collected the scattered papers from the gutter.

'Um…I suppose I am.' Nicola smiled and waited as Frances passed the pamphlets to another younger girl, who placed them in a box.

'We need more members.' Frances grabbed her satchel from under the table and hooked it over her shoulder. 'Want to join us?'

'I'm not sure…'

'Well, have a think about it. We meet each week. The address is on the back of that pamphlet I gave you. We want the movement to grow here in Australia. The 'Unfortunates' of this world need more voices, raised voices!'

'I didn't even know such movements were active here, the population is so small.'

Frances nodded. Her dark hair was cut so short it hardly moved. 'That's why we need more rallies like this one today. We must spread the word. We may not have the amount of people as England, but we still share the same problems. Injustice!'

An older woman, her face stiff with concern, drew up beside them. 'There's a problem, Frances. We can't use the George Street rooms anymore. Mr Haversham refuses to let us use them after last week's debacle. I'm off to seek out another venue. Any ideas?'

Frances sighed and pushed her hand through her short hair making it stand on end. 'We could always use my room if there's no alternative. It's small and the landlady might not like so many people in there, but keep it in mind as a last resort.'

The woman lightly placed her hand on Frances's shoulder for a moment. 'Thank you.'

'I'm sorry, Beatrice, it's not enough I know.' Frances's frowned. 'I'll talk to my brother. His current rooms aren't to his taste and he's thinking of renting out a house until he builds his own establishment in the country. I might be able to persuade him to let us meet there.'

Laughing sarcastically, Beatrice grimaced. 'Your brother would rather a herd of elephants marched through his rooms before letting us near him.'

Frances scowled. 'Yes well, I'm working on him. I think he's softening.'

Beatrice looked at Nicola and held out her hand. 'I'm Mrs Delaney.'

Nicola smiled. 'Nicola Douglas.'

'I hope to see you at another rally, Miss Douglas.' With that she was gone, busily tidying up and giving orders to the group of women who stood by the boxes and table.

Frances grinned. 'Beatrice believes that every woman is with us. Even those who say they aren't she thinks are simply in denial.'

Nicola watched the older woman efficiently organise the volunteers. 'Perhaps she is right.'

'Lord, I need a drink.'

Nicola blinked in shock.

Frances chuckled and, finding her other larger bag, she pulled out a skirt and wrapped it around her. 'No, not that type of drink.' She clipped the skirt into place and resembled a woman again. 'Fancy a cup of coffee? I'm as dry as a rock in summer.'

Relieved it was only coffee she wanted, Nicola nodded and fell into step with the unique woman. They crossed the street and then turned the corner. Frances led the way, obviously knowing where to go. She paused in front of a narrow, run-down shop and then pushed open the door. Inside, the long room held a number of small wooden tables and chairs and at the back, a man stood at the counter reading a small book.

'Good day, Pierre.'

The man smiled and waved before disappearing into a backroom.

Frances ushered Nicola into a chair by the window. 'Pierre will bring us a pot of coffee and some of his delicious pastry. He fled France owing money to his creditors but he's such a nice man and better still, a delightful cook.'

Amazed, Nicola gazed around the drab room, bare of all ornaments and colour. A young man with a hound dog face scribbled on paper and didn't look up. Beyond him sat a couple holding hands. The man looked relaxed, the woman seemed nervous. 'I'd never imagine this was a tea room.'

'Well, it's not really. It's a gathering place for people out of work, poor artists, rebellious politicians, unionists, adulterers, and any other clandestine meetings. Pierre feeds them, demands little money and asks no questions.'

Nicola listened with rapt attention and knew she led a closeted life, considering. Her father had been a middle-class boys' tutor. Her mother brought a small annuity to her marriage, so they'd lived comfortably, if not extravagantly. Her parents had shielded the worst of life from her, although her mother encouraged her to do good work for the poor. Her father had educated her as he would a boy, giving her balance between the two worlds. Yet, she had felt adrift in her world, not knowing exactly who she was or what to do. She was neither working class nor middle class, but somewhere in between and this uncertainty only increased when fate came and claimed her parents. She had no one and nothing left. Then she saw the advertisement to be a governess in the far reaches of England's empire…Australia, and Miss Rye's speech did the rest.

'Were you born here?' Frances asked as Pierre, curiously dressed in white trousers and shirt, placed a tray on the table. He gave them a stiff bow and without speaking left them.

'No. I've only been in this country a short time.' Nicola accepted the coffee that Frances poured for her. The tray held a plate of delicate pastries and she took one, suddenly feeling very hungry. The tart, filled with apple and cream, sticky and sweet, melted in her mouth. 'This is good.'

Frances winked. 'I told you. But don't let it become common knowledge or Pierre will have a seizure. He likes to keep it all on the quiet lest his past catches up with him.'

Nodding, Nicola smiled and took another bite. 'What about you? Have you always lived here?'

'Lord, no. I escaped England and my parents last year and followed my brother here, much to his surprise.'

'Escaped?' Fascinated, Nicola stared at her.

'Yes, escaped. Sounds tragic, doesn't it? I escaped my parents' noose-like hold on me and I escaped their wealth, which trapped me much more securely than poverty ever could.' Frances sipped her black coffee. 'My parents insisted I marry some son of a political friend that would further my father's interests in the government. I refused, and my life became hell. You see, my parents didn't like their children much and saw us as pawns to be used in games of wealth and power. I'd watched the way they used my oldest brother for advancement by making him marry a rich heiress. They wanted my second brother, Nat, to do the same, but he denied them the chance by purposely ruining his reputation. In the end they shunned him, and he became bitter.'

'How sad.'

'Yes.' A wistful expression flittered across her face. 'I love my brother, but my parents have done lasting damage to him. They treated him like something foul they'd trodden in. He changed from the laughing carefree brother I knew to a cynical sour man. When he left home, vowing to never return, I knew that my life would alter and that my parents would use me as their next project to gain more wealth and recognition. I couldn't let that happen. My brother wrote to me, thank God. And as soon as I could, I joined him here.'

'And now you're free.'

'And now I'm poor!' Frances laughed and played with her teaspoon. 'Nat has done well and keeps me alive, but I hate asking him for anything. My family has a history of taking and not giving. I refuse to act the same. However, he gives me an allowance and I use it to help the poor. I wanted to work but he wouldn't let me. So, I do charity work instead.'

'And the rights campaign?'

'That's something I do in my spare time, when I can. I'm passionate about it, but feeding the starving is more important at this present time. Anyway, enough about me.' She shook her head. 'I've not talked so much about myself in my life. You must have a way with you.'

Nicola paused from taking a sip of coffee and thought about it. 'Actually, you could be right. People have always talked to me; my parents, my father's pupils, the neighbours. I'm happy to listen.'

'So, tell me about yourself.'

'Not much to say. I'm a governess looking for work.'

Frances scowled. 'Another governess. There is barely enough work for the ones already here, do you know that?'

'Yes. I do now.' Sighing, Nicola glanced down at her small plate and its scattering of crumbs. 'Most positions advertised have a hundred or more women applying for them.'

'I see a lot of women in dire trouble at the soup kitchen. Too many come out here thinking they have permanent employment, only to find they have nothing and no one.' Frances drained her coffee and from her pocket pulled out a small watch on a chain. 'I've got to go.'

'Yes, of course. I too have been out longer than expected.' Nicola rose and fished in her purse for coins.

'No, leave that. Pierre and I have an agreement.' She laughed. 'No, not that kind of agreement.' She turned and waved to Pierre and nodded to the other customers.

Outside in the street, Frances hesitated, and a quizzical expression flitted across her face. 'I think you're a decent sort. Perhaps we can meet again?'

Nicola smiled at her honesty. 'I'd like that.'

'You mentioned you did poor work back home?'

'Yes.'

'Want to work at a soup kitchen tomorrow?' She raised her eyebrows as though daring her.

'Of course.' She didn't hesitate.

'I'll meet you on Lower George Street at ten o'clock. There's an alley running from it down to the harbour. I'll wait for you there.'

CHAPTER 5

*N*icola lifted her navy skirts high off the ground. A man leaning against a wall across the street whistled at the showing of ankle, but she ignored him and stepped over a puddle. Rain during the night had done little to wash away the grime from this area of the town. A stench from an unknown source made her want to cover her nose, but she hadn't a free hand. Clutching her skirts, she tried her best to keep them clean, although a glance at the dirty hem showed this was a forlorn hope.

'There you are.' Frances exited the entrance to an alley and greeted her with a grin. 'I didn't think you'd come.'

Nicola frowned. 'Why ever not? I said I would.'

'Yes, well many people say things they later regret.' Frances shrugged and slipped her hands into her drab skirt pockets. 'Anyhow, come along, we've got hungry people to feed.'

The dull grey day cast the alley into gloom. Noise and clamour from the harbour, docks and warehouses vibrated along the walls. Seagulls cried as they wheeled over the buildings. Further down the alley, people gathered in a straggly line; old men, women with babies on their hips and children peeking from behind their skirts. All wore the same doleful expression. The sunken eyes watched without interest as Frances escorted Nicola through the large double doors and inside an old disused warehouse. It took her a moment for Nicola's eyes to adjust to the dimness of the building. The only light came from the open vents high up in the walls. She guessed that over thirty people sat at the rows of planks that served as tables. Low chatter filled the room mixing with the shuffling of feet and the scraping of spoons.

'Right. You can serve beside me today.' Frances, her sleeves already rolled back, guided Nicola behind the long serving tables where two large pots of stew sat beside trays of bread chunks and stacks of bowls.

Nicola tied on the grey apron Frances provided while an older woman joined them. 'This is Mrs Lawson. She helps me to run this soup kitchen. Her son owns a bakery and from him we buy the two-day-old bread.'

Nicola didn't have time to do anything but smile and say good morning to Mrs Lawson as Frances gave her a ladle and pointed to the pot full of a watery vegetable stew. 'Fill each bowl as I send them along.'

Nodding, she took a deep breath and looked up at the first person to step before her.

Over an hour later, when the human line had finally stopped coming through the doors, Nicola helped Frances and Mrs Lawson to clear away. 'How many times do you do this?'

'Three times a week.' Frances heaved a long bench to one side to sweep under it. 'I'd like to provide it once a day, but funds are limited.'

'How many patrons do you have?'

'None. I pay for it myself, courtesy of my brother. Mrs Lawson supplies her time, which is wonderful because I

48

couldn't do it alone, but I have no wealthy gents passing me copious amounts of money to buy what I need. Though it isn't for the want of trying.'

'What about your brother. Can he not persuade his friends and acquaintances?'

Frances shook her head. 'No, he won't consider it and he ignores my begging. Besides, he already helps me with another project of mine and that's funding a small private orphanage in Parramatta. He says he is in this country to amass a fortune not spend one on other people's brats.' She sighed. 'He can be rather cold at times, but thankfully I know the real man beneath, otherwise I'd have nothing to do with him. He has no idea that the money he gives me to live on actually goes to others. He'd be horrified if he did.'

Nicola stopped her scrubbing of a table and stared, amazed by this woman's selflessness and commitment. 'Heavens, Frances. You are exceptional.'

'Nonsense. I do what I can, because I can, and I like helping others less fortunate.'

Mrs Lawson waved to them as she walked towards the doors. 'I'm off home now, ladies. Nice to have met you, Miss Douglas.'

'And I you, Mrs Lawson.' Nicola smiled.

Frances waved and called out her goodbyes before turning back to Nicola. 'I want to thank you for coming here today, Nicola.'

'I enjoyed being of use.' She rinsed out her cloth in the bucket of cold soapy water. 'Sitting around at the lodgings with nothing to do is tiresome. When I returned home yesterday after leaving you, I found a letter for me in reply to one of the advertisements I'd answered. The position had been filled before my letter even arrived on their doorstep.'

Frances swept her way towards the doors. 'I know it must be difficult for you. I am sorry. Although…' Frances turned to grin at her. 'While you aren't engaged in a position, perhaps I can claim your services here?'

Nicola couldn't help but laugh, realising she would enjoy being useful. 'I don't see why not.'

Suddenly a man stood in the doorway. He was dressed splendidly in a long black woollen coat with knee length black boots that gleamed even in the muted light of the large room.

Laughter left Nicola as though she'd been dunked in a tub of ice water. Her stomach clenched as Nathaniel West gazed at her. His violet eyes narrowed on recognition, but his expression gave nothing away however, as Frances greeted him.

'Why, Nat, what you doing here?' She kissed his cheek and Nicola caught a glimpse of her softer side. 'Come and meet my new friend, Miss Douglas. Nicola this is my brother, Nathaniel West.'

Nicola groaned inwardly. Why did it have to be him of all people?

Nathaniel hesitated. 'I'm afraid I have little time, Frances.' His frosty stare penetrated Nicola's soul before he bowed in her direction. 'Pleased to meet you, Miss Douglas.'

The distance between them was no more than ten paces, yet she felt as though it was a divide the size of the harbour. She inclined her head but remained silent and was rewarded by a sardonic lift of his arched eyebrow. She was grateful at least that he didn't mention their previous meeting.

Frances, attuned to their reaction to each other, looked at Nathaniel. 'You needed to see me about something?'

'Yes. I've invited a few friends over for dinner tomorrow evening and would be glad if you could join us.'

'Play your hostess you mean?' She folded her arms. 'You know I am unhappy about such things. I didn't come out here to don finery and be—'

He held his hand up, silencing her. 'I'm merely asking if you could, but if you are unavailable, I will understand.'

'You understanding? That'll be a first.'

His expression became stiff. 'Frances.'

'Oh, all right, but I'll only do it if Nicola is invited too. I need some female company.'

Nicola jerked. 'No!'

Both brother and sister blinked in surprise at her vehement rejection. Nathaniel folded his arms and his lips curved into a wry smile. 'I'd be delighted to include Miss Douglas in the party.'

'Oh yes, do come, Nicola.' Frances smiled. 'I do need support in a room full of smug men.'

Shaking her head, Nicola carried the bucket to the end of the room and untied her apron. 'I'm sorry, I'm unable to attend.' She refused to meet their eyes as she headed for the door. When she drew level with Frances she forced a smiled. 'I must go.'

'Please come, Nicola.'

'I cannot. Sorry.'

'Perhaps Miss Douglas is unused to polite society?' Nathaniel carelessly inspected his black gloves.

'Nat!' Shocked, Frances scowled at him.

He raised his gaze to Nicola and she swallowed back a sharp retort when a spark of something she couldn't define lit his eyes. He was challenging her. For a moment she wanted to laugh at him, mock him, but something stopped her. She wouldn't stoop to his level. 'Good day, Mr West.' She took Frances's hand and pressed it. 'I'll speak to you soon.' With head high, she turned and left them.

Watching her go, so proud and feminine, Nathaniel sucked in a breath. His groin tightened and his heart thumped against his chest like blacksmith's hammer. God, she is beautiful.

'Now what the hell was all that about!' Frances slapped his arm. 'She is my new friend, and you know I don't have many, so why did you act as though she was something you'd just wiped off your boots? You have more of Father in you than you think.'

'Don't *ever* say that.' He gave her a loathsome glare. 'I am nothing like him.'

'Then don't act it. You're better than that.'

He shrugged, slipping behind his comfortable mask of unconcern and gazed around, buying some time to gather his thoughts. 'Are you finished in here for today? Perhaps we could go have something to eat.'

'Don't avoid the question. Why did you behave like that to Nicola? She isn't some ignorant servant.'

'I'm hungry, Frances. I'd rather take you out than have you harangue me like a whore on a street corner. So, can we go?'

Frances marched away to lean the broom against the back wall and then, in jerking movements, she untied her apron. 'I don't understand why you have to act the arrogant swine all the time. I know you're not really like that.'

'Yes, I am.'

She stopped and looked at him. 'We aren't at home now. Mother and Father no longer rule us. You are your own man. There's no need to put on these acts of—'

'Enough, Frances.' Nathaniel walked out of the building not caring if she followed or not. He hated thinking of his parents, hated being reminded of how ill they used him. The past was gone.

'Don't you walk away from me!' Frances strode up alongside of him. 'Lord, Nat, you are one frustrating—'

He swung to face her. 'Why must you drag up the past all the time? I don't want to think about it or talk about it. Ever.'

She planted her feet apart and stuck her hands on her

hips. 'Then why do you act the way you do? If you're happy to leave the past behind then why do you put up all these defenses? You are no happier here than you were back in England or else you'd smile a lot more.'

He frowned. 'I do smile.'

'Your smile is usually a sarcastic lift of your lips. I should know as I'm usually on the receiving end of one.' She locked the warehouse doors.

Nat sighed and pushed his fingers through his hair. 'If I'd known that inviting you out for a meal would give me so much anguish I'd not have bothered.'

'Fine!' Frances spat, storming off. 'I don't need your bloody charity anyway.'

'Yes, you do!' Chuckling at her outrage and language, he ran and caught her arm. 'I love you, you mad wench.'

She stopped and gaped at him with her wide grey eyes.

He kissed her cheek and his smile, for the first time in a long while, was real.

'I love you too.' She softened her stance and linked her arm through his.

'You know, you'll never find a husband using that kind of language. It's bad enough you'll be wearing his clothes but to speak like him too, might be pushing the limits, dearest.'

She spluttered. 'A husband! Never!' Then looking up at him she sighed. 'I've got you, that's all I need.'

* * *

NICOLA EMERGED out of the tin bath's cooling water and wrapped a towel around herself. Her arms ached from carrying bucket after bucket of hot water upstairs but at least she was clean. Working at the soup kitchen was rewarding, but she couldn't take the risk of bringing disease back to the lodging and so, three times a week for the last two weeks, she'd bathed on returning from Lower George Street. Meg often laughed and made fun of her for constantly washing, saying she'd turn into a water nymph.

She dried her body and then donned clean undergarments. Sitting on the bed, she used the towel to dry her hair. On the small dresser, her parents watched from their portraits and she smiled back at them. After the long voyage out here and living in lodgings for months, she felt that her life back in England had all been a dream. Everything was so different now. Her foreign surroundings and harsh environment were the complete opposite to the softness of her old home and lushness of England's countryside. Still, she was here to start again and so far, she'd made some lovely friends. Mr Belfroy, God bless the man, had sold another couple of her sketches, but her stock was dwindling. She'd have to find the time to do more and even paint if possible.

'Nicola.' Meg's voice rang through the bedroom door.

She slipped on her night wrap. 'Come in.'

Meg pranced into the room and flopped onto the end of the bed, eyeing the bath. 'You all finished?'

'Yes, why?'

'Are you going to that awful woman's meeting this evening?'

'Yes.'

'Well since you don't like my ideas for an evening's entertainment, I thought I'd go along with you, if you don't mind.'

Nicola hid a grin, knowing that Meg only wanted some diversion from the occupants of the house and was not intrigued by Frances's issues at all. 'I don't mind.'

Meg sprang up and stepped around the bath to look out of the small window. 'I'm bored.'

'I know.'

Fiddling with the curtain, Meg sighed. 'I hardly see you anymore. That Frances takes up all of your time. If it's not the soup kitchen, it's all that rights nonsense. If it's not that, then it's going out on other charity work.'

'I like to be busy.'

'How do you expect to get employment though, when you're never home to write applications?'

Nicola frowned. It was true. She'd not looked for work in the last two days. She would have to find some form of permanent income soon. Frances, now a firm friend, expected total dependability, which Nicola would be happy to give if only she had a private income to meet her living expenses.

A scream echoed up from downstairs and for a second Meg and Nicola looked at each other in surprise. They heard rushing footsteps and suddenly both of them were whipping open the door.

Emily, tears streaming down her face, ran across the landing. 'Nicola, Meg, you must come!'

Nicola reached for her shawl and wrapped it over her shoulders. 'What has happened?'

'Mr Eldersley has collapsed in the kitchen!'

As the three women spun around and headed back downstairs, Deirdre Burstall came out of her room. 'What's all the fuss about?'

'Mr Eldersley has collapsed.' Meg shouted over her shoulder. 'Come and help.'

Racing into the kitchen, Nicola skidded to a halt near the crouching Mrs Eldersley, who held her husband's head and shoulders in her arms.

'Have you sent for the doctor, Mrs Eldersley?' Nicola whispered, kneeling beside the couple.

The older woman, her eyes blank, shook her head. 'It's too late for a doctor.'

Nicola turned to the women behind her. 'Bring Dr Armitage, Meg. Emily, make everyone some tea. Miss

Burstall go next door and ask for help. We need men to carry Mr Eldersley upstairs.'

Once the women scuttled to her bidding, Nicola gently rested her hand on Mr Eldersley's chest. Nothing. Leaning forward, she placed her ear above his mouth. Nothing.

'He dropped to the floor like a stone.' Mrs Eldersley whispered. 'We should never have started this business. His health wasn't up to it, that's why we left Mr Belfroy's employment. It was madness to start up this place, but Mr Belfroy insisted we could do it with his help. Seven months he's lasted since leaving Mr Belfroy's employment. He was a good coachman was my Jim.'

Nicola nodded and let her talk if it helped her. She felt for a pulse on Jim Eldersley's neck. Nothing. The man was dead.

* * *

THE TICK-TOCK of the clock on the mantelshelf sounded loud in the quiet room. The logs in the grate shifted, sending golden sparks up the chimney. Outside, the day had turned bitterly cold, but had remained dry for the burial of Jim Eldersley. Nicola gazed around at the seated black-clothed people, Mr Belfroy, Dr Armitage, a neighbour or two and the women lodgers. All held teacups and saucers, and once more Emily went around with the teapot and refilled their cups. If anyone talked it was in muted whispers, as though anything loud would shatter the silent reserve of the dear woman sitting in the chair by the fireplace.

Sighing, Nicola pushed a stray wisp of hair behind her ear and then rubbed the strain from her neck. The last three days had been testing.

For some reason the whole household had looked to her. Somehow, they'd all decided she would be in charge. Without thought, she'd taken the reins of organising the funeral and running the lodging house, but doing so had meant little time for herself, and little time to look for work. Mrs Eldersley, shocked and grieving, had taken to her room and stayed there until this morning, when Meg and Emily had washed and dressed her and led her out to Mr Belfroy's carriage.

Despite the tragic circumstances, she had enjoyed the position of leader. Her father told her many times in the school room she had a natural talent for leadership. Maybe she should take the teacher's certificate and become a teacher in a school instead of a governess.

Picking up the tea tray and with a brief smile at Meg, Nicola walked into the hallway. A knock at the front door halted her.

Meg came alongside. 'Here, give me the tray and you answer the door.'

'Where's the new maid?' Nicola whispered, glancing towards the green painted door that led to the kitchen.

'She didn't show up, the lazy baggage.'

'Why didn't you tell me?'

'You had enough to deal with. Emily and I made the tea and sandwiches. Miss Burstall even spent some of her money and bought that bottle of ginger ale and a neighbour bought the cake.'

After handing the tray over, she stepped to the door as the knock came again. 'You should have told me this morning,' she whispered.

'And give you more to worry about. Besides, Mrs Eldersley needed you.' Meg smiled and headed for the kitchen.

Nicola opened the door and a blast of cold air washed over her.

Frances stood on the step with her arms folded. 'Don't those lot in there know how to open a door when someone is knocking? And why are you answering it? Isn't there a maid?'

'I'm sorry, Fran.' Nicola blinked at the onslaught, her friend was not one for holding back she'd discovered.

'So, where have you been hiding? Why haven't you attended the rallies or the soup kitchen? Are you sick?' She peered closer. 'You don't look it.'

'No, I'm not sick.' Nicola stepped outside, pulling the door closed behind her for Frances's voice was become louder with every sentence. 'I'm sorry if I've let you down.'

'Stop saying sorry.' Frances snorted and raised her eyebrows at the closed door. 'Can't I come in? Are you ashamed to be seen with me? I'll not be changing my ways just to please some snotty gaggle of governesses, Nicola Douglas and you can tell them that from me!'

'Shush, Fran, please.' Nicola glanced back at the house. 'There's a funeral wake inside. We buried Mr Eldersley this morning. That's why I haven't been to see you.'

Frances's shoulders slumped, and she gripped Nicola's hands, her expression one of apology. 'Lord, why didn't you shut me up?'

'I couldn't get a word in, could I?' Nicola grinned.

'You should have sent me a note. I've been so worried.'

'I'm sorry, really, but there's been no time. Mrs Eldersley is grieving and I've had to run the lodgings.'

'Typical.' Frances tossed her head. 'Trust it to be you who looks after everyone.'

'I had no choice, no one else wanted the responsibility.'

'Of course not. They'd rather leave it all to you. The lazy good-for-nothing uppity-'

'No, it hasn't been like that, not really.'

'Can you come to a meeting tonight?'

'No, sorry. I have to look over the account books for Mrs Eldersley. The end of the month August bills have been arriving all week and she's not up to dealing with them. Also, this cold snap means we need more fuel for the fires. I have to order that and plenty more besides.'

Shivering as September's chill spring air inched inside their clothing, Frances pulled the collar of her black coat higher. 'I hate the cold, reminds me too much of England.'

Nicola glanced down and from beneath the coat, pale green skirts poked out.

'Yes, I'm wearing skirts, Nicola.' Frances huffed. 'I only wear trousers to make a statement, they aren't my normal everyday code of dress as you well know.'

'I'm pleased to hear it,' she replied cheekily, knowing it would irritate Fran. 'I am terrified of what you will wear from one meeting to the next.'

'You aren't funny, Nicola Douglas. Go back inside and see to them lot. I'll come again tomorrow.'

'Thank you.' She kissed Frances's cheek and returned inside to find the doctor was ready to leave, as were the neighbours.

Once they had left, she stepped into the sitting room and asked Meg and Emily to take Mrs Eldersley to her room, for the poor woman looked exhausted.

'I'll sit with her for a while, Nicola,' Emily murmured on her way out.

'I'll retire to my room also, Miss Douglas, I have letters to write.' Miss Burstall nodded to Mr Belfroy and followed the others out.

'A sad day, Miss Douglas.' Mr Belfroy announced, reseating himself on a chair by the fire.

'Indeed, it is.'

'Mrs Eldersley spoke just now of returning to England to join her sister, who is also a widow.'

Nicola slowly sat down in the chair opposite him. 'Really?'

'I encouraged her to go, for it is her heart's wish, but I will be sorry to lose her from my employ.'

Not knowing what to say, Nicola gazed at the fire, thoughts whirling around her head. If Mr Belfroy closed the lodging house, she'd have to find new accommodation and likely at a higher rate. Her finances would be further reduced. Oh, why couldn't she find work!

'I was wondering, Miss Douglas, if, once Mrs Eldersley has departed these shores, whether you'd be interested in running this establishment for your board and a wage of a hundred pounds a year?'

Blinking in surprise, Nicola wondered for a moment if she had heard correctly. Run the lodging house? Could she? It was a responsibility she wasn't prepared for, but one that she found she could do, if the last three days were any judge. Did it matter that she wouldn't be a governess? No, of course it didn't matter. The most important thing was having work. And by taking on this position she'd be making sure the women who came here were well looked after. Her initial surprise was quickly drenched in a flood of gratitude towards Mr Belfroy. Once more this kind honourable man had saved her. 'Thank you, Mr Belfroy, I accept your proposal.'

CHAPTER 6

*N*at shook the sweat from his eyes, ducking his head and weaving to the side, making sure he kept his shoulders and fists up high to protect his chin. From the corner of the chalked square, he made out the old hunched-back man, who stood and, holding the brass bell aloft, rang it heartily three times. Cheers and shouts went up, there was a surge towards the fighters but the organiser's men held the rowdy mass back.

'Christ man, what's taking you so long?' Tristan thumped Nat's back, laughing. 'You should have had him in the first minute. The man is lead-footed.'

Nat wheezed the air into his lungs and wiped the sweat from his eyes. 'I want to keep out of his reach, he can hit like a hammer.'

'Nonsense, man. He's like a windmill, arms everywhere.'

'Shut up will you and get me some water.' Nat closed his eyes for a moment, trying to block out the sight and noise of men baying for his blood. What possessed him to agree to this fight? He was no longer a young man of twenty. It'd been a few years since he celebrated his thirtieth birthday, which should have been enough warning to give up this sort of sport and stick to cricket. He hadn't been practising in months, and it showed.

Tristan thrust a crude tin cup into his hands and water sloshed over his wrist. 'It's only water, perhaps you need something stronger.'

'Sod off.' He gulped the water down just as the hunchback rang the bell again. Surging to his feet, he berated himself once more in agreeing to this madness. Already his opponent, some dockland fellow with missing teeth, had jabbed him in the ribs, which ached when he moved. Another lucky punch had caught his eye and likely tomorrow he'd have the bruise to show for it.

He raised his fists, keeping light on his feet as he'd been taught as a schoolboy back home in England. His wiry opponent gave a little jab, testing the way it was to be in this round, but Nat was tired of the game. It'd been a spur of the moment decision to enter the square, a desperate need to burn off some restless energy that bedding with his current mistress didn't do last night.

Weaving, ducking, he circled the opposite man, looking for a way to end the match so he could return to his club and drown his sorrows for another day. He thought of her then, the woman who'd haunted his mind. Nicola Douglas. His blood grew thick in his veins as an image of her face swarmed before him.

He never saw the punch, just felt the intense pain of the other man's fist hitting his jaw. The impact made him bite his tongue and the stinging pain joined the thudding ache of his face. He staggered, tasted blood. The crowd, mainly all working class, shouted encouragement to their champion and jeered at Nat when he readied himself again.

Anger cursed through Nat and brought him awake and

into focus. Thinking of that damned woman had been his downfall. He'd be on his back if he didn't concentrate.

Uttering a filthy swear word, he pivoted on one foot, danced a side-step and taking the fellow unawares gave him a quick three jab attack that sent the man to his knees. Nat jigged away, hopping from foot to foot at the edge of the square, waiting to see if he regained his feet, but the fellow knew he was beat and surrendered the purse.

Declared the winner by Mr Kent, the organiser, Nat was given the purse of four guineas. The unruly crowd went into a frenzy, the shouts and yelling growing into a deafening roar, as not many had backed Nat. He knew their thinking, a workingman's strength up against a toff who did nothing but sit around in his club all day. But who'd got the last laugh this time? Little did they know that he enjoyed physical pursuits and had been fighting since he was a small boy. Not many had the better of him.

'Excellently done, West.' Tristan once more thumped his back and gave Nat his shirt and coat. Nat winced, moving his shoulders to ease on the shirt over the wet stickiness of his sweat-soaked body.

'Let's get out of here.' Nat grabbed the rest of his belongings from Tristan. Now the fight was over, it wouldn't pay to stay in this rough neighbourhood. The four guineas was hardly worth it really, but then it'd never been about the money, just the sheer joy of beating another. However, today the win left him with a sour taste in his mouth that had nothing to do with the bloodied tongue and lip.

'Wait, I've yet to collect.' Tristan disappeared into the press of workingmen.

Nat groaned in frustration. Hanging around would only be asking for trouble. Already he was sensing a change in the atmosphere. He kept his head down but managed to glance around, taking in the situation. Mr Kent was arguing in the corner with five men, all baying for blood. They'd lost heavily by the looks of it. Shrugging on his jacket, Nat walked backwards a bit, heading towards the barn doors and the alley beyond. Damn Tristan, where was he?

'Mr West!'

Nat swung around and waited for Kent to wield a path through the thick of the crowd towards him. 'I've an appointment, Kent, got to go.'

'Can I book you in for another fight next month?'

'No, not this time.' He wasn't stupid. Kent had scored a high profit today.

Tristan joined them, hurriedly stashing coins into his bulging pockets like a child stealing sweets. 'Nice afternoon's entertainment,' he said with a grin.

'Let us go.' Nat made for the door, glaring at any man who made eye contact with him. Lord, he was stupid to risk his neck at these back-alley fights. If anything happened to him, Frances would be alone.

Once clear of the old barn, he squinted in the harsh sunlight. The squeal of pigs came from the slaughterhouse on the right. He shivered, despite the mild spring warmth of the September day.

'Shall we have a drink at the club?' Tristan replaced his hat as they headed left.

'I don't particularly care. I just want to be clear of that lot in there.'

'You think it could have turned ugly?'

'I'm sure of it. Too much money changed hands. Kent has pulled a fast one I think. He's seen me fight before but that was a new crowd.' As if to justify his words, a shout came from behind them. When Nat turned and saw the dozen or so men spilling out of the barn, yelling fit to be tied, his guts squeezed dread. He turned to Tristan and had to smile at the shock on his face. 'Well, friend, I hope you can run fast.'

* * *

'I THINK YOU SHOULD RECONSIDER.' Meg stood by the kitchen door, hands on hips.

Pushing a strand of hair back from her face, Nicola paused in listing the food in the larder. 'How could I? The income is needed.'

'But to run this place?' Meg's eyebrows shot up. 'To be at the beck and call of the likes of Burstall?'

'Is that so different than answering to a mistress of a family? I think not.'

'But as a governess you have some independence and superiority and respect. Who will respect you now?'

Fed up with Meg's argument, Nicola turned her back on her. 'I'm sorry Meg, I'm too busy to discuss this.'

'See, that's exactly what I mean. From now on you'll be harassed at every opportunity. *Miss Douglas, the breakfast is late. Miss Douglas, I need clean linen. Miss Douglas, must we have mutton for dinner again.* On and on it will be.'

'Like you!' Nicola snapped. Then at the hurt expression Meg wore, she felt instantly guilty. 'I'm sorry, Meg.'

Pulling out a chair, Meg sat at the table. 'I'm only thinking of you, Nicola. You are dear to me.'

'I know, and I thank you for your concern. However, I have made my decision. Mr Belfroy needed someone to carry on the good work he is doing by helping women in less fortunate circumstances. Running this place will be no less hard work than what I did at home, where I oversaw the house and helped my father in the school. I like being busy.'

'Very well, I'll say no more on the matter.' Meg toyed with the salt dispenser. 'I heard Emily being sick again this morning. She can keep nothing down for long.'

'I feel so bad for her.' Nicola paused again from counting the jars of chutney as knocking sounded on the door. 'Can you answer that please, Meg. If it is anyone for Mrs Eldersley, politely send them away, I don't want her disturbed.'

Meg left the kitchen and Nicola once more concentrated on the food stocks. She'd been in charge of the house for only a week and yet the ease in which she slipped into the managing role surprised her. This morning she had started to make inventories of everything in the house, from attics to cellar and outside. After breakfast she had spoken with Mrs Eldersley, who'd handed over the keys without murmur. In fact, Nicola suspected the older woman was relieved of the burden.

'Nicola!' Meg rushed back into the room. 'You are needed.'

'What is it?'

'New arrivals.'

Blinking in alarm, she untied her apron and smoothed her hair. 'I didn't expect…How many?'

'Three.'

'Three?' She hesitated by the door leading into the hallway. 'Is Mr Belfroy with them?'

Meg wrinkled her nose. 'No. From what I can gather they've heard about this place and decided to try their luck here without any introduction. I hardly think any of them has a penny to their name.'

'Oh dear.'

'Shall I send them away then?'

'Well, no…' Taking a deep breath, she raised her chin and headed for the front door where Meg had left them.

Nicola kept a welcoming smile on her face as she glanced over the small huddle of women by the door, despite her heart dipping in pity at the sight of them. Bedraggled, thin and with the air of hopelessness about them, three pairs of eyes stared at her. How could she turn them away? Isn't this what Mr Belfroy had wanted, a home for the unfortunates?

'Welcome. Please, won't you come through to the sitting room?' She waved them in and then turned to Meg. 'Bring in a tea tray and sandwiches, whatever we have,' she whispered.

The women stood just inside the door, not daring to wander further into the sitting room. Each held small amounts of luggage, their clothes faded and in parts frayed.

Nicola went to stand by the unlit fireplace that had been allowed to go out as this morning the sun had promised spring warmth and she'd opened the windows to freshen the room. 'Please, won't you sit down?'

'We are not entirely clean, Madam,' the tallest of the three answered, her cheeks reddening enough to match the colour of her hair beneath her bonnet.

'I'm Miss Nicola Douglas. I'm in charge of this lodging house. Please, I insist you sit.' She smiled warmly, hoping to put them at ease.

'I'm Miss Florence McIntyre,' the red-head responded, being the first to perch on the edge of the sofa. She looked up at the two women beside her. 'This is Miss Lydia Golding and Miss Susanna Nugent.'

'Pleased to make your acquaintance, ladies.'

'Do you have rooms, Miss Douglas? We heard that the fees here are very small, only five shillings, that's half of what we had to pay at the Governess Home. And we heard that if you have no money you can still stay, is that true?' Miss McIntyre's stare bore at Nicola, and she couldn't help but see the desperation in the other woman's eyes.

'Yes, it is.'

'Do you have rooms, or even just one room? We'll happily share.'

'Yes. We'll fit you all in somehow.'

The three women seemed to deflate in front of her eyes. At once and in unison, their shoulders sagged and they dropped their bags to the floor with obvious relief. Miss

Golding started coughing harshly, which made the other two crowd around her to comfort her.

Meg brought in the tea tray, her eyes flashing anger. 'That maid isn't worth the air she breathes!' Then, remembering their guests, she clamped her lips together and placed the tray on the small table as Nicola made the introductions.

Miss Nugent, a small thin woman with bright corn coloured hair and spectacles came to stand beside Nicola. 'Thank you, Miss Douglas. You have saved our lives. One more night in the open and I think poor Miss Golding would have perished completely.'

'In the open? You spent the night in the open?' Nicola gasped.

'Why yes, with no money we had nowhere to go. An innkeeper's wife down by the docks mentioned this place this morning when she found us sleeping in the lean-to behind her public house.'

Righteous indignation at their plight fired through Nicola. How could this happen. What was the government doing to allow such women to be homeless and without hope?

Meg handed her a cup of tea, her face solemn. 'You have a home here, Miss Nugent.'

'We are indeed fortunate,' Miss McIntyre said, between sips of tea. 'There are some ladies who never receive help and die alone.' Her voice had a Scottish accent.

'Yes, that's all too true,' Miss Nugent added. 'We must thank the Lord for His deliverance.'

Meg glanced at Nicola and rolled her eyes. 'In my experience, the Lord helps those who help themselves.'

'Thank you, Meg.' Nicola grabbed her elbow and steered her towards the door before she said anything else to cause offence. 'Can you organise to have a bath drawn. I'm sure the ladies require a bath after their unfortunate experience.'

Meg leaned in close. 'Where's that lazy Irish slut of a maid? She can do it.'

'I don't know,' she whispered, 'I haven't seen her all morning.' She straightened and with a smile turned back to the women. The absence of their useless maid was the least of her problems. 'Ladies, I'm afraid you'll have to share a room, as the house is rather full at the moment.'

'We don't mind, Miss Douglas.' Miss McIntyre stood and gathered the luggage. 'We are grateful for whatever you can spare.'

'Well, finish your tea while I organise the room.' Nicola bade for Miss McIntyre to resume her seat and left them. At the bottom of the stairs she closed her eyes for a moment. To accommodate the ladies would mean two of the current ladies sharing. She knew immediately that Miss Burstall would never share, and Miss Downing's plight meant she needed a room to herself. With a sigh, Nicola mounted the stairs, knowing her little bit of solitude that was her bedroom would now be gone, for Meg would have to share with her.

* * *

AFTER A SLIGHT TAP on the door, Nicola entered Mrs Eldersley's room.

'Miss Douglas,' Mrs Eldersley smiled in welcome from the bed. 'How are you faring downstairs?'

'I'm coping so far.' Nicola smiled, sitting on the wooden chair by the bed. 'How are you feeling?'

'Much better. Mr Belfroy sent me a message saying my ship leaves for England in three days' time and my cabin is all fitted out. He's tremendously kind.'

'Indeed, he is.' Nicola took her hand and patted it. 'Meg

says you've been eating well and have even made it downstairs on two occasions.'

'Yes. I know I could go down more, but the house is so full, and I do not feel ready to talk to strangers yet. Since my dear husband left us I feel so adrift. We were together for many years, most of my life actually, as we were friends since childhood.'

'I understand.'

'The sea voyage will restore me to myself again, I'm certain, and seeing my sister again will help fill the loss.'

'I sincerely hope so, Mrs Eldersley. You have shown nothing but kindness to many women and you deserve peace and contentment.'

'Some guilt remains that I am leaving you all, but I know you can do this work very well, Miss Douglas. You have the correct temperament and spirit and you are young.'

Nicola smiled. 'I must confess this path is something I never expected to take.'

'We should always seize what opportunities are given to us, Miss Douglas. Who knows what the future will bring?'

'Yes, that is true.'

Mrs Eldersley's expression grew serious. 'But you mustn't let your life be taken over by others.' She patted Nicola's hand. 'Do you understand? Make sure you have something of your own, too. Being old and alone isn't recommended, my dear.'

'I'll remember your words, Mrs Eldersley.' However, inside, she knew that her work would be her life. There wouldn't be many opportunities to find a husband and she wouldn't simply settle for anyone just to avoid being alone.

Resting back on the pillows, the older woman nodded. 'Now, Meg told me Mr Belfroy is arriving shortly. Is anything amiss?'

'I think Meg talks a great deal.' Nicola laughed. 'No,

nothing is wrong. I simply need to talk to Mr Belfroy in regards to the future of this lodging house.'

'But why? Do you have concerns?'

'No, not at all, but I must know how it all works. Taking in those three ladies yesterday put us at a stretch. I must know that Mr Belfroy is in agreement with it.'

'Oh, my dear, I can take that worry from you immediately. Mr Belfroy will never turn anyone away. His instructions to you will be the same as he gave me. Take care of the women and he'll take care of the rest. All bills are simply forwarded to him, once they've been checked.'

'I see.'

'Never think you are doing the kind man a disservice, for he supports this cause completely.'

'But the money...The food bill alone is substantial and then there is the fuel-'

'Dear Nicola, do not fret a moment longer. Mr Belfroy has the finance. Forget the bills and help these women find some respectability and security. That is your main and only concern here.' She smiled warmly, showing a glimpse of a forgotten beauty. 'This occupation needs someone young and industrious to make it a success. I was too old, too concerned with my Jim to fully participate, you understand?'

'Yes.' She nodded, feeling lighter of heart. 'I am going to be selfish and say that I wish you were staying with us. I need your guidance and counsel.'

'Nonsense, Nicola. You need neither from me. I've never known such a determined woman as yourself. I have no doubt you will excel in this work, and that you were sent here for this very reason.'

'I will never excel at anything if I don't find suitable servants to engage.'

'You let go the Irish one?'

'Yes, an hour ago.' Nicola sighed.

'Go to the docks when you know an immigrant ship has arrived. Secure them fresh off the boat before they have a chance to be corrupted by the ways of others. That's what I had to do when in need of maids for Mr Belfroy's house. It's undignified, I grant you, but it's always best to trust your own instincts on such things.'

Nicola left Mrs Eldersley's bedroom and headed downstairs to the sitting room. Thankfully, she found it empty and contemplated a few minutes sitting down reading the newspaper, but then remembered it was Wednesday and the soup kitchen needed her.

Kneading the knot of strain from her neck, she went out into the hall and took her cloak and hat from the hook on the wall. After an hour helping Frances, she'd visit the butchers and place an order before stopping at the haberdashery to buy some buttons and thread. Perhaps after that she could take a walk along the harbour. She quickly scrawled a note telling of her intentions. Smiling, she let herself out of the house. How funny it was when, not so long ago, she'd been terribly alone and now, she was surrounded by people, all she wanted was a peaceful hour's walk.

At the end of the street she caught a hansom to take her to Lower George Street, and within a short time she was striding down the lane to the old warehouse. As usual, the human lines crept slowly forward, and she smiled to some children she'd come to know and gave a penny she kept in her pocket to an old man, crippled with arthritis.

Finally, she made it inside and started to unbutton her cloak when she spotted Frances on the far side of the room and next to her was her brother, Nathaniel West.

Nicola's chest tightened as he saw her and gave her a wry smile. What was it about him that made her heart thump erratically whenever he was near? Why did she react to him? He was nothing to her, less than nothing, for she didn't like his arrogance, rudeness, or his superior manner. He was so much the opposite to Frances that she wondered how they could be related.

Still, their very connection meant, at times, she would have to be in his presence, and so she had to hide her confused thoughts about him. Nicola would act as he did, as though he was beneath her notice. She only hoped she could pull it off as well as he did.

CHAPTER 7

'Nicola, you came.' Frances beckoned her over.

With a sinking heart, Nicola weaved between the trestle tables and benches and joined them behind the cauldrons of soup. She gave Frances a kiss on the cheek, the whole time conscious of Mr West's stare. 'How are you, Frances?'

'Well, my dear. I'm so glad you came. I thought you wouldn't have the time now that lodging house has stolen you from me.' Frances turned to her brother. 'You remember, Miss Douglas?'

'Absolutely.' He bowed. 'Miss Douglas.'

'Mr West.' She inclined her head stiffly, noting the greenish-purple bruising surrounding his right eye and wondering what had caused it.

'Are you aware it is my sister's birthday today, Miss Douglas?'

Nicola smiled at Frances. 'No, I had no idea. Oh, you should have mentioned it before, Frances.' She hugged her close. 'My very best wishes to you.'

'Nonsense. Birthdays are awful days reminding a person how old they are getting, nothing to be celebrated in the least. I'm thirty, a disgusting age for a woman, neither young nor old, and definitely not worth rejoicing.'

'But celebrate we will.' Mr West turned to Nicola. 'I'm taking my sister out for the day once she has everything here underway, would you care to join us, Miss Douglas?'

'Oh, yes do, Nicola!' Frances urged, untying her apron.

Nicola shook her head. 'I don't think so, Frances. It's a family occasion. I can help here.'

'Pathetic excuse, Miss Douglas.' Mr West smirked, his eyes darkening in challenge. 'Birthdays must be shared by family and dear friends.'

'Nat's correct, Nicola. You are one of my dearest friends. I insist you join us. My day will be ruined without you.'

'Frances, I'm expected back-'

'We'll send a note to the lodging house and tell them to cope alone for a few hours. They're all grown women. Surely they can manage that.' Frances glanced up as two young women and Mrs Lawson arrived. 'Oh, our replacements. I'm naughty Nicola, as soon as Nat arrived wanting to take me out, I wanted you to come so I organised for two women to take our place.' She grinned like a cheeky child. 'Do put your cloak on, Nicola. I insist upon it.'

Within a short time, Nicola found herself back out on the street climbing into Mr West's elegant carriage. Frances had paid a young boy to deliver a message to the lodgings and despite her last attempts to forgo the entertainment, Nicola was beaten down by Frances's arguments that she must accompany them.

'Where will we go, Nat?' Frances grinned, looking mischievous. Today she wore a dark blue skirt and matching bodice with a white blouse beneath. A black hat covered her short hair and Nicola realised that when dressed properly, Frances West was indeed an attractive woman, especially when she smiled instead of wearing her usual scowl.

Mr West relaxed into the seat, giving the appearance of a gentleman at ease, but watching him, Nicola could tell it was a front to the world. His violet eyes were watchful, his smile strained and more telling to her was the tapping of his fingers on his thigh. Underneath his calm expression she felt tension radiate from him like heat. She didn't understand why she had such insight, especially in respect of this man, but something about him caught her awareness so acutely, she wanted to stare at him. However, when he raised a sarcastic eyebrow at her attentions, she blushed and looked away.

'I thought that since this was your special day, dear sister, that we would have a picnic. The weather is fine enough.'

'Wonderful idea.' Frances beamed. 'I haven't been on a picnic for...' She frowned. 'Well, fancy that, I can't even remember the last time I went on a picnic.'

'Probably because you spend all your time with the poor.'

'Don't start, Nat, please.' Frances's scowl reappeared. 'Not today.'

'No. I apologise.' Nat took her gloved hand and kissed the top of it. 'Forgive me.'

Frances smiled tenderly. 'Don't I always?'

Nicola shifted in her seat at their show of sibling love. Suddenly she felt more alone than ever before. There was no one to love her, to care for her as Frances had. Her father's love had been the one constant thing in her life. She had adored him, his kindness, his intellect, the way he would smile when she did something for him, the way he always had time to share with her. She'd felt his passing far more keenly than her mother's. When he died from a short illness a light went out in her world, and although she had her mother for another six months, they'd never shared a strong bond for her mother's continued ill health had made her a fragile woman for many years, one who took little interest in anything outside of her bedroom.

'Here we are.' Mr West tapped on the side of the carriage and the driver halted the horses at the top of a steep bank. A small jetty poked into the water and tied up at the end of it was a wooden boat. They'd travelled away from the city, keeping the harbour on their right, but around them the bush grew wild with only a few wooden shacks showing evidence of human occupation.

'Where are we, Nat?' Frances asked as he helped them down from the carriage.

'At an inlet. The river goes up to Parramatta, but we shan't go that far. Come along.' He handed them down the rough stone steps cutting into the bank and soon they were seated in the wooden boat and being introduced to a man, Bill Coates, who'd pull the oars.

'Now, Nat.' Frances frowned. 'We're too heavy for one man to row. Help him out.'

'Frances.' Nat laughed. 'I don't think-'

'You rowed at Cambridge, you can row us.' She settled into the boat and handed him one of the spare set of oars. 'Show us your strength, or is it beneath you to row two females to a picnic?'

'Is this some kind of test?' He fumed, sitting at the other end of the boat.

'I'm sure I can manage, sir,' Bill Coates mumbled through his full beard. 'The tide is with us.'

'Nay, Mr Coates, my sister, as is her habit, has set me a challenge, one I cannot ignore.' Shrugging off his fine grey jacket, he glared at Frances and set the oars into the water.

'Are you comfortable, Nicola?' Frances grinned, having won the battle.

'Yes, thank you.' Nicola adjusted her brown skirts, and aware that Mr West would be looking at her back the entire way, she straightened her shoulders and held her chin up. He'd never be able to accuse her of having bad posture.

The September sun warmed them and soon Nicola relaxed a little as the slap of the oars became a soothing rhythm. This was her first chance to be away from the city, and she took the opportunity to study their surroundings. The water was a dark brackenish-green but clean and flowing. Along the sandy banks going past, she spotted spindly pale wildflowers and plants she'd never seen before. Sometimes, a dwelling would appear, complete with a fenced vegetable garden, but generally the bush remained virgin. With the city behind them, the smell in the air changed too. Gone was the sourness of people's refuse and instead the sharp scents of eucalyptus and the softer tea tree retained their rightful place. Nevertheless, other softer scents vied for supremacy and it frustrated Nicola that she didn't know what they were or where they came from. She hated to be ignorant and vowed to find books at the library to redeem this flaw. This country was her new home, she would find out about it all.

'Select a spot to stop, Frances,' her brother ordered from the rear of the boat.

Frances craned her neck, scanning both sides of the river. 'Over to the right, Mr Coates. We'll beach on that sandy area between those two large gum trees.'

'As you wish, Miss West.' Coates strained on the oars and he and Mr West guided the boat to the shallow edge of the river, thrusting the bottom onto the sandy soil.

After Mr Coates helped Frances and Nicola out onto the

grass bank, he reached in for the wicker hamper and the red blanket sitting on top of it.

'Where shall we spread the picnic, Nicola? Frances asked, marching further into the bush.

Following, Nicola listened to the call of the native birds, one sounding like a whip cracking. Sunlight streamed through the gangling gum trees and she ducked under a thicker tree with small, thin green leaves.

'Under this tea-tree?' Mr West came up behind her and she spun around to gaze shyly at him.

Frances took the blanket and spread it out, covering the sparse dry grass. 'This is as good a place as any.'

Nicola knelt on the blanket and helped Frances unpack the variety of food while Mr Coates took out his own meal and wandered down to the water to sit under another tree to eat.

'I hope you are hungry, Miss Douglas.' Mr West smiled, sitting down opposite her. 'I asked my cook to include a good selection.'

'I'm sure we will be most spoilt.' Nicola kept her head down and concentrated on the handling of the food. Indeed, it seemed as though his cook had packed for an army. She laid out plates of game pie, boiled chicken, salads, bread, cheese and fruits.

'Open this, Nat, I'm parched.' Frances passed him a stone bottle and handed out cups.

He opened and sniffed the bottle. 'This is cider, Fran. Cook must have mixed up the bottles. I asked for tea.'

'Never mind, we'll cope.' Frances winked in a devil-may-care way.

'Cider, Miss Douglas?' He gazed at Nicola, his gaze intent. The bruising of his face and even the slight cut in his lip did nothing to distract from his attractive features.

'Thank you, Mr West.' She held out her cup for him to

pour, praying her hand wouldn't shake. Why did he have the ability to make her feel so…insignificant?

They ate in silence for a while, content to listen to the bird calls and then they spoke of small things, the bush around them, the passing of a small boat on the river. Every now and then they heard the rustle of some small animal in the undergrowth, but mainly the day's warmth and the constant chorus of insects settled peacefully over them.

'Lord, I'm so sleepy.' Frances laughed, pushing her empty plate away and draining her cup of cider.

'That was a wonderful repast, Mr West. Thank you.' Nicola began tidying up the blanket, eager not to make eye contact with the disturbing man opposite. Throughout the meal she had listened to his voice, watched the way his hands moved and felt flushed from the experience. What on earth was wrong with her?

'Leave that, Nicola. We can do it later. Lie down and sleep, I'm going to.' Frances, totally at ease, stretched out and, using her arms as a pillow, closed her eyes.

'I don't think I can…' She continued to stack the plates in the hamper.

'Oh Nat, take Nicola for a walk, will you. I'll not rest while ever she's clearing up like some kitchen maid.'

Nicola froze and stared at Mr West, who smiled and tilted his head, again the challenge clear in his eyes.

'Well, Miss Douglas, shall we take a walk. Perhaps I can show you a little of the bush? Though I confess my knowledge of it is extremely lacking, to my shame.' He stood without waiting for her answer and held out his hand to assist her to her feet.

'Thank you, Mr West, I should like that,' she lied, trying to smile and failing miserably.

'Yes, go you two and leave me in peace. It's my birthday after all.' Frances murmured.

Nicola stepped away from the blanket, putting enough space between her and Mr West so he wouldn't offer his arm. Her boots crunched the dry undergrowth releasing a new scent of the dusty earth.

'Frances may have told you that I've been looking at properties in the country?'

'Yes, she did mention it once I believe.'

He nodded and ducked beneath a low branch. 'I've been interested in some land near Camden. I thought to build a house there. On the few times I've visited I've asked the locals to teach me about the area. What grows there and so on. It is beautiful country out there. Macarthur picked well.'

Nicola stepped around a boulder and glanced at him, paying attention to what he had to say. It was the first time they actually shared a proper conversation. Although she had no idea who Macarthur was, she wanted to learn.

Mr West plucked a leaf from a low branch. 'I have much to learn, but I do find it fascinating. It is a harsher country than England and it weeds out weak men easily.'

'What do you think you'll farm there?'

'I haven't quite made up my mind yet. Sheep is a popular choice, but I don't think the acreage is enough to be truly successful in that venture. I thought perhaps to breed racehorses.'

'Racehorses. How interesting.'

'Yes, it is a burgeoning past time here, and a sport I think will grow handsomely.'

They crossed a shallow ditch and Nicola gathered up her skirts to avoid a prickly bush. 'Will you spend your time between the city and country, Mr West?'

'Yes. Though I feel the country will steal my affections rather too effortlessly. I have no love for the city. Away from the harbour, the city soon resembles streets of any other city in the world. That is far from captivating.'

'Yet, it is in the bowels of the city that your sister works so hard.' Nicola slowed down to smell a pale lemon wild-flower poking between two rocks, but found it had no scent.

'Frances is a unique woman and can survive without me being close by.'

'Do you think so?' Nicola looked up at him and their gazes locked. Her mouth went dry and she walked on. 'I-I've found Frances to be formidable on the outside, but inside she is the same as any other woman and needs-'

'You think I don't know my own sister?' He stopped walking and turned to her. 'I assure you, Miss Douglas, my sister's needs will always come first with me. She is all I have.'

'Then I hope when you marry, your future wife will also be Frances's champion.' Heavens what possessed her to say that? Had one cup of cider addled her brains?

He raised one eyebrow, his expression sardonic. 'My wife, should I ever consider marriage,' he whispered, 'will be a woman of compassion, Miss Douglas. No other will tempt me.'

She stepped back, swallowing hastily. 'I'm pleased to hear it.' She cleared her throat and continued walking, feeling flushed and unsettled.

'See this yellow flowering bush, Miss Douglas?' He paused to snap off a small branch festooned with yellow blossoms in the shape of furry balls. 'This is what they call a wattle. Beautiful, yes?' He handed it to her and their fingers briefly touched.

Nicola focused on the flowers, doing her best to ignore his closeness and the way it robbed her of breath. 'I wish I had brought my sketch book.'

'You draw?' He looked surprised.

'Indeed, Mr West.' She raised her chin in defiance to her pounding pulse. 'There is much you do not know about me.'

'Then perhaps I should remedy that?' He spoke softly, his words like a caress.

Flustered, she spun back the way they'd come. 'I think we should return to Frances before we lose our way.' She stalked off and only just heard his mumbled words that he wouldn't mind becoming lost with her.

CHAPTER 8

*N*icola walked into the study, a small room tucked behind the dining room, and closed the door on the women's voices. They'd just returned from seeing Mrs Eldersley onto her England bound ship. Now, back home again, Nicola was truly faced with the knowledge that the whole house depended solely on her.

She trailed her fingers across the account books piled on the corner of the desk. Could she manage the responsibility of caring for these women, of spending Mr Belfroy's money wisely?

Pulling out the top drawer, she took out her sketchbook and opened it to where the yellow wattle blossom lay pressed between the pages. She lightly touched the small delicate balls, remembering Nathaniel West and, as always, her chest constricted. In the three days since the picnic, she'd heard nothing from either him or Frances. Today she should have gone to the soup kitchen, but seeing Mrs Eldersley safely aboard took priority. Would he have been there at the warehouse?

A knock on the door had her snapping shut the sketchbook. She tucked it away and at the same time closed her mind on Nathaniel West. She had a job to do and that didn't give her space to think of him. 'Come in.'

Meg entered carrying a tea tray. 'I need to speak to you about that girl you hired yesterday. What's her name, Hannah?'

Nicola sighed and rubbed her forehead. 'What has she done now?' She sat at the desk, intent on balancing the account books before showing them to Mr Belfroy.

'Arguing with the new cook and she has broken another plate.' Meg grumbled, pouring out the tea. 'The way she's going, we'll all be eating straight out of the cooking pots, for we'll not have a solid piece of porcelain left.'

'She's new and Cook frightens her silly.'

'Cook frightens us all, but we don't go around dropping plates all day.'

'I'll talk to her.' She sipped her tea and sighed, it was refreshing and exactly what she needed.

Abruptly, a scream rent the air. Nicola stood, spilling her tea over her desk. 'What was that?'

Meg placed her cup on the tray. 'Likely Miss Golding has disturbed a mouse again. I'll go and find out. She is a useless-'

The study door was flung open so violently it hit the wall and bounced back, nearly clouting Miss Nugent as she raced in, her eyes wide and her face a ghastly grey-white. 'Miss Douglas!'

'Whatever is the matter?' A cold shiver ran down Nicola's back.

'You must come quickly,' Miss Nugent gasped. 'It's Miss Downing.' She grabbed Nicola's hand and pulled her from the room. Nicola lifted her skirts high and rushed after her.

On the stairs, Miss Burstall stood, her wide-eyed expression one of shock. 'Justice is what I call it. She had no other choice.'

They ignored her and continued up and into Miss Downing's room. There, Nicola skidded to a stop and Meg bumped into her. For a frozen second, she simply stared at the sight greeting her. Emily Downing, still dressed in her outdoors clothes, hung from a rope tied to the roof beam, below her, a tipped over stool. Miss McIntyre was crying, heroically trying to support Emily's weight away from the rope around her neck.

Nicola blinked and then the room erupted into chaos. She rushed forward to help Miss McIntyre lift Emily up and loosen the rope's strangle hold. 'Meg, get a knife quickly. Hurry!' Straining, she glanced at Miss Nugent. 'Run for the doctor!'

'I canna hold her any longer, Miss Douglas,' Miss McIntyre sobbed, her accent thick in her distress.

'Wait.' Nicola yanked up her skirts and climbed onto the bed. With strength she didn't know she owned, she heaved Emily higher. 'Don't let go, Miss McIntyre, I beg you!'

Meg returned with two sharp knives. Behind her, came the cook and the new maid, who began screaming hysterically. Meg climbed up beside Nicola, as did the cook and together they frantically sawed at the rope until they cried out because their muscles burned in their arms.

Miss McIntyre's sobbing became wails as her strength gave out. Finally, the remaining strands of thick hemp snapped and Nicola lost her grip. Emily and Miss McIntyre fell hard onto the floor.

Nicola scurried to Emily's side, but moaned deep in her throat when she realised the unnatural position of Emily's head. Her neck was clearly broken. Gently, hesitantly, she lifted Emily's head and straightened her neck. She looked down at the parted coat and carefully placed her shaking hand over the swollen stomach. Grief welled at the tragic loss.

'Nicola.' Meg touched her arm. 'The police are here.'

Frowning, she rose to her feet. 'The police?'

'Yes, two constables. Miss Burstall went for them.' Meg's tone matched the anger on her face. 'She was *lucky* enough to find two of them walking in the next street.'

Nicola turned to the door only to find Miss Burstall leading in the two constables. Revulsion at the triumph on the other woman's face turned Nicola's stomach. She greeted the men and then asked for everyone to leave, except Meg. With Meg's support she managed to answer the constable's questions and give a dignified account of Emily's life. However, when Doctor Armitage arrived, she gladly left the men to their work and headed downstairs to wait in the sitting room.

'Where's that cold-hearted witch, Burstall?' Meg demanded of the others the minute she entered the room.

'Don't, Meg. Not now.' Nicola took Meg's hand to calm her. 'I'll speak with Miss Burstall later.'

'She has to go, Nicola.'

'She will, believe me. That woman will be gone from this house before nightfall.' On shaky legs, Nicola crossed the room and sat by the unlit fireplace. Miss McIntyre reclined opposite on the sofa, looking exhausted her red freckles standing out on her pale face, while Miss Nugent passed around cups of tea with hands that shook so badly each cup was only half full. Of Miss Golding there was no sign and Nicola hoped she'd gone to bed. Her shattered nervous disposition would be too much for Nicola to bear at that moment.

The next few hours brought utter sadness to the house as the undertaker came and took Emily's body away. The constables left, as did Doctor Armitage while Nicola made the funeral arrangements. Mr Belfroy arrived, his face shadowed with haunting memories of his own recent loss. He sat silently near Nicola, content to let her and Meg deal with the unfortunate business.

When the uneaten evening meal had been cleared away, Nicola left the dining room, talking to Meg. The front door opened, and Miss Burstall entered the house. She hesitated on seeing Nicola and Meg.

'Miss Burstall.' Nicola raised her eyebrows, giving the other woman one of her most superior glares. 'You will pack your belongings and leave this house within the hour.'

Miss Burstall's top lip curled with contempt. 'Gladly, Miss Douglas. The idea of staying another moment within these walls upsets me greatly.' She brushed passed them and had taken three stairs when Meg stepped forward.

'May your conscience trouble you for the rest of your life, Burstall.'

Faltering ever so slightly, Miss Burstall's hand tightened on the banister and she looked down at them with a small smile. 'My conscience is quite clear, Meg Robinson. Is yours? You may have delighted in sharing a house with the likes of Emily Downing, but myself, I have higher standards that you can never hope to achieve.'

'I'd rather be dead than like you, you dried up old prune. You wouldn't know compassion and sympathy if you tried. I dread to think what kind of children you produce in your role as a governess. Their poor parents have no notion of whom they are hiring.'

Burstall took another step. 'I can say the same for you, too, Miss Robinson.'

Nicola stepped forward, hoping that what they all thought wasn't true. 'Did you have anything to do with Emily's decision to take her own life?'

'She made the choice, I didn't force her.'

Frustration flared in Nicola's chest. 'Explain yourself.'

'Let me just say that if Emily Downing found the need to

end her life I did nothing to prevent her. After all, what kind of future would she and her bastard have had?' Straight backed, she continued on to her room.

'Why you hateful, mean-faced witch!' Meg yelled and rushed forward.

'No, Meg.' Nicola barely managed to hold Meg still, for her spit-fire friend was intent on scratching Miss Burstall's eyes out and she was half tempted to let her.

Later, with the sun descending behind distant ranges, Nicola lit the lamps and drew the curtains, shutting the world out. The women had eaten a light supper and then retired to their rooms, leaving her and Mr Belfroy alone. She had ordered the fire to be lit, its cheery blaze comforting.

'No matter how hard I try, it still happens...' Mr Belfroy murmured, staring into the golden flames.

'What happens?' Nicola sighed, flexing her aching shoulders.

'They still die. Good young women still fill the church-yard no matter what I do.'

'Oh, Mr Belfroy, you mustn't blame yourself. You cannot save them all. You do so much as it is.'

'Not enough, Miss Douglas. Not enough.'

'Nonsense. I won't let you torment yourself with things over which you have no control. What occurred to Emily was tragic indeed, but I feel she was beyond saving. Her mind and soul had long been troubled by the events happening to her. She saw no future for herself because of the child. Can any of us be surprised by what she did? To her, in her mind, her life was already over. All she had to do was physically escape.'

'But it is the tragedy of her downfall that we must prevent, Miss Douglas. We must find these women, these good intelligent women, decent situations with the remuneration they deserve so they can live a life without hardship and degradation when they are out of work.'

'You cannot mend the entire population of unemployed women, Mr Belfroy. It is impossible.'

He jerked to his feet, his eyes damp. 'I must try, Miss Douglas. I cannot sit by idle.'

Nicola stood and placed her hand gently on his arm. 'Mr Belfroy, you, of all men, are the least idle. You know what good work you do here.'

He looked her directly in the eyes. 'It is not enough, my dear, and never will be.'

The following day, Nicola sat at her desk supposedly working, but she couldn't focus. Instead, she spent half an hour staring out the little window, which overlooked the neighbour's back garden. With a sigh, she put away her pen and wiped her tired eyes. Misery weighed on the house's occupants like a heavy chest cold.

Restless, she stepped to the door. Perhaps a swift walk would lift the mood. From the kitchen came the crashing sound of crockery being dropped and Cook's cursing at Hannah. Sighing, Nicola quickly donned her shawl and hat and slipped from the house before someone spotted her.

A slight breeze swayed the topmost tree branches. The bright sunshine made Nicola close her eyes and raise her face up to it. Spring flowers of daffodils, snowdrops and bluebells reminiscent of English gardens had burst into bloom in the small gardens she passed. She wished the lodging house had a good garden of its own, instead of the square patch of lawn and the one large tree in the middle. In fact, she wished the lodgings had more space entirely, both inside and out.

At the end of the street she turned left and not right as usual. The noise of the harbour and docks didn't appeal today, but a quiet walk around the suburban streets of

Double Bay suited her more. The houses in this area were well cared for, with large lawns and sweeping verandahs.

She'd walked for nearly ten minutes, admiring the blossom on fruit trees that offered up their scents from behind wooden fences, when she paused in front of one large two-story brick house set back from the road and with extensive lawns. On the gate a sign read 'For Sale'.

'For sale,' she whispered, her mind whirling with ideas. The house was well positioned on the high side of the road and the top floor would likely have a view of the harbour. Edging the lawns were tall palms, banana trees and immature Norfolk Pines, and all gave the garden a touch of some tropical paradise.

'Miss Douglas?'

Nicola whirled around to the slowing carriage. She hadn't heard it approach. Mr West poked his head out of the door. She sucked in a deep breath at the sight of him. How much easier her life would be without the bothersome reactions she had to this man. 'Good day, Mr West.'

He climbed down from the carriage and bowed over her hand. 'I didn't believe my eyes when I saw you there. You are the last person I expected to be here.' He looked up at the house. 'Do I have a contender for this house?'

She blinked in surprise. 'You are looking to buy this property?'

'Yes, I am. At least I'm thinking about it.' He grinned, tilting his head to study her. 'Does Mr Belfroy pay you so well that you can afford such a house?'

'You are making fun of me, sir.'

'Indeed, I am.' He glanced down at the ground and then back to her face. For once, sincerity clouded his eyes. 'I am ill-mannered, forgive me.'

'I am not so unbending as to not take a joke, Mr West.' She managed a small smile, not knowing why she wanted to make him feel better. Blushing, she turned back to view the house. 'If I was fortunate enough to be able to purchase this house, I'd turn it into a home for governesses and middle-class ladies in need.'

'Really?' His bland expression gave no hint of his thoughts. 'Would you care to see inside? I have the keys.'

She stepped away, shaking her head. 'Thank you, but no. It is futile to torment one's self for things they can never have.'

His soft smile transformed his handsome face into something so wondrous, of such startling male beauty, Nicola felt robbed of all thought. He held out his hand. 'Indulge me, please.'

Mindless, she allowed him to guide her through the gate, up the path and onto the wide verandah. She stood still as he unlocked the door and then he ushered her inside the square entrance hall.

Rooms led off the hall left and right, but the main feature, a magnificent central staircase dominated it. Nicola ran her hands over the polished timber banister and gazed upwards at the large landing at the top.

She glided from room to room, the drawing room, front parlour, the library and dining room. In some rooms, the cornices were moulded in designs of cherubs and flowers, others had mock silk Chinese wallpaper covering the top half of the walls, differing in colour in each room, while the bottom half was timber panelled. Large windows let in plenty of light. She finished her tour in a study decorated in dark red.

'It is a worthy house, yes?'

She turned to him and nodded, unable to speak. The house was the exact kind she would want to live in.

'I will buy it,' he whispered, 'I'll buy it for you.'

Nicola stared at him as though he'd spoken a foreign

language. His words floated around in her mind, but made no sense.

'Nicola,' he took her hand, 'may I call you Nicola? It's such a beautiful name and suits a magnificent woman such as you.' He stepped closer, his eyes darkening as though burning with some inner fire. 'Nicola, marry me, please.'

'Mr-marry? You?' She couldn't breathe.

The corner of his mouth lifted. 'Is that so awful?'

'But you do not know me, or I you.'

'Then we must rectify that.' He brought her hand up and gently placed his lips to it and the strength went from her legs.

'I cannot marry.'

'Why ever not?' He laughed lightly, though she found nothing funny about it.

'Because…because I am a governess…'

'And there is a law against governesses marrying?'

'No, but…' Her mouth went dry as he lowered his head, stopping inches from her face.

'Nicola, marry me. I'll make you happy. I promise.'

As if pulled by an invisible string she swayed forward, their lips touching, but the physical contact sprang her drugged mind awake and she jerked back, shocked at her behaviour. 'I must go!'

'Nicola.' His violet eyes held a promise of delights, of hidden sensations that he could give her.

'No. Don't call me that. You…we…' She touched her lips with her fingertips, frightened by the intensity of him. It was as though the very air about them was charged. Trembling, she walked backwards, putting space between them. If he touched her she believed she would lose her mind, she was sure of it. How could he arouse such desperate feelings in her from a mere glance of those eyes of his? She was terribly afraid that if he laid a hand on her she would beg him to never stop...

'Nicola, please...'

'I cannot.' She shook her head, not knowing her mind.

'Why?' His pained passionate plea broke her heart.

'We are too different! I know nothing about you.'

'Let me court you, please.'

'No. We aren't even friends. You—' Choking on a sob, she fled the house and the tantalising Nathaniel West.

CHAPTER 9

*S*tanding, hands on hips, Nicola glared at the cook lolling on the floor, her legs spread wide and an empty bottle of gin nestled in her arms. The beginnings of a meal lay scattered across the table. 'Mrs Nesbit, will you get up!'

'Can't. Me legsth won't work...' She hiccupped and laughed.

Nicola glanced at Meg who, having divested her outdoor clothes, came to stand beside her. 'Mrs Nesbit is drunk.'

Meg sniffed. 'Half her luck.'

'Meg!'

Shrugging, Meg headed for the hallway. 'Let her sleep it off.'

'And have no dinner?'

'Who can eat anyway?'

Nicola gave the intoxicated woman a small kick in frustration. 'You have no decency. Now get up.' When the cook fell sleepily to one side, Nicola cursed and stormed from the kitchen. In the study, she stopped by the window and massaged her temples. The day had been trying enough with

Emily's funeral without coming back to find Mrs Nesbit in that state and the maid nowhere to be found. Why did this country have such dreadful servants? They'd both have to go, but who'd replace them? She shook the thought away, not prepared to deal with it today.

A slight tap interrupted her thoughts and the door opened to reveal Mr Belfroy. 'Ah, Miss Douglas, sorry to disturb you.'

'Not at all, Mr Belfroy, do come in.'

He stood just inside the door, his hat brim being mangled in his thick fingers.

Nicola frowned, for the kind man was usually at ease in her company. 'Is there something I can help you with?'

'There is indeed, my dear.'

'Sit down, please.'

'I cannot stay...' He straightened, taking a deep breath. 'I was wondering if you could manage a few more ladies here.'

'More?'

'I've found a small hostel down near the Rocks area. A disgusting place with a ruinous reputation.' Anger flashed in his weary eyes.

'And there are ladies there? Governesses?' She couldn't help sounding doubtful, as the Rocks area was notorious for habituating the worst sort of people.

'Yes, at least one lady is, or was. She is in very poor spirits.'

'But you think there could be more than one lady?'

'I'm certain of two staying there. The-the other woman, Miss Rogers, needs immediate help. She is with child... Unmarried. Not a governess, but a lady's maid recently arrived from England. Her virtue was stolen aboard the ship. There is an inquiry into the matter...' His shoulders sagged. 'I'm sorry this has come so soon after Miss Downing. I quite understand if you refuse-'

'Of course, we must help them.' Nicola started for the door. 'Give me a moment to gather my things.'

'You are a good woman, Miss Douglas.'

'Who can turn their back on those in need?' She smiled grimly, thinking of Emily Downing and how she hadn't been able to help her. Pushing the thought away, she marched into the hallway. This was her job, her duty now. It was what she had agreed to do. Besides, keeping busy kept her mind off a certain handsome man with the eyes that seemed to burn through her soul.

In the carriage, Mr Belfroy gave her more details as they made their way through the poorest area of the city to the infamous Rocks area. 'I do understand, Miss Douglas, your reluctance in accommodating more women. The house is becoming too small.'

'And we have unreliable staff, Mr Belfroy, to help us.'

'Well, you'll be pleased to know that I have put my house up for sale and the proceeds will be used to purchase a more spacious house for you.'

Nicola stared at him. 'Oh, Mr Belfroy, is that necessary?'

'You know our predicament, it is the least I can do.'

'But where will you live?'

The carriage slowed and Mr Belfroy opened the door to the sharp noises of the docks. 'I shall rent an adequate apartment in town. My needs are small since I have withdrawn from society. I much prefer to have things this way. There is no point in trying to persuade me, my mind is made up.' He descended from the carriage and then helped her down.

Nicola gazed around in disgust. She had only been to this foreshore end of the Rocks once, with Frances, and had never wanted to repeat the visit. She was amazed at the difference a few hundred yards could make, for up on the hill, wealthy families lived in style. Yet down at the water's edge, the worst kind of debauchery occurred. The fresh salt breeze from the harbour couldn't remove the rot of human refuse. Mean little alleys criss-crossed the streets at this point of the harbourside. Docks and wharfs had long been established here, but with the flourishing industry came the lowest aspects of society, who frequented the public houses, brothels and opium dens. Effluent and general rubbish crammed the sides of the road, the buildings were rundown and in various states of ruin. The smell of rotting refuse filled her nose, making her gag. How could anyone live in such conditions?

'This way, my dear.' Mr Belfroy took her elbow and guided her around the stinking piles of goodness knows what and into a laneway boarded by stone terrace houses rising up the steep incline. 'The hostel is further along, and, if one can be generous enough to say so, it's in a slightly better street than this one. Only, the carriage is too wide for it.'

She nodded, holding a handkerchief to her nose and prayed they wouldn't be attacked and robbed. A mangy dog peed against a wall and from the opposite side of the street a rough-looking man emerged from a doorway and stared at them.

At the end of another dirty, neglected street, Mr Belfroy entered a two-story building. Its upper floor held a balcony from which hung copious amounts of washing.

Inside the dimly lit corridor, they made for a decaying staircase. At the top, a man and a woman, barely decently covered, leaned against a wall chatting. Nicola glared, fighting the urge to speak her mind about their slovenly ways, but Mr Belfroy turned left and she shuddered at the thought of being left behind. In another room a door was opened showing a couple kissing on an unmade bed. Nicola stared at the sensual way the man stroked the woman. Her stomach tightened for she immediately thought of Nathaniel West. Hurrying along, she blocked out other images and sounds coming from various rooms. It seemed the place was nothing more than a brothel.

The second last door on the right was open. Mr Belfroy knocked but the woman on the bed didn't respond. 'Miss Rogers, I have returned as promised.'

Nicola entered the badly lit room and crept closer to the rusty iron bed. 'Miss Rogers, I'm Nicola Douglas.'

The woman, her eyes sunken and with dark shadows bruising the delicate skin beneath, turned to stare at her. 'You must go away.'

'Why?' Nicola crouched beside the bed.

'Because I am bad, terribly bad.'

'I'm sure that is not true.' Nicola smiled in reassurance. 'Come, gather your things. I wish for you to return home with me.'

'You don't know what I've done…I carry a child.'

'Yes, I'm aware of that.'

'I was wanton.' Her face screwed up in misery. 'He promised to marry me, but he abandoned me. I had nothing…He took my money, everything and left only empty promises. I hate him, but not as much as I hate myself for my weakness…'

'Come, let me help you.' Nicola aided the thin woman, dressed in rags, to stand. Her body was wasted from starvation, yet her stomach was large with child. Images of Emily clouded Nicola's mind as she helped Miss Rogers out of the room. Could she really go through it again? Was she strong enough to bear this woman's burdens too?

'I shall give the child away to the orphanage,' Miss Rogers murmured, slipping her feet into scuffed shoes. 'You will help me to do that?'

'Yes.' Nicola aided her to the door, filled with despair for this poor woman.

'Thank you. Then I may start again, move away… I always

wanted to visit Africa, or even India... Yes, that is what I'll do.' Decision made, Miss Rogers breathed a deep sigh and sagged against Nicola as though the act of talking had taken her last strength.

Mr Belfroy stepped forward and took Miss Rogers by the waist and half carried her. 'I'll take her down to the carriage and then return for you. Miss Barker's room is the next room along.'

Nicola left them and headed down the dark silent corridor. She tapped on the door and it was wrenched opened by a tiny woman dressed entirely in black, holding her bag. 'Miss Douglas?'

'Yes.'

'Oh good, Mr Belfroy mentioned you might come for me. I'm Miss Georgina Barker. I've been waiting, you see, praying you would come for me. Mr Belfroy did speak of me?'

'Yes, he did. I'm here to take you back to the lodging house I manage.'

'Oh, thank you.' She bustled out of the room and slammed the door with a resounding bang. 'Good riddance to this fifthly place. Once I'm in respectable accommodation I know I'll find work more suitable than what I've been doing.'

'Which was?'

Miss Barker stormed down the corridor. 'Needlework. Not that needlework isn't respectable, it is, but I'm a teacher. I've been taking in needlework for the last few weeks, but then my glasses broke, and I've been unable to afford to have them replaced and I cannot work without them. Sadly, things have rather gone downhill from there.'

Nicola had to hurry to keep up. 'Were you originally a governess, Miss Barker?'

'Indeed yes. But now I plan to take the Teacher's Certificate and teach in a government school. Mr Belfroy said he'll pay for me until I have a position. The man is a saint indeed.'

Miss Barker chatted all the way to the carriage and, once inside it, she smiled at Miss Rogers. 'Cheer up, we'll be just fine now.' She took Miss Rogers's hand and held it all the way to the lodgings as if it was the most natural thing in the world to do.

* * *

'DARE you not face me anymore, Nicola?'

Nicola looked up from her desk and frowned in surprise as Frances strode into the study. 'Good day, Frances. It's a pleasure to see you.'

'Is it?' Frances marched to the desk and threw her gloves on it. Today she wore her split trouser-skirt and also her scowl. Her hair stood on end as though she'd raked her hands through it numerous times. She looked like she was either ready for war or just participated in one.

'Are you upset at something?'

'Yes, damn you.'

Nicola slowly rose to her feet, dropping her pen onto the books she'd been working on. 'What have I done?'

'You refused my brother. Why, I'll never know.' She paced the room. 'For two weeks he's been unbearable, far worse than usual, drinking and whoring, and I had no idea why until finally this morning he told me that you had refused him. I'm stunned beyond words that he even asked you. After all, marriage was never something he strived for, he was always happy with his little liaisons.'

Nicola winced and glanced down at the desk. She had made the right choice then. Mr West was totally unsuitable as a husband. Drinking, whoring... She felt sick at the thought.

Frances continued pacing, her movements jerky. 'And you were the last person I imagined him to propose to. If he ever married I expected him to pluck a dainty flower from the highest rung of Sydney's society, that would have been just the thing for him to do, something for him to throw back into mother's face, since she's done nothing but belittle him since birth, telling him he'd amount to nothing. Of course, she was made correct because Nat did exactly as she said he would do, just to hurt her as she hurt him with her disparaging words.' She sucked in a breath. 'But you... Now that I never could have believed...'

'Perhaps he thought by marrying me, someone beneath his station, would also antagonise your mother?' She swallowed past the hurt.

'No...' Frances shook her head. 'This went much deeper than revenge. A flighty disgustingly rich colonial heiress would have been revenge on mother, someone who would even look down on mother as unimportant would have been revenge, but not you.' She rubbed her forehead. 'I don't understand it.'

'That makes two of us.'

'Why did you refuse him? Oh, I know he can be a bear at times, but underneath his prickles and bad moods he is a good man.'

'I—'

'I've never seen him in such a state. Even when our parents treated us worse than a farmer does his animals, he'd always put on a brave face to the outside world. But now...' She paused near the window and stared out. 'He said he'd buy you a house. Nat never buys anything for anyone. He takes care of himself first, and me too, of course, but he's always kept everyone else at a distance.' She slowly turned, and her eyes filled with tears. 'It breaks my heart to see him so...without hope...'

Nicola swallowed past the tightness in her throat. She'd never seen Frances emotional before. 'I'm sorry, Frances.'

'But why did you refuse him?'

'You said it yourself. I'm hardly the perfect choice, so much so that even you cannot believe it to be true.'

'Never mind me. You didn't reject him because of me. So why did you?'

Nicola held her hands out and shrugged. 'There are many reasons really. I like what I do here. I don't think I could bend to a man's will now. I enjoy my freedom and independence. I never thought I would marry. I have my work.'

'But don't you want a family of your own?'

'Yes...perhaps. I have dreamed of it occasionally, but I don't think being a wife and making calls will fulfil me for the rest of my days, Fran. And no man, no matter how good a husband, will allow his wife to work all the time as I do, as *you* do.'

'Nat is unlike most men.'

'Your brother and I are very different people. He hardly knows me. Will he contend with me helping those less fortunate for I will not give it up.'

Frances sniffed and shrugged in a most unbecoming way, like a little lost boy.

At her fragile stance, something rarely seen with Frances, Nicola's heart melted. She crossed the floor and held her friend tight. 'You know I'd adore having you as a sister, but I believe your brother would ask for more than I can give him. He'd want his wife to be his social equal, which I'm not and never will be.'

Nodding, Frances pulled away. 'I understand, naturally I do, for I am the same. No man will put up with me and my actions and beliefs. Are you certain though, that rejecting him was the right thing to do?'

'It has to be. We are opposites.' Moving back to the desk, Nicola sought to change the subject, she had already spent countless hours tormenting herself over Nathaniel West. She didn't like how her body respond to him, how her mind went stupid at his nearness. No, she believed Mr West had asked her to marry him on impulse, on a whim of fancy. If he'd been a true suitor would he have left it so long before seeing her again?

She searched for a large piece of paper and finding it handed it to Frances. 'Look what Mr Belfroy has done? He's bought a larger house for us, and I am to manage it.'

'A bigger house?' Frances studied the document. 'My, that is a grand home.'

'Yes, a proper place for women. It is to be called Belfroy's Home for Governesses and Middle Class Ladies. Those who don't want to stay at the government governess home for whatever reason, including those women who have...who have been abused, or with child and who cannot stay at other places...'

'Middle class?' Frances dropped the paper as if scalded. 'Surely the poor women of the city need help too.'

Nicola gathered up her papers. 'Well, yes, but they are not what this home is catering to. I'm also going to be running an agency. A place where educated women can record their names and potential employers can come and inspect the list for suitable applicants. We shall advertise in the newspapers.'

'I'd be happier if you also took in the poor women of the district and homeless children.'

Pausing from tidying up her desk, Nicola looked at her. 'Fran, there are already places like that, orphanages and such like.'

'There is always the need for more, Nicola. You know that.'

'I'm sure there is, however, there is also the need for this type of home so women who are not used to living in such primitive conditions can be cared for.'

'Yet, the poor must remain in their own filth, is that it?'

'No. You know I don't mean any such thing.'

Frances placed her hands flat on the desk. 'Then why turn your back on the lower classes?' She sneered.

Annoyed, Nicola glared. 'My role is to help fellow women such as myself. I cannot mix the two classes together in one home, that will not do, and you know it. I cannot do everything. Why are you arguing with me in this way?'

'Why are you determined to advance one sort of woman over another?' Frances fired back.

'The poor have many champions, but governesses and educated women do not. There are charities for the destitute, but none for middle class women. I thought you, of all people, would understand my desire to do what I can for these women.'

'What I understand is the lack of compassion you and Belfroy are showing to women of a lower class, who could, with your help, rise above the desolation surrounding them.'

'Why must *we* do it all, Frances?' Nicola couldn't fathom her unfairness or accusations. 'If you are so passionate to do more than you are, then find the sponsors to create a home for the poor, as we are doing.'

Frances laughed with mock humour. 'You think it is so easy, or that I haven't tried? Good God, it's all I spend my waking hours on, but unlike you, I do not have a wealthy man behind me, whose sole crusade is to help others. I have to manage with the measly handouts that I can beg for.'

'I haven't the answers, Frances. I'm simply doing the best I can with what I have. I'm sorry your ambitions to help the poor aren't met with more support, but you mustn't blame me for helping others the way I am.'

'Listen to you, Saint bloody Nicola.' Frances's face grew red with anger. 'Don't you patronise me from the safety of this house, where everything is provided for you. You have no idea how the poor live and what it takes to survive each day.'

'And you do?' she snapped. 'You, who left an upper-class home and society in England because you wanted freedom from your controlling parents? You would know less than I do about being poor? I hardly think so!' Stressed at the disintegration of their friendship, Nicola collected the few things she needed from the desk. 'I haven't the time to stand here and explain my actions to you, Frances. I am to meet Mr Belfroy within the hour.'

'Perhaps my brother never stood a chance with you because another has beaten him in the contest?'

Locking her desk drawer, she jerked at Frances's innuendo. 'What do you mean?'

'Mr Belfroy can give you just as much as my brother can,' Frances's top lip curled in revulsion, 'perhaps you see him as a future husband, someone who will not be long on this earth and who will leave you a generous widow to do as you please?'

Nicola gasped, horrified. 'How can you say such a disgusting thing to me?'

At once Frances's expression altered from anger to shock. 'Oh, Nicola, oh forgive me. I'm sorry, truly.' She held out her hands, shaking her head. 'My temper is impossible. I am unforgivable. I meant none of it, you must understand. Words run out of my mouth, always have done, and trouble follows immediately.'

Feeling her friendship betrayed and sullied, Nicola stepped away, towards the door. 'Even in anger, once some words are spoken they are beyond forgiveness.' She dipped her head in farewell. 'Excuse me, I am late. Goodbye, Frances.'

* * *

NAT POURED another brandy and handed it to Frances, who still cried silently in the chair by the window. Her tale of the argument she had with Nicola caused him more pain than he'd show. At first, he wanted to throttle Fran for being so senseless and rash. Her temper, like his, had been a problem since childhood, and usually those on the receiving end didn't matter to them, until now. Why did she have to ruin the one good friendship she'd ever had? And because of it, he'd not have the link to Nicola, which might have allowed him to watch over her from afar.

He crossed to stand on the other side of the window. Together they watched the street traffic below. For the last couple of weeks, he'd done his best to drown his sorrows in any way he could, drinking, staying out at clubs until sunrise, sleeping with a bevy of women, gambling. None of it had worked. He still woke from sleep and Nicola was his first thought and the hollow pain would claw at him again. How had he fallen for her so hard and so fast? It repulsed him that he'd allowed his emotions to get the better of him.

It was rather hilarious that for all his adult life he'd had no desire to marry. His parents' soulless marriage helped to confirm that decision. Yet, the moment he realised that marriage to Nicola would be something positive and even joyous in his life, he'd found rejection once again. Only this time the rejection from Nicola hurt far more than his parents had ever done. His parents' deplorable behaviour was constant and he could always trust in that continuing, uncaring attitude they had, but with Nicola, he'd been blindsided. He never saw it coming. Ever since that fatal night in front of the theatre when she had given him a look of utter loathing, he'd been captivated and intrigued. For her, he wanted to be good and decent, to earn her approval at every opportunity. Only, his boorish manners had revolted her, and rightly so. He didn't know how to undo the damage.

He sighed, despondency weighing heavy on him. 'You will write a letter of apology, Fran.'

'Yes.' She nodded, dislodging more tears. 'Though I cannot blame her if she never reads it and I never hear from her again.'

His heart constricted at the thought. Despite Nicola's refusal of his marriage proposal, which he knew was untidily done, his affections remained true. When had he known she was the woman for him, he wasn't certain. Only, he couldn't survive a day, an hour, without thinking of her. He ached to hold her and see that soft smile she wore. He wanted her like no other woman in his life and it damn well confused him no end.

'You have to go to her, Nat.'

Frances's words broke into his thoughts and he jerked straighter. 'Go to her? I think not.' The very idea brought him out in a cold sweat.

'Who else will plead my forgiveness? I hardly think she'll agree to see me.'

He felt torn in two. Yes, he wanted to see her, but could he actually face her so soon after his rash proposal? Shaking his head, he went to the cabinet and poured himself more brandy. When had he ever been a coward? Not until Nicola Douglas entered his world and brought his heart to life.

'Please, Nat, please do this for me.'

'Haven't I extricated you from enough situations?' He gulped from the glass.

Frances wiped her eyes with a white linen handkerchief. 'I will beg if that is what it'll take.'

He swallowed the rest of his brandy in one swallow. 'Very well. I'll go, but I hope you've learnt a lesson from this, Fran. Good friendships aren't so thick on the ground that they can be ruined without thought.'

'I know, and you don't have to lecture me, brother,' she

snapped. 'I hardly see you surrounded by that many men you can call friend.'

'Frances!' He stared at her in astonishment. 'Will you control your mouth?'

She closed her eyes wearily. 'I'm sorry. Oh, I am hateful.'

'You need a bridle,' he scoffed, lifting the brandy bottle to fill his glass again, only he paused, and set it back down. If he were to call on Miss Douglas a clear head would be wise.

'When will you go?'

'Tomorrow. In the afternoon. I have appointments in the morning.'

'Be sincere, Nat.' Frances gave a wobbly smile.

'Naturally.' He turned away to hide his shaking hands, hoping the amount of alcohol was the reason for it and not the thought of facing Miss Douglas.

* * *

'NICOLA?' Meg lowered the morning's newspaper. 'Where are you going at such an early hour?'

'There's an immigrant ship in the harbour, docked only last night. I'm going down to see if I can find some servants. A new employment agency has opened near Circular Quay.' Nicola straightened her pale blue skirts and adjusted her hat in the mirror above the fireplace.

'Well, find a cook if you can, breakfast was intolerable. A decent kitchen and house maid would be nice too.'

Nicola rolled her eyes. 'I'll do what I can. You could come with me, you know.'

Meg shifted slightly on the sofa. 'Not today. I thought I might-'

Miss Nugent raced into the sitting room, waving a letter at Nicola. 'Oh, Miss Douglas, you'll never guess my excitement.'

'A position, Miss Nugent?'

'Yes.' Her face broke into a wide grin. 'I have been accepted by a Mrs Farmer, from the Hawkesbury district. Isn't that wonderful?'

Nicola patted her arm. 'I'm extremely pleased for you.'

'Thank you. I am so relieved. I shall have three children to teach and an annual salary of seventy pounds. It's not as much money as I'd have liked, but it is better than none at all.'

'I agree.' Nicola smiled, checking the money in her reticule. 'I hope you'll be most happy there.'

Meg stood, throwing the newspaper on the occasional table. 'When do you leave?'

'Tomorrow evening. Mr Farmer is in town at the moment, but is returning home tomorrow and I shall go with him.' Miss Nugent nearly skipped in her excitement.

'I'll arrange for Mrs Nesbit to provide a nice farewell meal.' Hoping the cook would be sober enough to prepare it, Nicola headed out into the hallway for her parasol. 'I must go.' She left the house and hurried down the street. At the corner she caught an omnibus to take her into the city.

Once at the docks, Nicola waded through the stream of humanity that always seemed to be in this area and headed to the agency. The quay surged with activity. The cries of swooping seagulls added to the noise of men unloading ships, of the clip-clopping of horses on the street, of the clanging at the iron mongers, the screeching of hawkers.

At the doorway leading to the offices, Nicola found a large group of people waiting their turn to enter, while inside the people were crammed cheek to jowl. Disheartened, she had no wish to stand around for an hour or so waiting her turn, and so leaving the office, she headed away from the harbour and up towards the city centre, hoping to do a little shopping.

Shying away from Lower George Street, to save bumping into Frances, whose behaviour still hurt her, Nicola crossed Bridge Street and entered the haberdashery on the corner.

After buying reels of cotton, needles, buttons and ordering white linen to be made into table cloths for the new establishment, she asked for them to be delivered and left the shop. She continued on, happy to window shop. It felt indolent to be away from the house, the women and the work ahead of her, but a morning spent doing nothing wouldn't hurt just this once. Soon they'd be moving into the new house Mr Belfroy bought in Glebe and then there'd be weeks when she'd not have a moment to herself.

Walking along Macquarie Street, Nicola headed towards the Inner Domain. She dodged a cat that streaked out between two carts and flew past her skirts. A little boy holding his mother's hand squealed, wanting to chase after it, but a command from his mother had him contentedly walking again. Nicola gazed after him for a moment. The small boy glanced over his shoulder, finger stuck in his mouth, large blue eyes unblinking and Nicola smiled.

The door to a large stone building on her right opened and two men and a woman strode out, talking. Nicola's step faltered as she recognised Nathaniel West as one of the men. He was facing slightly away and had not noticed her. After shaking the man's hand, he kissed the woman's hand and tipped his hat to her. Nicola couldn't take her eyes off him. That man, only eight feet from her, had asked her to marry him. It defied logic. How was it possible for two people to go about their lives when one of them has proposed marriage and the other has rejected it?

Nicola took a step back, hesitating on whether to cross the road or return the way she'd come. Meeting face to face with Mr West wasn't an alternative. She stood on the edge of the street waiting for a wagon to rumble by, willing it to move faster so she could escape.

'Miss Douglas?'

Nicola, half turned, momentarily closed her eyes and prayed for courage. Summoning a smile, she spun back to him. 'Mr West. How delightful.'

His wry smile made her heart skip a beat. 'Come now, Miss Douglas, we both know delightful isn't the correct word in this case. Perhaps...awkward would be more fitting?' He took her hand and bowed over it. 'You are well?'

She nodded, blushing. 'As you see.'

'Would you indulge me in a walk, Miss Douglas? There are things I must say.'

'No, sorry, I…'

'Please?' His eyes softened with the plea.

Hoping her trembling didn't show, she swallowed and wondered at her reasoning when she said she would.

They walked for the length of the street, content to let the city noise, the pedestrians and traffic occupy them for a time. Nicola didn't know how to start a conversation with him. Her mouth seemed to have shut tighter than a clam. Would he propose again? She hoped he wouldn't, for she utterly believed she wouldn't know how to refuse for a second time. And did she want to?

Sneaking a peek at him from under her hat brim, she sighed inwardly at his handsome profile. Not many women would refuse such a man. So, why had she?

'If you are not tired, we could cross over and walk through the Domain?'

She glanced up at him and smiled nervously. 'I am not tired.'

He raised his hand as though to place it over hers, but slowly lowered it back to his side. 'I had intentions of calling on you this afternoon.'

'Oh?' Her stomach clenched at the thought.

'On Frances's behalf.'

'I see.' Disappointment echoed through her, which made her frown in surprise. What did it matter if he wasn't coming to see her for himself? What did she expect? It was intolerable to be so confused and it was all his fault.

'She is extremely distressed, Miss Douglas, and begs your forgiveness.'

Nicola gazed over to the harbour in the distance. The park was littered with people enjoying the warm day. She wished she strolled peacefully and without this man beside her. How could she enjoy the park and the view when her head swam with thoughts and questions and her body...

'Will you forgive her?'

She bowed her head and went to sit on a bench under a large Norfolk pine tree. Arranging her skirts, she avoided looking at him. 'Do you know what she said to me, Mr West?'

'I do. She had no right to say what she did, and she knows that.' Taking off his hat, he ran his fingers through his dark hair and Nicola watched him in guilty pleasure. He caught her staring and smiled a slow smile full of warmth and something else, something devilish.

Jerking to her feet, Nicola fiddled with her reticule. It was madness to be in his company. She lost all reason with him near. 'I must return. Thank you for the walk.'

His hand shot out and stopped her as she went to rush by him. 'Don't go...please.' The anxious concern in his eyes melted her resistance.

'Tell Frances I do forgive her.' She stared down at the grass, her mind whirling. Why did she have such a response to this man? Her traitorous body yearned for his touch. This was never in her plans when she sailed from England. She came to teach, to have a career and be independent, to rely on no one.

'Nicola…' He said her name on a sigh as soft as a night's breeze and she swayed gently towards him. His hand inched up her arm, burning the skin beneath his fingers. 'Look at me…'

She dragged her gaze to his face and saw the same yearning reflected in his eyes. His lips parted and she sucked in a breath, thinking he would kiss her, but a child's cry from nearby broke the magic around them and they both jumped guiltily.

'I must go.' With one hand she lifted her skirts high enough for her to hurry from him, her cheeks burning, and her breath caught in her throat.

CHAPTER 10

A bang from above her head made Nicola wince. The labourers she'd hired to move the furniture from the old house and into the new one were clumsy and lazy. Already they had dropped a crate of kitchen crockery and broken several things inside. Between them and the maid, Hannah, there would be nothing left.

'Nicola,' Meg called from the other room.

Sighing, she left the unpacking of the drawing room and crossed the entry hall to the parlour opposite where crates and furniture were piled haphazardly. 'What is the matter? And must you call me as though I'm your dog? I am extremely busy and do not need to keep running to you.'

'Oh, do shush, Nicola. Lord, you'll have a heart seizure if you don't calm down, and then how will we be? Now come, look what just arrived.' Meg beamed, pointing to the huge display of flowers sitting on the new piano Mr Belfroy had delivered this morning. 'Read the card.'

Nicola took the little white card from the bouquet and read.

Wishing you all the very best of

115

happiness in this new venture,
Frances and Nathaniel West

'How kind of them.' Meg sniffed the white roses nestled amongst the lilies and greenery. 'You are fortunate to have such friends.' She grinned, running her fingers over the piano keys. 'As well as me, of course.'

'Of course.' Nicola laughed and tucked the card in her skirt pocket. There wasn't time to ponder on the gift now, or on those who had sent it, she had so much more to do.

'Have you eaten?'

'No. Have you seen my list?'

'Upstairs I think.' Meg played a little tune and then closed the piano lid.

Another loud bang overhead caused Nicola to groan. 'Those men!'

'I'll go up and speak to them. You find Mrs Nesbit and ask her to make you some tea and a plate of something.' Meg paused by the door. 'The unpacking of the whole house doesn't need to be finished in one day, Nicola. Do calm down and rest. Mr Belfroy will be upset if he thought you were working too hard, and think of us! What on earth would we do if something happened to you?' Her eyes widened in innocence and she laughed.

'Go on with you.' Smiling, Nicola waved her away and then turned her attention to the parlour. The room was of a good size and decorated in hues of blue and cream. A new sofa and chairs had arrived shortly after the piano and a large bookcase now stood on the far wall next to the fireplace. With some touches of home comfort this room would be a nice place for the women to sit and write letters, read or simply relax.

Leaving the parlour, she went down the hall to the next door on the left, the dining room. The long polished table, chairs and a serving side table were all in place. Opposite the dining room was Nicola's study. In here, boxes crowded the desk and carpet. None of that would be sorted today.

Voices at the front drew her out of the study and back into the hall. Miss McIntyre, a natural leader and organiser, was shepherding in Misses Golding, Barker and Rogers. Nicola smiled at them. 'Welcome to your new home, ladies.'

'It is so big, Miss Douglas.' Miss Barker stared up at the landing above. 'We will surely lose ourselves and each other here.'

'I do not think we will be of a small number for long, Miss Barker,' Miss McIntyre said in her Scottish accent and stepped closer to Nicola. 'I thought we should come and help here. The last cart was packed just as we left and is on its way. There is only cleaning left to do back at the old house and I have instructed Hannah to make a start. I hope that meets with your approval?'

'Certainly, Miss McIntyre, and thank you for your help.' Nicola squeezed her hand, acknowledging her friendship and kindness.

'What can I do to assist you now I'm here?'

'Actually, I've yet to inspect the state of the bedrooms since the moving men started. Miss Robinson is up there now, but I have the kitchen to check on and-'

'Leave upstairs to me, Miss Douglas.'

'Thank you.' Turning to the ladies, she gestured to the staircase. 'Please, ladies, go up and select a bedroom. For now we have one each, but I am sure that will change soon enough. Oh, and open the windows if you please. The rooms are stuffy in this heat.'

Their chatter drifted up the staircase behind them. Hearing the rumble of wheels on the gravel drive, Nicola took a deep breath and went outside into the warm October sunshine. She still found it strange to have warm weather in the months that she always associated with cooler temperatures. Back home in England the leaves would be falling from the trees, the nights turning cold with winter approaching.

Another cart pulled up in front of the double doors with the last of the furniture. While giving instructions to the two men, who climbed down to untie the ropes, she noticed Mr Belfroy's carriage turning into the gates. The circular drive was not large and with two carts in front of the house the carriage had to stop on the curve of the drive. Nicola walked down to meet it, and at the same time, made notes on improvements for the gardens, which were neglected and overgrown with weeds. But the back garden looked promising with an abundant orchard and vegetable patch.

'Miss Douglas!' Mr Belfroy climbed down from the carriage and bowed over her hand. 'How is it all coming along, my dear?'

'There is some upheaval, naturally. Moving six women, staff and a household of furniture isn't easy.'

'Indeed not.'

'Later, I would like to speak to you about hiring outside staff.'

'Yes, yes, later, I promise.' He beckoned to the person inside the carriage. 'Come out, dear boy, and meet my friend, Miss Douglas.'

Intrigued that Mr Belfroy wasn't alone, Nicola's eyes widened as a tall man, dressed in a brown suit with a cream shirt and cravat, stepped out from the carriage. He held his top hat in one hand and with the other he pushed back his over-long hair, the colour of wet sand. He must have been at least six foot four, a height Nicola had rarely seen.

'Good day to you, Miss Douglas.' He spoke with an accent she hadn't heard before.

'Welcome, sir.'

Mr Belfroy bustled forward. 'Miss Douglas, please meet

Mr Hilton Warner. He is my cousin's son, but his mother and I grew up like brother and sister, so Hilton calls me uncle.'

Nicola found her hand taken and kissed. 'If I'd known Australia held such beauties, I would have travelled here long ago.' His tanned face broke into an easy smile, crinkling the corners of his hazel eyes.

'Where are you from, Mr Warner, if I may ask?'

'America. The North, but you won't hold that against me, will you Miss Douglas?'

'I'm sure I won't, Mr Warner.' Nicola smiled, and gestured to the front door. 'Please, won't you come in? Though I do apologise for the state of the house. I'm not even certain I can offer you refreshments at the moment.'

Warner boldly held out his arm and after a brief hesitation Nicola placed her hand on it. 'We don't need refreshments, Miss Douglas, for we can drink of your beauty.' He frowned as she chuckled. 'Was that too overdone?'

'Indeed, it was, sir, but I'll forgive you.' Laughing, she led them inside, where she gave him a guided tour, while Mr Belfroy spoke to the ladies about their job prospects.

Upstairs in one of the bedrooms, Nicola and Mr Warner paused to stare out of the window at the view of the water in the distance. Nicola glanced at the tall American. 'When did you arrive in the country, Mr Warner?'

'Yesterday evening.' He leaned against the wall beside the window and gazed at her.

A little flustered at his attentions, she fiddled with the lace curtain, which was in need of a good wash. 'And you came specifically to see Mr Belfroy?'

'No, that wasn't the only reason. I came to open some trade routes for my businesses.'

'How interesting. May I ask what kind of business?'

'Exports and imports between my country and this one.'

He folded his arms casually. 'My uncle is a clever man, I think.'

'Oh?'

'His passionate endeavours to help abandoned females brings him into contact with admirable women such as yourself. I wish I had thought to champion such a cause and therefore be forever surrounded by elegant loveliness.'

Nicola stiffened. 'I can assure you, sir, that Mr Belfroy, your uncle, is most respectful and in no way—'

'Whoa! Hold up there, Miss Douglas.' Warner pushed off the wall and stepped closer. 'I meant no disrespect.'

'That is not how it sounded, Mr Warner.'

'Then I shall beg your forgiveness for my crassness.' Teasing replaced the concern in his eyes. 'I am indeed backward in my manners, Miss Douglas. I meant no harm with my clumsy humour.'

She nodded. 'Yes, indeed. I am too sensitive on the subject. Unfortunately, I have seen the ugly side of our situation and, no doubt, will continue to do so.'

'My uncle spoke of the atrocities suffered by good women who only long for decent work. While I am here, I hope to help in any way I can.'

'Really? That is pleasing.'

'I have promised my uncle that I will invest in this house and charity.' He looked around the room. 'I think you will need all the extra help you can get.'

'Very true.' Nicola sighed, staring at the faded wallpaper, its rose pattern hardly visible anymore. 'I have plans, Mr Warner. This house will be a shining example of our abilities to cope as single, educated women.'

'Will you tell me all about your plans over dinner?'

She shied away from his earnest expression. 'I don't think that would be possible.'

'Why?'

'There is so much to do here. I have days of organising and we could get new arrivals at any time...'

Warner smiled. 'Have you run out of excuses now?'

Unable to help herself, she returned his smile and sighed. What harm would there be in having dinner with this man? 'Very well. Where shall I meet you?'

'On my ship.' He turned and waved out towards the distant harbour. 'I'm staying aboard my ship. The captain is my partner.'

'I see. How exciting.'

'You will come?' He looked as hopeful as a boy at Christmas.

'Only if I can bring my friend, Meg, Miss Robinson.'

'Excellent. Let's say tonight, around seven?'

She raised her eyebrows at his eagerness. 'Tomorrow, around eight?'

He threw his head back, laughing. 'I like you, Miss Douglas. Tomorrow it is then.'

The following morning, despite her desperate need to organise the study, Nicola gave in to Meg's insistent urging to accompany her shopping.

As they alighted from the omnibus in the city centre, Nicola was close to regretting asking Meg to be her companion tonight, for the younger woman had done nothing but talk about it since dinner the previous evening.

Entering a dressmaker's shop, Meg chuckled. 'I do believe I nearly fell in a faint when you asked me to attend this dinner party.'

'Keep your voice down, Meg.' Nicola glanced at the women milling around the bolts of cloth and stands of clothes. 'You will promise to behave tonight, won't you?'

Inspecting a burnt orange silk dress, Meg winked. 'I always behave.'

'I mean it, Meg.' Nicola spotted a table full of hosiery on sale and inspected a few items.

'Your American is quite dashing.'

'He's not my American.' Nicola glared at her, hoping she'd be quiet.

'His voice sends shivers down my spine.' Meg giggled. 'I simply tingled all over yesterday when he said goodbye and kissed my hand.'

'Meg,' she threatened in a low murmur. After selecting some hosiery, she moved on to another stand showcasing straw boaters just arrived from England. Beside the hats was an assortment of lace gloves on shelves.

'I do hope the ship's captain is as handsome as your American. But if he isn't, no doubt I'll put up with him for your sake. They must be rich, owning a ship. I should wear something marvellous just in case.'

Tossing down the lace gloves she'd been considering, Nicola turned away. 'I'm leaving. You're impossible.'

Laughing, Meg grabbed her hand and prevented her from departing the shop. 'Oh now, Nicola, don't be so stuffy.'

'I should have known better. I shall cancel tonight.'

'Nonsense. I won't hear of it.' Meg pouted and then grinned. 'I'm sorry. I'll behave.'

'I don't know why I agreed to Mr Warner's request. I'm not usually so impulsive, really.'

'You agreed because he's handsome and intriguing. Who could resist such an offer of dinner on board the man's very own ship!' Meg picked out a deep red dress with white lace around the bust line and sleeves. 'This will be perfect for me.'

'Where did you get the money for such a dress?'

'My aunt, naturally. She sent money two days ago.'

'Good, then you can pay some board.'

'Oh, Nicola, you do know how to spoil a day!' Meg stormed away to another table full of lace and silk ribbons.

Unperturbed, she followed her. 'You know the rules. Those who can pay must do so.'

'I swear I'll never tell you anything again.'

'Don't behave like a child, Meg.' Nicola turned away and headed for the door.

'Where are you going?'

She stopped. 'To tell Mr Warner we won't be dining with him tonight. If you're going to behave like a spoilt child and—'

'Oh, all right. I'll pay for my keep.' Meg huffed and flounced out of the door.

'It's only fair, Meg, and you know it.'

'All I know is that Mr Belfroy found a defender in you. I bet you count the peas in the pot to make sure the cook hasn't cut you short.'

Nicola laughed. 'Perhaps I do.' She tucked her arm through Meg's and they headed down the street.

'Nicola? Nicola!'

She searched the pedestrians for the person who called her name. Across the road Frances waved. Beside her, Nathaniel stood staring.

Summoning a smile, Nicola waited for them to join her and Meg. 'It's good to see you, Frances, Mr West.' She'd not seen Frances since their argument and the hurt lingered faintly. She kept her gaze from Nathaniel, not needing to look at him to feel his daunting presence which filled her senses.

'How are you?' Frances smiled. Today she wore a lemon dress and looked prettier for it.

'I'm well.' Nicola turned to indicate Meg. 'You remember my friend, Miss Robinson?'

After the pleasantries, a suffocating awkwardness sprang up and Nicola glanced down at her shoes, trying to think of something interesting to say, but her mind was blank of everything except Nathaniel West, who stood opposite to her.

'Did you receive the flowers, Miss Douglas?' Mr West asked.

Appalled at her lack of manners, Nicola became flustered. 'Yes, indeed. Thank you very much. They are lovely.'

'Would you care to come to dinner, Nicola, and you too, Miss Robinson?' Frances asked, her hand reaching out to settle lightly on Nicola's arm. It was a gesture of apology, of hope, and Nicola covered Frances's hand with her own and smiled.

'Tonight?' Frances grinned, her expression one of antic-ipation.

'Thank you, Miss West, but we have an engagement for tonight.' Meg raised her chin, her eyes laughing at Nathaniel. 'Nicola and I have been invited to dine on Mr Warner's ship. He is newly arrived from America and has taken a special interest in our dear Nicola.'

'Meg!' Nicola gasped, her cheeks burning. She looked at Nathaniel whose eyes seemed to have turned from violet to steel grey. A pinched whiteness surrounded his lips, which were tightly clamped together.

'Well, that is wonderful for you both.' Frances's voice shook a little. 'An American would have so many new and interesting things to talk about. I hope you both have a lovely evening.'

'Frances, you know the address of Mr Belfroy's new establishment, the Governess Home?' Nicola swallowed nervously.

'Yes, I do.'

'Then perhaps you would care to come for tea tomorrow, around four?'

'Thank you, I-'

Nathaniel stepped forward. 'Does the invitation include me, Miss Douglas?' His direct stare dared her to refuse him.

'In-indeed, sir. You are most welcome. Though...though the house is not yet ready for us to entertain properly...'

'We shall see you at four then. Good day, ladies.' He bowed and taking Frances's arm, marched away.

Nicola sagged and put a shaking hand up to her throat. Why did he have the power to reduce her to a witless and nervy fool?

'Come, Nicola.' Meg dragged her down the street. 'Time is getting away and we have much to do before tonight.'

CHAPTER 11

*T*he hired cab halted on the road alongside the moonlit quay and Nicola descended the step to the ground. It seemed that all of Sydney congregated at the quay tonight. Golden light spilt from the street gas lamps and some of the ships in the harbour had strung up colourful Chinese lanterns, giving the harbour an air of gaiety and excitement. So many people mingled, laughter and chatter filled the warm spring night air.

'Oh, how did I forget?' Meg came to stand beside her and stared around, eyes wide with anticipation.

'What did you forget?' Nicola couldn't help but get energized by the cheerful atmosphere in the dock area.

'The navy!' Meg clapped her gloved hands. 'Two naval ships are in the harbour. See, over there.' She pointed to two large ships riding at anchor in the harbour. 'I read about it in the newspaper yesterday. One British and one French. They have joined together to hold a special ball on board the British ship. Everyone who is anyone will be there.' She paused as a wealthy couple glided past, the woman's jewels dazzling in the light. 'I confess, Nicola, if your American and his captain are as dull as dead fish, I will slip away and join the fun over there.' She giggled, but there was a glint in her eyes that made the joke seem less light-hearted.

'If you do that, Meg Robinson, our friendship will be over for good.'

'Oh, come on then.' Meg sighed dramatically. 'Let us go aboard and see what Mr Warner has to entertain us.'

They strolled down the quay until they reached the plank walkway for the Lady Hilton.

'Ho there, ladies.' Mr Warner, all smiles, hurried down to meet and escorted them up onto the deck. 'Welcome aboard.' He held out both arms for them to take. 'Shall we go inside? The captain and I have sent the crew ashore and we've made use of the saloon. I'm afraid as mere men it lacks the decorative touches of a female, but I hope you'll be comfortable enough.'

The saloon held a long red carpet under a solid looking timber table highly polished. Tall candelabras around the room created a welcoming glow and shone on the silverware. In the centre of the table was an elegant glass bowl on a stand filled with exotic fruits of pineapple, oranges and grapes, which hung over the edge, tempting the most selective of palates.

The far door opened, and a man entered. Nicola liked the look of him at once. He appeared to be young, but close up she depicted the lines on his handsome face and the seriousness of his grey eyes. She guessed him to be about thirty, a few years younger than Mr Warner.

'Miss Douglas, Miss Robinson, please meet my partner and captain of this ship, James Pollings.'

'Ladies, welcome.' Captain Pollings bowed over their hands and then indicated for them to sit at the table. 'I hope dinner will be to your satisfaction. My cook is an old man, but good at his craft.'

Nicola sat down and adjusted her skirts, glad she'd bought a new gown in pale green with cream lace on the bodice and sleeves. As she glanced up, she noticed Meg staring openly at the captain. She kicked her under the table, all the while smiling at the two gentlemen. Meg jerked, blinked and lowered her head. Nicola beamed a wider smile to cover her friend's behaviour. 'Is this your first time to Sydney, too, Captain, like Mr Warner?'

'No, Miss Douglas. I had the pleasure of sailing into this fine harbour last year. It was that trip which prompted me to talk to Hilton about furthering our business interests.'

Mr Warner poured wine for them all. 'Our country is still suffering the effects of the civil war, you understand. It will take time for trade to recover as it once was.'

'Did you fight?' Nicola asked, alarmed at the quietness of Meg, who now studied her empty plate as though it held the answers to the world's mysteries.

'Absolutely, as Yankees. We both fought.' Warner grew serious. 'I can happily say that I'd be a contented man if I never saw another rifle or cannon again, but that is the way of many a man's thinking after war.' He straightened and raised his glass. 'To tonight.' He gazed fondly at Nicola as they all raised their glasses. 'May this be the beginning of lifelong friendships.' They echoed his sentiments as the first course was brought out.

As the cook and his young helper served the courses throughout the next few hours, Nicola found herself truly relaxed. The captain and Warner were wonderful hosts. At times they all spoke together, and at others they would break off into smaller conversations. She was amazed at Meg's solemnity, she spoke little, but paid great attention to the captain's every word. Had the handsome captain swept Meg off her feet? It hardly seemed possible.

'Nicola is an uncommon name, Miss Douglas. One I have

rarely heard,' Warner murmured, sipping brandy as the last of their plates were taken away by the cabin boy.

She wiped her mouth with the napkin, replete from the fine meal of potato and leek soup, a beef stew, and lastly, cooked whole apples in a treacle sauce. 'My father was called Nicholas. My mother named me after him.' She smiled, thinking of her father and how he would have enjoyed the conversation with these two intelligent men.

'Tell me about him.'

Talking about her father was an easy assignment and they swallowed up another hour discussing not only her father but teaching and world events.

Warner topped up her glass with more wine as the clock on the wall chimed midnight. 'I was named after my mother's family. She was a Hilton before marriage.' He grinned, his hazel eyes lingering on her face.

'The Lady Hilton is named for her?'

'No, for my grandmother. She was a very special lady.'

'Are all your family still in Boston?'

'Yes. My parents and sister.' He ran his fingertip around the edge of the glass. 'I would like to show you my home, Miss Douglas.'

Her heart fluttered. 'I am certain I would enjoy it, Mr Warner.' She looked away, concentrating on Meg's rapt expression as she listened to the captain's soft voice. Nicola wished she could hear what they talked about, so she could join in and take Mr Warner's attention away from her. She felt rather overwhelmed by it.

'Would you come, if I asked?'

She stared at him, wondering if she heard correctly. 'I hardly think it is possible, Mr Warner.'

'Why?'

'I have a position here, responsibilities. I cannot simply relinquish them to sail to America. My income is only what I receive from Mr Belfroy. I do not have the means to be free to roam the world as I wish…' She blushed, knowing she had spoken too much, revealed too much.

'Forgive me.' He bowed his head. 'I let myself run away with half formed ideas and expect everyone else to be the same. Thankfully, not all are as impulsive as me, or the world would be in a terrible state, would it not?'

She smiled, admiring him for the way he had apologised and averted her from further embarrassment. Standing, she caught Meg's attention. 'Thank you, Mr Warner, Captain Pollings, for your wonderful hospitality and your friendship. I know I can speak for Miss Robinson as well as myself in saying tonight has been very enjoyable for us both. However, it is very late, and we must be going.'

'Yes, I thank you too.' Meg stood and crossed the room to gather their shawls.

Warner came to stand next to Nicola and helped her wrap the shawl around her shoulders. 'I was hoping we could meet again tomorrow. The four of us could perhaps take a walk in the Domain, or take tea somewhere?'

'Yes, excellent idea, Hilton.' Captain Pollings nodded, smiling at Meg. 'Shall we collect you around two o'clock?'

'I…we will look forward to it, Captain, won't we, Nicola?' Meg's eyes begged for Nicola to agree.

'Yes. Thank you.' Then she remembered the afternoon tea arrangement with Frances and Nathaniel. Warmth flooded her face as she looked at Warner. 'I just remembered, I have guests tomorrow.'

'Then the next day,' Meg urged, eagerly staring from one to the other.

'The next day it is, Miss Robinson.' Captain Pollings kissed her hand.

They lingered outside on the deck, listening to the music drift across from the naval ship and staring up at the stars.

Eventually they headed down to find a transport home. The area was still busy and hired hansoms were in great demand despite the late hour.

'I'll be counting the minutes until we meet again, Miss Douglas,' Warner whispered, his face shadowed in the street lamplight. 'You have no idea what meeting you has done to me.' He raised her hand to his lips and the fluttering in her heart started again.

Before she could reply a couple sauntered past, and Nicola stared coldly at Tristan Lombard and his chattering female companion. Meg, thankfully, failed to notice him as she listened to the captain. Then, with surprise, Nicola stared at the next couple following Lombard.

Nathaniel West strolled with a bejewelled young woman clinging to his arm. The woman giggled up at him, her demeanour adoring. One of her hands travelled up his chest, her painted red nails playing with a button on his waistcoat. Nathaniel's step faltered as he recognised Nicola. His benign expression became a grimace as he glared at her and Warner's joined hands. He gave a stern nod in her direction and walked away.

Nicola was grateful the dim lighting hid her heated face. She felt tainted, that the whole evening was ruined, for she was certain Nathaniel would think the worst of her being out so late, that he wouldn't consider a quiet dinner on a ship would be anything but innocent. He'd think she was no better than him, having a companion. Oh, she wanted to stamp her foot like a child. She wanted to slap his sardonic face. She wanted to... She wanted to go home to bed and forget she had seen him with another woman on his arm.

Well, again she'd been reminded how he gave his attentions freely. Frances had spoken of his liaisons before and this confirmed it. She had escaped from a commitment to which only one of them would have been loyal.

* * *

THE FOLLOWING MORNING, after a dreadful night's sleep, where she dreamed of being on a sinking ship and the only rescuer was Nathaniel, but he kept rowing away from her, Nicola was determined that work, and lots of it, would be the only way she could get through the day. As she counted the linen sheets returned from the laundry, she prayed that Nathaniel would cry off today and only Frances would call.

'Nicola!' Meg raced up the stairs as though the hounds of hell chased her.

Scowling at Meg, Nicola turned back to the shelves of linen in the closet. 'Whatever is the matter? Can you not wait until you are near me before talking, instead of yelling the house down?'

'Come downstairs.' Meg's eyes glowed with inner happiness. 'Quickly, now.' She snatched the list and pencil from Nicola's hands and flung them onto a shelf then pulled her from the closet.

'Really, Meg...'

Downstairs, Meg ushered her into the drawing room, which had been transformed to resemble a flower shop. They both stood on the threshold and stared in wide-eyed amazement. Every conceivable surface held stands of flowers. Perfume thickly scented the air and the riotous colour nearly hurt Nicola's eyes.

'Where? Who?' Nicola crossed the room, gently touching the odd flower. 'I've never seen so many flowers in one room before.'

'Captain Pollings and Mr Warner. Together. For us.' Meg twirled. 'Oh Nicola. How they must esteem us to go to such length, such expense. Have you ever seen such a display of affection?'

'No...'

'Nor I. They must have bought every flower in Sydney!'

'How do you know the flowers are from those two gentlemen?'

From a small occasional table, Meg fished out a square cream card from between two stands. 'To two of the most glorious beauties on Australian soil. Although these flowers are nothing compared to your individual loveliness, we hope they can brighten your day as you both have brightened our world. Sincerely and forever yours, Mr Hilton Warner and Captain James Pollings.' Meg looked up and sighed with dreamy rapture. 'I know they did it together as a thank you and so it is all very proper, but the effort it must have taken them this morning... That alone deserves our devotion.'

'Devotion? A little too strong, don't you think?' Nicola swallowed the emotional lump in her throat. No man had ever bought her such a display of flowers. In fact, the only time she'd received flowers was the sprig of Wattle blossom Nathaniel gave her at Fran's birthday picnic. Her gaze swept the room again. All this was such a romantic gesture. She wasn't used to men giving her attention. What was she to do now? How did other women cope? Was there a ritual she needed to learn? Why didn't she know these things? No books had taught her about this. Panic gripped her.

Perhaps, instead of helping her father to teach boys, she should have been asking her mother for advice on matters of the heart, but at the time her frail mother had never seemed to be the one who would happily divulge private knowledge, and if Nicola was honest, the thought of courting and courtship itself had seldom presented itself in the forefront of her daily occupations.

She stared at Meg, who skipped around the room, bending to sniff each of the bouquets. 'What do we do about all this?'

Meg laughed and clapped her hands. 'Do? Why, we do

nothing, except write a thank you note. Oh, and hope they have more surprises for us.'

Nicola stepped back towards the door. 'No, I don't want more surprises.'

'Why ever not? They are so handsome and-'

'We hardly know them, Meg.'

'This is how we get more acquainted, silly. Lord, Nicola, there is much you know about things that don't matter so much, but there's even more you don't know about the important issues, such as love and romance.'

Nicola left the room with Meg's words ringing in her ears. How true they were. She could teach a child to spell their name or find England on a map, but when it came to men, romance and matters of the heart, she knew very little. Still, it only confirmed her belief that she was meant to be a governess, to be a spinster, all her life.

She retreated into her study, where she could lose herself in accounts and household issues until Frances arrived, but as she sat at her desk, she felt such a heaviness in her chest, a weight pressing down making it hard to breathe.

A knock sounded at the door and she turned when it opened. Mr Belfroy stood there, wearing an apologetic smile. 'Forgive my intrusion, Miss Douglas.'

Standing, the worry over men eased a little as she concentrated on the dear man who came forward and kissed her hand.

'I'm sorry to interrupt.'

'You can never interrupt me, Mr Belfroy, I am always at your service.'

'Indeed, you are good.' He leaned heavily on his cane, the other hand held his hat.

'Shall I take those for you?' Nicola gestured to his belongings, wondering why Hannah, the maid, hadn't done her job properly when answering the door.

'No, thank you, I cannot stay. I have only called for a moment, to discuss with you an idea my nephew mentioned to me this morning.'

'Mr Warner?'

'Yes. He thinks we should hold a ball, a charity ball, in honour of this house and the fine women in it.'

'A ball?'

'To raise funds for you all and the upkeep of the house.'

'But I thought you had sufficient…Forgive me, I don't want to appear to be rude-'

'Oh no, you must not worry yourself. Indeed, I have the money, but it is the future Hilton is thinking of, a future when I will not be here, or you…'

She blinked, not comprehending. 'I don't understand, sir.'

Mr Belfroy perched his buttocks on a wooden chair by the unlit fire, his knees creaking as they bent. 'Miss Douglas, for this house to continue long after I am dead, money needs to be raised. A charity must be created and maintained by a board of trustees. Hilton believes so and has convinced me of the same.'

'I see.'

'A ball will only be the beginning, but it will be a way to announce the efforts of this house, to make people aware. If we have patrons and donations, the longevity of this house will be assured.'

Nicola slowly sat, her mind whirling. 'I confess I am surprised at this turn of thinking. I never imagined we would need outside help. Perhaps that was short-sighted of me.'

'No, my dear, it wasn't. I was the same as you. But we have talked before of your future plans to include a teaching school for young ladies, and perhaps an orphanage here, and all those other wonderful ideas.' He held his hands out wide. 'I am not going to be here for many more years, my dear. Naturally all my fortune is left in trust for the Home, but it will not last forever. You must see the sense in having extra income and help for the long-term health of this enterprise?'

'Yes, of course...' But she didn't. She didn't like the thought of strangers being involved, of them having their say in the way she ran the house.

Mr Belfroy creaked to his feet, his cane tapped the floorboards at the effort. 'Now, I'll leave you to think it over. You may have ideas that need further discussion and my nephew tells me that he is to meet with you tomorrow, so you'll have plenty to discuss then. We can speak again later in the week, yes?'

'Absolutely.' She rose and walked with him to the front door.

He turned and patted her hand. 'I understand your hesitation, my dear.' He gazed around the hall fondly. 'It is hard to allow others into your private world, I know that only too well. However, we must think of those who are in need of our help. The more people assisting us, the more women and children we can aid.' He smiled. 'Take care, my dear. Until next time.'

'Good day, Mr Belfroy.' She watched him walk, leaning heavily on his cane, towards his carriage.

'Miss Douglas?' Miss Barker came to stand in the doorway beside her, a letter in her hand.

'Yes?'

'I have received correspondence from a fellow governess I met last year. A Miss Regina Clarke.' Miss Barker held up the letter as proof. 'Her current situation will end in November and she'll be needing accommodation then. Is she welcome here? I can vouch for her honesty and manners.'

'She is welcome, Miss Barker. We never turn anyone away.'

'Thank you, Miss Douglas. I shall write to her immediately stating the terms of the Home. She will be able to pay her way to start with.'

'Very good, Miss Barker. Assure her we charge very little.' Nicola watched the carriage trundle down the drive and at the same time, noticed another waiting to turn in. Her heart sank. It was Nathaniel West's carriage. She crossed her fingers behind her back, hoping Frances had borrowed her brother's carriage and he remained at home.

'We have another visitor?'

Nodding, Nicola straightened her shoulders and lifted her chin. 'Yes, a friend of mine. Will you ask Mrs Nesbit to send a tea tray into the parlour please, Miss Barker?' With a determined step, Nicola went to meet the carriage. She pasted a smile on her face as Nathaniel climbed from the carriage and helped his sister down.

'Nicola.' Frances, wearing a brown skirt and pale gold blouse, hugged her warmly. 'What an excellent position the house is on.'

'Yes, we are fortunate to have this rise. It affords us views to the harbour in the distance.' She inclined her head to Nathaniel, who looked resplendent in a dark grey suit, the jacket of which was knee length. 'Good day, Mr West.'

'Miss Douglas.' He bowed towards her, his eyes again assessing.

'Won't you come in?' She smiled but couldn't look him in the eyes. She led them into the parlour, away from the drawing room and all its flowers. That was something she didn't want to explain.

For the next fifteen minutes, Nicola and Frances chatted about the soup kitchen and gossiped on the latest society happenings. The whole time, Nicola was aware of Nathaniel standing by the window, sipping his tea, watching her.

'You may be surprised to know, Frances, that future plans here will now include a small orphanage.'

'Really?' Frances grasped Nicola's hand. 'That is excellent news. I am so happy you changed your mind, Nicola.'

'Well, it makes sense doesn't it? We'll have all these teachers, why not put them to work?' She laughed softly.

Frances chuckled. 'A perfect solution indeed.'

'I hope you will be able to help us, Fran, when the time comes.' Nicola glanced over at Nathaniel and caught him staring at her. Blushing, she looked back at his sister. 'There, I do listen to you on some things.'

Frances sipped her tea. 'I'd be delighted to help.'

'We hope to include a school for young ladies as well.' Nicola leaned forward eagerly, excited to share her plans. 'The school will instruct young ladies in all manner of household duties, as well as some refinement. But I want to stress the importance of making these girls adaptable to all situations...' She paused as Nathaniel left the window.

'Mr Belfroy's wealth must be beyond anyone's imagining for him to fund such ventures.'

Nicola lifted her chin. 'No, you are quite wrong, Mr West. We are hoping to become a charity. With donations and patrons, we shall be in the position to help more people than just governesses.'

'What changed your mind, Nicola?' Frances placed her teacup on the tray. 'Once you would have rejected such a notion.'

'I was never against helping those less fortunate, Frances, but governesses also need to be cared for. We cannot forget them. However, with Mr Belfroy's generosity in providing the house and having extra land to build on, we can do more. An orphanage will be beneficial to both causes, the children can be taught by the governesses awaiting situations.'

Nathaniel took a sip from his teacup. 'Tell me, Miss Douglas, are the governesses under your care allowed to... shall we say...dally with the opposite sex?'

'Nat!' Frances snapped.

Nicola raised an eyebrow, giving him one of her cold looks. She knew he was referring to seeing her last night with Mr Warner. 'We are not in a prison, sir. The women stay here at their own will and have such freedom as they desire.'

'Perhaps they misuse such freedom? And what of the Home's reputation? Women of easy virtue wouldn't attract the money needed from wealthy patrons. The scandals will—'

'We have no women of easy virtue here, sir.'

'I believe you have a woman staying here who is in the delicate state of being with child and is not married.'

'Her trust was abused, and she was ill-treated by a man who promised her marriage. Her situation was—'

'And she isn't the first, is she? What does that tell you?'

Nicola tightened her grip on her saucer, wishing she could fling the object into West's gloating face. Why did he alter his manners so much? One minute he was adoring, and the next finding fault and rude. 'I—'

Frances leaned forward. 'You don't have to explain, Nicola.' She gave her brother an icy stare. 'Why do you, Nat of all people, make such an issue of this? You know what happens, how it happens. Nicola and Mr Belfroy are providing a place for these women, something I am unable to do despite my best efforts. Why do you attack her for it?'

'I am merely stating the fact that donations and patrons will depend on your reputation here. Is this a house for fallen women or for unemployed governesses?' Nathaniel placed his teacup down on a nearby table, his gaze never leaving Nicola.

'I can assure you, Mr West, our reputation here will be above reproach. No patron will regret being involved.'

ANNEMARIE BREAR

'Then perhaps I should become one?' He gave her a secret smile. 'Will I be your first or has another beaten me to it?'

Her heart seemed to somersault in her chest at his meaning. 'Any donation will be gratefully received, Mr West, and you are most welcome to be one of our patrons, but no, you won't be the first.' Let him make of that what he will, she was beyond caring.

Nathaniel's hands clenched by his side, his eyes narrowed with barely concealed hostility. 'I think it is time we left, Frances. I have appointments.'

'Yes, very well.' Frances rose, looking from Nicola to her brother and back. 'I will see you again soon, Nicola?'

'Certainly, Frances. You are welcome to call any time.' Nicola rose and turned her back on Nathaniel. Hateful man.

CHAPTER 12

*N*icola stared out over the water at the boats gently riding at anchor. On this warm afternoon at the beginning of November the Domain was busy with families picnicking on the grass and listening to the brass band playing. Couples strolled, children played, dogs barked. She sauntered with Mr Warner, while Meg and the captain lagged behind, eating fruit tarts bought from a stall on the edge of the parkland. For the last few weeks the four of them had developed the habit to walk each Saturday afternoon in the Domain.

'What game is that, Miss Douglas, is it cricket?' Warner pointed to where a crowd had gathered around to watch men playing a bat and ball game.

'Yes, it is. A popular game for men.'

'I saw it played once in England I think, but it was some distance away.'

'Shall we watch it for a while?' She headed to the boundary of the field. 'My father very much enjoyed playing cricket. He was considered rather good at it too as a young man. He would often allow me to take part when he had a game with his pupils. Naturally, my mother was appalled by the idea, but Father said girls had just as much energy as boys.'

They weaved through the crowd to get close to the action. One of the batsmen hit the ball high, sailing it over the fielders' heads. The throng cheered.

'Why Nicola, look who the batsmen are.' Meg laughed, coming up alongside. 'It's Mr West and his friend Mr Lombard.'

Nicola peered. The middle of the pitch, where the two men stood talking, was a good distance away, but as one of the men raised his head to grin at something the other said, Nicola instantly knew it was Nathaniel. She watched avidly as the men took their positions again and the bowler ran and sent his delivery down the pitch. Nathaniel hit it comfortably, the pleasant sounding crack of leather on willow echoed to them. The ball raced away for the boundary once more and he and Lombard ran between the wickets.

'He's awfully good,' Warner murmured.

Nicola nodded, not trusting herself to speak. There was something about watching Nathaniel being so physical that stirred a primal need deep within her. She couldn't take her eyes off him.

From out in the middle of the field, the umpire signalled a halt to the proceedings and all the men came off to have a cool drink and sit in the shade of nearby trees. Nathaniel stood only ten yards away, drinking out of a tankard and laughing with a group of friends. She'd never seen him like this. Before he'd always been immaculately dressed, but today his billowy white shirt gaped out from his pale moleskin trousers, his dark sweat-dampened hair clung to his forehead and his knee-high boots had mud stains on them.

As if some unseen force made him aware of her presence,

he turned his head and stared straight at her. Nicola forgot to breathe.

'Miss Douglas?'

Nicola blinked as Warner lightly touched her arm. 'Um…pardon?'

'I said, I hoped you do not mind my interference, Miss Douglas?'

'Interference?' Her numbed mind didn't understand a word he was saying.

'About the charity ball.'

'Oh. Oh, I see. Sorry.' She forced herself to look away from Nathaniel and at Mr Warner. 'No, I don't mind. Not at all.'

'It is my desire to help.'

'Yes, and it is most welcome.'

'Shall we continue walking?' As they stepped away from the gathering, he took her hand and gently placed it over his arm. 'I felt setting the Home up as a charity complete with a board and patrons would lessen your work and responsibilities, but I apologise that so far it has done none of that.'

Nicola looked back over her shoulder at Nathaniel and found his attentions were focused on two young women within his group. The pain of that was unexpected, but soon overcome as Warner smiled down at her. 'You are kind to think of me, Mr Warner. However, the responsibilities were never a concern to me. I enjoy my role and am thankful every day for Mr Belfroy's trust and employment.'

'Do you wish to do this forever?'

She shrugged one shoulder and adjusted the hold of her parasol. 'Forever is a long time.'

'Do you think of having a husband and family?' His fingers softly caressed hers.

She removed her hand from his arm, alarmed that she liked his caress. What was wrong with her? First Nathaniel and now Warner. Was there some hidden wanton inside her just waiting to escape? Had the years of spinsterhood now made her man crazy? Perhaps she needed to steer clear of them both? She stopped to admire the view, her thoughts churning.

'You are uncomfortable with this subject?' He stood very close.

'There are some moments when I think of those things, but usually I am too busy to consider my own private future.' Nicola sighed and stared down at her pale green and white striped skirt, bought only last week at Meg's horrified insistence because apparently, Mr Warner had seen all of Nicola's clothes at least twice over. 'The day is too beautiful to talk of serious issues, Mr Warner.' She looked up and smiled.

He grinned and again took her hand and slipped it through his arm. 'You are quite correct, Miss Douglas. Will we talk instead of the ball?'

They walked on and Nicola relaxed. She enjoyed his company very much. All the times they'd spent together he had made her laugh. He was witty and funny, very courteous and considerate. He charmed her effortlessly and made her feel light-hearted. Within a short time of being in his company she could forget the harshness of the world and be carefree. 'The invitations for the ball are being accepted at a furious rate. There are so many people I do not know and will have to greet at the door. I'm extremely nervous.'

'I will be beside you. Together, we'll fumble our way through.' He winked. 'Anyway, my uncle knows everyone worth knowing in Sydney and will be right beside us. So many people are curious about him, since his withdrawal from society. The gossips will be in a frenzy.'

'Poor Mr Belfroy. He'll never step foot outside his door again.' She grinned. 'I cannot imagine I will get everything done on time. There is still much to do and only a week left to do it.'

'Meg is helping you, and the other women?'

'Yes, they are. Miss McIntyre is priceless, so good and helpful.' She dodged around a ball thrown by a small boy to the left. 'Although Meg is more of a hindrance then a help sometimes.'

'I'll encourage James to take her out driving more, to spare you.'

At the mention of the captain, Nicola paused. 'Do you...I mean...does he...' She frowned. 'I'm not expressing myself well.'

'What is it?' His eyes softened, and the caress of her fingers started again. 'Ask me anything.'

'It's Meg and the captain. In the five weeks since our dinner on your ship, when they first met, the captain has been very attentive to Meg.'

'You wish he hadn't been?'

'No...unless...unless he is only playing with her affections. If he has no thought to her emotions and the hope he is building within her, then I feel he should—'

'Keep his distance?'

'Yes.'

He brought her hand up as though to kiss it, but quickly drew it down again. 'Let me put your fears to rest. James is very much in love with your dear Meg.'

Her step faltered. 'Love? Are you sure?'

'Entirely sure. He told me so.'

'But he will sail away and leave her.'

Warner shook his head. 'No, not at all. He has every intention of proposing. When he sails from this harbour, he fully expects to have her by his side as his wife.'

The news shook Nicola more than she anticipated. Meg married. Meg gone from her life?

'You are shocked. Does the news upset you? I apologise.'

'I-I am surprised, that is all.'

'Did you think him not an honourable man, one who would play fast and loose with her?'

'No…' What had she expected? She didn't know, but not marriage and for Meg to leave the country.

'You will not tell her, will you? It is meant to be a surprise. He wants to propose at the ball.'

'Of course, I won't tell her.' They walked to the end of the path and turned to retrace their steps. 'When do you think you will sail?'

'That, I cannot answer.' His smile flickered, and an uncertain look came into his eyes. 'There is much it depends on.'

'Oh? Your business interests?'

'Yes, those, and interests of a more personal nature.'

They walked on in silence for a moment until Warner stopped and guided her over to sit on a bench overlooking the water. 'Your friendship has become very important to me, Miss Douglas.'

'As yours is to me.'

'We have spent a good deal of time together these last five weeks.'

'True…'

'I've enjoyed each occasion we've met. I have come to admire you greatly.'

'Thank you, and I you.' She glanced up as a seagull squawked overhead, rising and falling on the air current.

'Miss Douglas, would you consider marrying me?'

Nicola turned to him so quickly, her neck creaked. 'Marry you?'

'Is that so terrible a concept?' He tilted his head, chuckling.

'No, no, not at all. Only, I never expected it.'

'Why? You must know how much I want to be with you.

Not a day goes by without my wanting to be with you in every sense.'

'I don't know what to say.' He wanted to marry her. That this good, decent man wanted her made her giddy with girlish pride. Yet, she couldn't help thinking of another proposal asked of her...

'I wasn't going to mention it for a while yet, but...' He smiled sheepishly, 'I'm terrible at keeping information to myself.'

She gave him a wide-eyed stare. 'Are you sure you and the captain haven't been drinking some magic marriage potion?'

'Maybe we have!' He laughed, but quickly sobered. 'Will you think about it? I know it is a shock and an important decision. Marriage to me will mean living in America, but we will travel, too. I can provide for you, Nicola, and will love you in the way you deserve.'

Touched by his sincerity, his affection that was evident in his manner, she reached out and squeezed his hands. 'Thank you, Hilton. Thank you for allowing me this choice and for caring for me. I will think very hard about this, I promise.' At the edge of the park she spotted a hansom cab idly waiting for a fare. 'I must return to the Home. Two new governesses arrive on the evening train.'

'Nicola,' he stood, towering above her, 'I'll give you a few days alone to think. Perhaps at the ball you can give me your answer?'

She nodded, too emotional to speak, and left him.

* * *

NATHANIEL ADJUSTED his white silk cravat in the mirror above the fireplace, his fingers not heeding his brain. It was times like these he wished he had engaged a decent valet and not relied on his useless butler. 'For the love of God!' In temper he yanked at the thing, ripping it off from around his neck and threw it across the sitting room, just as Frances entered.

'Nat, heavens.' She stooped and picked it up from the floor. 'Here, let me do it for you.' With deft movements she tied and fussed with it until it was a snowy silk perfection. 'There.'

'Thank you.'

She crossed to the far chair where she had left her shawl. He studied her dress, the finest he'd ever seen her wear. The shimmering gold silk and cream lace ensemble gave her a healthy glow and she'd chosen to add rose buds to her short hair, which thankfully she'd been growing once more. Pouring himself a brandy, he realised she had gone many weeks without wearing her ridiculous trouser-skirt outfit. Hopefully, she was tired of shocking people, though it hardly mattered now. All of their society knew of her peculiarity for shocking others.

'You've started drinking early.' Frances frowned, wrapping the shimmering shawl around her shoulders.

'I detest balls.'

'Poppycock. You love them and always have done. It gives you the perfect excuse to dance with all the pretty young women, and to flirt with the older married ones. You are at your best at a ball and don't you dare deny it.' She gave him one of her triumphant looks which meant she knew of his secrets and wasn't afraid to use them against him.

'Is there nothing about me you don't know?' he asked, ushering her out the door.

'Yes, there are a few things, which worry me, and there are some things I'm sure I'd rather not want to know at all.'

'Am I such an open book then?' he joked, helping her into the carriage and then climbing in after her.

'Don't make me laugh, brother.' Frances scoffed. 'You are

anything but open.' She gave him a sly look. 'I know that you are still enamoured of dear Nicola.'

He blanched and leaned back into the leather seat to keep his face in shadow. 'What makes you think that?'

'Don't toy with me. You cannot keep your eyes from her.'

'One can look at a beautiful painting without the need to buy it, sister.'

'Not you. When you want something you usually get it.'

'Not always.'

'And not with Nicola it seems. Yes? Though it's hardly surprising she thinks nothing of you when you antagonise her the way you do.'

'Can we talk about something else before you ruin the entire night?'

Frances gasped and pushed forward in her seat to look at him properly. 'So there still is something. I knew it!'

'Gloating is unattractive in a female, Frances.'

'Why can you not make it up with her?'

'When did it become your business, I wonder?'

'Nat, please... She is my good friend and you are my brother. Of course, I would be thrilled to see you joined as one.'

'And Miss Douglas would rather walk through fire.'

'You know this for certain?'

'Without question.' He tried to ignore the pain this brought.

'But are you honest in this? Do you really mean marriage, a true marriage? You must be sure about it. We've seen the consequences of unhappy partnering at first hand.'

'Stop talking, Frances, I beg you.'

'Good lord, you've never entertained the idea of wedlock before.' Frances groaned. 'Oh my, I think I might have told her that too.'

'Frances!'

'You must talk to her again, Nat.'

'I have, several weeks ago.'

She gasped again. 'And?'

'And I was rejected most vigorously.' He gave a sarcastic smile, which became a grimace as the hurt renewed in strength.

'I suppose it is to be expected. You two didn't become friends from the start. She's seen too much of your bad ways and been on the receiving end of your cutting words. And I've spoken of your ghastly women numerous times.'

'Thank you,' he murmured with heavy sarcasm. 'Tell me again why I have anything to do with you?'

She slumped back on the seat. 'And that dashing American has been paying attendance to her. He's been in her company constantly. I've hardly seen her myself. You stand no chance against him for he is supremely handsome and so tall. I've heard of women swooning just by hearing him talk. It's his accent, you know.'

Nat gritted his teeth. He'd like to do injury to that *dashing American*. It seemed the whole of the city had become drawn in with that man!

'Lord, I do hope she doesn't marry him. I'll never see her again.'

He felt as if someone had punched him in the gut. If Nicola married another, his life would be over. It was bad enough her rejecting him, but at least if she lived her life as a spinster working for the Governess Home she'd be close, and he could watch over her from a distance. But to have another man touch her, for him to receive her love... No. He couldn't bear that.

'Perhaps you should again ask her to marry you, Nat, before he gets the chance.'

'I'll think about it.' He ground out between clenched teeth. 'Now drop the subject, please.'

'Well, don't leave it too long, for heavens' sake.' She gave an unladylike sniff of disapproval. 'If you'd been nicer when you first met Nicola things might have been very different by now.'

'Indeed.' Didn't she know he'd already gone down that tortuous route? Didn't she think he'd done nothing but punish himself repeatedly?

'Find your charm and work it on her, Nat. I'm begging you.'

'She sees through it, Fran.' He sighed at the truth of it. 'She thinks nothing of me and she is correct to do so.'

The carriage slowed outside the assembly hall and within minutes they were walking into the building, divesting their outer clothes and waiting in the line to be greeted.

'Mr Warner is standing next to his uncle Belfroy,' Frances whispered. She craned her neck to look beyond the tall man in front of them. 'Is Nicola there?'

Nat grasped her elbow and they stepped forward. He studied Warner. The man laughed at something a guest said and then he turned and brought Nicola into view, laying a possessive hand on her arm. Not that she seemed to mind. Her face glowed with good health and happiness. Her beauty radiated out to Nat like a beacon. He'd never seen her looking so magnificent. Tonight, she wore a shimmering gown the colour of which changed in the lamplight like mother-of-pearl. No woman came close to her.

His throat went dry as they inched closer and finally he shook hands with old Belfroy before moving on to Warner.

'So glad you could attend tonight's festivities.' Warner's accent grated on Nat's raw nerves.

'Wouldn't have missed it,' he muttered, watching Frances and Nicola embrace each other.

Warner cupped Nicola's elbow. 'This is Miss Nicola Douglas, the—'

'I know Miss Douglas.' Nat dismissed him with a nod and stood in front of Nicola. Her lovely eyes dispelled his anger and as she smiled tentatively at him, he fought the urge to crush her into his arms. 'Good evening, Miss Douglas.'

She held out her hand and he took it, relishing the warmth of it. 'Thank you for coming, Mr West.'

'Will you save me a dance later?'

'That I will.' She lowered her gaze and he felt the need to move on as others came along the line.

Frances took his arm and they walked into the reception room, nodding to acquaintances. Was all of Sydney here tonight? How long would he have to wait before he could claim his dance?

Christ, he needed a drink. From the corner of her eye, Nicola watched Nathaniel leave the room and enter the ballroom with Frances. Thank heavens no one could see her inner turmoil. Seeing Warner and Nathaniel shake hands was too much. It alarmed her the effect both men had on her. What was she to do? Warner expected an answer tonight, but she couldn't give him one. Flustered, she turned and found Miss McIntyre behind her. 'Oh, Florence, will you stand in for me? I need…'

'Absolutely, Miss Douglas. You've been standing there for an hour, go sit yourself down for a moment or two.'

Smiling her thanks, she left her position by the door, only Warner touched her arm, halting her before she could leave the room.

'Is everything all right?'

'Yes, completely. I just need a drink of water.' The concern in his voice and the look in his eyes made her feel guilty.

'I shall get you one immediately.'

'No, please. I need a moment.'

'Has something upset you?'

'No.'

He frowned. 'You've been avoiding me all day.'

'I have been busy all day. Much depends on tonight's success.'

The band struck up from the other room and he gave her a cheeky smile, the seriousness vanishing as if it had never been. 'I beg the first dance from you. You cannot deny me that?'

'I...' All she wanted was a quiet moment to herself, something she'd not had for the last week with organising new arrivals at the house and the entertainment and requirements for tonight.

'Please?' His boyish charm pulled at her heart.

'Oh, very well.' Her hand on his, they glided into the ballroom and joined the others for the first waltz of the evening.

Dancing in his arms affected her more than she imagined. He was so much taller than her, and with his handsome face and friendly manner he drew smiles from the gathering, and a flutter of fans from the females as he elegantly twirled her around. What woman would say no to this man? She had tried to think rationally about the proposal and what it would mean. Living in America would be exciting, having Hilton's love would be wonderful, but something nagged at the back of her mind - a sense of being suffocated...

When the music stopped, Frances was instantly beside her, whisking her away to the refreshments room. 'You two appear to be great friends.'

'What do you mean?' Nicola nodded her thanks to the maid who gave her a glass of fruit punch.

'You seem very comfortable with him, that's all.' Frances accepted her glass and they sauntered away into a corner.

'We've spent a lot of time together recently, so familiarity is a consequence of that. He's been heavily involved in establishing the charity, plus the preparation of tonight and the equipping of the Home. There were so many things we needed, more beds and furniture...'

'The way he looks at you has nothing to do with furniture.' Frances sipped her drink, merriment in her eyes.

'He's asked me to marry him, Fran.' She sighed, relieved at finally having told someone.

Frances's face drained of colour. 'And your answer?'

'I haven't given it yet. Why are you so shocked?'

'I'm surprised that's all. He's not been here long.' Frances concentrated on her drink. 'Do you love him, Nicola?'

'I don't know.' She smiled at a passing couple and said good evening to another before turning back to Frances. 'I think I do, but I'm frightened it is more of a brotherly love. I like and esteem him...' She nodded to another gentleman as he passed and lowered her voice. 'How do I know what is real? It's all so complicated.'

'Many marriages are made without love. Is that what you want?'

'No, but I think I could love him easily.'

'I see.' Frances rubbed her finger around the rim of her glass. 'And then there is my brother.'

Nicola searched Frances's face for any hidden clue to her thoughts. 'Yes.'

'He has feelings for you, but you do not return them.'

Nicola's stomach clenched, she felt slightly sick. 'I-I am not sure that is completely true either.'

Frances paused in raising her glass. 'Which part?'

'Both.'

'Oh, Nic. All I can tell you is that my brother has never been inclined towards marriage or towards any one particular woman. No lady has captured his heart. Until you came along.'

'Captured his heart? A little dramatic don't you think?'

'He is capable of loving someone, Nicola, despite his behaviour at times.'

'But that is the problem. His behaviour. He isn't one for marriage, is he? He likes his...companions. How could I believe what he says is the truth?'

'He wouldn't say it otherwise. There would be no need. He must really mean it for him to even think of uttering such words to you. He is so private and reserved.'

'I could not bear to have a husband who-who...would seek comfort elsewhere after marriage. The humiliation would be too much.'

'Nat is many things, Nicola, but I do not believe he would do that to you. Unless you gave him just cause. Some women do not care for the activities in the bedroom.'

'Heavens, Fran!' She looked wildly about, heat suffusing her face. 'This is hardly the place for such a discussion.'

Frances gripped Nicola's hand. 'You mustn't marry the American. Not if you don't love him.'

'I know, but...but a part of me wants to. He would be easy to love... I've said that once already, haven't I?' She sighed, torn about making a decision she believed she'd never have to consider. 'I know Warner would care for me, he'd support my interests, he already does.'

'But his home is in America.'

'Yes.'

'And I thought you wanted to make your home here and do good deeds here.'

'I do, but would your brother allow me to work as I do now. I hardly think so.'

'Miss Douglas.'

They both jumped guiltily and spun around to face Mr Belfroy and another gentleman.

Mr Belfroy offered his arm. 'Miss Douglas, may I have

your attention for a moment to introduce you to some friends of mine.'

'Yes indeed.' She squeezed Frances's hand and then took Mr Belfroy's arm just as Nathaniel walked towards his sister.

Nat bowed as the party went by and turned to Frances. 'What was your little talk about?'

'Wouldn't you like to know?' She pulled at her lace collar. 'I can't breathe in this heat.'

'You both looked as guilty as each other when I approached, both deep in conversation by the look of it.'

Frances placed her glass on a passing footman's tray and then took Nat's arm. 'I need air.'

Puzzled by her anxious expression, Nat guided her past the guests and out through a set of French doors to the paved courtyard. Roses grew in wide plant pots. In the distance a horn sounded in the harbour. Frances sat on a stone bench and fiddled with the flimsy rosebuds in her hair.

He studied her. 'Talk to me, Fran.'

She flashed him a quick smile and then stared down at the ground. 'Do you truly love Nicola? The whole 'ever after' sort?'

His chest tightened at the mention of her name. 'Yes.'

'She believes you aren't genuine.'

'You were discussing me, in there?' The champagne he'd recently drunk roiled in his stomach.

'The American has also asked for her hand in marriage.' Fran jerked to her feet and paced. 'You have to do something, Nat, or we'll both lose her.'

He braced his feet apart, hoping it would steady him for at the moment he felt as weak as a newborn kitten. Sweat broke out on his forehead. 'Has she answered him?'

'Not yet. He expects her reply tomorrow, or even tonight, I think.'

He swore violently under his breath. How rotten was his

luck? Was he to go through life forever being overlooked? This time it was his own damn fault for letting his heart rule his head. He didn't need this agony. It was much better to use the women of the night and leave his days free to do as he pleased. Why ever had he thought to marry, to be with just one woman? All along he'd known it wasn't what he was about.

'Nat?'

'I have to go.'

'No, Nathaniel.' She caught his arm in a grip that was stronger than most men's. 'If you think I'll allow you to slink away and deal with this by getting drunk in some brothel for days then you'd best think again.'

'Fran, don't interfere.'

'Then don't be a coward, for God's sake.'

He straightened, fury burning with hurt. 'If you were a man I'd knock you down for that remark.'

'If I'd been a man I would have knocked you down first!' She scorned. 'If you give up on this chance of happiness, I'll never forgive you. I mean it, Nat. You need Nicola. She's the only person who'll save you from yourself.'

'But she doesn't need me.'

'I believe she does. If she wanted Warner she'd have said yes the moment he asked, but she didn't.'

He threw his head back and groaned. Staying that way, looking up at the blanket of diamond stars, he let her words sink in. Could he fight for her? He'd never backed down from a fight in his life. Right from boarding school he'd fought for whatever he wanted, or sometimes just fought for the hell of it. Strangely, his father's face swam before his eyes. Disappointment. That one word summed up his relationship with his father. They disappointed each other in every way. His father wanted a son he could be proud of, but nothing Nat ever did earned praise or even a smile. Of course he now knew that his father didn't like him, never had from boyhood. As a child he expected that all parents tolerated their children, but this wasn't so. He'd learnt at school that some parents actually cared for their children. But not his, and it was reaffirmed every holiday when his parents were too busy to spend any time with him. It didn't take long for him to learn that loving them was a waste of time. In fact, causing scandal was a fun way to annoy them even further.

'What are you thinking about?' Frances whispered, standing behind him.

He blinked, refocusing on the stars and felt the ache start in his neck from his position. 'Our parents.'

'Why? Why now at this time?'

He stared down at her. Loving her had proven he was capable of the emotion, something which he'd often wondered about when growing up. For her, he tried to be a good person, though at times it was hard to live up to her expectations as much as it'd been his father's.

Frances took his hands in her own. 'Let go of the past, Nat.'

'Is it possible though? They say we are shaped by our parents' deeds.'

'We are better than them. We care for others, not just ourselves like they do.'

'I never wanted a family or a wife. I never thought I'd be competent at honouring either. Then I met Nicola and found something missing in my life.' He walked over to the bench and stood so still he could hear the music from inside and the odd horn from the ships in the harbour. 'I would be a good father.'

'I don't doubt it.'

'I would love my children, teach them, let them know they were important to me.'

'Naturally you would. You are not our father, Nat.'

'It hurts, loving her, Fran.'

'I know, dearest.'

'Do you remember one of my friends back in England, Donald Kilkenny?'

'Vaguely.'

'He killed himself when we were about twenty. I spoke to him only the day before he shot himself. I saw him at Waterloo train station. He looked simply awful, hadn't washed or shaved for weeks. He'd lost weight, had grey skin, looked like a corpse.' Nat slipped his hands in his jacket pocket. 'He'd been in love, you see. Adored this girl who had rejected him. When I'd heard that Donald had killed himself over that girl, I was disgusted. I was disgusted at Donald for being so stupid to allow his heart to rule his head. I didn't understand, I couldn't fathom how any man could feel as Donald did. But I do now.'

Frances jerked, eyes wide. 'You're not going to kill yourself, are you?'

'No. I couldn't do that. I have to take care of you. Yet, I recognise the need to deal with the pain of loving someone who doesn't love you.'

'Oh, Nat.'

'She is everything to me, Fran. I want to see her, be with her always. I hunger for her smile. I ache to hold her…' He shrugged and gave her a wry grin. 'There now, you can never say again that I keep things to myself.'

'Thank you for confiding in me.' She kissed his cheek.

He drew in a long deep breath and gathered his courage. 'Nicola promised me a dance.' He strode to the door, but quickly returned to Frances and kissed her cheek. 'No sister could be better than you.'

She gave him a lofty stare. 'I know.'

'Come, we Wests have a fight on our hands.'

CHAPTER 13

*N*icola stood hand on hips, tapping her foot and fighting the urge to scream like a fishwife at the new kitchen maid, Bessie. This was the last thing she needed to deal with this morning. Hannah, the other maid stood in the corner of the scullery with Mrs Nesbit the cook, their eyes wide with anticipation of a 'set to'. Nicola drew in a deep breath. 'Bessie, I understand that you only started here yesterday, but at your interview you assured me of your competence and experience. However, the jobs you have done today show no evidence of this. The breakfast pots weren't cleaned well enough, you left ashes in the grate in the drawing room, you refused to listen to Mrs Nesbit's instructions and now you've been accused of stealing.'

Bessie, one hand on her hip and the other hidden into the folds of her apron, smirked. 'I ain't stolen nothin'.'

'Hannah is certain you've taken a piece of jewellery from Miss Peacock's chest in her room. Is this so?'

'Nope.'

'Then to settle this matter I will have to search your belongings and your person.'

'No, you ain't.' Bessie edged backwards.

Movement at the door leading into the corridor had them all turning. Miss McIntyre and Meg stood on the step.

'Yes?' Nicola sighed. She'd had only an hour's sleep since the ball last night and her eyes felt as though they had sand rubbed in them.

Meg stepped down into the kitchen. 'You've a visitor.'

'I can deal with this, Miss Douglas.' Miss McIntyre strode forward, her height and stern manner seemed to shrink the room. 'You go and deal with your visitor and then go up to bed. You need your rest.' She turned to Bessie. '*You*. Don't think for one minute you have been forgotten. Miss Peacock has searched every room in this house and her brooch is nowhere to be found. However, Miss Shaw swears on the Bible she saw the brooch on Miss Peacock's table this morning when you were in the room changing the sheets. So, let us start again.'

Nicola slipped from the room with Meg following. They were content to let Florence deal with the servant. Nicola hoped Florence would never leave, she'd be lost without her help and support.

'Nicola.' Meg halted her in the hallway.

'Yes?'

'I've hardly seen you this morning. We haven't had a chance to speak of my engagement.'

Nicola grasped Meg's hand. 'You know I'm delighted for you. I told you that last night.'

'I know, but there were so many people around. Do you truly believe I'm making the right decision?'

She glanced up the hallway. 'Meg, I have someone waiting. Can we talk later?'

Nodding, Meg stepped away towards the study. 'Can I use in here to write to my mother?'

'Of course.' She smiled. 'I'm dreadfully tired, but later we'll talk, I promise. Oh, and Meg?'

'Yes?'

'The captain is a fine man.'

A wide smile lit Meg's face. 'Yes. He is.'

Nicola turned for the drawing room, stifling a yawn behind her hand. What she wouldn't give for a few hours' sleep.

As she entered the room, Nathaniel stood up from the sofa, a soft smile playing on his lips. 'Miss Douglas.'

'Mr West.' She didn't expect him and immediately put a hand to her hair to tidy it. After leaving the ball at sunrise, it felt like she'd been asleep only a second or two before being woken by a frantic Miss Peacock, wanting her to confront Bessie. Her appearance wasn't up to visitors, especially Mr West, who seemed to have slept well and looked rested and refreshed in his smart dark suit. Last night they had danced just once, but her heart skipped as she remembered how close her held her, how his gaze never left her face. He had smiled and complimented her the whole time and in his arms she'd felt secure, wanted, and she liked that feeling.

Nathaniel softly tapped his hat against his leg. 'I'm sorry to call unannounced, but I was wondering if you'd like to take a drive with me this afternoon?'

'Oh…'

'Frances will be with us also.'

'I'm afraid I haven't had much sleep and am frightfully tired.'

'How about I promise to stop for a while to give us a chance to nap under the trees?' His smile spoke straight to her heart, which didn't help matters.

'Well…'

'Three o'clock?'

'Um…'

'That's settled then.'

He stepped forward, took her hand and kissed it. 'Until three.'

'Er, yes.' She stared after him as he left the room. It had happened so quickly. She gazed down at the spot he'd kissed on her hand. He'd kissed just above the knuckle of her third finger on her left hand. Did it have a particular meaning or was she just imagining it? Lord, she must be tired. Sleepily, she turned for the stairs and her bedroom.

Later, refreshed after a few hours' sleep, Nicola washed and changed, taking extra care with her toilette, as the minutes ticked by towards three o'clock. She shouldn't have agreed to go. Warner was expecting her answer and she was surprised he'd not called before now. Thankfully he hadn't pressed her last night for an answer. He'd been surrounded by interested people the whole night and she was grateful for it.

A soft knock preceded Florence, who quietly closed the door behind her. 'Oh good, you're awake.'

'If there are more problems, Florence, I really don't want to know.' She sighed, collecting her white lace gloves from the bedside table. With a last look in the mirror, she smoothed her dove grey skirt.

'I had to let that trollop Bessie go.' Florence stood tall and determined. 'I hope you don't mind, or think I'm taking advantage of the trust you've put in me, Miss Douglas.'

'Did she steal the brooch?'

'Aye, it was in a secret pocket in the bottom of her skirt.'

'Then you did the right thing.' Nicola heard the long case clock on the landing strike three times. From outside came the muted crunch of carriage wheels on the gravel drive. 'I'm going out for a few hours with Miss West and her brother. But when I return I need to talk to you.'

'Oh?' Florence followed her out of the room. 'Is it bad news? Have I done wrong?'

'No, it's an offer for you. A position.' Nicola smiled. They descended the stairs together and at the bottom Nicola collected her parasol from the stand by the door. She turned to Florence. 'If you are willing, Mr Belfroy has accepted my proposal to pay you a wage and be second in charge here.'

'Oh my.' Florence gaped in surprise.

'I'll talk to you later about it, but it'll give you something to think about.' Nicola patted the other woman's shoulder and opened the door to reveal Mr West.

'Afternoon, ladies.' He bowed.

Nicola ignored the way her chest tightened at the sight of him and, after saying good-bye to Florence, accompanied him outside. She stared in confusion at the waiting transport. 'A gig, Mr West?'

'Yes, Miss Douglas.' He helped her up onto the seat and then ran around the other side to climb aboard. With a flick of the reins the horse trotted down the drive.

'Where is Frances? Are we to collect her from somewhere?'

'Unfortunately, my sister has business elsewhere and cried off. She sends her apologies.'

Nicola held onto her straw boater and parasol when the horse picked up speed as they left the city behind. 'So, it is just the two of us?'

'And the horse.' He grinned.

'Mr West—'

'Please don't fret, Nicola. I promise you'll come to no harm.'

She swallowed with difficulty. That he'd called her Nicola affected her more than being alone with him on this drive. What were his plans, his intentions, by doing this?

He glanced at her before concentrating on driving again.

'Have you ever been reckless? Done something that raised people's eyebrows in surprise?'

'No.'

He laughed. 'You haven't lived then.'

'People can be happy without having to test the boundaries of what is right or wrong.'

'Only someone as good as you would say that.'

'Which shows how different we are, Mr West.' Her shoulders sagged. Why did he continually accentuate the differences between them? Why couldn't he, just for once, be charming and attentive without any hidden undertones? Hilton managed it, why couldn't Nathaniel? Was it so hard to do? Was he simply unable to have a polite conversation? 'Please turn the horse around, Mr West. I wish to go back.'

'Come, Nicola, don't spoil the afternoon.'

'You already have by—'

'By wanting you to myself for a moment?' He shot her a quick glance. 'Is that so appalling?'

'If you wanted to talk to me alone, we could have stayed at the house and walked the lawn.'

He laughed. 'You, alone at that house? Impossible.'

'Mr West—'

'Nicola, please, allow me an hour of your time, I beg you.'

Once the dirt road narrowed and became no more than a rutted track in the middle of dense bushland, Nat slowed the horse to a walk. The wheels creaked over the uneven path. 'I have broken social laws, I know, but—'

'But you've always done what you please, yes?' she snapped. 'You may not care what people say, but I do, Mr West. I have a position of trust and respectability. I have a reputation!'

'Nicola.' His eyes sent a message of apology.

She took a breath, her anger wilting under his tender gaze.

Reining the horse to a halt, they sat quietly. His hands dangled between his knees, holding the reins loose in his fingers. 'Frances tells me Mr Warner proposed marriage to you.'

She remained silent, knowing he didn't need her to confirm it.

'It felt like someone had stabbed me in the heart.'

Staring at his profile, she didn't know what to say. Was he sincere? Words were so easy.

'Will you marry him?' His voice was barely a whisper.

'No.' She closed her eyes against the knowledge of what her heart already knew. She couldn't marry Mr Warner, not while Nathaniel West affected her such as he did. 'I doubt I'll ever marry.'

'What a stupid thing to say.' He scoffed, leaning back in the seat.

'Why is it stupid? A woman like me—'

'A woman like you needs to be married, loved, adored. Don't pretend otherwise. You're passionate, caring, and intelligent. You'd make any man a fine wife.'

'Thank you.' She smiled faintly, a little afraid by the depth of sincerity in his tone. Again, her heart seemed to liquefy and she frowned at the response. Was this love or compassion? How could she know? 'Let us walk.'

Without waiting for his assistance, she scrambled down from the gig, nearly tripping on her skirt in the process.

He quickly joined her, but his ready smile and usual witty remarks were lacking as they stepped though the dry undergrowth. She'd become used to the crisp clean air of the bush now, of the loud native birds that squawked their song instead of trilling it like English birds did. Sometimes she missed the damp density of the woods back home, but she also found a strange contentment in the harsh Australian bushland. Perhaps she identified with the struggle of the plants and animals to survive, the hardiness of their existence. Yet, their beauty still showed through as though resolute in letting nothing diminish their right to live.

Nicola stopped to study the unusual yellow flowers growing on a large bush. 'Do you know what this flower is called? I've seen it before and always admired it.'

Nathaniel stopped close beside her and studied the long cylindrical flower, that stood straight and proud amongst its needle type leaves. 'It's called a Banksia, I believe. There are red ones too, I've seen them along the coast, and they also have different shapes.'

'It looks spiky.' She reached out to touch it gently and found the spikes were actually soft petals. 'No, they aren't sharp.' Smiling, she glanced at him under her lashes. 'I should have brought my sketchbook. I'm ashamed at the small amount of sketching I have done since arriving. My mother would be displeased if she were alive.'

He stood quite still. 'Do you miss your parents?'

'Yes, very much. My father was such a tremendous man, generous, knowledgeable, amusing. I adored him with every ounce of my being. His death was a blow I thought I would never recover from.' She looked up from the flower into his eyes. 'You're the first person I've been able to admit that to.'

'Then I am deeply honoured.'

'Oh, I've talked about him before, many times, but I've never acknowledged the pain of his death. When my father died, for the first time in my life I felt lost, without guidance, unloved.' Nicola walked on, amazed she'd spoken so personally to him. Her parents were a treasured part of her that she rarely shared with anyone, fearful of the ache that talking about them brought, but surprisingly, she had mentioned them to both Hilton and Nathaniel, and she didn't know what to make of it.

'Look at this one, Nicola.'

She turned as he bent down near a large rock. Crouching beside him, she examined the fragile pink flower on a long stem. 'No, don't pick it, let it be.' The yellow wattle he'd given her on Frances's birthday picnic was still in her diary, to add another would be accepting too much. 'I wonder what it is called.'

'It has the appearance of an orchid, don't you think?'

'Why, yes.' She grinned at him. 'You are knowledgeable about flowers.'

'No, not really. Though I grew up having access to a very impressive and varied collection of plants from all over the world. My mother collected them. She had an immense green house built adjoining the conservatory at the side of the house. My father used to rage at the amount of money she spent on paying botanists. She commissions them to find her beautiful and rare plants.' He carefully touched the tiny pink and white spotted petals. 'The odd time I spent with her in the greenhouse was the closest I ever came to being her son, instead of a person sharing her house at holidays.' He stood abruptly and cleared his throat.

She watched him, the sudden stiffness of his manner, the pulse ticking along his jaw. He still suffered from his parents' actions. 'We should go back.'

'Yes, we don't want to become lost.' He took her elbow and led her back to the gig.

'Perhaps next time we can bring a picnic and I'll remember my sketchbook.' She didn't look at him as he helped her up onto the seat.

'Will there be a next time, Miss Douglas?' His eyes widened and there was humour lurking in their violet colour.

'Not if you call me Miss Douglas there won't be.' She raised her chin in mock severity. 'I have become quite used to you being unconventional and calling me Nicola.'

'So, you forgive me for taking you out today?' He grinned, climbing onto the seat.

Adjusting her skirts so that a few inches of the leather seat showed between them, she nodded. 'I will overlook it this time, but Mr West,' she paused to stare at him, 'play straight with me and we'll never have a cross word, I promise.'

'For you, Nicola, I will do anything.' He took her hand and kissed it, then straightening, he flicked the reins and they made for the Home.

* * *

ADJUSTING her position on the stool, Nicola scrutinised her sketch of the front of the Home. The house was in proportion and again she counted the windows to make sure she had included them all. The trees and gardens were positioned properly... She added a few more strokes to the tallest tree on the right of the house and using the side of her little finger shaded below it to add dimension. Yet, something wasn't quite right with the curve of the drive. Head bent, she concentrated on fixing the problem.

A small brown butterfly fluttered over the page and landed on the edge of the sketchbook. She paused, admiring its hues of orange-brown. The still November day was heavy with sunshine, which brought out the bees and insects. Another glance up at the house scared the butterfly away and she watched it flitter among the recently planted gardens, which thanks to their new gardener, were taking on shape and colour.

'Excuse me, Miss?'

Nicola turned on the stool and brought her hand up to protect her eyes from the sun's glare. 'Yes, may I help you?'

The woman, carrying a small portmanteau, walked closer.

Her bonnet, a little old fashioned shaded her face, and her faded grey dress emphasized her thin figure. 'Is this Mr Belfory's Governess Home?'

'That's correct.' Nicola stood and placed her sketchbook on the stool. 'I'm Miss Douglas, the manageress. Are you looking for a place?'

'I'm Sara Bent, lately arrived from the Shoalhaven district. My last position finished earlier this month and I've been unsuccessful in gaining another. I have a letter from my employer.' She awkwardly held her luggage and tried to open it.

'Miss Bent, please, we shan't worry about that right at this moment.' Nicola stepped closer and laid a calming hand on the woman's arm. Up close, Nicola realised the woman was young, no more than twenty at the most, and for some reason Sara Bent reminded her of herself when she first arrived. 'I'm sure sharing a pot of tea will be a far better way for us to become acquainted. Shall we go inside?'

'Miss Douglas, first I must be made aware of the rate.' Worry clouded Miss Bent's blue eyes. 'You see, I recently sent some of my wage home to my mother and I also paid the arrears off my debt to the FMCE Society.' Her shoulders sagged. 'Although I am very relieved to have cleared my mind of these debts it has left me short. I assumed I would find a place again straight away. However, it's been harder than I thought. I've known no other family than the one I met onboard the ship. They, the Macalister's, hired me when their nurse failed to show up as we were ready to sail.'

'Why did you leave that family?'

'The mistress decided to return to England to finish her daughter's education. She felt I couldn't teach the finer arts such as painting and music to the satisfaction she required.' Miss Bent raised her chin. 'The fault was not mine, Miss

Douglas. Mrs Macalister had grand notions that weren't suitable to a small country place such as the Shoalhaven.'

'Come, you can tell me more inside. It is too hot out here.' Nicola collected her sketchbook and together they walked towards the front door.

When they reached the first step, Miss Bent stopped. 'I can pay a pound for my lodgings. How long will such an amount allow me to stay?'

Nicola's heart softened at the sight of this proud young woman. 'If you paid me a pound, Miss Bent, how much would that leave you until you secured another situation?'

Miss Bent lowered her lashes, a faint blush covering her thin cheeks. 'About four shillings.'

'Then save your pound.' Nicola took the portmanteau from her and found it extremely light. 'Is there anything is this?' She smiled, meaning it to be a joke.

Tears shimmered in Miss Bent's eyes. 'Only undergarments. I had to sell my books and...and even my clothes. I made the mistake of staying at a hotel and they charged me an exorbitant amount.'

'Never mind, we'll soon have you put back to rights again.' As they entered the hall, Florence came out of the parlour. 'Oh, Miss McIntyre, we have a new guest, Miss Bent. Can you show her up to one of the rooms, please?' Nicola turned to Sara. 'I'll order you a tray of something and would you care for a bath?'

'That would be very acceptable, thank you.' Miss Bent untied her bonnet and took it off, revealing raven black hair. She put a hand up to the lank ribbon securing her plait. 'It's been too long since I've been able to wash properly, especially my hair.'

'Miss McIntyre, we have some spare clothes, don't we? Miss Bent is in need of a dress or two.'

'Yes, indeed, Miss Douglas, leave it to me. I'll see that Miss

Bent is comfortable.' Florence replied, gesturing for their new guest to precede her up the staircase.

Nicola smiled at her. 'Thank you.' She lowered her voice as Florence passed. 'I think she'll be hungry and rather exhausted. Let her freshen up before the others descend on her.'

Florence gave an understanding nod.

Nicola turned away and headed for the kitchen. As always, when she received a new guest, she had mixed emotions about it. Part of her was happy to be able to provide a room to a needy lady, but then part of her found it depressing to witness such misery, such hopelessness.

She had to try harder to find these women worthwhile employment.

HEADS CLOSE, scrutinising the building plans, Nicola listened to the foreman's explanations and didn't realise she had a visitor until Mr Warner stood beside her. 'Oh, Mr Warner.'

'I'm sorry to disturb you, Miss Douglas.' He smiled, bowing.

'Not at all.'

'Meg told me you'd be down here. She says this is where you are each day.'

'Yes, things are happening at a rapid pace.' She thanked the foreman before slipping her hand onto Warner's arm, who looked dashing today in a pale fawn suit. 'Come and look at the progress of the orphanage. The roof on the dormitory has been completed, and the school room is nearly ready for its windows.' She led him between stacks of timber, roof slates and labourers, who were hammering, sawing and working hard in the afternoon heat.

'It's all very impressive, I must say, and so quick.'

'Money has been flowing in since the ball. So many people have responded to us and it's all thanks to you.' She smiled gratefully at him.

Hilton peered into a window opening. 'Don't thank me yet. Soon you'll be surrounded by yelling children. How on earth will you cope then?'

She laughed, light-hearted at the success so far of the Home. 'There are enough of us to manage. Some of the women are studying for their teacher's certificate. We're hoping the government will acknowledge us as a legitimate school and provide funding for teachers' wages.'

'Do you ever stop, Miss Douglas?'

'Why should I stop?' She frowned. 'I have so much to do.'

He looked away and walked over to inspect a pile of stone. 'You will not want to leave here.'

Her enthusiasm for the project faded at his sad expression. She was being unfair to him, cruel even and that wasn't like her. It'd been weeks since the ball and for weeks she'd been dodging his questioning gaze whenever they were together. She never allowed them to be alone and kept putting off making a final decision about his proposal. Nicola bowed her head, knowing the time had come.

'Miss Douglas.' He took her hand and she looked up into his eyes. 'I knew my answer on the night of the ball.'

'How?'

'When you danced with Mr West. No one looking at you as closely as I was would have detected the subtle way your fingers caressed his shoulder as you danced.'

She jerked back. 'They didn't.'

His smile mocked her vehement denial. 'Yes, they did. You might not have let your face show your feelings, but I could tell. When in love, your perception of some things becomes very clear,' he shrugged, 'though in others not so clear.'

Shaking her head, Nicola headed back to the house. He was mistaken. 'You are quite wrong, Mr Warner.'

'Please, let us be honest in this, for I hold our friendship in high regard.'

She paused by the garden arch leading into the small courtyard behind the house. Bees buzzed over the trailing roses. 'I too, value our friendship.'

'I'm glad.' He took her hand again. 'I would hate to lose it.'

'I am sorry I cannot marry you, Hilton, really I am. I wish I could say yes because you would be a genuine husband, a man to be proud of and one any woman would be thankful to have.'

'But you did think about saying yes?'

'Oh, of course.' She squeezed his hand. 'I was quite close to saying yes. I promise you that.'

He nodded and managed a weak smile. 'Then I can ask for no more.'

'I'm sorry.'

'No, don't be. There is no need. We cannot rule our hearts, can we?'

'I do not love Mr West.' Her heart hammered in her chest at the mere thought. She wouldn't surrender to Nathaniel West.

Chuckling, he leaned over to kiss her cheek gently. 'Dearest Nicola, you should not deny what is nature.' He turned and swept his arm out to encompass the whole estate. 'All this is noble and splendid, but to receive a person's love, to have some form of…of connection with another, that is what makes us truly human.' He smiled and patted her hand. 'Now, I must go. James and Meg are turning the ship upside down in preparation for their marriage. James's neat cabin has been transformed with clutter, but they are happy and enjoying every second of it.'

Nicola walked with him around the side of the house to

the drive and his uncle's carriage. 'Yes, I have hardly seen Meg lately. She is a whirlwind of activity at the moment. Though she was hurt that her family refused to travel to see her wed.'

'It is their loss, for it is easier for them to travel to Sydney from Melbourne, than from Melbourne to America. They might be missing their last chance to see her for a long while.'

'America. Such a long way. I will miss her. The house will be quiet without her.'

'I hope you'll miss me also?' He grinned, opening the carriage door.

'Absolutely. You've been a very good friend.'

'Good, that makes me feel better.' After climbing in, Hilton sat near the window and smiled at her. 'I'll be travelling along the coast until Christmas, so I'll not see you for a little while.'

'Travel safe then. We'll meet again at Christmas.' She stepped back as the driver flicked the reins and the carriage lurched forward. Taking a deep breath, she watched the carriage rumble away and prayed to a God she didn't really believe in that she'd done the right thing in refusing Hilton.

CHAPTER 14

'I'll miss you,' Meg whispered, hugging Nicola tight. They stood in the captain's cabin of the *Lady Hilton*, having returned there after Meg's wedding just a couple of hours before.

'Not as much as I'll miss you. You'll be rather busy, I feel.' She chuckled through her tears.

'Oh yes.' Meg's grin was full of mischief. 'I cannot wait for tonight, and every night!'

'Meg!' Nicola roared with laughter. 'You're impossible.'

'I know!'

Sobering, Nicola sighed, knowing her time was short with this passionate friend of hers. 'It was a beautiful wedding. Everything has gone off perfectly.'

'I never expected this, you know.' Meg swung away to open a drawer near the bed. The captain's quarters now included another room. One of the adjoining cabins had been knocked through so Meg and her new husband could have a place in private to sit and relax.

'Never expected what? To marry a ship's captain?'

'To marry at all.' Meg grinned. She did a little twirl,

causing her light blue dress to flare out at the bottom. 'I'm so happy I could burst. Not even my mother and aunt's failure to attend today can diminish my joy at having James as my husband. He's a good man.'

'And he loves you.'

'Yes. Aren't I lucky? I'm not sure I deserve him, but I'll make him a good wife.'

'I believe you will.'

'Though I wish you had fallen madly in love with Mr Warner, then I wouldn't be going to America alone.'

'Sometimes I wish I had too.' She glanced around the cabin, seeing Meg's little touches and then she spotted the framed sketch of the harbour she had drawn as a present to the newlyweds. Nicola realised that she'd already made one long journey and this country was where her future lay. She brightened. 'Imagine all the new places you'll see and the people you'll meet. I want you to write long letters, telling me everything you experience.'

'I will, and you must let me know how the women get along and all your plans.' Meg stepped closer to Nicola and held out her hand. 'This is for you.'

'For me?' Surprised, she took the little box from her and opened it. 'Oh, Meg!' Nicola gasped, not believing her eyes. On a bed of velvet lay a gold chain and suspended from it was the half-crown given to her by the First Mate the day she landed. 'This is my lucky half-crown?'

'Yes. I stole it out of your room and James had it made into a necklace for you.'

'I don't know what to say.'

Meg lifted the necklace out of the box and fastened it around Nicola's neck. 'Every time you look at it or feel it against your skin, you'll think of me, and our friendship. Remember, I was your very first friend in this country, and I know at times I've tried your patience, but you do mean a lot to me and I wanted to show it.'

'Thank you.' Tears spilled, and she smiled sadly at Meg, upset at the thought of her leaving. 'I am so amazed you've done this. Thank you.'

'Although I won't physically be here, I'll be here in spirit.' Meg kissed her cheek and Nicola embraced her.

'It's a wonderful gift.'

'We had some fun, didn't we?'

Nicola raised her eyebrows. 'Oh yes. However, there were times when our opinions differed on what fun exactly was.'

Chuckling, Meg re-secured the white flowers in her hair. 'Remember that time I put vinegar in Burstall's tea?'

'Heavens, yes.' Nicola chortled 'And the time you hid Miss Golding's Bible and she searched for it all day. Or the time you convinced Mrs Eldersley that it was Wednesday when it was actually Tuesday, and she went out and complained to the grocer about him not delivering her order.'

Meg collapsed onto the bed in a fit of giggles. 'Such fun.'

Her laughter dwindling, Nicola sobered. 'I sincerely hope you live a long and happy life, Meg.'

'You must do the same.'

'I'll try.'

'You need to marry Mr West.' Meg gave her a saucy look as she straightened her skirts. 'Find out what it is to have a man, Nicola, and I guarantee that West would know how to please a woman.'

'Meg!' Nicola felt her cheeks grow warmer, but Meg just burst into a peal of laughter.

Nicola shook her head at her. 'You're outrageous.'

'I know, and won't you miss me!' Laughing, arm in arm, they went back out to the guests on deck.

Warner came to Nicola's side and Meg left them to talk to her guests. 'Soon we are to part, Miss Douglas.'

'Yes, sad as it is.'

'At least I got to spend a beautiful Christmas with you. It'll be one I'll never forget.'

'Me too.' She thought back to last week when the Home had rung with the joyous celebration that was Christmas. Despite the governesses being out of work, for one day they put all that despondency aside and enjoyed themselves. Mr Belfroy, Warner and the Captain had joined them for a wonderful meal. Although she hadn't seen Frances and Nathaniel on the day, she saw them the day after. Frances had bought her a beautiful peacock blue satin scarf and Nicola in return had given her a pair of cream kid gloves.

Her hand went up to the brooch she wore. She fingered the diamond and emerald flower, Nathaniel's present to her, one which was far too valuable for her to accept at first. Only he refused to take it back, saying he'd be deeply insulted if she spurned his gift. His present to her meant more than she cared to admit.

'James says the wind is favourable.'

She concentrated on Warner. 'That is good. And the tide turns in about four hours?' she asked, admiring how dashing he looked today in his best suit of dark brown, the colour of rich chocolate. His overlong sandy hair, this morning neatly slicked down, now lifted with the breeze sweeping off the harbour.

'Indeed. Are you staying a while longer after the guests have gone ashore?'

'I'm afraid not. A new governess is expected to arrive this afternoon and there are other things awaiting my attention.' She couldn't tell him that Miss Rogers was due to give birth any day now.

'I'm sad not to have these last few hours with you. But I'll always have the memory that I danced in the New Year of eighteen sixty-eight with you. I'll treasure that.' He spoke the words out over the sea, but she heard the subtle hurt in them.

She recalled the New Year dinner and dancing party, he'd hosted on this ship only a couple of weeks ago. It'd been a grand night. 'I'm sorry, Hilton.'

'Don't be.' He smiled down at her and tucked her hand in his arm. 'Come, let us eat and be merry.'

Much later than Nicola expected, she walked up the driveway to the Home, having paid the hansom cab at the bottom of the hill. She'd wanted a few minutes more to herself before the demands of the home occupied her. Leaving Meg and Hilton had been bittersweet, but it was over now and she wished them well. They had their life and she had hers.

She stopped and studied the house, her home. If only she knew what the future held. Would running this house be enough? Had she made the wrong choices along the way?

'Miss Douglas!' Miss McIntyre raced out of the front door, her skirts held up in one hand.

'What is it, Florence?'

'Miss Rogers,' Florence gasped on reaching her.

'The child?' Nicola rushed towards the house.

'Aye, Miss Douglas. Not born yet, but she's had pains for hours.'

'Have you sent for the midwife or Dr Armitage?' In the hall she unpinned her hat and then pulled off her gloves.

'The doctor is away attending a factory accident and the midwife is delivering twins somewhere. She said she'd come as soon as she can.'

'Is it terribly bad yet?'

Florence joined her as they headed up the staircase. 'Bad enough, but she's not screaming. I've given her a wad of cloth to bite down on.'

At the bedroom door, Nicola paused. 'I've never attended a birth before, Florence. Have you?'

'Aye, Miss. Plenty. My mother had six and my eldest sister had seven.'

'Right.' Taking a deep breath, Nicola opened the door and pasted a smile on her face. The air in the room was stale and the closed curtains threw it into a depressing gloom. 'Open those curtains, Florence, and a window. The evening is warm.' She turned to the woman on the bed. 'Now then, Miss Rogers. I hear we have a baby arriving shortly.'

Miss Rogers raised her head to nod weakly. She looked exhausted already. Her damp black hair clung to her face, which was the colour of uncooked dough, except for the two red spots on her cheeks. In the last few weeks she'd not gained much weight and Nicola feared the poor woman wouldn't have the strength to expel the child.

Florence stepped closer to the bed. 'Miss Rogers, I'm just off downstairs to get some water and a few things. Miss Douglas is here and will stay with you.'

'The doctor?'

'He'll be here soon as he can.' Florence smiled and left the room.

Nicola sat on the chair drawn up to the bed. 'How long have you had the pains?'

'Five hours or so. But my back has ached for three days.' Her face screwed up in agony as another pain assaulted her body.

Spying a water jug and glass on the bedside table, Nicola quickly filled the glass and put it to Miss Rogers's lips. 'This will make you feel better.'

'I think I need more than water, Miss Douglas.'

Grinning, Nicola placed the glass down and then took hold of Miss Roger's thin hand. 'May I call you by your Christian name, Penny?'

'Yes, I would like that.'

'Well then, Penny, you lie back and rest while you can.'

'I have written instructions.'

'Instructions?'

'In case I die.' She waved feebly to the drawer by the bed.

'Oh, you mustn't think like that.' Fear gripped Nicola's insides.

'The child, if it survives, is to be adopted by a good family that I have already found.'

'And what if you survive, which I'm certain you will, what of the child then?'

'It is still to be adopted. In the envelope is the family I found. Mr and Mrs Walker.'

'Walker?' Nicola leaned back in astonishment. 'How did you find this family? You've not left the house since you arrived.'

'Mr Belfroy helped me.'

'That was his business when he visited you last week?'

'Yes.'

'Why didn't you mention it to me? I would have helped too.'

'I heard about the plans of building an orphanage here…' Penny winced and groaned. 'You'd talk me out of it.'

'But we can care for the child here. You don't have to give the baby up if you—'

'No! I don't want the child here.' Another pain robbed her of breath. It was some minutes before she could speak again. 'I have arranged everything, Miss Douglas. I hope you will adhere to my wishes?'

'Naturally.'

'The envelope, is in the drawer, will you take it? Once the child is born, will you send for the Walkers? Mr Belfroy assures me they are a nice couple. They plan to travel to New Zealand and start afresh.'

Nicola opened the drawer and took out the pale envelope. 'I'll do everything as you wish for it to be done.'

'Thank you.'

Florence hurried into the room carrying towels and a large bowl of water. 'Doctor Armitage's gig just turned into the drive, Miss Douglas. All will be well now.'

Nicola patted Penny's hand in relief. 'There now, that is good news. I'll go and change my dress and will return shortly.' Standing, she slipped the envelope into her skirt pocket. As she left the room, she couldn't dispel the grief weighing on her. A baby's birth should be a joyous occasion, but not this time. Anger replaced the sadness when she thought of all the unmarried women who were taken advantage of and who would bear children they didn't want, while the fathers continued their lives untouched.

* * *

NICOLA PUT her hand up to shade the baby's face from the dawn's first rays of light that streamed in through the bedroom window. Behind her, Penny slept an exhausted sleep. Gazing at the baby boy she held, Nicola felt a strong urge to never let him go. His tiny face, newly washed, was a soft rose pink colour. She noted every detail; his closed eyes showed the fine fan of eyelashes, his nose nothing but a delicate bud, the purse of his little lips. Quite simply she was in awe of him. A baby. Not just any baby, but one she'd seen fight his way into the world. She had watched his chest expand with his first breath, heard his first cry. The miracle that was birth left her speechless and teary. While Dr Armitage and Florence took care of Penny, the baby had been thrust into her hands and she'd been responsible for wrapping him and keeping him warm.

'Miss Douglas,' Florence whispered at her shoulder.

'Yes?'

'I'm heading off to bed for an hour or two. You should do the same. He'll be fine in the basket.'

'I'll stay with him for a bit longer, but you go and rest.' She smiled at Florence, who covered her mouth as she yawned.

Florence glanced down at the baby, moving the blanket aside to see him better. 'He's a good-looking little chap, isn't he?'

'Yes.' Nicola couldn't help but feel proud of him, as though he was her son. 'shall I take the basket into my room?'

'Might as well. Miss Rogers wants nothing to do with him.' Florence picked up the basket and together they left the sleeping mother and crossed the hallway to Nicola's room.

'Thank you, Florence, but go to bed now. I'll see to this little one.' Nicola shooed her out the door and once alone, went to sit on the bed. Gently she placed the baby down and instinctively laid alongside of him. Bringing him closer into the curve of her body, she sighed and closed her eyes.

'Nicola. Wake up.'

Nicola opened her eyes, blinked, and stared at Frances. 'Oh. Frances.'

'What on earth are you doing?'

Lifting her head, she looked at the tiny fellow, who was now stirring awake. 'Don't raise your voice.'

'Raise my voice?' Frances stood, hands on hips, her usual scowl in place. 'I nearly had a heart attack when I walked in. Miss Barker said for me to come up, but she gave me no inkling of what I'd find.'

'It's a baby, not a gargoyle.' Carefully, Nicola rose and gathered him into her arms.

'What are you doing with a baby?'

'He was born early this morning, to Miss Rogers.'

'So why is he sleeping with you?'

The baby cried as Nicola climbed from the bed. 'His mother doesn't want him.'

Frances's eyes widened. 'Please don't tell me you are to have him?'

'No, how could I?' She tutted, though something inside her wished she could. 'He's to be adopted.'

'Good.'

'No, it's not good. He should be with his mother. Is it his fault that his father is a blackguard?'

'Stop being naive, Nicola, for heaven's sake. You know how the world works. You should do, you've seen enough evidence of it.'

Pacing the room didn't help soothe the baby who now was wailing lustily. 'He must be hungry.'

'Have you a wet nurse?'

'No. I'm not sure if Miss Rogers arranged for one...' Nicola winced as the baby's cries became piercing. She didn't hear the knock but was thankful when Florence entered the room.

'My, he's some lungs on him, Miss Douglas.'

'Florence, he needs feeding and I have to send word to the Walkers.' Warm wetness filled Nicola's hand through the baby's napkin. 'Oh dear, he's wet, too.'

'Give him here to me, Miss.' Florence deftly took the child and cradled him to her. 'I'll take him to the kitchen and see what we can do. Perhaps Mrs Walker can come today?'

'I'll wash and change my clothes and then send word to her.'

Silence descended once Florence left with the baby. Nicola washed her hands in a bowl on her dresser. 'I'm sorry I wasn't prepared for your visit, Frances.'

'A baby arriving would disrupt the best laid plans, I should think.'

'I wish his appearance was under happier circumstances.'

Nicola selected a pale apricot skirt and bodice from her wardrobe. 'I wish something could be done for him to remain with his mother.'

'Wishing is for children, Nicola,' Frances snapped.

'Why are you in such a bad mood for?'

Sighing, Frances slumped onto the bed. 'Forgive me. I am not fit for company. I should have stayed home, but I needed to talk to someone.'

'What has happened?'

'My mother has sent for Nat and I to return home. Our father has died. We only received the telegram informing us this morning.'

Amazed at the news, Nicola went to sit beside her. 'Will you return to England?'

'I will not go. There is nothing for me in England, and my mother is ashamed of me and my views. No, I shall stay here.' Frances twisted her fingers together. 'I'm afraid Nat might go though, and it bothers me greatly. He is all I have and if he were to leave...'

Nicola found it hard to breathe. Her stomach twisted like a spring. Nathaniel gone, for good? Her mouth went dry. 'But he cares little for your mother.'

'True. However, he is her son, as I am her daughter, and there is always something inside that makes it hard to turn your back on them completely. Although Nat would refuse to acknowledge it under threat of torture, I believe he's been waiting for the day when our parents would make amends for the hurt they've inflicted.'

'But he wants to make a life in this country. Your mother has your older brother for comfort.' She bit back the insane urge to shout that she wouldn't allow either of them to leave.

'My older brother, Gerald, is worse than useless. It seems he's married to a woman my mother doesn't care for. Hardly surprising. My mother writes that my sister-in-law has no intellect, is as quiet as a mouse and cannot play cards well, that alone is a capital offence in mother's eyes.' Frances grinned. 'My mother is a diligent card player. One of the best female competitors in London, of her circle, of course.'

Unable to sit still, Nicola jerked up and paced the room. 'Would he…I mean, would Nathaniel stay permanently in London?'

'Well yes, it's very likely. The estate goes to my older brother, but apparently Nat and I haven't been left out of father's will, which we imagined would happen. Our father was an unlovable tyrant, but in death, he's been fair for once. There are businesses and houses for us, and all manner of things.'

'But your brother left England for a reason. He wanted to start again in this country, to build a life here.'

'Heavens, don't romanticise it, Nicola.' Frances gave a mock laugh. 'Nat came here because it was as far away as he could get from our parents.'

'I see.' She didn't see anything, she only felt ill at the thought of Nathaniel leaving.

'There's nothing keeping him here now. He knows I'll be fine, if a little lonely.' Frances pulled out her watch from her pocket. 'Oh lord, I'm dreadfully late. There's a rally on in Macquarie Street against the new Contagious Diseases Act.'

'What is that about?'

'Locking up prostitutes for examination. Oh, I can't explain it now, I'm far too late as it is.' She kissed Nicola's cheek. 'Thank you for listening, even with all you have to deal with. You're a dear friend.'

'You know I'm here for you whenever you need me.'

'I'll come again soon. Good luck with the baby.' With a final wave, Frances scooted out the door.

Nicola gently lowered herself down onto a wooden chair by the window. She felt fragile, hollow. Only now that

Frances had gone could she concede to the deadening pain that squeezed her chest. Nathaniel gone. How would she survive never seeing him again?

No, he cannot go.

He said he loved me.

His mother rejected him, she cannot have him back.

But then, she had rejected him also.

Why had this happened? The pain grew unbearable and she pressed her fist into her chest hoping to ease it. God almighty. No, she couldn't...surely not... Did she love Nathaniel West?

How could she care for him? How could she overlook his drinking and whoring, his uncharitable views on women? How could she respect such a man?

But she *did* love him. Somehow there must be something worth loving within him for she was not the only person who cared for him. Frances adored him. He couldn't be all bad, could he?

She wanted to smile at the relief of finally being able to admit what she felt. A tear fell onto her hands, and then another. What a cruel twist of fate, for it was all too late.

The baby's cry reached her, growing closer. Quickly she wiped her eyes and went to the bed for her fresh clothes. She had responsibilities, duties to carry out. People depended on her. In her mind, she listed all the good things about her professional life. Yet, in her heart, she cried for the fool that she was. Nathaniel would go, and she would remain and it was no one's fault but her own.

CHAPTER 15

'*E*xcellent shot, Miss Clarke.' Nicola clapped before moving into position to hit her ball through the hoop. She hadn't played croquet for some time and was delighted that the latest governess to arrive, Miss Clarke, had asked if it was possible for them to create a croquet lawn at the side of the house.

Nicola's aim was off, and the ball missed the hoop. She laughed softly. 'I need to practise I think. You are far too good for me.'

Miss Clarke, a small dainty woman of twenty-eight years, looked bashful. 'My previous employers enjoyed the game very much and encouraged me to let the children play as often as lessons allowed. I'm afraid I rather have the knack for it.'

'Then we shall have regular games of it. I think we all need the exercise.' Nicola gestured over to the other women seated on chairs around a table groaning under the weight of afternoon tea treats. Florence hovered around them, unable to sit still for a minute. Miss Barker was poring over the newspaper, reading out snippets to Miss Golding. Misses

Shaw and Peacock were chatting, sipping their tea and Miss Bent was reading a book of poetry.

Smiling, Miss Clarke played another shot. 'The women here are most kind. We are lucky to have such comfortable accommodation.'

'Indeed.' Nicola looked up at the bedroom windows of the upper floor and noticed Penny standing at her window, watching them. The Walkers had collected the baby boy four days ago without Penny even seeing the child. Nicola sighed, recalling how upset she was when the Walkers left the house, carrying their new son. Thankfully, they seemed nice people, but she couldn't help feeling the loss of the baby.

'Miss Douglas, who is that man?' Miss Clarke nodded towards their visitor.

Nicola's heart somersaulted as Nathaniel stopped to announce himself to the women at the table. 'That is Mr West.' She drew in a laboured breath. 'He is a friend of mine.' A friend? She groaned inwardly at the statement. Their kind of friendship was such unlike any she'd experienced before. How *did* one turn friendship into something else, especially when one has refused the other before?

While Nathaniel chatted with ease to the women, she watched him unobserved. Once again, he'd filled her with confusion. In equal turns he'd been able to anger, frustrate and irritate her, yet at the same time captivate and fascinate her. Now his presence brought out other emotions, concern, secret joy at his nearness and fear - fear of him leaving. At last he turned in her direction and lifted his hand in acknowledgment.

She waved back, placing the croquet mallet on the ground. 'Excuse me, Miss Clarke.' Suppressing the urge to hurry, she walked sedately towards him and he met her halfway.

'Good day, Nicola.' His tender gaze nearly brought her to her knees.

For a moment she simply looked at him, absorbing his presence. 'How are you, Mr West?'

'Well, and you?'

'Fine, as you see.' She wished she'd worn one of her better dresses today. Not expecting visitors she'd worn her plain grey and didn't even have a lace collar on to brighten it. She despaired over her hair, which was bundled up into an unbecoming net because it needed washing.

He looked towards the half-built dwellings further down the back of the property. 'Would you care to show me the progress?'

'Certainly.' She flashed a brief smile and fell into step with him. 'How is Frances?'

'She was well enough when I shared breakfast with her this morning.'

'Good.'

'She told you about our family news.'

'Yes. I was sorry to hear it.' Nicola skirted a tree, glad its shade hid her hot face. 'My sympathies to you.'

'Thank you.' They headed down the slope and into the chaos of the building site.

Swallowing, her mouth dry, she tried to think of something witty to say and failed miserably. He looked so well today, dressed superbly in a dark suit. How had she failed to see the real man beneath the cold exterior? Her father had said many times that she was a good judge of character. Why then, did she allow herself to think of Nathaniel as shallow, heartless even? One only had to see how he loved his sister to know he was deeper than first imagined.

'How many governesses do you care for here at the moment?' Nathaniel stopped to study the closest building, the shell of the schoolhouse.

She focused on her role as manageress, something she could do without thought, or damage to her heart. 'Oh, er, nine, but I've received word from two others. They arrive next week and Flor–Miss McIntyre's two younger sisters from Scotland will be joining us when their ship docks next month. But a lady in need could knock on the door at any time. We never turn anyone away.'

'When do you expect to have these buildings finished?'

She frowned at the debris of the work site. Strewn timber, stone, piles of sand and mortarboards littered the yard. 'I'm not sure. Hopefully before the middle of winter.'

'Has worked stopped because of the lack of funds?'

'No, no, definitely not. The board has been most generous.'

'Then why aren't the workmen here?'

'They stopped yesterday because of the rain and today they simply didn't turn up.' She nibbled her top lip, feeling responsible that the men weren't doing as they should.

'Are you confident in the men's ability?'

'Um…yes…' She shrugged. 'I've never managed the construction of buildings before. Perhaps they do take some advantages, I'm not sure…'

Folding his arms, he planted his feet apart. 'If you'll allow it, I'd like their names. I'll speak with them and see if we can speed things up a bit for you.'

'Oh, that is most kind.' Her heart did a little skip. She knew he wasn't so bad. 'Thank you.'

'I'd like to see it all settled for you before I go away.'

The happiness which had flooded her, now disbursed like water from a broken dam. 'You mean to travel to England then?'

'Yes. In a fortnight. I'm busy tying up my affairs here.'

'I see…'

'As a patron of the Home, I thought I'd do as much as I

can while I'm in the country. Once in England, I'm afraid other concerns will be my main focus.'

'Naturally.' She tried to keep her voice light. Now faced with the reality of the situation, one which she had hoped wouldn't actually eventuate, she felt as though she'd entered a dark cave without a light. How was it possible she could end up wanting this man so badly it obliterated everything else? Why wasn't she content to remain a spinster and be devoted to her work? 'Do you hope to return to this country again one day?'

Nathaniel bent down and picked up a narrow piece of timber. 'I don't think so.' He inspected the wood as though it was the most interesting thing he'd seen.

Nicola kept her face passive, despite the need to howl like a baby. 'Your mother will be pleased to have you home.'

'I doubt the feeling will remain long. She-damn!' He dropped the piece of wood, and flinching, peered at his hand. 'A splinter.'

'Let me look.' Impulsively, she stepped closer and took his hand. Only after she cradled his hand in hers, did she realise the intimacy she'd created. His head was so near, his chest mere inches from her breast. She focused on the splinter in his palm, aware of the warmth of his hand, the smell of him, a mixture of soap and leather. 'I think you'll require a needle...to get it out...'

When his other hand came up to caress the back of her neck, she leaned into it and closed her eyes. 'Nicola.' His voice broke. 'How can I leave you?'

'I-' She bowed her head, her throat full of emotion, cutting off the words her heart wanted to say.

'Do you feel anything for me?' he whispered, his fingers stroking the soft skin beneath her hair. 'I beg you to ease my misery.'

'How can I do that?' Her body felt laden, the rawness of

emotions weighing her down, drowning her in their intensity.

Nathaniel rested his forehead against the side of her head, his nose nuzzling her hair just above her ear. 'Make me stay.'

'Is that possible?' she whispered, closing her eyes to the sensations warring within her.

'I'll do anything for you, anything.'

At the sound of tears in his voice she pulled away to look into his eyes and there she found the sincerity of his love. 'What can I do?'

'Marry me, love me.' He took her hand and placed it against his cheek. 'I'll be all that you ask.'

'Will you, truly? Will you allow me to work here?'

'As my wife you'll not need to work, I'll take care of you.'

'And I want to take care of them.' She lowered her hand away. 'Don't you understand? What I have done here is important to me. I cannot abandon it.'

He expelled a heavy breath. She saw the fight in his eyes, on his face, and stiffened. A second more, and then he relaxed, and gave a wry smile. 'What you do to me woman!'

'Do you accept that I must continue to work here in some capacity?'

'Yes, very well. If it makes you happy, then how can I argue?'

'And there's more.'

'More?' His violet eyes widened.

She stepped back, needing the space to think clearly. 'If I were to-to agree to-to marry you-' He went to speak but she held up her hand. 'Let me finish. If I were to marry you then, then I insist on complete honesty between us.'

'Of course.'

'I would not, that is to say, I refuse...'

'What? Tell me.'

Taking a deep breath, she raised her chin. 'If you went

with another woman after our marriage I would leave you instantly. I will not be made a fool of.' There she had said it.

A slow smile altered the seriousness of his expression to one of burning ecstasy. 'My love, with you by my side, in my bed, no other woman exists.'

Nicola felt the heat rise to her cheeks, and a delicious melting in her lower stomach, but she still gave him her most serious glare. 'I mean it. If you tire of me, then you must say so immediately, and we will work something out so that-' She was silenced by his kiss and she clung to him.

He lifted his mouth away from hers just enough to speak. 'You talk too much, Miss Douglas.'

'Nathaniel, I'm serious in this.'

'So am I, my darling.' He captured her lips again, crushing her into his arms. 'You are all I want. Now say my name again...'

For a moment she thought to pull away, but as his lips moved against hers, she surrendered to the desire growing inside her. Tentatively, she slid her hands up his arms, across his shoulders and into his dark hair. She smiled inwardly when he quivered and drew her even closer. Feeling his lips on hers was ecstasy in a way she'd never imagined.

Eventually, they separated to drag air into their lungs. Nathaniel grinned down at her, kissing the tip of her nose. 'I adore you.'

She didn't doubt it for a moment. His love shone from his eyes as he gazed at her. Gently she placed a fingertip to his lips, savouring the feel of him, rejoicing in the freedom of touching him. This is what she'd been missing from her life. There was no use denying anything anymore. Nathaniel had been right. She wanted to be loved completely, as a woman should be by a man.

For a long moment they simply gazed at each other, content to acknowledge their feelings openly.

'I'd best return to the house.' She smiled shyly. How easy it would be to stay in his arms, but the women would be wondering what had happened to her.

He held her about the waist, preventing her from walking away. 'Another few minutes more.' He bent and kissed her neck, causing her toes to curl at the decadent deliciousness of it.

'I have things to do...'

Pouting like a small boy, he played with her fingers. 'When will I see you again? There isn't much time before I sail.'

She jerked as if slapped. 'Sail? What do you mean? I thought you wanted to stay?'

'I do, but it's all arranged.' He smiled and kissed her fingertips. 'I will go to England, see mother and do what needs to be done and then come back.'

'But I thought you wanted us to be married?'

'I do, my love, and we will when I return.'

All pleasure seeped out of her. 'How long do you expect to be in England?'

'I'll be as quick as I can.' He frowned and touched her face. 'I don't want to be away from you.'

She stilled. 'How long?'

'Including travel time, I suppose it'll take eight months or so.' He brought her back into his arms. 'We'll announce our engagement before I sail and then marry on my return.'

Standing stiffly in his arms, she attempted to make sense of it all. 'I thought you would stay if I agreed to marry you.'

With one finger he tilted her chin up so he could look into her eyes. 'What am I doing wrong?'

'You're leaving me.'

'But I assumed you wouldn't mind so much, that only my heart would be affected by the absence. You have your work here and—'

'And I want you beside me.' She glanced away, ashamed of herself. 'I'm being selfish, forgive me. Of course, you must go to your mother.'

His hands slid down to her hips and he snuggled her into his body. 'My mother can go hang.' He winked. 'I must have been off my head to even consider leaving now I finally have you.'

'No, Nathaniel. I'll not make you choose between us.'

'Nonsense. I made my choice a long time ago. My mother doesn't deserve my loyalty. You are to be my wife. You are the woman I love. You will always come first.'

'Are you sure?'

A devilish glint entered his eyes. 'Perhaps I should show you then?' He picked her up and swung her around.

She squealed with laughter. 'Put me down, you fool.'

Holding her in his arms, he grew serious. 'Can we be married soon?'

'It takes three weeks for the banns to be called. Is that soon enough?'

'No, but I suppose I'll manage it somehow.' He lowered her feet to the ground and then took her hand and kissed it.

Nicola smiled. 'Will we go and tell the others?'

He nodded. 'But first, can we get this damn splinter out?'

Chuckling, she wrapped her arms around him and they strolled back to the house.

* * *

RAIN LASHED THE WINDOW, encouraged by a wicked wind intent on doing damage to anything not tied down. The heat of the past week ended with a violent storm. Shivering at the cold draught that blew under the door, Nicola ran her pencil down the list in front of her. She frowned at all the things she had to do this week. However, even this enormous amount of work demanding her attention couldn't stop the smile on her face when she thought of Nathaniel.

A slight tap on the study door preceded Florence, who carried a notebook and pen. The opened door allowed the musical notes of someone playing the piano to drift in. 'Can I disturb you for a moment, Miss Douglas?'

'Indeed, Florence, anything is better than reading this list that never diminishes.'

'Well, you've had a busy couple of weeks preparing for your wedding.'

Her wedding. She smiled at the thought. Soon she'd be Mrs West. Underneath the papers scattered across her desk was a scrap of paper she'd used to practise writing her new name. 'So, Florence, what can I help you with?'

'It's about the two new ladies who arrived yesterday, Miss Forbes and Miss Shellings. It seems they won't be staying for only two nights after all. Their departure has been delayed. They won't be sailing to New Zealand on tomorrow's tide.'

'Oh, dear.' She tapped the end of the pencil against her cheek. 'What is the hold up?'

'The captain told them he's still waiting on supplies or some cargo or something. He thinks they'll now sail on Sunday's high tide. The women are worried you may not allow them to stay those extra days. I think there is a problem with money. Neither of them have much and they are concerned you'll charge them more if they stay.'

'Why would they think that?' Nicola pulled the bell rope behind her desk, hoping that Hannah would answer it this time. It was always a gamble whether or not the maid was in the kitchen and even then, she'd take forever to answer the call. 'Tell them they are welcome to stay as long as it takes, and we won't charge them extra. I know the room they're sharing is small, but it is better than being cooped up in their cabin waiting for Sunday.'

Florence nodded and checked her notebook. 'I also wanted to talk to you about Mrs Nesbit. It's her birthday tomorrow, and although she's just our cook, I thought it might be nice if we had a little ceremony at midday and perhaps a cake or something?'

'Yes, we should mark the day for her. She has been diligently trying to keep her drinking under control. So we can use this as a reward, too.' Nicola opened her diary and turned to tomorrow's date. 'I have an appointment in the morning, but midday is free. Can you organise it?'

'Consider it done.'

The small clock on the mantelpiece above the fire struck five o'clock. Nicola closed her books. 'I have to start getting ready for tonight. Where is that silly maid?'

'Likely sitting by the kitchen range with her feet up, eating cook's food for your dinner party.' Florence stood and tucked her notebook under her arm. 'I'll go stir her up a bit.'

'I ordered a bath. I want to wash my hair for tonight.'

'You go on up, Miss Douglas. I'll see that your bath is prepared.'

Nicola walked around the desk and softly squeezed Florence's arm. 'What would I do without you?'

'I believe it's the other way around.' Florence scoffed with a grin. 'I'm just glad Mr West is allowing you to continue working here after your marriage. We'd be lost without you.'

'Mr West had no choice in the matter.' She laughed, heading out the door.

Crossing the hall, she entered the dining room, which shimmered with golden light spilling from numerous candelabras and the odd lamp. Nicola inspected the tablecloth for marks and adjusted some of the place settings. A large glass vase sat in the middle of the table filled with wild flowers. All was in order and Nicola sighed with relief. This small dinner party to formally announce her engagement to Nathaniel meant a lot to her and she wanted it to be perfect. Even though Nathaniel had wanted to be married as quickly as possible they agreed it wouldn't be feasible and had set the date for February twenty-fifth.

Going upstairs, she pondered on the last few weeks since she agreed to be Nathaniel's wife. Each day he had arrived to spend time with her, sometimes bringing Frances, sometimes alone. The change in him surprised her. Gone were the quelling looks and challenging words that she associated with him on first acquaintance. Now his whole manner spoke of his love, his happiness, and she felt empowered by the knowledge that she brought him this joy. Making another person so happy was addictive. That Frances was also incredibly excited helped smooth Nicola's small doubts that she was doing the right thing. Despite Nathaniel's assurances that he'd never look at another woman again, she couldn't completely forget his past.

'Miss Douglas.'

Turning at her bedroom door, Nicola smiled at Miss Rogers, who peeked out from her room. 'Yes, Penny?'

'May I have a word, please?'

'Is something wrong?'

Miss Rogers inched forward, glancing up and down the hallway, as though fearful of someone overhearing. 'I would like to ask a favour, if I may?'

'Oh?'

'I received word of a ship sailing for Africa. It leaves on the outgoing tide tonight. I've managed, only this morning, to secure a passage on her.'

'Really?' Nicola's eyes widened in surprise. 'Are you certain this is what you want to do?'

'Completely certain. I need to begin again somewhere new, where my past isn't known.'

'I understand.' Though she couldn't help feeling sorry for

the woman, she did wonder how she could easily walk away from her child, a child she'd never seen or held.

'I beg that you allow me to leave without fuss and cere-mony. I want no one to know.'

'But—'

'Please, Miss Douglas. I ask you to do this one last thing for me. I know I cannot expect more from you. You've done so much already.'

'Penny, I—' Nicola broke off as Miss Shaw left her bedroom and came towards them, holding aloft a book.

'Oh Miss Douglas, Miss Rogers, I have just finished a most marvellous book. It's...' Miss Shaw faltered on seeing the seriousness of their faces. 'Forgive me, I didn't mean to intrude.'

'It is nothing, Miss Shaw.' Nicola smiled. 'I'd be delighted to hear about your book later, if you will tell me.'

Nodding and ducking her head, Miss Shaw scuttled past them towards the stairs.

Penny stepped back into the shadows of her room. 'I cannot stay here another day and suffer the pity I see in their eyes when they look at me.'

'They mean well.'

'I know, but I cannot live normally again here.' She gestured behind her. 'I'm all packed. I only ask that you send for a hired cab for me at ten o'clock. I'll travel straight to the docks and board the ship.'

'I'll see that the cab is here at that time. Do you have a forwarding address?'

'No. Not as yet. I will write to you.'

'Do you want me to inform you of your child's progress, should I hear of anything?'

Shaking her head, she retreated further into the room. 'No... It is done. He is a Walker and nothing to do with me now. A clean break is the best thing. I hope you appreciate that.'

'I'm trying to, yes.'

'Thank you for everything, Miss Douglas.' Slowly the bedroom door closed and as Nicola was left staring at it, some of her happiness vanished. On a night when she'd be formally engaged, something she never thought would happen to her, another woman would be painfully beginning a new journey alone and unloved. It wasn't so very long ago that she had done the same thing.

CHAPTER 16

'*C*ome on, West. Can we finish this game or what?'
Tristan Lombard leaned his hand on the end of the
billiard table, holding his cue with the other. 'I thought we
were going to attend that card game upstairs tonight? I hope
we can make a good show of it and I can earn back some of
my losses from last month.'

Nat, bent over his cue, glanced up at Lombard. 'Actually,
I'm not in the mood for cards tonight.'

'Oh, what?' Lombard swore fluently. 'You're jesting,
surely?'

In one clean movement, Nat sunk a red ball in the middle
pocket. He straightened. 'I'm quite serious.'

'But I thought after a few hours of cards we could go to
the rat pit. I won well there last week.'

'And I told you last week that I'd not be attending any
more rat pits.' He shivered despite himself. 'I cannot stand
rats.'

'Nay, what kind of man are you?' Lombard scoffed. He
crouched down to eye up the balls on the table. 'You've
become a bore lately.'

'Is that so?' Nat grinned. Lombard was like a spoilt child when he didn't get his own way. 'Listen, if you want to play cards or attend the rat pit, then go.'

'It's no fun on my own.'

Laughing, Nat got into position again and made his next shot to the top right-hand pocket. 'You can never be alone at those events.'

'It's not the same though. I can hardly converse with the undesirables that gather there.' Lombard drank heavily from his whiskey glass. 'If you don't want to play cards, then what do you want to do?'

'After this game, I'm going home. I want a clear head tomorrow as Nicola and I are meeting decorators at the house.' Nat caught his friend's grimace at the mention of Nicola's name. This wasn't the first time Lombard had given such a reaction. 'You have a problem, Lombard?'

'No, what makes you say that?' Unable to meet his gaze, Lombard shifted around to the other side of the table.

Nat watched him, recalling each time since he told of his marriage plans how Lombard had sneered and ridiculed. At first he'd let it wash over him, his happiness at having Nicola as his fiancée obliterated every other thought from his head. Yet now, as once again Lombard's expression showed his feelings, Nat wanted to get to the bottom of it. 'What are your thoughts on my marriage?'

Lombard sniffed and inspected his cue. 'I have none.'

'As my friend though, you must be pleased for me?'

'If it's what you want, then all is good.'

'But you must have an opinion?' Nat kept his voice light and effortlessly took his next shot.

'Not really.' Lombard shifted from foot to foot. He took out his pocket watch and flicked open the top. 'Time's getting on. Shall we call it a night?'

'In a minute.' He stood his cue stick upright and used it as a prop to lean on. 'So, you have no opinion of my marriage, of my future wife?'

'Why should I have?'

'Well, as my friend, we shall be entertaining you. I'd hope that you'd be comfortable in my home.'

Giving a chuckle, that held no humour in it, Lombard pulled at his starched collar. 'I'm sure once the novelty of being a newlywed has worn off, we'll no doubt be seeing you in the clubs again and things will go along as normal.'

Frowning, Nat chalked his cue tip and then moved around the table, going behind Lombard, to line up for another shot. 'Novelty of being a newlywed?'

'Why, yes. After all, your wife will hardly keep you interested for too long and then things will return to how they were.' Lombard grinned. 'I'll make sure I leave you some women. I cannot bed them all, though I might have a good go at it.'

'Keep them. I think my wife will satisfy me.'

Lombard laughed loudly. 'What, a prim governess? Are you mad? It's hard enough to believe you are actually marrying her, but to think she will satisfy you is insane.'

Fighting back the burning urge to haul Lombard across the table by the throat, Nat instead gave him a strained smile. 'You seem to have little faith in my choice of partner.'

'I think you've lost your wits.' Lombard relaxed his stance, falling for Nat's show of good nature.

'How so?' Nat raised an eyebrow, fighting for calm.

'Well, you've been hot for her since you first saw her last winter. But instead of just throwing her skirts over her head and scratching your itch, you've treated her like she was some noble lady.'

'Ah, I see.' His fist tightened on the cue stick. 'I should have treated her like a whore from the Rocks.'

'Utterly so, my good man.' Lombard nodded, his expression serious. 'But it's not too late to pull out of the agreement. Pay her off. Those women are always desperate for money.'

'Right.' He stepped away from the table, pretending to consider the angle of his next shot. Rage churned his gut, making his hands tremble with the need to throttle Lombard.

Unawares, Lombard went to the drinks cabinet in the corner and poured himself another whiskey. 'No one will blame you for cutting ties with her. She isn't of our class. Most will think you've had a lucky escape.'

'Who are they exactly?'

'Friends from the club, acquaintances.'

'Had a good laugh, have they?' Nat took his shot and missed. He straightened. 'Your turn.'

'No, no one is laughing, Nat. It's more a case of pity.'

'Pity.' A red mist seemed to cloud his mind. He walked around the table, as though heading for the drink's cabinet. 'Do they think I'm so stupid as to marry a woman just so I can bed her?'

Lombard shrugged. 'Why would you marry a governess anyway? Just set her up as your mistress and be done with it. She doesn't deserve your name.'

'I happen to think she does.' Nat ground out between clenched teeth.

'Really? How tragic. What happened? Have you filled her belly all ready?' Lombard snorted and chalked his cue. 'It's a shame really. I always fancied giving her one myself. I bet she'd have an arse as smooth as—'

With a roar that hurt his throat, Nat dropped his cue and lunged for him. The force of his charge threw them both onto the floor, knocking over a lamp table as they did so. Amidst the broken glass of the lamp and whiskey glasses, Nat straddled Lombard and punched him in the face. The crunch of Lombard's nose breaking gave Nat a sense of satisfaction, but it wasn't enough as pain cursed through his hand, making him even madder. He hauled Lombard to his feet and gave him a one-two to the stomach, instinctively knowing he could do damage there but not to his hands.

Lombard sank to his knees, coughing and spluttering.

Nat stepped back, aching for the man to do or say something else so that he could smash his teeth in. 'Get up Lombard, you coward. Get up and fight.'

'Go to Hell!'

'Get up I said,' he yelled, jerking him up by the lapels of his jacket.

'Let go of me, you bastard.' Lombard spat in Nat's face. The shock held him immobile for a moment, then he flung the scoundrel away into the tall bookcase by the window. Books rattled on the shelves, several toppled to the floor. Just as Nat brought his fist back to smack Lombard again, the door burst open and in rushed three men.

'I say, what the devil is going on here?' The proprietor of the club, Atkins, glared at the mess.

Nat jerked forward, intending to punch Lombard again, but a call from the door made him lower his fist.

'Enough, West. No more.' Jones-Parker, an older man, walked further into the room. 'Leave him.'

Nat glared at them all. 'Has anyone else got something to say about my future wife?'

Puzzled, the men looked at him as though he was mad.

Atkins came in and righted a chair. 'Why would we, Mr West?'

'Well if any of you do have something to say, then let me hear it now and we'll deal with it.' He sucked in a ragged breath. 'Because I'm telling you this, if I hear one derogatory word about my wife in the future I'll know where to come looking. Clear?' Nat swept his gaze past the older men in the room and out to the gathering spectators in the hall.

No one moved or spoke a word as he shouldered his way out of the room and left the club.

* * *

'HERE'S TO THE HAPPY COUPLE.' Mr Belfroy raised his glass high.

Nicola, seated next to Nathaniel at the head table, felt her cheeks achingly protest at the amount of smiling she was doing today. She gazed around at the room full of friends; Frances, Mr Belfroy, the women from the Home and the staff. Other people had witnessed their marriage, many of them acquaintances of Nathaniel's, but it was the presence of those she'd grown close to that mattered the most.

'As much as I'm enjoying today,' Nathaniel whispered in her ear, 'I'll be happier when we are alone together.'

She lowered her lashes at his forwardness, the heat rushing to her cheeks. 'You mustn't talk like that. These people are here sharing our special day. You cannot wish them away.'

'The day is yours and mine. I wouldn't care if no one had come. You are all that matters.' He took her hand where it rested beside her plate and kissed the back of it. 'When will they leave?'

Nicola laughed softly. 'Don't be rude.'

'Can we not slip away?'

'No.' She nudged him playfully. 'Eat some more and be less impatient.'

'Hark at you, only married a few hours and already giving orders.' He grinned. 'Promise me you'll not turn into a shrew overnight.'

'I promise nothing, Mr West.' Her eyes narrowed with a

sauciness she didn't know she possessed. 'Who knows what tonight will bring?'

His expression altered from light-heartedness to some-thing more serious. He leaned towards her, his fingers playing with hers. 'Tonight will bring many things, my darling, that I do promise.'

Desire was written on his face and she found it difficult to breathe. 'Nathaniel…'

'Sweetheart, don't look at me like that in front of all these people. I'm barely controlling myself as it is.'

She straightened in her chair, and after a small pressure on his fingers, she let go of his hand and turned back to their guests. Lifting her head, she smiled at Frances, who was looking their way, and Frances raised her glass to them in silent salute.

For the next hour, Nicola ate and drank while mingling with her guests. Even when they were on opposites sides of the room, she was aware of Nathaniel's presence. Whenever she looked across at him, she found his heated gaze on her, the wry lift of his lips.

'When did you change your mind?' Frances murmured in Nicola's ear.

Nicola spun around, giving her a quizzical look. 'Change my mind about what?'

'Marrying my brother, of course.'

'Oh, I don't know exactly when. He sort of grew on me.' She laughed.

'He has a habit of doing that.' Frances swallowed the last of her wine. 'But there must have been a moment when you knew you had to say yes to him?'

'I suppose so, yes.' Nicola stared down at the glass in her hand, remembering. 'I think the turning point was when I held Miss Roger's baby. I suddenly, desperately, wanted a child of my own. I wanted Nathaniel's child.' She looked up at Frances. 'I realised that I wanted a family of my own. Then, you came and told me that Nathaniel was to return to England and I felt as though my whole world had collapsed.'

Frances nodded. 'I thought so. Your face drained of all colour when I told you. Such a reaction hinted that you weren't as unaffected by my dear brother as you liked to believe.'

'Aren't you the clever one, then?' She linked her arm through her new sister's-in-law's. 'Have you moved all your things into the house?'

'No, not yet. I told Nat I'd not move into your house until you are in the country, to give you some time alone together.'

'There was no need to do that. We are leaving in two days' time. The house is large, and I hate the thought of you living in that tiny room in Margaret Place. That whole building should be condemned.'

'Nonsense. It is a perfectly suitable place for me to live. I'm close to the soup kitchen and—'

'All right.' Nicola held up her hand, laughing. 'Don't get started.'

Frances chuckled and kissed Nicola's cheek. 'Here comes my brother. I think he wants you to say your farewells.'

With her hand tucked through Nathaniel's arm, Nicola circled the room, thanking people for coming and accepting their good wishes. Within half an hour, she and her new husband were in the carriage heading for their new home in Double Bay.

Nestled against Nathaniel's side, she yawned, her body swaying with the movement of the carriage.

'Tired, my love?'

'A little. I was up so early and it's been such a wonderful day.' She put a hand up to her hair, hoping it'd kept in place and remained presentable. Never in her life had she fussed about her appearance as she did this morning. Frances, who'd arrived at the Home to help her dress, had laughed at her nervous cries that she wouldn't look beautiful on today of all days. Her dress, a pale peach satin over white tulle, had fitted perfectly. Miss Shaw had scooped up her hair and pinned it, adding peach ribbons and white rosebuds. All the women agreed she looked lovely. Mr Belfroy, when he arrived to escort her to the church, had confirmed it by becoming a little teary at the sight of her coming down the staircase.

'A perfect day.' Nat kissed the top of her head.

'Yes.'

'Have I told you how beautiful you are?'

'I believe you have, but I'm always interested to hear you say it again.' She rubbed her cheek against his shoulder like a contented cat.

'I am looking forward to seeing you wear light colours now.'

She stared at him. 'Light colours?'

'Yes.' He moaned pathetically. 'Do you know, that apart from the charity ball, I have only seen you wear browns, greys, and dark green and blue?'

Nibbling her bottom lip in thought, she tried to picture all her clothes and what she'd worn when with him. 'I never gave it a moment's thought.'

'Well, now, as my wife, I want to see you in colours like this.' He plucked at her peach dress. 'Lemon and sky blue, pink, sprigged cotton, lavender and pale green.'

She grinned, liking this new side of him. 'I will try my best, husband.'

'Good. You'll have a dress allowance, make sure you use it with my needs in mind.'

She laughed at him and they shared a sweet tender kiss as the carriage slowed.

'Here we are.' Nathaniel opened the carriage door as the driver halted the horses on the drive. 'Our home.'

Nicola stepped down and gazed at the house, the one that had been for sale she'd seen all those months ago, the one in which Nathaniel had originally asked her to marry him. 'We'll be happy here. I know it.' She glanced at him and smiled. 'Thank you for buying it.'

'How could I not?' He kissed her gently. 'How could I let strangers live here, the place where I first kissed you, touched you. This house was meant to be ours.' Taking her by the hand, he led her along the path and inside.

In the entrance hall, Nicola paused, soaking in the truth that this was her home now and she was married. During the week, her belongings had been packed and brought here. She and Nathaniel spent as much of their spare time as they could, wandering the house, discussing improvements, ordering furniture, interviewing staff. Yet none of it seemed real. Until now.

'Ah, Mrs Rawlings.' Nathaniel greeted the housekeeper, employed four days ago.

'Welcome home, Mr and Mrs West.' She bowed her head.

'Thank you, Mrs Rawlings.' Nicola liked the older woman, who, recently widowed, had been the best of those she'd interviewed for the position. Along with Mrs Rawlings, they'd hired a cook, parlour maid, kitchen maid and a gardener.

'Would you care for a tray of tea to be brought in for you?' Mrs Rawlings said, standing to one side as they walked into the drawing room.

'Nicola?' Nathaniel raised his eyebrows in question.

'Actually, I've had enough to eat and drink.'

Nathaniel turned to Mrs Rawlings. 'Thank you, but we'll call if we need anything.'

'Very good, sir.' The housekeeper closed the double doors as she left.

The setting sun cast fingers of light through the windows of the drawing room. Nicola liked this room, its colours of pale green, gold and white soothed her, yet held the subtle classic feel. With a weary stretch, she relaxed on the cream striped sofa and longed to kick off her shoes. Nathaniel walked to the window and stared out for a moment before crossing to stand before the empty fireplace. His restlessness made her grin.

'What amuses you?'

'You do.'

'How so?'

'You don't know what to do with yourself, do you?'

He frowned and then laughed. 'No, not really. What does one do after a wedding breakfast? By rights we should be on our way to some honeymoon destination.'

'I don't need a honeymoon. All this,' she waved her arms out wide to encompass the room, 'all this is enough for me. I don't want to be in some strange place surrounded by people in whom I have no interest.' She rose and stood in front of him. 'A warm comfortable house, our home, and you in it are all I want. Besides, in two days' time we travel to your country property. That shall be our honeymoon.'

'The property is ours, not mine.' He gathered her into his arms, holding her tightly. 'Two days ago, I went to see my solicitor and made my will. I had your name added to the deeds of all the properties I own. Should anything happen to me everything I have, the businesses, everything, will be yours.'

'Oh, Nathaniel.' Surprised by this show of devotion, she could do nothing but gape at him.

'I wanted to make sure that you would never know poverty again.'

213

'I don't know what to say.' She wrapped her arms around his neck and brought his head down, so she could kiss him. He returned her kisses as eagerly as she gave them. His tongue flicked between her lips, encouraging her to open her mouth and when she did, she was overwhelmed by the intensity of his passion as he deepened the kiss. She gripped his upper arms, her legs suddenly weak. She never thought it could be so wonderful, so primal. Nat grounded his hips against hers and her body arched, wanting more.

Deep in the pit of her being, a hot yearning awoke, sending out unfurling coils of need that made her body sensitive and responsive to the man who held her.

'Is it too early to go upstairs?' he murmured, his breathing now shallow gasps while nibbling the soft skin beneath her ears.

'I don't think so…' She moaned as he kissed a path down her neck. 'Besides…it's our home and we can do what we want in it.'

He took her hand, and giggling like naughty children, they crept upstairs to their bedroom suite, hoping Mrs Rawlings or the new parlourmaid wouldn't see them.

Nathaniel locked the door behind them and dragged her into his arms. 'God, you are magnificent. I cannot believe you are mine. I want to love you, Nicola, love you properly, forever.'

'It is what I want too, my darling.'

He raised his head to give her a devilish grin. 'I hope you're prepared to not sleep tonight, my sweet girl.'

She laughed, feeling carefree and beautiful when he gazed at her. 'Do I seem to care about that, husband?' She raked her fingernails down the fine material on his back. 'I feel like I've waited my whole life for tonight.'

'You and me both, my love, you and me both. But I must go slowly. I want to appreciate every second.' He led her to the stool in front of the dressing mirror and sat her down. Standing behind her, he slowly found the pins holding her hair and removed them. The small flowers followed the pins and then he ran his fingers through her hair, letting it fall freely down her back. 'You have such beautiful hair, Nicola. It's like burnished copper.'

She smiled and leaned against him, watching him in the mirror as his hands travelled down to undo the buttons of her gown. He slipped the satin material down off her shoulders and bent to kiss her exposed skin.

'Nathaniel...' Closing her yes, she gave herself up to the whirling sensations he created within her.

Again, his fingers worked, this time on her corset, loosening the stays until the garment came away from her body. He cupped her breast through the linen chemise, kissing her neck and collarbone. 'Nicola...'

She stood and stepped around the stool and into his arms. 'You are overdressed, husband.' She teased, unravelling his cravat and tossing it aside. After planting a kiss on his lips, she unbuttoned his waistcoat and then his shirt, the whole time watching his eyes and how they darkened with desire when her fingertips touched his skin.

Nathaniel drew her over to the bed and eased her down gently. 'Are you afraid?'

'Of you? Never.' She gave him a saucy smile, one she never thought she could produce so easily and then laughed. Rising up onto her elbows, she grinned. 'Do you sleep with your trousers on, Mr West?'

He threw his head back and laughed. In a flash he launched himself onto the bed, grabbed her by the waist and spun her under him. The surprise attack made her giggle like a young girl, but then she saw the humour fade from his eyes to be replaced with such love that she wanted to cry at the beauty of it. She touched his cheek, adoring this man with every ounce of her being.

Nathaniel traced the line of her jaw with his finger. 'I love you, Nicola.'

'I know.'

'I would die for you.' His expression changed to one of nearly sorrow. 'Do you think you can really love me, for all my faults?'

She brought his head down to kiss him with all the love she had inside. 'I already do, my darling. You just need to believe in it.'

CHAPTER 17

*N*icola woke up and stretched, frowning as she realised she was alone in the bed. In the last six weeks she'd grown used to having Nathaniel beside her when she opened her eyes in the morning.

Sunlight streamed through the window and from the dressing room she heard the sound of splashing. She thought of the lazy mornings they spent in the country and the hours of idle occupation as they grew to love their property in Camden.

Nathaniel emerged from the dressing room, drying his face on a towel and wearing only his trousers. She admired his broad chest and the light scattering of fair hair there. His arms were brown from the days toiling in the sun as he worked beside the labourers in shaping the property to his liking.

'Good morning, sleepy head.' He grinned, coming over to give her a long leisurely kiss.

'What time is it?'

'After nine.'

She flung back the sheets. 'You should have woken me earlier.'

'I thought you could do with an extra hour of sleep.' He threw the towel on a nearby chair. 'We were so late coming in from the country last night, you looked exhausted.'

'I was, but I had planned to go up to the Home earlier than this. There's so much I have to do.'

He pulled her into his arms. 'Frances will be waiting for us down at the breakfast table. She hasn't seen us for weeks and will likely have missed us, so don't rush off.'

She nodded and gave him a quick kiss. 'I won't, but if I don't get washed and dressed soon my day will be ruined.' She rubbed her forehead in annoyance at seeing all their luggage piled in the dressing room. A broken carriage axle on their way home yesterday had held them up for hours. When they finally arrived at the house in Double Bay it was close to midnight and Nicola had gone straight to bed after giving Frances a brief hug.

While washing, her new maid, May, knocked on the door. Nathaniel, now fully dressed, gestured for her to come in as he headed for downstairs.

'Good morning, May.' Nicola smiled, liking the girl. She had employed her during their stay at Camden. At seventeen, May was old enough to be sensible and young enough to be trained as Nicola wanted. Although, having never had her own maid before, Nicola found she and May were both learning together as they went along.

'Morning, Madam.'

'I'll wear the lemon skirt and bodice today.'

'What would you like me to do with your hair?' May's dimples and sweet manner had earned her the friendship of the entire Camden household immediately, that and also being from a local family. Nicola hoped the girl would settle into the city just as well.

'I'll only have something simple today as I'm in a hurry. I'll be wearing my straw boater anyway.'

'As you like, Madam.' May, her expression serious, took up the brush and set to the task.

'Did you manage to sleep much last night?' Nicola asked, adding a light spray of perfume to her neck and wrists.

'A little bit, Madam. You know how it is when sleeping in a strange bed at first.'

'Yes. You must write to your family and let them know you've arrived safely.'

'I will, Madam.' May scooped Nicola's hair up, securing it with pins and a silver flowered clasp at the back. 'I'll tell them how lovely this house is too.'

'It is a handsome house.' Nicola smiled as May perched the straw hat on top of her head, tilting it forward a little to show off Nicola's hair arrangement at the back.

While May worked, Nicola thought of the house in Camden, so different to this one. Their country property was single storey, with a wide encasing verandah. She had spent weeks putting her own touches to it and working in the garden with the outdoor staff. Free from the responsibilities of the Home, she'd found the six weeks in the country, just her and Nathaniel, deeply relaxing and fulfilling. She'd been able to learn more about the man she married and found her feelings for him intensify. Often, they would dress simply and, taking a picnic, walk to the small creek that ran through their land. They'd lay on a blanket in the sunshine and talk and eat, content to be quite at times, or even doze in the shade of a tree. Nicola realised those precious hours had done much to strengthen their relationship, to create the strong foundations of their marriage.

'There, Madam, all done.'

Rising, Nicola gave a last look in the mirror and satisfied she was presentable, headed for the door. 'Thank you, May.'

She glanced in the direction of the dressing room. 'I'm afraid you'll be busy unpacking today.'

'Leave it with me, Madam, I'll soon have it all sorted.'

Downstairs, Nicola entered the breakfast room and found Frances and Nathaniel deep in conversation.

On seeing her, Frances jumped up from her chair and hurried to embrace her. 'Oh, I'm so happy you are back. I was just telling Nat how much I missed you both.'

They broke apart and sat at the table. Nicola poured herself some coffee and selected a slice of toast from the stand. 'How are you? I'm sorry for last night, but I couldn't keep my eyes open a second longer.'

'Heavens, I understand. Nat was telling me you had a dreadful journey home. Next time take the train.'

'We will, but I wanted to go by carriage, so we could stop as we wished and see some of the places we were passing. Also, we had an invitation to stay a night with some new friends, the Forresters. He is the brother to Nathaniel's solicitor. They live in Campbelltown and I didn't want to arrive covered in soot. But, yes, next time we'll definitely go by train. I've learned my lesson well.' Nicola grimaced at the memory of waiting by the roadside for a replacement vehicle to come and collect them after their carriage broke an axle. Then as darkness crept over the countryside, rain began to fall, making them thoroughly cold and miserable.

Nathaniel laughed. 'I'm not sure how I'll be able to hold my head up at the club again. Whenever we go into the country from now on, it'll be by train.'

'Well, you're home now.' Frances sipped her coffee. 'And I hope you'll not be off on adventure again for a while. This house is far too large for me by myself.'

Nathaniel put down the newspaper he'd been glancing at. 'Next time we go to the country you'll have to come with us.'

'We did invite you to join us.' Nicola raised her eyebrows at her while biting into her toast.

'It was your honeymoon.' Frances rolled her eyes. 'You didn't need me there spoiling your fun. But tell me, did you like the house, and the town?'

'Oh, very much.' Nicola spread jam onto her toast. 'We made a few alterations and decorated. I also designed the front garden while Nathaniel had the stables extended.'

'Plus, we planted a beech grove.' Nat winked over the top of his paper.

'Yes, and Nathaniel instructed for a lake to be built and willows to be planted on the edge of it.'

'Willows, a lake?' Frances looked from one to the other. 'I'm wondering if this is really my brother, the man who hates to spend money on such frivolous things.'

Nicola looked from Fran to Nathaniel, the warmth leaving her face. 'Did I spend too much? You should have said, Nathaniel. I should have known, especially as we decorated this house before our wedding. I can cancel—'

He reached over and took her hand. 'Darling, do not listen to my sister. I am quite able to finance the refurbishment of two houses.' He sat back and gave Frances a scowl. 'Mind your own business, Frances, please, and stop frightening Nicola with your stories of how bad a person I am. You'll undo all the good work I've done in the last several weeks.'

'I wasn't. I was merely stating the fact that you hate spending money.'

'Only on things that have no value or concern to me, which in this case doesn't apply.' He lifted up his newspaper again.

'I'm sorry, Nic.' Frances gave an apologetic smile which split into a grin. 'Do tell me more.'

'We received so many invitations and met a great deal of

people. As a thank you to the friendship offered to us during our stay we held a wonderful dinner party last week. I was very nervous. I've never organised such an occasion before. We had twenty-four couples and five courses.'

'I'm sure you did a wonderful job of it. If you can run a women's home, you can hold a dinner party.'

Nathaniel lowered the newspaper, his expression one of mischief. 'Fran, you would have been proud of our Nicola, she was adored by all the men and made friends of their jealous wives. Not an easy task I grant you.'

'This is a side of my sister-in-law I've not seen.' Frances's eyes widened. 'With all this excitement I'm surprised you returned home at all.'

'I did enjoy my time there and look forward to staying at the house each year.' She poured more coffee into her cup, thinking about how comfortable she'd been in the country with Nathaniel. 'Actually, Nathaniel and I have decided that we'll spend three or four months each year at the country property. Camden is a growing town and the people are friendly. Autumn seems to be the perfect time to be there as it's not too hot or too cold.'

Agnes, the parlourmaid, entered the room carrying a small tray which held the morning's post. She placed it next to Nathaniel and then turned to Nicola. 'Excuse me, Madam, would you care for a fresh pot of coffee?'

Nicola gave a questioning look to Nathaniel and Frances, both shook their heads. 'No, thank you, Agnes. We have sufficient.'

'Very good, Madam.'

'How have you found the staff, Frances?' Nicola asked after Agnes had left carrying some of the dirty plates from the sideboard.

'They've been rather good and cared for my every need.'

'I am pleased. We were here only a short time, a couple of

days before we left for the country and I wasn't able to get a thorough opinion of them. I'm glad you moved in to supervise them.' The clock in the hallway struck the hour. 'Have you called in at the Home recently?'

'Two days ago.' Frances dabbed at her mouth with a napkin. 'They are all missing you tremendously. Miss McIntyre had the women and staff in a frenzy of cleaning in readiness of your homecoming.'

'Ah, but this is Nicola's home now,' Nathaniel murmured.

'Oh, shush, Nat, you know what I mean. They all think so highly of your wife. You have to share her, you understand.' She turned back to Nicola. 'Miss Shaw obtained a position in Parramatta and Miss Clarke also has a situation up in the north country near Armidale.'

'How excellent. I cannot wait to see them and hear their news.' Eager to check that all was in order at the Home, she hurriedly finished her meal.

'Darling,' Nat looked at her fondly, as one would do an impatient child, 'The Home will not fall to ruin just because you have some breakfast.'

'I know. It's just that I have missed them.'

'Shall I drop you off on my way then?'

'Are you ready to leave now?'

He swallowed the last of his coffee. 'Yes, come along then.' He sighed, but his eyes held humour and devotion.

'You might as well drop me off at the soup kitchen as well.' Frances rose from her chair.

'Isn't the soup kitchen open tomorrow, not today?' Nicola asked, collecting her gloves from the table in the hall.

'Yes, but also today too. The demand has grown so much that we have to open an extra day.'

'Can you afford to, Fran?' Nathaniel asked, pulling on his leather gloves.

'Can we afford not to?' Fran shrugged helplessly.

'I'll come and help you tomorrow.' Nicola squeezed her hand. They continued chatting out to the carriage and on the way to the Home.

Nicola waved them away from the front steps of the Home and then turned to find the door being opened and most of the women rushing out to greet her.

'How well you look, Mrs West.' Florence McIntyre beamed, the others chorusing the same sentiments.

'I've missed everyone.' Nicola ushered them inside, smiling and greeting them individually. 'How are you all?'

The women started talking at once until the hall rang with noise.

'Enough!' Florence clapped. 'Lord above, you'll be sending Mrs West deaf within the hour at that rate.' She turned to Nicola. 'Would you prefer to have the business side of things done first, Mrs West, and then take tea with us afterwards?'

'Superb idea, Florence.' She thanked the women again for their homecoming and headed for the study.

Once seated behind her desk, she found the account books opened for her inspection. She smiled at Florence, who sat stiffly in the chair on the other side of the desk. 'How's it been?'

'Quite good, Mrs West, we've—'

'Florence, please, while we are in each other's company I would prefer it if you called me Nicola. I'm not used to my new title as yet and I feel, between the two of us, that we are friends enough to be less formal.'

Florence looked startled at the request. 'Are you sure?'

'Definitely. So, it is agreed?'

'Yes, thank you...Nicola.'

'Good. Now, to business. The letters you sent to me while I was in the country were a great help. I felt I could relax knowing you had everything under control.'

'Thankfully, we had no emergencies while you were away.

Mrs Nesbit only got drunk once and Hannah broke just three plates.' Florence let out a long breath, as though grateful that's all that happened.

'My sister-in-law tells me Miss Clarke and Miss Shaw have gained situations?'

'Oh yes, indeed. Most happy they are too. Miss Shaw leaves tomorrow and Miss Clarke on Friday.'

Nicola concentrated on the figures before her. 'When do your two sisters arrive, or have they already? There was some delay was there not?'

'I'm expecting them any day. I told them to send a telegram from Melbourne if they are able to get shore leave there. But I've heard nothing so far. I scan the papers each day for news of sightings of their ship.' A worried frown appeared on Florence's face. 'I do hope all is well with them.'

'I'm sure everything is, Florence. Sometimes we just have to be patient. The journey from Scotland to this country is extensive, as you know, and at the mercy of the others for much of it.'

'Upstairs I have prepared the end room on the right for them. Does that meet with your approval? They'll be happy to share. Fiona is sensible and will not have brought much with her and Fanny is of a slight build. So, they'll hardly take up any room.'

'I'm sure they are delightful girls. They've come a long way, so do make sure they are comfortable. I know you do not want any favours for them, being your sisters, but since you've offered to pay for their keep out of your wages, then they deserve the same considerations as all the other women here.' Nicola smiled.

'Thank you, Mrs-Nicola. At seventeen and fifteen, I'm hoping they'll find work soon enough.'

'I'm sure they will. Now, the schoolroom and orphanage. I'm most eager to see them. Are they finally finished?'

'Yes, the orphanage dormitory is, but not the schoolroom, there have been problems with the foundations. It seems a spring runs beneath the ground and it's causing subsidence. I'm afraid the foreman's conversation about it all goes over my head and I understand very little.'

'I'll ask my husband to speak with the builders. We shall need to put advertisements in the newspaper and spread the word that we can now take paying students. I'll have to talk to the women about this too. Do you know of any who are eager to teach in the schoolroom?'

'Miss Peacock has expressed a desire to, as well as Miss Barker, who received her teacher's certificate yesterday. She passed her exams exceedingly well.'

'Excellent. That is a good start. I will help out when I can too.' Nicola turned the page of one of the accounts books and studied the figures. 'Have you seen Mr Belfroy?'

'Yes, only yesterday morning. He came to see if you were returned from the country and to celebrate Miss Barker gaining her certificate.'

'He is well?'

'The same as usual, I think.'

Nicola nodded and reached for the occupancy ledger. 'We have two new arrivals?' She frowned, not remembering any new faces earlier.

'Mrs Patterson and Miss Nelson.'

A look of uncertainty crossed Florence's face. 'What is it?'

'Nothing really…'

'But something?'

'Mrs Patterson is a kind lady, but…um…quite elderly. Nearly seventy, I'm afraid. She keeps to her room a great deal.'

Nicola blinked in surprise. 'Seventy years old?'

'She has excellent references. She came out to this country last year with a new family, after spending most of her life with a noble family in Ireland, who sadly didn't offer her a pension and so she had to find a new position. Unfortunately, the situation with the new family didn't work out and now she is here. She told me quite adamantly that her health had been perfect up until the voyage out when she caught a chill. Since then she has constantly been unwell.'

'I feel at her age she will have trouble finding another position and if her health is bad, then perhaps she will do well to stay here awhile to recuperate. I doubt she should be working at her age. We'll look after her.' Nicola scanned Mrs Patterson's details in the agency book. 'How has the agency been doing? Any interest from prospective employers?'

'Not too many as yet. The enquiries have been for housemaids. As you can see we have plenty of women listed, but I feel we need to advertise the agency more.'

'I agree.' Nicola took out her diary from the top drawer. 'I'll make arrangements to do that in the morning.'

They talked business for another fifteen minutes until eager for a cup of tea, they left the study and went to the parlour where the women had gathered. While enjoying a splendid morning tea, Nicola chatted to the women, met Mrs Patterson and Miss Nelson and then toured the new building work.

By midafternoon, Nicola was again busy at her desk. Mr Belfroy had been to welcome her back and they had discussed business for an hour and done another tour of the buildings.

Rubbing her neck muscles, Nicola leaned back in her chair. While absent, the Home had gone along smoothly with Florence at its head. She didn't know whether to be pleased about it or hurt that she was replaceable. Before her marriage, the Home and the women in it had been everything to her. It was difficult to let go of some of the control.

Her thoughts returned to the conversation she had with

Frances at breakfast. The mention of Nathaniel's money disturbed her. She had no real thought to his wealth before and now wondered just how rich he was. He never seemed to be concerned about such things, but then he might be hiding it from her. Money was one subject they had not discussed.

After a slight knock, Nathaniel popped his head around. 'Am I disturbing you?'

His warm loving smile made her tingle. 'No, you aren't disturbing me.' She rose as he came into the room. 'I didn't expect to see you for hours yet.'

He stepped behind the desk and took her into his arms. She sagged against him as they kissed. There was no better feeling than being held by him. 'I missed you.'

She cupped his cheek in one hand. 'And I you.'

'Really?' Doubt clouded his eyes.

'I did.'

'I thought you'd have been far too busy to think of me.'

'Even when I'm full of activity I miss you.' She kissed him, seeing the signs now of his lack of confidence where her love was concerned. He'd been damaged by his cold upbringing and it didn't take much for him to doubt her affections.

'Good.' He caressed her fingers of one hand, kissing each one in turn. 'I met with my solicitor and a few other business partners, Jonas Cox and Matthew Wright, but I couldn't concentrate.'

'Shall we go home?'

'Have you finished here for the day?'

'Yes. There's always tomorrow.'

He frowned. 'I thought we could spend tomorrow together.'

'I promised Fran I'd help at the soup kitchen and I've advertisements to place in the newspapers.' She kissed him again, hating to see the disappointment on his face. 'I promise you that we'll spend the day after together.'

'I'll hold you to that.' He let her go so she could pack away her books and gather her things.

In the carriage going home, Nicola held Nathaniel's hand, her mind whirling with thoughts on how wealthy her husband might or might not be. By the time they reached the house she'd made the decision to talk to him about it. She knew most women didn't trouble themselves about finances, but she wasn't most women. Indeed, she wondered if she'd have a battle on her hands in getting information out of Nathaniel. After all, some gentlemen refused to discuss such matters with their wives, believing it to be none of their business. Would Nathaniel be the same?

In the drawing room, Nathaniel spoke to Mrs Rawlings, and ordered some tea. Nicola nodded at the housekeeper as she left the room and sat down on the sofa beneath the window.

'You're wearing a frown, sweetheart. Is something wrong?'

Now was a good a time as any to mention her worries. 'I've been thinking about what was said at the breakfast table this morning.'

It was Nat's turn to frown. 'About what?'

'Money.'

'Money?'

'More accurately, your finances.'

'Sweetheart, I told you not to worry about that. You are free to decorate both houses as you please.'

Restless, Nicola stood and walked to the empty fireplace. 'We promised each other that we'd always be honest.'

'I am being honest.' He reclined on a leather wing-backed chair, watching her.

'Then will you tell me the extent of your wealth, or lack of it? I know you have businesses and houses, but I don't know all the details. If my name is on the deeds, then I should know.'

Agnes brought in the tea tray. 'Will I pour for you, Madam?'

'No thank you. I'll see to it. Thank you, Agnes, that will be all.' Nicola, anxiously waiting for Nathaniel's reply, set out the cups and saucers.

'I will tell you everything you want to know. There will be no secrets between us.' He sat forward on his chair and stopped her from fiddling with the tea tray. 'Come over here.'

She squealed as he pulled her onto his lap. 'Nathaniel, no. Mrs Rawlings might come in, or Agnes.'

'Let them. We are newly married. It's expected.' He grinned and then kissed her deeply, showing his passion for her. 'I've been waiting to do that all day.'

'Behave yourself.' She playfully slapped at his chest, though secretly enjoying the naughtiness of being on his lap in the middle of the afternoon. 'Be serious, please.'

'Very well.' He sighed and gave her a wry look. 'Apart from the inheritance back in England and the two properties, this one and the Camden house, I have shares in a sheep station in Queensland. I have a one eighth share in a coal mine near Newcastle. I own a complete terrace of houses here in Sydney. I own a pottery factory in Parramatta.' He grinned. 'That was an impulsive purchase to annoy a gentleman I didn't like and who wanted to buy it himself.' He shrugged suddenly as if to mentally dismiss it from his mind. 'I recently bought land in Melbourne, plus I have two factories there. What else...'

'I had no idea.' She stared at him, amazed. 'Why did you not mention this before?'

'I didn't think you were interested. Not many ladies are.'

'Well, I am certainly interested. You should know me well enough by now to know I would be. I'm not some dim-witted woman content to spend her days in frivolous occupations such as gossiping about latest fashions, buying useless things and paying calls. Why I—'

As usual, he silenced her with a kiss. 'I am fast learning just how clever my wife is. I'm also learning that when she starts a tirade I have to stop her quickly or I'll get no peace.'

She played with a button on his waistcoat. 'I want to learn about your businesses.'

'And you shall.'

'Promise?'

'Absolutely. We'll start next week. I want you to know everything there is to know in case something happens to me.'

Her heart constricted. 'Don't say that, Nathaniel.'

'It is a way of life, darling. We have to be prepared. Look at my mother. She's fallen apart now my father has gone. Yet, when he was alive they hardly got on at all. And my brother is a useless article.'

'I still feel guilty for you not returning to England.'

'Nonsense. I am free to make up my own mind. I've been doing it long enough.'

'I never thought myself as a selfish person before, but I am, and am ashamed to be so. I couldn't bear to be parted from you.'

He held her closer, nuzzling her neck beneath her ear. 'Only death will separate us, my love, that I can promise you.'

CHAPTER 18

*N*icola, reading a letter from Meg, swayed in the carriage, as the driver, Timms applied the brakes. She frowned at the rough ride, but continued reading, excited to finally hear from her dear friend.

...THEREFORE OUR STAY in Rio was longer than expected, and I seemed to be the only person who didn't mind this inconvenience. I cared nothing for the ship's repairs, only that it afforded me to spend more time in Rio. I adore Rio, there is so much to see and do. The colours and flavours, the scents and people all amaze me. There is such heat, such passion. Oh, the sights I've seen, Nicola. Some would shock you, I declare, but others, with you being so clever minded, would interest you vastly.

NICOLA SMILED, wondering what Meg had seen and frustrated that her wayward friend hadn't seen fit to give more details, but such was Meg, she supposed.

. . .

You will be surprised, I think, to learn that I am very happy in my marriage. James is a wonderful man and is no way dull or strict. He gives me such freedom to go ashore alone when we make port at different places. He is a busy man but makes the time to spend with me. I am most in love with him, which is fortunate.

'I am indeed happy for you, Meg,' she murmured. Her own happy marriage gave her the insight to how Meg must feel.

I will tell you though that our dear Hilton is still not himself since leaving Sydney. I truly think you broke his heart and it will never be mended. But perhaps that will change when we arrive in Boston and he is home among his own people again. I have grown rather fond of him and James wouldn't be without him of course...

'Mrs West.' Timms's call through the open window stopped her reading and she looked up.

'Yes, what is it, Timms?'

'There seems to be some sort of blockage ahead, Madam. An overturned cart, as far as I can tell. I can't turn the horses or go around it. We'll have a bit of a wait it seems.'

'Blast. Where are we?' A horse and rider blocked her view from her opposite window.

'Bridge Street, Madam.'

Folding the letter away into her reticule, she nodded and prepared to descend from the carriage. 'I will walk from here, Timms.'

'I will meet you in Charlotte Place, Madam?'

'No, I don't know how long I'll be or how long you'll be getting through all that.' She waved towards the build up of vehicles. 'I'll catch the omnibus to the Home. You go back to the house when you can, my husband may need you later.'

'Right you are, Mrs West.'

Once on the footpath, Nicola steadied her hat as a gust of wind tunnelling down the street threatened to dislodge it from its pins. She remembered Mrs Eldersley mentioning that April was known for its winds. Well, it would be May next week, surely the gales would be gone by then?

Dust swirled around her legs and she grimaced at the state of her dress hem. It was all well and good for Nathaniel to want her to wear light colours, like this pale green stripe, but the practicalities of doing so weighed heavily on the negative. Still, she didn't have to launder the clothes and donning such beautiful dresses gave her selfish pleasure.

The church bells struck the hour of twelve and she hurried away down an alley to escape the confusion of the road blockage. Weaving through the streets, she kept her head down to keep the wind and dust from her eyes. A part of her wished she could cry off the appointment with the printer, but she'd promised Florence to check the progress of the leaflets for the school since Florence was busy with her newly arrived sisters. She ducked down another narrow alley, finding it the quickest way to Charlotte's Place.

'Well now, if it isn't Mrs West.'

Surprised, Nicola glanced up and found Tristan Lombard in her way. Beside him, leered a rough looking man. 'Good day, Mr Lombard.'

'It seems as though married life suits you, Mrs West. You have never looked so lovely.' Lombard's insolent gaze roamed her from head to toe and back again.

'Thank you. If you'll excuse me, I have an appointment.' She attempted to move past him, but he stepped in her way, blocking her path. Surprised, she stared at him.

'You have time to chat with an old acquaintance?'

'I don't actually. Forgive me, I'm already late.' She forced a smile in his direction, not meeting his eyes. Something about the man always made her shudder.

'How is my friend, Nat? He hasn't been seen in the club for some time.'

'He is a busy man.'

'Well, what man wouldn't be when he has a wife as beautiful as you in his bed?' He leaned closer. 'I know that's where I'd be if you were mine.'

'I beg your pardon?' She gave him a scathing stare, her dislike of him going up another notch. How could Nathaniel have anything to do with such a horrid person?

'Well, something extraordinary had to have captured his interest enough for him to marry you, wouldn't you say?'

'Excuse me.' She stepped around him, but he caught her elbow in a crushing grip.

'Don't be so hasty, Mrs West. We have much to talk about.'

She winced at the pain in her arm. 'There is nothing we have to discuss. Let me go.'

'Did you not miss me at your wedding? I was to have been Nat's attendant. Did he tell you why I wasn't there?'

'He said you were away in the country on business.'

Lombard smirked. 'A lie, Mrs West, a damned lie.'

The blood ran cold in her veins as she stared at him. 'Let me go, please.'

'On your wedding day, I was still recovering from a busted lip and swollen eye, courtesy of your husband.'

She raised her chin. 'Then-then likely you deserved it.'

His wolf-like smile frightened her. 'I'll beg to differ on that. Your husband has a temper, Mrs West. You should be careful not to entice it. Nat's a fine boxer. Did he tell you that was one of his pastimes, knocking men's teeth out?'

'He has mentioned he boxed, yes.' Why did Lombard bear

her such animosity? She shivered, afraid of his threatening presence.

'But not that he did the same to me?' He chuckled. 'No, I can see by your face he didn't reveal that information. However, I expect there is much about his previous life he hasn't told you.'

'I haven't the time to talk to you. Please let go of my arm.'

'In a moment.' He paused, his eyes narrowing with anger or hatred she didn't know which. 'Tell Nat that I'll be waiting for his apology.'

'You'll be waiting a long time, I think, especially after the way you are treating me today.'

'Tell your husband, that unless he does right by me, I'll let loose certain information about his private dealings with a certain Mr Carstairs.'

'What do you mean?' She stared, her mouth dry at the warning.

'Pass the message on, if you please.'

'I insist you tell me what you mean.' She had the urge to strike his impudent face.

'You cannot demand anything of me, Madam. In this case I hold all the cards. Simply tell Nat to contact me or I'll spill everything I know about Carstairs and his dealings. If Nat hasn't lost all his reason, then he'll know what to do.'

'He'll not react to your intimidation, Lombard.'

'And I'll not lose another penny because he has a fancy to become an honourable married man, particularly when he's only married a strumpet of a governess.'

'How dare you!'

'Oh, I dare, Madam, I dare.' He grimaced, curling his lip up as if what he saw disgusted him. 'I cannot believe West has thrown away so many lucrative financial opportunities because of you. Well, he might suddenly want to be right-eous, but I do not, and I'll not grow poor because of it either.'

'I don't know what you're talking about.'

'Give him my message.' He squeezed her arm cruelly and then thrust her from him, before bowing like a gentleman. 'Good day, Mrs West.'

Incensed by his disrespect, her temper flared. 'Go to Hell, Mr Lombard, and take your message with you. I'll not do your dirty work. I have never liked you and am glad Nathaniel has rejected your friendship. I'm pleased he gave you the hiding you deserve.' She stopped, alarmed at her own viciousness and at the expression of calm rage on Lombard's face.

He turned to the silent man next to him, gave one nod and then quietly walked away up the alley.

Nicola, frozen to the spot, watched wide-eyed as the rough-looking fellow smiled, showing black rotten teeth. She backed away, hitting the wall behind her, but he advanced quickly, too quickly for her to respond. He slammed one hand over her mouth and then she felt a sharp burning pain in her side.

Gasping, she held her side, confused at the pain and its source. Taking her hand away she staggered at the sight of the sticky blood soaking her gloves. Her knees buckled, and she slid down the brick wall to the damp cold cobbles.

'Don't scream, missy,' he threatened, leaning over her, 'or I'll bone you as clean as a butcher's carcass. You just lie quiet now until I've gone.'

She held her side, reeling as the pain hit her in repeated waves without let up. 'No! Help me,' she begged on a scream.

'I said to shut it!' He drew his hand back and she screamed again as his fist came down and spun her into blackness.

* * *

NAT FLICKED the lace curtains aside and stared at the empty drive for the umpteenth time in the last ten minutes. He glanced over his shoulder at Fran, who sat knitting on the chair by the fire. 'Are you sure she didn't mention her plans for today to you?'

Fran huffed and gave him a quelling look. 'No. I told you, she has likely been held up at the Home. Miss McIntyre's sisters arrived yesterday, and she would be listening to the latest news from them.'

He tapped his fingers on his leg. 'She's never this late. It'll be dark soon.'

'She's only at the Home, for goodness sake. Go there and fetch her if it will soothe you.'

'No, I'll seem overbearing.'

'You are.'

He gave her a lopsided grin and turned away from the window. 'I am not overbearing at all. I am a concerned husband.'

She laughed at that. 'Be a concerned brother then and pour me a Madeira.'

'What are you trying to knit this time?' He went to the drinks cabinet, poured the drink and handed it to her.

'I need to make five scarves for a family who just lost their father.' She gave him a sarcastic glare. 'And I can knit, thank you very much. True, I am not exceptional at it, but I'll improve with time and practice.'

'You are too good. I hope they appreciate your kindness.' Wandering back to the window, he searched the street. Nicola had never been this late. A gnawing feeling twisted his gut. The door opened, and Agnes came through, carrying a basket of logs for the fire. 'Agnes, tell cook to hold dinner until Mrs West is home.'

'Yes, sir.' Agnes unloaded the wood and placed a piece on

the flames. 'Cook was just mentioning the same thing to Timms, sir.'

'Timms?' Nat frowned. 'Why is he home? Didn't he take my wife this morning?'

'Yes, sir, he did. She sent him home.'

Nat stormed from the room and down the hall to the kitchen. Fran called him, but he ignored her. He opened the kitchen door harder than he meant to, startling the cook and Mrs Rawlings. Both bobbed their respect. Timms jerked to his feet from a chair by the door where he'd been polishing his boots.

'Timms, why aren't you with my wife?'

'She told me to return home, sir. We were caught in a road blockage. She didn't want to wait and decided to walk.'

'Walk to where?'

'Charlotte Place, sir, to see the printers.'

'And afterwards, do you know of her intentions?'

'To go to the dressmakers and then back to the Home.'

'And she didn't want you to meet her there?'

'No, sir. She said for me to come back here in case you had need of me. She said she'd catch the omnibus.'

Nat clenched his jaw at her damned independence. 'Get the carriage out. We'll go to the Home and collect her.'

'Yes, sir.' Timms hastily pulled on his boots and after taking his jacket off the hook on the back door, hurried out into the yard.

Nat turned to the housekeeper and cook. 'I apologise that the meal may be ruined, Cook.'

'Nay, sir, I'll sort it out, never fear.' She bobbed her head, her double chin wobbling.

He left the kitchen and met Frances in the hall. 'I've ordered the carriage.'

'Yes, I thought you might.' She put on her cloak and gloves as Agnes joined them to collect his outdoor clothes for him. 'I will laugh at you over this, you know. Such fuss just because she's a little late.'

'She's two hours late, Fran.' He took his hat and gloves from Agnes. 'If something had held her up, she would have sent word.'

The time it took to travel to the Home served to further tighten his stomach into knots. Nat prayed she was there, yet a part of him knew she wouldn't be.

In the Home's parlour he spoke to the women gathered, asking them if they knew the whereabouts of his darling girl.

'I'm sorry, Mr West.' Florence, the only woman standing, twisted her fingers together. 'Mrs West left here about eleven o'clock. She was going to the printers. She said she'd be back by three and when she didn't arrive I assumed she'd gone home.'

He glanced at Frances, and the worry he felt was reflected in her face. 'We'll go to the printers first and see what time she left there.'

Frances stood, nodding. 'Thank you, ladies. We'd best be going now.'

'You will let us know when you find her, won't you?' Florence asked, walking with them to the front door.

'We will.' Frances squeezed her hand.

Putting on his hat, Nat noticed that his hand trembled. Frances saw it too and covered it with her own. 'We'll find her, Nat.'

He managed a brief smile, but his facial muscles felt stiff with the effort. As he helped her inside the carriage, the sound of hoof beats on the drive made him pause.

'Who could this be?' Florence said from the doorway. 'It's nearly dark.'

Nat stepped back to see the rider come into the golden light spilling from the doorway.

The rider, no more than a youth, dismounted and swiped off his cap. 'Who is in charge here?'

Florence stepped forward. 'I am. Can I help you?'

'I'm from the hospital. A lady has been brought in and the doctor believes she is associated with this Home.'

Nat thought his heart would stop. 'A lady?'

The youth nodded, causing his blond hair to fall over his eyes. 'Doctor Harper thinks she might be the lady who held the charity ball last year, which he attended.'

'Hurry, Nat!' Frances demanded from the carriage door.

'Timms follow this fellow.' Nat, with one foot on the folding step, looked back at the boy. 'Take us there.'

'Yes, sir.' The boy grabbed the horse's reins and heaved himself back into the saddle.

'We mustn't become over-imaginative, Nat. She could have merely sprained an ankle,' Frances said, gripping his arm as the carriage careened down the drive and along the roads into the city.

'Don't be ridiculous, Frances. If it was only a sprain she'd have told them her name.'

'Yes, of course. Sorry, I wasn't thinking.'

Agitated, he flung his hat off onto the opposite seat and ran his hand through his hair. 'She must be unconscious. Perhaps received a blow to the head.' He bit back a moan of agony at the thought.

'Yes, she may have fallen and banged her head. It is very likely, the roads are so uneven.'

He closed his eyes, willing her not to be badly hurt, but they sprang open again as the carriage slowed and turned into the hospital drive. In the darkness, he felt disorientated, but lamplight showed up the front door and before the horses had come to a complete stop, he threw open the door and jumped down. He waited fractionally to help Frances and then they were hurrying through the hospital entrance to the office on the right.

'Come this way, sir.' The youth on horseback had followed them in and was now gesturing for them to go with him down a wide corridor to the right. Nat followed blindly, his mind in turmoil and Frances clinging to his arm. The boy turned left and then right again into a large ward, lined with beds. He stepped up to the nurse seated at a desk. 'I've brought these people here. They might know the lady Doctor Harper was examining earlier.'

The nurse rose, and smiling kindly, came towards them. 'I'm senior Nurse Orwell. Please wait here while I fetch the doctor.' She disappeared through a doorway behind her desk, returning a few moments later with a small bespectacled man.

'I'm Nathaniel West.' He searched the doctor's face for any hint of bad news.

'How do you do, Mr West. I'm Doctor Harper.' He held out his hand to be shaken.

Nat, his patience at an end, hastily shook it. 'My wife has been missing and—'

'Ah, I see. Did you marry Miss Douglas from the governess home?' Harper nodded as if it all made sense to him now. 'I remembered her name about ten minutes ago. I thought it was her, as I attended the ball, you know, but I couldn't think of her name at first. I was about to send for Mr Belfroy.'

'How is she? Can I see her?' Nat stepped forward. If the man didn't take him to her shortly, he'd not be responsible for his actions.

'Yes, yes, come along.' Harper bowed to Frances and then waved towards the door he'd come out of. 'I have her in a room by herself, so she can be assessed.'

Nat followed Frances into the bright white-washed room.

The room held a bed and a chair. Under the window was a narrow wooden table. Nat heard Frances's small gasp and he closed his eyes. He stopped, unable to move or open his eyes in fear of what he might find.

'As you can see, Mr West, your wife has been attacked. Her left eye has closed shut due to swelling and bruising and she has a lump on the back of her head. The main injury is the stab wound.'

Nat's eyes flew open. Stabbed! He stared at the slim figure of Nicola lying under the white sheet. 'Is-is she dead?' He swayed. She looked dead. His beautiful girl, his darling Nicola looked dead to him. Please, God, please don't let her be dead.

He blinked, realising he'd missed what the doctor said. 'What did you say?'

Harper walked to the bed and felt Nicola's pulse. 'I said that the knife hit her hip bone and skimmed off it. I can't see evidence of any organs being damaged by the blow. Although deep, the wound is clean. I've stitched it and believe she will recover fully from this attack.'

'Why isn't she awake?' Fran's voice came out on a choked whisper. She sat on the chair by the bed, tears filling her eyes.

'I've given her laudanum.' Harper felt Nicola's forehead. 'The pain was rather intense, but she's resting peacefully now.' He straightened. 'If you'll excuse me, I need to check other patients. I'll be back shortly.' With a nod he left the room.

From his position by the door, Nat stared at Nicola's damaged face. How could anyone have hurt her so savagely? For what purpose? A burning rage filled him. He clenched his fist, fighting the urge to smash someone or something. There was a roaring in his ears. His jaw ached from tension.

'Nat.'

He jerked his gaze away from Nicola to Fran.

'Nat, come closer, take her hand. We need to tell her we're here and that she is safe.'

'I cannot.' And he couldn't. He was physically unable to move. His heart cried out to her. He longed to gather her into his arms and hold her forever, but he simply couldn't.

'Don't be silly, Nat.' Frances frowned, her whispers growing more demanding. 'Come over here. She needs you.'

He took a step back, the desire to flee the room so strong he could hardly resist it.

Frances rose, her expression close to loathing. 'Nathaniel West if you leave this room I'll never speak to you again.'

He sucked in air, not knowing he'd held his breath. Panic gripped him. 'Fran…' His chest tightened. His eyes stung.

'Oh, dearest.' Fran ran to him and held him hard against her. For an instant he wanted to repel her embrace. He needed air. He needed…

He needed his love, the one he'd die for.

Through tear-blurred vision he gazed at his darling. She'd been in pain, hurting, crying and he'd not been there. Why wasn't he with her? Why did he ever let her out of his sight? She was too precious and meant so much to him, so why hadn't he been there to stop this?

How would she ever forgive him?

He closed his eyes, feeling the hot tears roll down his cheeks. He couldn't remember the last time he cried, and it felt foreign, strange.

'Nat.' Fran smiled up at him, her eyes as wet as his. 'Sit with her. Let her know you're here.'

Allowing her to guide him to the bed, his legs heavy and heart even heavier, he drew nearer to Nicola's bedside. This close, the bruising on her swollen eye appeared worse, her skin so pale. Pain, a psychical pain in his chest rendered him to his knees beside the bed.

He grabbed her hand and kissed it, laying the palm

against his cheek. 'Nic, my dar...darling.' He cleared his throat. 'Sweetheart, it's me, Nat. I'm here. I'm holding your hand.' When there was no response he glanced up at Frances standing beside him.

'Perhaps it's the laudanum.' Fran laid her hand on his shoulder.

'I want to take her home.'

'You can. As soon as she is better.'

'She can get better at home.'

'They won't allow you to move her, and we don't want to, not yet.'

He gently touched her hair, always so soft. If only he could hold her, take the hurt from her. 'How could anyone do this to her?'

'I don't know.'

'I'll find the culprit.' He got to his feet, still holding Nicola's hand. 'I'll find the person who did this and I will kill him.'

CHAPTER 19

a dull ache spread from Nicola's side, engulfing her whole body it seemed. From one eye, she watched the nurse and doctor move to the end of the bed and murmur to each other. They'd finished examining her and changed the bandage on her hip. She'd liked to have known what they said, but tiredness won over curiosity and she closed her eyes.

Whispers woke her. Opening her good eye, she waited for her vision to clear. Frances sat beside the bed, whispering to a nurse who stood in the doorway.

'Thank you, nurse. I'll sit with her for an hour or so.' Frances turned back, and her eyes widened when she saw that Nicola was awake. She held her hand. 'Dearest.'

'Fran.'

'How are you feeling?'

'I don't know. I feel nothing for the moment.' She frowned, wondering why. 'Earlier it hurt, my side.'

'Yes, dearest, it will for a while. The doctor is happy with your progress though and says that he'll reduce the amount of laudanum, if you can handle the discomfort.'

'Laudanum.'

'Yes, for the pain.' Frances fiddled with straightening the sheet and blanket. 'If you have less of the drug you'll be clearer in your mind, but the pain might be too much for you.'

'I understand.' She moved her head a little, taking in the stark white room. 'Where is Nathaniel?'

'Home. I left him shaving.' Fran smiled, patting Nicola's hand. 'He hasn't slept for two days and last night I begged him to sleep, wash and change his clothes.'

'Two days?'

'Yes.' Frances brushed Nicola's hair back from her forehead. 'You were attacked on Thursday morning and today is Saturday.'

Nicola swallowed with difficulty, her throat dry. Images, no more than flashes, played in her mind of the attack. Lombard's face, the rotten teeth of the man with him and then pain. 'How did I get here?'

'A woman found you and she called to a passing dray. The driver brought you here.'

She nodded, though remembered none of it. 'Can I have some water, please?'

'Of course.' Frances dashed to the narrow table under the small window. She fussed with the water jug and cup. 'The water isn't very cold, nearly warm in fact.'

'It'll be fine.' With Frances's help she sipped the water, savouring the moisture in her mouth. Twinges in her side made her wince, but drinking the water was worth the effort.

'Nicola.' Frances took the cup away and shifted on her chair. 'Dearest, do you know who did this to you? Do you recollect anything?'

'Yes, some.' She was remembering more and more, Lombard's threats, the alley. She'd been reading Meg's letter on the way to the printer. 'Is Nathaniel coming here today?'

'Absolutely.' Frances rolled her eyes. 'He's been unbearable. It's the worry, I know that, but my patience was coming to an end with him. He wouldn't leave you, he shouted at everyone, including the poor constables that came. I was embarrassed and furious with him yesterday.'

'I'm sorry for causing all this trouble.'

'Nonsense. It's hardly your fault, is it? Nat will be so happy to see you awake properly. Likely now he'll behave as he should.'

Nicola's eyelids grew heavy. 'Tell the doctor I don't want any more laudanum.'

'I will. You rest and then we'll talk again.' Fran bent over and kissed her cheek. 'I'll still be here when you wake up.'

When she next awoke, she found the room dull with a greyish light. The only sound was the clicking of Frances's needles as she sat knitting on the chair by the bed. When relaxed, her sister-in-law was a handsome woman, especially now she'd grown her hair longer and wore elegant clothes more often than not. A splatter of rain hit the window and in the distance came the rumble of thunder. 'What time is it, Fran?'

'Oh! You gave me a fright.' Frances put her knitting away and leaned forward. 'How did you sleep?'

'Well.'

'I think you slept for about an hour. It's nearly midday. There's a huge thunderstorm happening outside. Miss McIntyre called in to see you. Everyone at the Home sends their very best.'

'That's nice. Is Nathaniel here?'

'No. He was, but he went again.' Fran smoothed the blanket down. 'He's gone back to the police station. Cannot sit still for a second, never could.' She grinned. 'Do you want some more water?'

'Please.' She hated feeling so helpless. She wasn't one for

being sick. The legacy of caring for her mother for years made her unwilling to place that duty on another. The drink refreshed her, though the pain returned, stronger than before.

'How are you feeling?'

'Sore.' She looked to the doorway, wishing Nathaniel would come through it. She missed him, wanted his arms about her, to see his smile.

'The police inspector will come this afternoon, Nicola. I told the doctor you had woken and talked to me earlier.'

She thought of Lombard, his threat and the man who drew his knife. 'What do the police know?'

'Nothing. That's why they are keen to talk to you.'

For a moment she wished it was all over and done with, then her courage returned. She wasn't a coward and would deal with this mess, but how she prayed it'd never happened. 'I don't know what to do, Fran.'

'About what, dearest?'

'About the incident.'

Fran held her hand in both of hers. 'Simply tell the police what you know, they'll take it from there.'

'I'm scared to.'

'Why?'

'Because it was Tristan Lombard and his man.'

Frances reared back in her chair, her grey eyes wide. 'Tristan Lombard, Nat's friend? He stabbed you?'

Emotion welled in her chest and she closed her eyes. Fran had lost the colour in her cheeks and Nicola could only imagine what the news would do to Nathaniel.

'Tell me, Nicola,' Fran shook her hand, 'Tell me everything.'

She wiped the tears from her good eye, not daring to touch the puffy bruising on the left side of her face. 'It's my fault really. I shouldn't have provoked him, Tristan, I mean.

He stopped me in the alley and although he was rude, I should have ignored his bad manners and kept going.'

'I never did like the man.' Frances fumed. 'I told Nat plenty of times to stay away from him, he's a bad one is Lombard.'

'He made some disgusting remarks as to why Nathaniel married me and I lost my temper. Lombard was also angry, angry at Nathaniel over some business…' She rubbed her forehead, desperate to remember everything she could. 'Carstairs. Lombard mentioned Carstairs and that he would tell people about him and Nathaniel.'

'What did he mean?'

'I don't know for sure, but whatever it is, it mustn't be good, as I feel Lombard has some hold over him. Lombard said that Nathaniel had to go see him. He'd lost money or something and it was Nathaniel's fault.'

Frances sagged against the chair. 'I cannot believe this.'

'And I lost my temper and told him to go to Hell.' Nicola picked at the blanket, recalling the fear she'd felt as the other man advanced on her. 'Lombard gave a nod to his man, who then attacked me.'

'Oh, dear God.' Frances looked ill. 'This will…Lord, we cannot tell Nat, he'll go mad. Murder will be done.'

Nicola's bottom lip trembled, and more tears fell. 'What can I do, Fran?'

Nathaniel stepped from behind the door, his expression stiff as though cast from granite. 'You will do nothing.'

'Nat!' Fran jumped to her feet. 'No, Nat. This is for the police to decide, not you.'

'The man will be dead by nightfall.'

Nicola watched him, amazed at his self-control. He'd brought the smell of rain with him and droplets glistened on his coat. He looked so powerful, so handsome. She held out her hand, aching for him. 'Nathaniel.'

He blinked but remained unmoved.

She willed him to come to her for if he left the room filled with his cold rage then murder would be done as Fran said it would. His eyes, those beautiful violet eyes she adored, narrowed and his hand twitched. He fought within himself. 'Nathaniel. I need you.'

Nathaniel jerked as if slapped. His eyes focused on her and in an instant he'd thrown off his coat and was beside her, scooping her up into his arms. He held her so tight she couldn't breathe and the wound in her side throbbed.

Her words had the effect she knew they would. She had never needed anyone in her life and he knew it. Often since their wedding day, he'd joked that she could go on living without him, whereas he would die if she ever left him. Being independent, she had agreed it was true. She required no one. Only now, after being married to this man and loving him so intensely, did she realise that she did need him, desperately.

She leaned back in his arms, ignoring the soreness each movement made, and gazed up at him. 'Do you love me?'

He kissed her repeatedly. 'You know I do.'

'And you don't want to leave me?'

'Never, my darling, never.' He cradled her head in one hand, his love shining from his eyes.

'Then you will not go near Tristan Lombard.' She felt him tense. He went to speak but she silenced him with a finger against his lips. 'I will not be married to a criminal, do you understand, nor will I be a widow.'

'Nic-'

'No, Nat. You must listen to me. Frances is right,' she darted a glance at Frances, lowering her hand from his mouth, 'if you go near Lombard blood will be shed and I couldn't stand it.'

'He has to pay.'

'And what of the threat concerning Carstairs? I want the truth of it.'

Nathaniel let go of her and went to stand by the window. 'Carstairs and I did business together, along with Tristan.'

'Illegal business I take it?' Frances barked, folding her arms.

'Yes. We imported fine goods but didn't pay tax on them.'

'Oh, Nat.' Frances shook her head, the disappointment in her tone matched how Nicola felt.

'We did three shipments last year and were meant to do two more this year, but,' he gazed apologetically at Nicola, 'I backed out of the agreement when you agreed to marry me.' He drew in a deep breath. 'When Carstairs learnt of my plans he scrapped the whole idea and left Sydney. However, when he left, he also took our money for the cargo with him. I could afford to cover the loss, but Lombard couldn't.' Nathaniel ran his hand through his hair. 'I only learnt of Lombard's descent into debt after we returned from the country. He'd always been a gambler and strayed close to ruin many times, but usually he managed to pull himself out of it, but not this time.'

'Is this the only illegal business you've done?' Nicola forced the words out.

'Yes. I only got involved because I was drunk the first time we agreed to do it. The danger of it excited me.' He shrugged as if confused at himself. 'Only, that feeling didn't last as long as I expected. There is no excuse for my behaviour. At the time I found my life dull and empty. I was simply trying to find something to do…'

Frances slumped into the chair, a look of reproach on her face.

Nicola sighed, tiredness pulled at the back of her eyes and she felt sore all over. 'We need to decide what to do.'

'We cannot tell the police now,' Fran snapped.

Nathaniel stepped forward. 'I'm sorry it has come to this. I never imagined my family would become involved and hurt. I will deal with Lombard accordingly.'

'No!' Nicola and Frances cried together.

'I won't do anything ridiculous. Trust me.' He came and sat down on the bed and took Nicola's hands in his.

'You will lose your temper. I know it.' She had to prevent him from doing something stupid, but how? She couldn't watch him day and night.

'I promise you I won't even see him. I'll simply make inquiries.'

Leaning back against the pillow, the energy drained from her. 'I just want him gone. I'd be very happy if he left Sydney and never returned. I couldn't bear to face him again.'

'I'll see that it is done.' He kissed her. 'I promise.'

She closed her eyes. 'I'm so tired, Nathaniel. I don't like being tired.'

'Then go to sleep, my love.'

'Will you stay with me?' At least if he stayed with her for an hour or two it might give his temper a chance to cool.

'Nothing will part me from you.'

She felt him kiss her on the head and then she gratefully sank into oblivion.

* * *

'WELL, LOOK AT YOU.' Frances grinned as she joined Nicola in the parlour. 'You seem much better today.'

'I feel it.'

Frances picked up Nicola's sketchbook from the table beside the sofa. 'You have been sketching?' She flicked through the book. 'That's a splendid one.' She laughed, holding up a drawing of herself. 'You've made me far prettier in this than I am.'

'Nonsense.'

'Are you tired? With this being your first day downstairs we don't want you becoming exhausted.'

'I am recovering very well. Being home is such a pleasure but being allowed downstairs is even better.' Nicola curled her stocking-covered toes up towards the heat of the roaring fire. A newspaper lay open on her lap. Despite being home for a week, Nathaniel had insisted she stay in bed and rest. After the fourth day she was weary of staring at the same four walls. She'd read books and written letters, even had visitors, but by the fifth day she'd begged to be allowed downstairs.

'Do you need anything?' Fran asked, jabbing the fire with an iron poker.

'No, thank you. Agnes comes in every ten minutes and Mrs Rawlings every half hour.' Nicola laughed. 'Between them, I want for nothing.'

'No doubt Nat gave them strict instructions not to leave you alone. I'm sure he believes you'll be in the carriage the minute his back is turned.'

'That's something he need not worry about. Just walking a few steps pulls at my stitches.' She grimaced at the thought of the sharp pain she got when she moved too quickly. A few times she had to hold back a scream as Nathaniel touched her in the night, not thinking as he slept. For all that though, she was happy to be beside him again and out of the hospital.

'You'd not want to venture out anyway, it's freezing today. In the few years I've been here I've never known May to be so cold and we have months of this ahead of us. I think I would die if I ever had to return to England. I'm too used to the warmth now.'

Nicola watched the flames, remembering England and the whiteness of a snow-covered countryside. 'Where have you been today?'

'The soup kitchen this morning and then I called to see a few families in Newtown. I managed to buy a good quantity of bread loaves and the baker even offered to drive me to deliver them.'

'The baker?' Nicola hid a smile behind her hand. 'That wouldn't be the baker from Phillip Street, would it?'

Fran gave her a cool stare. 'And if it was?'

'What is his name?' Nicola played dumb, knowing it drove Fran mad. 'Lawson, is it? John Lawson?'

'You know damn well it is.' Frances sniffed. 'What of it pray?'

Nicola stared with a raised eyebrow. 'You seem to be spending a lot of time with him lately.'

'Don't be absurd. He offers me good deals, so I can feed a few families. There is nothing to make of that. His mother has been a good friend to me regarding the soup kitchen.'

'It wouldn't be the worst thing to happen, you know, being attracted to a man.'

'Stuff and nonsense, Nicola West.' Fran sat straighter in her chair. 'Just because you are happily married, don't you dare think you can turn into one of those matchmakers we both detest.'

Nicola smothered a chuckle. Fran's denial said so much. From what she knew of John Lawson, he was a sensible man in his mid-thirties, never married and took over his father's bakery when he died in a cholera outbreak some ten years ago. Nathaniel had gained this information when she happened to mention to him that Frances was calling in at the bakery most days.

'Did you have any visitors today?' Frances asked, relaxing her stiff posture.

'Yes, ladies from the Home.' The humour left Nicola as she recalled the visit this morning. 'Sadly, Mrs Patterson is ill with a bad chest and Doctor Armitage fears she won't recover. Florence has found a position for one of her sisters. Fiona is to be an apprentice seamstress in George Street. Miss Peacock has gained a situation in Goulburn and two more ladies have arrived.'

'And the orphanage?'

'We now have five children, all siblings. Their parents died, both drowned in a boating accident last Sunday. Apparently, they went out fishing and the recent bad weather has churned the sea up most considerably. The boat, well hardly a boat, nothing more than a little wooden skip Florence said. Anyway, it overturned, and they were lost.' She tapped the newspaper on her lap. 'There is mention about it on page six.'

'How tragic.'

'Indeed.' Nicola folded away the newspaper. 'I miss being at the Home. Oh, I know it is well run by Florence, the woman is exceptional. But I like being there, doing my bit. The charity board met last Tuesday, and I should have been there. I'm feeling rather disconnected. First, because of my wedding and being in the country, and now this injury. Everything is going on without me.'

'You'll be back there soon enough.' Frances smiled.

'That's just it. I don't think I will be. At least not all the time as I used to be.'

'You mustn't think like that. Doctor Armitage said you'll recover properly in a few weeks and your life will be as it was before.'

'Not entirely.'

As the clock on the mantle struck the hour of four, the parlour door opened and Mrs Rawlings sailed in bearing the tea tray. Behind her followed Agnes with another tray full of cakes and biscuits. 'Here we are, Madam, a lovely cup of tea for you and Miss West.'

Bemused, Nicola gently swung her legs down from the

sofa and winced at the tightness it caused in her side. 'I didn't order tea, Mrs Rawlings.'

'I know, Madam. Mr West said this morning I was to keep you supplied with tea and light food to speed your recovery.'

'Did he now?' She shook her head at his thoughtfulness. She had a feeling he'd never relax again.

The housekeeper placed the tray on the low table in the middle of the room and stepped back so Agnes could do the same. 'Will I pour, Madam?'

Frances leaned over and picked up the pot. 'No, thank you, Mrs Rawlings, I'll do it.'

'Very good, Miss.' Mrs Rawlings ushered Agnes out and closed the door.

'She's a good housekeeper, Nicola.'

'Yes, we are lucky to have her.'

Frances passed the teacup and saucer to her, her expression quizzical. 'What did you mean that your life wouldn't be as it was before?'

Nicola took a deep breath, not knowing whether she should part with her new-found secret. In the end, she couldn't resist. 'Can you keep a secret?'

'Need you ask?' Frances leaned back in her chair, the tea forgotten.

'You'll not have to keep it for long, only until Nathaniel comes home.'

'How intriguing, do tell.'

'Doctor Armitage was here this morning and he examined me because I...'

'Oh, Nicola, please don't tell me you have something seriously wrong with you? I couldn't bear it.'

'No, let me finish.' She reached over and took her dear friend's hand. 'I asked him to come because I...I thought I might be with child.'

Frances's grey eyes grew wide. 'A child?'

257

Nodding, Nicola waited, hoping she'd be happy for her. 'Doctor Armitage confirmed it.'

'A baby!'

'Yes. I can barely believe it myself. Wishing and hoping for a child is different to actually achieving it and I must admit I'm a little scared as well as delighted.'

Tears filled France's eyes. 'I'll be an aunt. Oh, Nic.' She jumped up and hugged Nicola, laughing and crying. 'This is wonderful, thrilling news. A baby in the family.'

'Nat will be pleased, I hope.'

'Pleased?' Frances clapped, joy radiating from her face. 'He'll be like a dog with two tails. He's wanted children, wanted to be a father, more so since meeting you.'

'I'm going to tell him tonight.'

'Yes, do. After all that's happened, he'll be overjoyed.' Frances sat back in her chair when the door opened, her look of happiness fading as Nat walked in. His face was pale and anxious.

'Nathaniel? You're home earlier than I expected.' A shiver of fear ran down Nicola's back. 'What is it?'

He held up his hand, showing a yellow piece of paper. 'A telegram came to my office, from Melbourne.'

'And?' France frowned. 'Why is it affecting you so much? Is it bad news?'

'That depends on your opinion.' He gave a brief sad smile. 'It's from our mother.'

'Mother?'

Nathaniel sighed deeply, at this moment looking his thirty-four years. 'Her ship, the *Ira Jayne* docked in Melbourne to disembark some of its passengers and Mother thought she'd take the opportunity to warn us of her impending arrival.'

Nicola looked from one to the other, their shock mirroring each other. One part of her wanted to say, it is only your mother, but the other side of her, the sensible part, knew that such words were useless. Nathaniel and Frances had both told her stories from their childhood concerning their parents. Tales, which were far from the happy reminiscences they should be.

How was she going to accept a woman, her own mother-in-law, into her home when she'd been responsible for such hurt towards two people she loved so dearly?

'She cannot come, Nat.' Frances's wooden tone hung heavy in the air.

'We cannot stop her now, Fran. She is on her way and will arrive by the week's end.'

'Then meet the ship when it docks and tell her to return to England.'

Nicola gave Fran a sympathetic smile. 'That is impossible, Fran. I doubt that she will agree to that after journeying for over a month or more.'

'Then she can stay in a hotel.' Frances jumped to her feet. 'She can stay with the very devil if she wishes, but she cannot stay here!'

'And how will that look to people?'

'I don't care.'

Nicola rubbed her temples, trying to think of a solution. 'It will be expected that she comes to this house. As her daughter-in-law, I am expected to care for her needs. I won't be accused of ignoring her and not doing my duty.'

Frances paced, glaring at first Nat and then back at Nicola. 'You don't know her. You don't know how she corrupts your mind without you realising it.'

'Calm down, Frances.' Nat sighed. 'You haven't seen her for nearly three years and I haven't for five. Father's passing might have changed her.'

'Nathaniel's right, Fran.' Nicola nodded. 'We have to give her a chance.'

Nat looked at her and she held out her hand to him, which he gratefully took. 'I'm sorry, my darling.' He kissed the top of her head. 'This was the last thing I expected.'

'There is nothing for you to apologise for, my love. It is hardly your doing.' She placed his palm against her cheek. 'We shall weather it. Besides, she may have changed. Wouldn't that be splendid?' She forced a smile, hoping it would be so.

CHAPTER 20

*L*ater that night, while snuggled together in bed, watching the shadows on the wall dance, Nicola felt Nathaniel's long sigh. 'You must not worry.'

He caressed her thigh lightly, careful not to touch the bandages on her hip. 'I cannot help it. That she should come here, to the one place where I am happy, just pains me.'

'If she has never been close to you or Fran, then why does she come?'

'Only my mother can answer that. She delights in playing games. Likely she became bored at home, or perhaps curiosity overcame her when she received my letter containing the news of our engagement. I haven't written to her since February and I wondered why she didn't respond. Now I know. Instead of writing she decided to travel here instead and see for herself how Fran and I get on.' He moved his legs restlessly and the thick white blankets rippled in the moonlight streaming through the windows. A small fire glowed in the grate behind the protective screen.

Nicola, her arms wrapped around his waist, marvelled at how one woman could cause this upset to her own children.

Her hand strayed to her stomach, which held only the slightest bump. 'You and Fran must try to put the past behind you. I'm not suggesting that it'll be easy but raking it all up will only continue the hurt. Perhaps your mother has changed. You must at least give her the chance to put things right between you.'

'And if she hasn't altered, what then?'

A streak of devilment flared within her. 'Then send her on the next ship back.'

His hand roamed over her stomach, joining her hand on the swell below her bellybutton. Nathaniel grinned. 'All this sitting around has made you grow fat, my love.'

'Indeed, I have, but that is not the only reason.'

Yawning, he buried his head into her neck. 'Oh?'

She nestled in closer to him, loving the feel of his body against hers. 'I believe your son or daughter may have something to do with it.'

He slowly raised his head to stare at her. 'Do you mean…'

'A baby.' She smiled, pressing his hand onto her stomach more. 'Our baby.'

His face lost all expression. 'A baby…'

'It does happen, you know.' She laughed.

'I'm to be a father.' He closed his eyes and pulled her into his arms so tightly she thought he might break her stitches apart. 'Oh my darling, wonderful girl.' He kissed her repeatedly. 'I love you. Thank you. Thank you.'

She leaned back and threaded her fingers through his dark hair, tears blurring her vision of his wondrous look. Never in her life had she felt more secure and loved as she did at that moment. 'I'm glad I make you happy.'

'Happy?' He kissed her again, a long slow kiss full of love. 'I'm the happiest man alive. When?'

'Well, I haven't had my monthly show since before we

were married. Dr Armitage estimates around the end of October.'

'October.' Stunned, Nathaniel pulled back the sheet and went down the bed to put his lips on her stomach. 'October.'

'Or early November. Babies arrive when they wish to.' She teased his hair, roughing it up.

He plumped up his pillows, laid back and then gathered her into his arms. 'I will be a good father, not like my own, I promise.'

'I know you will. I never thought otherwise.' She softly tugged at his sparse chest hair, her head comfortable against his shoulder. 'This might not be the best time to bring this up, but I must ask.'

He kissed her hair. 'Ask what?'

'Have you heard anything of Lombard?'

'No, not yet. I've cast a wide net, but he's as slippery as an eel. I've had reports that he's gone into hiding, but I'll bide my time. He'll show his face one day.'

'You must never put yourself in danger, Nathaniel. We have a lot to be grateful for now, with the baby coming. I will not lose you to the likes of Lombard. He's not worth it.'

'I know, sweetheart, I know.' He held her close, but she was unable to sleep, her mind dwelling on Lombard and her mother-in-law.

* * *

GINGERLY SITTING down behind her desk at the Home, Nicola smiled at the women gathered in the room. She'd spent an hour with them in the drawing room, listening to their various pieces of news and now wished to get some work done. 'I am perfectly well enough to sit here and check the accounts, ladies.'

Florence, who'd been out and only just returned, crossed

her arms and didn't appear satisfied by the statement. 'Does your good husband know of you being here?'

'No, he doesn't and what's more he doesn't need to know. I will be back in my parlour before he is aware of it.' She gave Florence a meaningful look. 'And you aren't to tell him either, Florence McIntyre.' Nicola raised a knowing eyebrow. 'I am as capable of sitting here as I am at home.'

'You're a brave woman, Mrs West.' Miss Bent smiled.

Florence glared at the women. 'I hope to God you've not tired Mrs West. She's been through a terrible ordeal and I'll—'

'Miss McIntyre.' Nicola raised her eyebrows, hiding a laugh as the woman's annoyance brought out her Scottish accent more thickly. 'The ladies have been very good and aren't deserving of your displeasure.'

'Even so, I'm sure you'd like some time to yourself. Come, ladies.' Florence steered them all out, except Miss Bent, who approached to the desk.

'I was wondering if I could have a word with you in private, if you please?'

'Of course.' Nicola indicated for her to sit down as the women filed out of the study. 'Oh, Miss McIntyre?'

'Yes, Mrs West.' Florence held the door.

'Will you join me in half an hour, please?'

Florence nodded, her back stiff with authority. 'shall I order you a tea tray too?'

'Bring it with you when you come back.'

'Very good, Madam.'

When the door closed, Nicola rested back in her chair and smiled at Sara Bent. The young woman had put on a small amount of weight, filling out her thin frame. 'You wished to speak with me?'

'Yes, Mrs West.' Miss Bent sat on the edge of the chair, her shoulders rigid. 'I wish to inform you of my impending marriage.'

Surprised, Nicola stared. 'Marriage?'

'Yes. In the past two months I have been on friendly terms with Mr Greenwood, Frank Greenwood, of Greenwood Butchers in Macquarie Street.'

'I see. He owns a butcher shop.'

'No, his father does. However, it will be Frank's one day. It is a good business and old Mr Greenwood is a widower and a nice man.' Miss Bent blinked rapidly, a sign of her nervousness. 'Please do not think of me as being unscrupulous while you were ill. Everything between Mr Greenwood and myself has been completely proper and correct. We met by chance while out walking one evening. From there we have become friends and strolled in the Domain a number of times. He is a good man, Mrs West.'

'And he proposed to you?'

'Yes, last Sunday, after we went to a musical performance. I've been thinking it over and this morning I sent him my reply.'

'So, you have thought about this very seriously? You haven't accepted simply because you see no alternative?'

'Oh, no. Indeed, I haven't thought about anything else. I haven't been able to sleep because of it weighing on my mind. But I reasoned that this is a good chance for me. I'd have the security of marriage, my own home and a family. Mr Greenwood senior said I could send for my mother, if I wished, but I doubt she'll come.'

'Well, that is generous of him indeed. When is your marriage to take place?'

'At the end of June. Is it possible for me to stay here until then, or must I leave now since I'm no longer looking for a position?'

'We are not so full that we are turning people away for

lack of beds, so you are welcome to stay until your marriage. You might find the other women will enjoy having such a happy diversion to think about.'

'Thank you, Mrs West, you are very kind.' Miss Bent stood, seemingly more relaxed. 'I shall go tell Mr Greenwood of my staying here.'

'You may also tell him that I wish you both well.' Nicola grinned. 'And you may hold your wedding breakfast here if you wish. Mr Belfroy loves nothing more than a good wedding. He will probably offer to give you away, if it pleases you.'

Miss Bent's eyes widened. 'Oh, you are generous, Mrs West, thank you, and to Mr Belfroy, too.' She dashed from the room.

Nicola let out a long breath, content to hear some good news. She opened the account books and checked the figures. A pile of correspondence sat next to the ledgers and she idly picked up one or two. Most were invitations for various dinner parties, but some were letters from previous women who had stayed at the Home. Normally, she would be eager to read the mail, but today her mind was occupied with the arrival of Nathaniel's mother. Her ship was due to dock within the hour. She knew she should be at home, preparing her welcome, but the quietness of the house this morning had driven her mad. Both Nathaniel and Frances had left early to clear their schedules for the afternoon meeting, leaving Nicola alone to worry. In the end, she had ordered the carriage and visited Mr Belfroy for an hour before coming here to the Home.

A tap on the door heralded Florence. 'Nicola,' she whispered, her face wan. She crept closer to the desk, glancing back over her shoulder.

'What is it?'

'It's old Mrs Patterson. I'm afraid she's died.'

'Oh, good heavens.'

'I went in to her room, to give her a cup of tea and thought she was asleep. But she wouldn't wake up. Then I realised.'

'Dr Armitage did say she might not recover from her chest cold. She was frail and weak.'

'And old.' Florence sighed, her smattering of freckles stark against her pale skin. 'Imagine dying amongst strangers. How intolerable.'

'The poor woman. I only met her a few times, hardly got to know her at all.'

'She was kind, knowledgeable and happy to listen to anyone who ventured into her room.'

'We must let Dr Armitage know.'

'Yes. I'll see to it.'

'I'm sorry to leave this on your shoulders, Florence, but my mother-in-law arrives this afternoon from England.'

'Of course you must return home. I am capable of dealing with this.'

'You deal with everything.' Nicola gave her a brief smile of thanks. 'This Home couldn't run without you. I used to think I was the main force here, but not any longer. You've filled my role with ease.'

'I never intended—'

Nicola held up her hand. 'No, don't apologise in any way. This was obviously meant to be. I will tell you that I am with child. So, your position here will only grow in importance.'

'Oh, Nicola. I'm so pleased for you. A baby, how wonderful.'

'It is wonderful. Can you just keep it to yourself for a little while? I'll tell the ladies another time.'

'I'll not mention it, I promise. You know, I will never take your place, Nicola. You are too much the essence of what this home is about, what it is built from.' Florence gave a mischievous smile. 'Besides, once the child is born I know you'll be back here, even if it's only for an hour a day.'

'I confess this Home is a part of me and I can never relinquish my love of it.' She raised her head proudly. 'We do good work here.'

'And it'll become more important as the orphanage and school grows.'

Standing, Nicola reached out for Florence's arm. 'Walk out with me. I cannot concentrate on the books today.' She grimaced. 'I might as well go home and prepare to meet my mother-in-law.'

Florence fought a smile as they left the study and walked down the hall to the front door. 'Is she so bad?'

'Apparently. I believe the word dragon and her name are linked, or so Fran tells me.'

Laughing, they headed out to the carriage, where Timms waited anxiously for her and Florence helped her to climb inside. 'Oh, I forgot to mention that Miss Bent is engaged to be married.'

'I suspected something of the sort.' Florence frowned mockingly. 'She was taking a great many walks.'

Chuckling, Nicola closed the door and leaned out of the window. 'I am happy for her. I'm glad she will be settled.' She sobered. 'Now, it may be a few days before I can escape my family duties but send a note should you have need of me and let me know of the funeral details. Good bye.'

Timms set the carriage rolling down the drive and out into the street. Nicola smoothed out the skirts of her sky-blue dress and fiddled with the white lace around the bodice. Should she change when she got home? The time it took for ships to dock and passengers to disembark was unpredictable. It could be hours before she arrived. The closer to home she got, the worse her nerves grew.

When Timms drew the horses to a halt in the drive,

Nicola climbed down, her stomach tied in knots. She hoped Nathaniel and Frances were home. Mrs Rawlings scurried out of the front door, her actions so unlike her that Nicola paused.

'Madam, I am glad you are home.' Rawlings panted on reaching her.

'Is something the matter?'

'I don't know where to begin.' Flustered Mrs Rawlings flapped at her face, but suddenly she tidied herself and became professional again. 'Mrs West has arrived.'

'Mrs West?' For a moment, Nicola was confused. She was Mrs West. Then it became clear. 'Mr West's mother is here, *already*?'

Mrs Rawlings nodded, her expression one of aversion. 'Yes, Madam, been here for twenty minutes, she has, and is most put out. I haven't had the time to send for you as she's run me ragged. I can barely draw breath from running to do her bidding and her uppity maid thinks she can tell me what to do as well, but I soon put her straight.'

'Good gracious me.' Despite her aching injury, Nicola hurried up the path and through the door. In the hall, she hastily unpinned her hat and smoothed her hair into place. 'Where is my husband,' she whispered to Rawlings.

'I haven't seen him since breakfast, Madam, or Miss West.'

Nicola paled. They hadn't met their mother off the ship? She closed her eyes momentarily and prayed to some unseen deity to help her through this first meeting. Chin held high, shoulders back, Nicola summoned a smile and sailed into the drawing room.

At the window, a woman dressed in a glorious dress of dove-grey silk edged with black lace, slowly turned towards her. Silvana West gave Nicola a glacial stare from steel grey eyes, Frances's eyes, only Frances's were warm and soft, Silvana's were cold and hard. 'And who might you be?'

Ah, so the games begin. Nathaniel was right. Nicola hesitated. The woman would have seen her descend from the carriage and seen her speak with Mrs Rawlings, from those clues alone she would know Nicola was her son's wife. 'I may ask the same of you, Madam, since you are the stranger here, not I.'

'If this is how a stranger is treated on her arrival...' she glanced at Nicola's wedding ring, 'Then I would look to your role more diligently, Madam.'

'All guests are treated well in my home, especially when they are invited.'

The barb struck home and Silvana's eyes narrowed. 'Where is my son?'

'You mean my husband?'

'My God, don't tell me he's married *you*.'

'Who did you think I was?'

Lips squeezed tight together, Silvana drew in a deep breath, her nostrils flaring. 'I'll never understand that boy, never!' She looked around as if searching for an escape.

'I'm sure—'

'Why didn't he meet my ship? Did you prevent him?'

'Not at all. Why would I?'

'He never could be relied on. I had presumed he'd changed at least in that.'

'Your son has changed in many ways and—'

'Don't presume to tell me about my ungrateful child.'

Angered, Nicola gripped her skirt. 'When Nathaniel left this morning, I understood he would be going to the quay to meet you. Perhaps he had other more *pressing* business to deal with.'

'I am Silvana West.' She tossed her head, nearly dislodging her magnificent wide brimmed hat, with its profusion of black feathers. 'I refuse to be spoken to in such an insolent way by a former governess.'

'And I am Nicola West. This is my home, and I refuse to be spoken to this way also.'

'How did you snare my son's affections?' Silvana's contemptuous look made Nicola grit her teeth in anger. 'My son had no wish to marry, he said it often enough. Yet, somehow, you've managed to secure him. From what I gather from the staff here my hope of Nathanial marry well is dashed. A governess. How will it be borne? What is your family, your connections?'

Nicola stiffened, the insults hitting her like darts. 'That is none of your business.'

'Ah, so you must not have any otherwise you'd happily mention them.'

'I am not answerable to you. How dare you enter my home, uninvited, and insult me?'

Noise from the drive had both of them glance out the window. Nicola sagged at the sight of Nathaniel helping Fran down from the gig. Her first thought was to run out to them and beg for them to rid her of this awful woman, but when she glanced back at Silvana she found the woman had tears running down her cheeks. Nicola blinked, certain her eyes were playing tricks on her.

Silvana drew out a flimsy scrap of black-laced linen and dabbed at her eyes just as Nathaniel and Fran stepped into the room.

'Mother.' Nathaniel stopped and frowned. 'We are sorry to have missed you at the docks.'

'Oh, my darling boy, and sweet Frances, my dearest daughter.' Silvana ran to them and embraced them to her, sobbing as though her heart would break.

Amazed at this turn around, Nicola simply stared.

'Come now, Mother, no more crying.' Nathaniel gently extracted himself from her, but Silvana clung on to Frances.

'Oh, my dear, dear children. How I have missed you so. It

has been too long, much too long. Nathaniel,' Silvana turned back to wave her handkerchief at Nicola, 'your wife has been so kind to me. I'm delighted by her.'

Nicola's mouth gaped. She stared at Silvana as though the woman had lost her mind, maybe she had? Then she noticed that Nathaniel was beaming, the joy clear in his eyes.

'I cannot tell you how pleased that makes me, Mother. Nicola makes me very happy.'

'My dearest son.' Silvana simpered, gripping his hand. 'Your happiness is so important to me.'

He smiled, his eyes at first wary, but then they softened. 'I'm relieved you are not angry with us for missing you at the wharf. Business held me up, and I'm sure I missed you by only minutes, but I'm glad you managed to make it here without mishap.'

'Are you tired, Mother?' Fran murmured. She seemed stunned for words by her mother's emotional display.

'A little, my dear, but I shall rest in a minute.' Silvana held Fran's hands and sighed. 'How well you look and so beautiful.' She led a bewildered Frances to the sofa. 'Come sit by me and tell me everything about your life here. I want to know it all. I have missed you so very much, both of you.'

As if in a daze, Nicola reached for Nathaniel when he came to her side and slipped his arm around her waist. Together they watched mother and daughter talk as though their relationship had always been close and loving.

'Mother has changed significantly,' Nathaniel whispered, his expression clearly showing his confusion and shock. 'She never shows emotion. I never would have believed it. Father's death has changed her a great deal more than I expected.'

'It is early days yet,' Nicola warned quietly, wishing she could speak of what had occurred between her and Silvana only minutes before. How could she tell of Silvana's horridness when now she was all sweet and loving? They'd not believe her. She hardly believed it herself.

'If she comes with the desire to make amends, I won't reject her. She is after all, my mother. I think she might need me now.'

'Of course, but let us wait and see, yes?'

'I have a good feeling about this.' He kissed her cheek. 'Mother,' Nathaniel stepped forward, 'we have some excellent news for you.'

'Oh, what is that, dearest?' Silvana's affectionate gaze swept over them.

'You are to be a grandmother. Nicola is with child. It is due in late October.'

Nicola, watching her mother-in-law closely, saw the flash of tightness around her lips at the news before her stiff smile widened and she rose to embrace them both. 'Why darling, this is such splendid news, and well worth that terrible journey to hear. Now, is it possible to have some tea?'

CHAPTER 21

*O*pening the parlour door, Nicola stopped when she saw her mother-in-law sitting at a small table playing cards. Before she had a chance to back out of the room, Silvana looked up, her expression filled with loathing. 'Oh, it's you. I'm waiting for the tea tray, but your servants are lazy and very inferior to those back home.'

Nicola turned away. 'I'll find the maid for you now.'

'Leave it. The quality of your cook's talent is severely lacking. I'm sure I'm better off without. Her meals are quite deplorable.'

Bowing her head in acquiescence, Nicola stepped back, wishing to leave the room and Silvana's presence. After four days of her mother-in-law's company, she knew what a superb actress Silvana was, and her mind-playing was a feat to behold. Since her arrival, Silvana had held her son and daughter in the palm of her hand, giving them the love and attention they'd always longed for. Yet, the minute she was alone with Nicola, Silvana turned into a shrew, spewing forth her venom and spite and Nicola had no idea why.

'I will tell you, or should I say, prepare you,' Silvana

paused, making certain she had Nicola's attention, 'That I'll do my very best to have Nat and Frances back in England before the year is out.'

For a long moment Nicola couldn't take in what she heard, then the meaning rang clear. 'You want them to return to England with you for a short time?'

'No, you stupid girl, for good. There is no need for them to be here.'

'They have built a life here.'

'Nonsense. Don't be so dramatic.'

'I doubt your success in this, Madam.'

'Oh, I'll be victorious in this as I am in everything else I plan.' Silvana packed away the deck of cards and smoothed down the skirt of her resplendent dark blue silk gown. 'I need my son in England.'

'You have a son in England.'

'Gerald doesn't have Nat's business acumen and he is losing the family money not accumulating it, plus his wife is useless.' She shrugged elegantly as if talking about the weather. 'Wives are dispensable, like you and her, but sons are not.'

'My husband will not leave me.' Nicola fought for calm, though it was difficult. 'I am soon to have Nathaniel's first child. He will not want to be parted from me.'

'A child is of no consequence until it's grown. We'll send for it then.'

Send for her child as though it was nothing more than a parcel? 'You are insane to think Nathaniel will agree.' Stunned, Nicola could only stare.

'Quite the opposite actually.'

'You might have fooled Nathaniel and Frances into believing you have changed from the unfeeling harridan you were, but I could—'

'You could do what?' Silvana stood and glided to the

ANNEMARIE BREAR

window. 'You can do nothing, for my son has always wanted
love and attention from his father and me. I know his rebellious behaviour stemmed from his childhood. The silly boy
wouldn't grow up, always wanting a pat on the head like
some puppy.' Silvana tossed her head in disgust. 'He was sent
away to school to make a man out of him and, as you can see,
it worked.'

'If he has any decency it is because Frances never gave up
on him and loved him through it all. That and the fact he
escaped you as soon as he could helped to prevent him from
becoming a complete blackguard.'

'You know nothing.'

'I know a lot more than you think. Nathaniel has told me
such painful stories of your neglect in your role as mother to
him and Frances. You should be ashamed of yourself.'

Silvana waved her away like an irritating fly. 'What is
done is done. The future will be different. They will come
home with me and forget this backwater.'

'And you think I'll calmly let you do this?'

'Yes. I'll see that you and the child are generously
provided for until the child is of an age. Then it will travel to
join us and go to a proper English school.'

'And what of my husband's love for me?'

'That will soon fade. Distance is a great healer.'

'Nathaniel cannot be ruled and will not simply give up me
and everything he has worked for to return to a place where
he was unhappy.'

'Ah, you don't understand.' Silvana gave her a cold look.
'What you fail to consider is Nat's loyalty to his heritage.
Gerald didn't inherit all of his father's businesses and money,
because my husband knew his eldest son well and that
Gerald could never cope with such responsibility.' She picked
up a figurine and placed it down again with a curl of her lip.
'No, Nat showed how he could make money, and this

impressed his father greatly.' She walked behind the sofa, trailing her fingertips along the top of it. 'This morning I gave Nat some letters, letters that will show him how much his father respected him. After reading them he will know his duty.'

'Why didn't his father write to him in the last few years instead of when he was ill?'

Silvana's eyes widened innocently. 'Oh, my husband didn't write those letters. I did, at least I paid for them to be written.' She smiled, her expression sly as a fox.

'I will tell Nathaniel all of this.'

'And willingly hurt him?' Silvana frowned and pursed her lips. 'Do you want to affirm all those years of…neglect? My son might be in his thirties, but he still hasn't grown up. He still longs for the love of his parents. Now he has it. Answer me this, have you ever seen him so happy as he is now?'

Nicola swallowed. It was true. Nat smiled and laughed continually, content to finally have a complete and loving family around him for the first time in his life.

Silvana's ugly smirk ruined any beauty she possessed. 'Do you want to be the one to dispel his happiness? Do you think he'll thank you for it?'

'You are truly evil.' Nicola tensed as Silvana walked up very close to her.

'You haven't even seen the worst of me yet.' Silvana twisted the tender skin under Nicola's arm, making her cry out. 'You say one word of this to my children and I'll see that you disappear. Nat mentioned some unpleasantness recently, what was the name…Lombard, was it?' Silvana's eyes glinted. 'Yes. I can see that he will come in handy.'

'Why would you do this?' Nicola whispered, horrified. Surely the woman wouldn't go to Lombard. No, she couldn't possibly…

'Because I always get what I want.'

'You won't, not this time.'

Silvana's eyes narrowed to flints of steel. 'I see that you will be a problem.' She gave Nicola a loathing glare. 'I'll have to deal with you.'

Shaking, holding her burning arm, Nicola watched her mother-in-law swish from the room. Her hand slipped over her stomach as if to protect the baby inside. For the first time in her life, she didn't know what to do.

* * *

THE TINKLING of crystal and the low murmur of conversation filled the elaborate dining room. Nicola sipped her red wine, her headache pounding. She carefully watched and listened to her mother-in-law across the table. As the weeks dragged by, Nicola kept her troubling thoughts about Silvana to herself, not wanting to upset Nathaniel or Frances. However, the pressure of staying clear of her mother-in-law and pretending to be happy when she wasn't was taking its toll on her.

This dinner party given by a business associate of Nathaniel's was a lavish affair, the guests being wealthy people of Sydney. Usually she would have enjoyed such a night, but Silvana's presence meant she had to be on her guard, never allowing herself to be alone with the spiteful woman. Thankfully, Silvana had spent the beginning of the evening attached to Nathaniel and praising him to all within earshot.

A young man, with bright blond hair sat on Nicola's left and he turned to her with a crooked smile. 'Mrs West, you are not eating.'

She looked down at her plate, the delicious meal of roast pigeon, half consumed. 'I don't have much of an appetite tonight.' Forcing a smile, she racked her mind for this man's name, but couldn't remember it, and her headache grew worse. The room grew stuffy. If only someone would open a window, even for just a minute, to let in the cool winter air.

'Perhaps something else might suit you?'

'Lord, no. I'll not put the staff to any trouble. I doubt I could eat anything at all, actually. My head—'

'What an ungrateful person you are, daughter,' Silvana whispered from across the table. 'The food is simply divine.'

Nicola's hand clenched on the snowy white tablecloth. She blushed with embarrassment as the people closest turned in her direction. She also hated it when Silvana called her daughter. 'I am not ungrateful at all, Silvana. I'm simply not feeling my best tonight that is all.'

'Then we'll send you home so you can rest.' Silvana's expression appeared caring, but Nicola saw the hardness in her eyes. 'Our hosts have many entertainments to amuse us for hours yet. I'm sure seeing your long face will only ruin the night for everyone.'

The young man beside Nicola tilted his head. 'That is hardly true, Madam. My parents wouldn't consider an unwell guest as being rude.' He turned to Nicola. 'Would you like to go upstairs to one of our rooms and lie down for a while?'

'That would be lovely...Mr Channing.' She sighed in relief at finally recalling his name. He was the son of Nathaniel's friend and their hosts. 'However, I shall go home I think.'

'Of course.' He signalled to a footman behind them and the man quickly bent over. 'Mrs West isn't feeling well. Alert Mr West that she wishes to go home and collect her wrap.'

The footman nodded and walked to the end of the table where Nathaniel sat talking to their hostess. Nicola missed Nathaniel's reaction to the message as Silvana was talking again.

'All this fuss over such nonsense,' she twittered brightly to the older gentleman on her right. 'I declare a trifling headache is hardly worth all this effort.'

'You have suffered no effort on my behalf, Madam.' Nicola grounded out, standing. Mr Channing stood also just as Nathaniel appeared beside her.

'Darling, you are unwell?' He peered anxiously at her as if to see some injury.

'A headache, my love,' she whispered, blushing deeper at the attention she now had of the entire table. 'I just need to go home and rest.'

Their hosts came alongside of Nicola, full of concern, but she urged them back to the table and their guests, before thanking Mr Channing for his assistance.

Silvana rose dramatically. 'And I was enjoying myself too.'

Nicola gave her a cold stare, anxious to be away from her for a few hours. 'Then you must stay, Silvana, I insist.' She turned to Nathaniel, lowering her voice. 'Stay with your mother and enjoy the evening. I'll have Timms drive me home and then he'll return for you both.'

He walked out of the room with her to the waiting maid, who held her silk wrap. He placed the flimsy golden material around her shoulders. 'Sweetheart, I want to come with you.'

'I'll be fine, really. You stay with your mother. Fran will be home from her meeting by now. If not, I'll go to bed and have Mrs Rawlings bring me up a cup of cocoa.' She kissed his cheek. 'I'll likely be asleep within minutes.'

'Are you sure?'

She cupped his cheek when he kissed her softly. 'I'm perfectly sure.' As she turned away, she noticed Silvana standing in the doorway, a cold calculated look on her face. Nicola shivered as the butler opened the front door, but she knew it was in response to her mother-in-law and not the cool night air. How long could she hold up against the awful woman?

* * *

THE LITTLE BELL tinkled as Silvana entered the small dressmaker's shop. She paused and looked around the dingy interior, which despite the owner's best efforts still held the appearance of poor quality. However, for her assignment today it proved to be perfect.

'Ah, Mrs West, I take it?' A woman in her forties, her grey-streaked hair put up in a tight bun, stepped from behind the counter.

Silvana inclined her head and searched for any customers.

'There's no one here but me, Madam.'

'Good.'

'Your man is waiting out in the lane behind the shop.' The dressmaker led Silvana through a curtained doorway and into a back room piled high with crates of material and articles of her trade. After opening a rear door, she stopped to allow Silvana to go outside.

On the step, Silvana hesitated. From her silk reticule, she pulled out a small purse of coins and placed them in the woman's hand. 'You never saw me.'

'Your man has already paid me, Madam.' The woman said, though she grabbed the purse.

'I am buying your silence some more.' Silvana stared intently into her eyes. 'You may prove useful another time.'

'At your service, Madam.' The woman bowed and disappeared back inside, closing the door.

Taking a deep breath, Silvana turned and hurried up the narrow mean yard to the lane beyond. A man sat on a cart, for all the world looking like a tradesman making a delivery. Silvana waited for him to climb down and then she finally stared into Tristan Lombard's face.

'Mrs West.' He tugged the brim of his hat and smirked as though this was a huge joke. 'Like my attire?'

'Shut up, you fool. And don't ever say my name again. You think this is a game?' She gripped her reticule in frustration.

Lombard reddened and straightened up. 'Listen, Madam, I'm not some street urchin you can insult on a whim.'

'No, but you need me as much as I need you. So, let us begin.' She glanced around the lane nervously.

Lombard folded his arms, watching her intently. 'Why are you doing this? I'm no admirer of your son's wife, but your plan is—'

'My plan makes sense. I want Nat and Frances back in England with me. I need them there and the family will benefit from Nat's money. This country,' she grimaced, 'will never prosper. It will never rival England and so they are wasted here.'

'And so you think they will simply follow mother duck home?'

'Don't be impertinent.' Silvana's jaw cracked and she realised she'd been clenching her teeth. She forced herself to relax, to concentrate on the job at hand. 'All that keeps my son here is his wife. With her gone, he will come home. I shall make sure of it.'

Lombard leaned against the cart, humour lurking in his eyes. 'I'd like to see the mighty Nat West be brought under control by his mother. He's too sure of himself by far.'

Silvana stiffened. 'Are you willing to help me in this or not? Because if you think this is some joke—'

His expression changed, became serious. 'You want me to get rid of Nicola West. That is far from being a joke.'

'Are you able to do such a thing without making a mistake?' She lowered her voice. 'There are to be no traces left behind.'

'There won't be.'

'It happened last time. Nat is after your blood over that stabbing.'

He leaned in closer to her, a look of evilness in his eyes. Despite herself, she took a step back. 'That was just a warning. I assure you, Madam, this time it will be perfect.'

CHAPTER 22

I thought when you were with child you put weight on, not take it off?' Florence laughed, bending to wipe the last desk in the row.

'Yes, I believe so.' Nicola forced a smile, hiding her true emotions. She finished stacking books on the shelf on the far wall of the schoolroom and turned to survey their work.

Three neat rows of desks and chairs waited for children to occupy them. The chalkboard was in place behind the main desk at the front, the floorboards were swept, the two windows cleaned, and the little black stove was shining and filled with kindling ready to be lit. Finally, the schoolroom was ready to be used after weather delays, setbacks in the building of it and the government's hindrance in allowing them to be recognised as an official place of learning. However, tomorrow the orphaned children, now numbering twelve, would begin lessons, as well as any children from the surrounding streets.

'What is it?' Florence had closed the gap between them. 'You've been quiet for weeks now, much quieter than your normal self. Everyone has mentioned it.'

'Would you prefer I didn't come here so much then?' She smiled through her misery. Outside the orphaned children played, their laughter drifting through to them.

'Don't talk nonsense. We are all happy that you spend so much time with us. Your efforts in the last month have really made a difference with the agency. Why half a dozen women have arrived here and left just as quickly with situations secured. None of that would have been possible without your energies and commitment.'

'I like my work here.'

'But there's something more, isn't there?' Florence's concern touched Nicola deeply. 'You haven't been your usual self. I declare I haven't heard you laugh for at least two months.'

Laugh? Nicola couldn't remember the last time she laughed. 'I'm sure you are exaggerating.'

'You are pale, and your eyes look troubled, Nicola. I'm not the only one who sees this.'

Except my husband.

Nicola squeezed Florence's hand and moved down the row of desks. 'I am perfectly well.'

'Do you think you can fool me? I know you too well. We've shared the same house and worked too closely not to. I know all of your moods and emotions now.' Florence pulled out two of the chairs. 'Come and sit a while. You have worry lines on your face that weren't there a couple of months ago. You may have a bit of a stomach now, but your arms and shoulders show a thinness that's not natural. Why aren't you eating properly? Come, talk to me.'

Sighing, feeling heavy and cumbersome in her eighth month of pregnancy, Nicola lowered herself onto the small chair. 'There really isn't anything to talk about.' But even as she spoke, her chin wobbled. Suddenly, she was stifling the sobs that had been building for months.

Florence held her close, rubbing her back in long smooth strokes. 'Unburden yourself, I insist. You know it'll go no further.'

Sniffling and rummaging in her skirt pockets for a handkerchief, she tried to stem the flow of tears, but they seemed unstoppable now she'd finally given in to the release. 'I don't know how to speak of it.'

'Start at the beginning. That's usually the best place.'

'My mother-in-law, Silvana, detests me.' Nicola twisted the handkerchief in her fingers. 'I wouldn't mind that so much, for I do not like her either, but you see, she hides her hatred under a coating of false smiles and kind words. She has captured Nathaniel and Frances in her spell. In front of them she is a devoted loving mother, one they have never had before, so of course they are so happy to receive such attention.'

'And you canna tell them how she treats you?'

'No. I see their pleasure and cannot ruin it for them. Though I know Silvana is only acting in that regard, too.' A ragged sigh escaped her. 'I have tried to cope, but she is becoming more spiteful to me every day. She is also very clever and is never caught doing it. She waits for them to leave the house and then she starts on me.'

'That is why you are spending all your days here.'

Nicola nodded. 'She monopolises Nathaniel and Frances's time and I cannot bear to be in her company. So, I come here to work, to forget her until it is dark and I must return home. Yet, I use my condition as an excuse and stay home when they go out to the theatre or to a function.'

'Oh, Nicola.'

'I should have seen this coming from that very first day.'

'Can you not speak about this to your husband?'

'No. It would break his heart. I won't do it to him. He's finally getting the love from his mother that he's been waiting his whole life. Frances is the same. Her relationship with Silvana is growing and Frances is amazed that her mother is showing interest in her charity work. Silvana even worked at the soup kitchen the other day! How could I take all that from them?'

'But doesn't Mr West see the difference in you, as I do?'

Nicola smiled lovingly. 'I allow him to think the baby is taking all my energy. You must understand, Nathaniel is not himself lately. His mother's attentions have surprised him in a way he never expected, plus he is to be a father. All of these changes have altered our lives. Besides, we never seem to have a minute alone lately.'

'When does she leave to sail home?'

'She won't decide on a date. Last night at dinner she hinted that she might go in the New Year. How can I bear another four months of her company?'

'Well, I know one thing. Tonight, you will stay here with us. I'll send a note to your home and tell them we are having a meeting or something and you'll be back in the morning.'

Nicola stood, her back aching from the uncomfortable chair. 'No, it is impossible. Thank you though, for caring.'

'You mustn't let this continue, Nicola. You'll become ill and you need your strength for the birth.'

Taking a deep breath, she shrugged. 'I cannot eat at the same table as her.'

'Come into the house, we'll have luncheon and you will eat it all. Mrs Nesbit hasn't been drunk for a month now and is cooking up a storm. Yesterday, she baked two dozen macaroons for the children, despite her yelling every five minutes that they are under her feet and she'll take a horsewhip to them.' Florence gave an exaggerated wink and slipped her hand through Nicola's arm as they walked outside. 'Perhaps we'll take the horsewhip to your mother-in-law instead.'

Leaving the schoolroom, Nicola smiled at Miss Barker

and the children playing. They seemed happy and she knew they were well cared for. Hopefully they would grow to be good people. When she looked up towards the house she saw Mr Belfroy walking slowly down towards her. 'I didn't think you were calling by today, Mr Belfroy.' Her smile disappeared on seeing his troubled face, an expression she knew all too well. 'What is it?'

'Ah, Mrs West, Miss Florence.' He tipped his hat to them as the drizzly rain started. They hurried back up the slope through the trees. Behind them, Miss Barker called the children into the dormitory.

Inside, Nicola shook the raindrops from her skirt. 'You shouldn't be out in such weather, Mr Belfroy.'

'It wasn't raining this morning when I started out, and I'm glad I did venture outdoors today as I found a dear lady in need of our help.'

'Oh?' Nicola gestured into the study and followed him in with Florence. 'Where did you find her?'

'She's recently arrived from New Zealand but has had severe misfortunes in both that country and this. Her name is Jane Percival.' Mr Belfroy creaked onto a chair by the small glowing fire. 'I found her walking down Macquarie Street, the look of her was the first clue to her dilemma. She had the worn face of a lady who has endured too much. I watched her for a while. She was looking in shop windows and reading the little cards on display, you know the type that list rooms to let or positions offered. I spoke to her about them and she told me of her need for employment.'

'Why didn't you bring her with you?'

'She wouldn't take my assurances that I meant her no harm. I believe she has been mistreated dreadfully in the past.' He leaned on his cane placed between his knees. 'I told her to wait at her lodgings and I'd fetch you to her.'

'I'll get my cloak.'

'Nicola,' Florence stepped forward, her eyes full of meaning, 'perhaps I should go?'

'No, thank you, Florence. I'll do it. I need to have something to do or go mad.'

'Very well. I'll organise a bed for Miss Percival and food for you on your return.'

In the hall, as they readied to leave, Miss Hunt, a newly arrived governess came out of the parlour, her face glowing with joy. 'Oh, Mr Belfroy, Mrs West, Miss McIntyre, you'll never guess my news.'

'Happy news I gather?' Florence asked, helping Nicola with her cloak.

'Why yes, I've been appointed as a companion to Mrs Carlisle, who is returning to England a fortnight tomorrow.'

'Are you pleased to be sailing to England, Miss Hunt?' Nicola asked, pulling on her gloves.

'Yes, very much so. I never thought I would, but I feel my luck has run out in this country. I've managed to pay back my debt to Miss Rye's Society and am now free to do as I please.'

'Then I'm happy for you.' Nicola patted the younger woman's shoulder. 'We'll have a celebration meal next week for you.'

Once in the carriage, Nicola leaned against the seat, grimacing as her back ached. How she wished Silvana was also returning to England in a fortnight.

* * *

'As fast as you can, Timms.' Nat called up to the driver as he opened the carriage door and climbed in after Frances. Once they were seated, the carriage lurched forward on its way to George Street.

'Why the rush, Nat?' Frances scowled, adjusting her hat.

'My appointment at the dressmakers isn't until one. I thought we could share a meal somewhere. I've been at the soup kitchen all morning and am famished.'

'I've business to deal with. I'll have to drop you off, I'm sorry.'

'Well thank you for stopping to collect me. I didn't want to be caught in the rain.'

He reclined against the seat and stared out the window at the passing traffic and buildings. A light rain fell from low grey clouds. The dismal day suited his mood and the errand he was on. A note had been passed into his hands this morning concerning Lombard. The stupid fool had surfaced again at one of the gentlemen's clubs last night. Nat's gut clenched at the thought of getting hold of his onetime friend.

'Nat?'

'Hmm?' He turned to Frances, his mind full of Lombard.

'I wanted to talk to you about Nicola.'

'Oh?' His thoughts turned to his darling wife and he frowned. Lately she seemed out of sorts, but he put it down to the pregnancy. She was working too much, too. He rarely saw her, only at night, and usually she was so tired she would fall asleep the instant they climbed into bed.

'I think something is wrong with her.'

His heart squeezed painfully. 'How do you mean, wrong?'

'She's not sleeping or eating properly.' Frances's grey eyes grew anxious. 'I saw her last night. It was very late, around two in the morning. She'd been in the study getting a book. She wore only her nightclothes and I could see how pale and thin she is.'

He nodded. Nicola's weight loss on her arms and legs had worried him as well, but again he put the blame on the growing child inside her. 'I'll encourage her to eat more. The child is likely taking all her energy.'

'I might suggest we spend the day together tomorrow.

Just the two of us...oh, no I can't I promised mother I'd go sailing on the harbour with her and some friends.'

'I'll organise something.' Nat rubbed his chin, thinking. 'It's been too long since we had time alone. Her days are filled with visiting the Home, I've let my business occupy my time and Mother's arrival has dominated everything.'

'Nicola has been sadly neglected, Nat. We must do better.'

'Yes, you're right, as always.' He smiled. 'I'll buy Nicola some jewellery. I don't buy her enough pretty things. She never asks for anything.'

'Because that's not Nicola's way. She's too good for you.' She chuckled.

'I know that.'

'Mother likes her, so that is something.' Frances tapped her reticule. 'There have been times in the last few months when I have believed I was dreaming. It is incredible to think of our mother being here and of her behaviour, which is so different to how it was back home.'

'True. I couldn't have been more surprised by Mother's affections. Such a radical change gave me many doubts, but we've talked at great length about the past. She admits her dealings with us were shameful, but she knew no better, it was how she was raised.'

'I'm sorry it took so long and Father's death, for her to admit it though. Our lives could have been very different.'

Nat grasped her hand. 'The past is done with. Although I was sceptical at first, and disbelieving of her intentions, Mother has done everything she can to make things right again between us. We must accept Mother's apology and forgive her. She is trying to make amends and I cannot reject her.'

'I have forgiven her, but it is hard to forget her coldness sometimes. My childhood, and yours, was quite ruined because of her and father.'

He glanced out the window, remembering his childhood and the loneliness of it. The bond he always wanted with his father would never be now, but he had a chance with his mother, and despite the pain she inflicted on him as a child, he couldn't refuse her offerings of love now. He'd waited too long for it. 'She says she has changed, and she is trying to show us. Can we turn our backs on her when she is trying so hard to make it up to us?'

'It wasn't easy, Nat, when she first came. I expected the worst.'

'You weren't alone in that.' He'd spent many sleepless nights curled up with Nicola, wondering at the change in his mother. Weeks of her showering love on him, showed him how wonderful it was to be cherished by a parent. Now, the love he'd always wanted to give his mother came pouring out. In part, he had to thank Nicola for change within himself, because her affection and devotion had shown him that to love another is not only fulfilling, but also healing.

'Sometimes I fear all this happiness won't last, Nat,' Fran whispered. 'I'm not used to it.'

'Nor I, dearest.' He squeezed her hand. Then, as the carriage slowed to a halt at the top of George Street, he opened the door for her. 'I'll be home at five.'

Frances paused half out the door. 'Oh, before I forget, has there been any news on Lombard?'

Nat kept his expression neutral and lied through his teeth. 'Nothing substantial yet.'

As the carriage rolled away down the street, he let out a breath and thought of the distasteful business ahead. If Lombard thought it safe to return to town, then he was greatly mistaken.

Peering out of the rain splattered window, Nat recognised the grim old buildings along the wharfs at Wooloomooloo Bay. A weather-beaten inn, with the grand name of The Shining Star Hotel stood at one end of an ugly street and here Timms halted the horses. Nat climbed down and shivered in the cold rain-filled wind blowing off the water.

'Is this the right place, Mr West?' Timms called down.

'I believe so, Timms. Stay here, I'll be back shortly.' Nat crossed the road and headed into the hotel. Inside the doorway, he paused to allow his eyes to adjust to the murky room. Smoke from the ill-kept fireplace and the patrons' pipes hung in a thick pall at ceiling height. A few villainous looking men straddled chairs by the dirty window, each had a grubby hand around a tankard. Quietness settled over the room as the barman and his two other customers turned to stare at him from their position at the bar.

'Can I help you, sir?' The barman, a big, balding man with a long black beard, leaned his podgy hands flat on the bar top.

Nat stretched to his full height, giving each man in the room a careful assessment. 'Indeed, you can, friend.' He stepped to the counter, slid his hand across it towards the barkeeper and lifted up his fingers to reveal the wad of money under his hand. 'A simple transaction, my good man,' Nat murmured.

The barkeeper's eyes grew wide at the amount of money he saw. 'Which would be?'

Nat leaned closer, dropping his head and shoulder to shield them from the others. 'Tristan Lombard.'

The barman straightened, grabbed a cloth from beneath the counter and plucked a glass from the shelf behind him, which he wiped vigorously. 'Can't recall him.'

'Is that so?' Nat grinned, knowing the game. 'Very well. I'll have my friends, the town's officials, close down this hotel by tomorrow night until they have checked your licence and who knows how long that might take.... Good day.' He turned to leave.

'Wait.'

'Yes?' Nat lingered a moment as the barman shifted his weight from foot to foot, swallowed and then ever so slightly tilted his head to the right, indicating the door in the corner.

'Thank you.' Nat slid his hand across and placed the money near the cloth on the bar. Without looking back, he left the barroom and went through the door in the corner. The narrow corridor was dark and smelt of damp. Beyond a steep staircase was another door, partly opened, showing a crude kitchen area.

Taking a deep breath, Nat looked up at the dimness of the landing above and then took the stairs two at a time.

'Where is Nathaniel?' Nicola asked Frances, divesting her wet outer clothes in the hall.

'He said he'd be home for five o'clock.' Frances, her eyes bright and cheeks red, took Nicola's hand. 'Come join mother and me in the parlour, we're drinking some fine Madeira.'

'How many have you had?' Nicola smiled, entering the hot room. A fire blazed and the dark green curtains were drawn against the dismal weather.

'Not nearly as many as I would like.' Fran giggled, dragging her across the room to sit on the sofa. 'Mother started way before I did, I tried to catch up.'

'Are we celebrating?'

'I've had a very good day.' Silvana, who sat opposite, announced. 'Everything is as it should be, or it will be soon.'

Nicola stiffened at Silvana's scowl and her low words. 'Good evening, mother-in-law.'

'It was a good evening until you came home.' Silvana's lip curled, something Nicola was used to seeing.

'Mother!' Shocked Frances straightened from her collapsed position at the end of the sofa.

'Well, really, Frances, I find it quite sh-shocking that she is never home.' Silvana hiccupped. 'Nicola, you allow your servants too much free-freedom. Why my son married you I'll never understand.'

Hiding a delighted smile at her mother-in-law's slip of behaviour, Nicola raised an eyebrow. 'Your son married me, Madam, because he loves me, and if allowing my servants too much freedom is my only flaw, then I will be most pleased.'

'Only flaw!' Silvana spluttered. 'Don't make me laugh.' She gulped down the last of her drink and held her glass up to Frances. 'More, if you pl-please.'

Frances slowly rose to her feet, the colour draining from her face, and took the glass. 'Perhaps you've had enough, Mother?'

'Do you dare to tell me what to do?' Silvana's tone was icy. 'I take orders from no one. I refused to take them from your father and I'll not take them from you either.'

'I wasn't ordering you, Mother, simply suggesting that...'

Silvana stumbled up from the chair. 'Be quiet, damn you.'

Nicola rose also, although it was difficult with her large stomach. 'I think a lie down is in order.'

'Shut it, you! How dare you even speak to me, you're nothing but a trollop. I know all about you and your kind.'

'Mother!' Frances gasped, instantly sober.

It dawned on Silvana that she'd gone too far, and she covered her mouth, sinking onto the chair. 'Dear God.' She reached out to Frances. 'Dearest, oh how could I have behaved so badly? I've drunk more than I care to admit. I-I'm so dreadfully sorry, Fran.'

'I think it is Nicola you need to apologise to.' Frances

stepped away from her mother's hand, a look of disgust on her features.

Gathering herself, Silvana smiled lovingly at Nicola. 'You must forgive me, Nicola dearest. I am not one who is used to strong liquor. I-I'm not myself, you see...' She squeezed out a tear to go along with her begging tone. 'Say you'll forgive me, I implore you.'

Nicola saw through her act. Yet, as she had continued to do since the woman arrived, she pretended otherwise. 'I think, perhaps, you should go and lie down.'

'Er...yes, of course.' Silvana reached out for her, but Nicola recoiled as if burnt.

'Mother, I advise you to retire for the night.' Frances rang the bell and immediately the door was opened by Mrs Rawlings. 'My mother is unwell, Mrs Rawlings, will you escort her to her room, please?'

'A pleasure, Miss West.' Rawlings gave Nicola a quick glance before helping the older woman from the room.

Nicola moved past Frances and grabbed the iron poker from its stand and jabbed at the roaring fire to reduce the flames. The crackling sparks going up the chimney was the only sound in the room. She straightened, putting the poker back on its stand. 'What were you celebrating to cause you to drink so much?'

'Mother had some good news, but I can't think if she actually told me what it was.' Fran shivered and rubbed her arms. 'Am I wrong to think that this isn't the first time my mother has been unkind to you?'

Nicola stared into the orange embers falling beneath the grate. 'I think enough has been said this evening, Fran.'

'Then I am correct.'

'I'll go upstairs and change.' Nicola turned, and keeping her gaze lowered, moved past Frances.

'Have Nat and I been so blind?' Her anguished cry halted Nicola as nothing else would.

'You've wanted the mother you've always dreamed of. There is nothing wrong in that.'

Tears gathered in Fran's eyes and slipped over her lashes as if they were in a race. 'What has she done?'

'Fran, I'm rather tired...'

'Mother is the reason why you aren't eating or sleeping and why you spend all your time at the Home. I want the truth now. What has she been saying?'

'Hardly anything at all.' How could she shatter Fran's happiness? She tried to think of an excuse to leave but gazing into her dear friend's face she realised that excuses wouldn't work.

'You're lying.'

'She...she mentioned that she wants you and Nathaniel to return to England with her.' Nicola shrugged as though they were discussing social gossip.

'And?'

'And that...that she would prefer it if I stayed here.' The hurt of those words clawed at her chest.

Fran blinked. The shock clear on her face. 'How have we been so stupid...so gullible?' She went to embrace Nicola, but habit made Nicola jump out of the way.

'What is it?' Anger now replaced Fran's astonishment. 'You recoiled from Mother too. In fact, you jumped as though you'd been scalded.' She jerked forward and grabbed Nicola's arms. 'I demand the truth.'

Nicola opened her mouth to speak but her voice dried up.

Frances glanced down and frowning, pulled up Nicola's sleeves that displayed old and new bruises received from Silvana's pinches. A punishment Silvana had delivered at every opportunity.

'Mother did this to you?' Fran gasped, disbelievingly.

She could only nod.

'Why?'

'She...she hates me. I'm not good enough for her family and so she punishes me with vile insults and pinching when no one is here.'

'I cannot believe it.' Fran stared at the bruises, stroking them gently. 'I should have known her concern wasn't genuine, but it was so nice to be loved by her at long last...'

'I know.'

'She used to pinch me, too...' Fran looked up, her face the colour of putty. 'Why didn't you tell us?'

'I didn't want to make you and Nathaniel unhappy.'

'I knew something wasn't right.' Fran's chin wobbled, anger blazed in her eyes for a second before desolation replaced it. 'I-I said to Nat only today, in the carriage, that there was something troubling you.'

'I wanted to speak up, truly I did.'

'Oh, Nicola.' Bent like an old woman, Fran stumbled over to the sofa. 'What have we done? What have we *done!*' Her heartbreaking sobs filled the room and Nicola rushed to offer what comfort she could.

'This will crush Nat.' Fran choked on a sob.

Nicola stiffened. 'No, it won't. I will make sure it doesn't.'

* * *

ON THE HOTEL LANDING, Nat opened the first door on the left, an empty bedroom. The next door revealed the same, as did the third. The last door was locked. He knocked.

'Who is it?'

Nat grimaced, recognising Lombard's voice inside. 'Barman,' Nat said gruffly behind his hand.

'I don't want to be disturbed.'

'Got a note for you.' Nat waited, heard a thump and a

several swear words and then the pleasing sound of the lock being drawn back. When the handle turned, and the door opened a crack, Nat put his shoulder to it and shoved.

'What the hell?' Lombard fell backwards onto the floor.

Nat got his balance quickly and hauled him up by his shirt. 'Did you miss me, Tristan?' he asked, just before he smashed his fist into Lombard's face. The pain of bone on bone ricocheted up his wrist and he bit back a groan.

Lombard hung off Nat like a limp doll. 'West, look, you don't need to do this.'

'Don't I?' Nat brought his fist down again, smashing the man's nose. The renewed pain in his hand made him drop his hold of Lombard.

Howling, Lombard writhed on the floor, blood spewing from his nose. 'You bastard! Ah God, Christ almighty,' he gasped, swearing, crying.

Nat stood over him. 'How pathetic you are. Get up.' He dragged Lombard to his knees and brought back his fist again.

'No, for the love of Christ, no. I can't take anymore.'

'Don't be a girl, I've only hit you twice.' Nat spat, leering close. 'My wife was stabbed.'

'I'm sorry, so sorry. I never meant for that to happen.'

'You coward, you can't even own up to it. You did want it to happen. Own up to it. Say it, for God's sake before I kill you!' Rage brought Nat's fist down on Lombard's cheek. This time the pain of it made Nat cradle his fist in his other hand and swear violently. He had to stop aiming for the face and use the stomach instead.

Lombard, blood covering his face, scrambled away, crab-like, his pitiful wails filling the room. 'I'm sorry, Nat. Enough, enough. I never meant for it to go this far.' He spat blood. 'I-I just was desperate... I needed Carstairs's shipment, you knew that. My debts...'

'You've always got debts! I've bailed you out time and again and this is how you repay me?'

'I'm sorry, Nat. I'll never go near her again, I promise, no matter what.'

'Too right you won't.' Nat advanced, the urge to kick his teeth in too strong to resist.

Holding his hand up, crouched over like a wounded animal, Lombard begged. 'Enough Nat, no more, please. I'll not do it, I promise.'

Nat stilled. 'Do what?' He waited for Tristan to say more, but the man just cried, dribbling blood down his white shirt. 'Do *what*, you bastard?' Nat hauled him up again. 'What had you planned?'

'It was her plan, not mine. I didn't want to get involved but she offered a lot of money - money that I need.'

'Who?' Nat racked his brain trying to understand his meaning. 'Tell me or I'll kill you now, you worthless piece of scum.'

'I can't.'

'You will.' He shook him like a rag doll. 'Whose plan and what was it?'

'She wanted me to get rid of your wife.'

'Who did?'

'Your mother!'

The room spun. Dizzy, Nat dropped Lombard like a sack of coal, uncaring of anything but the one word whirling around his brain. Mother.

A pain so acute ripped his chest apart. It felt like a red-hot poker was thrust through his body aimed straight for his heart. He stumbled. The surroundings blurred then came back into focus making him feel sick. Silence pounded in his ears. Instinct told him to run, to hide from the hurt, but a burning ember of fury grew, replacing all thought.

As though his feet had grown wings, he dashed from the

room, down the stairs and out of the barroom. Out in the street he ran through the rain, splashing across puddles to the carriage. 'Home. Now!' He shouted to Timms and threw himself into the carriage.

The drive home in the deepening darkness seemed interminable. He couldn't think or feel – was numb to all sense as his rage built. His nerves were shredded raw by the time Timms halted the horses in front of the house. The wheels hadn't fully stopped before he jumped from the carriage and bolted inside. The parlour door opened as he made for the staircase. He jerked around and stared at Nicola. Anguish clouded her eyes. She looked so forlorn and lost and his heart shattered into pieces. She *knew*. She knew his mother had deceived them.

She'd known all along.

For a moment he couldn't move, couldn't breathe.

'My love,' she said softly, 'There's something I must tell you.'

'Nic…I…'

She glanced at his red and bloody hand gripping the banister and frowned. 'Will you come with me?'

Emotion burnt his throat, draining his anger. He couldn't do it again. He couldn't go through the pain of seeing his mother's ridicule, of knowing she never cared for him. 'Where-where is she?'

'Your mother is upstairs in her room sleeping. No, don't go up.' She held out her hand and he forced himself to go to her.

In the parlour, he allowed her to guide him to the sofa and she sat beside him. The warmth of the room felt stifling and he pulled at his stiff collar.

She held his hand. 'How did you find out?'

'Lombard.'

Nicola shuddered, and he wanted to drag her into his

301

arms, but couldn't. He felt detached, frozen. Where had his rage gone? He understood anger. He'd lived with it long enough to find it a strange comfort. But this numbness was new to him and he didn't like it. He felt out of control of the situation.

'What of Lombard?' Nicola murmured, as if afraid to say his name.

'I found him. I went to confront him about what happened to you, but he also gave me further information, details which I never expected.'

'In regards to your mother and me?'

'Yes.'

'What did you do to him?'

He raised his hand and studied his swollen knuckles. 'He'll live. Unfortunately.'

'He is another one who belongs in the past now.'

A deep sigh left him. How had he let his life get so unmanageable?

'Do you love me, Nathaniel?'

He stared at Nicola, uncomprehending. 'You know I do. You are my life.'

'Am I enough to make you truly happy?'

'Yes.'

'And you will love the child, too?'

'Yes. Nicola, I—'

She nodded, holding his hands tightly. 'Do you remember the time we spent in the country after our wedding?'

'Of course.' He shifted in the seat, needing to get up and move about but she held him fast.

'That was the happiest time of my life, I think.'

He blinked, watching her. Where was this leading? He wanted to deal with his mother and talk to Frances... Oh God, Frances! He had to tell her.

Nicola smiled, a warm loving smile he hadn't seen for

many months. 'I would like our baby to be born at the country property.'

His heart restricted at the thought of holding his child. He longed to hold his son or daughter. But now wasn't the time to discuss this.

'We have a bright future ahead of us. We have love and we will have a wonderful family.' Nicola leaned over and kissed him softly on the lips. 'I love you completely, without restraint or conditions.'

Nat closed his eyes and felt a hot tear roll down his cheek and then another. How had he deserved this wonderful woman? 'Nic...'

She cradled his head against her breast and let him pour out his misery.

Sometime later, he straightened, feeling exhausted but better. He'd accepted what his mother had done. Now he just wanted to get rid of her for once and for all.

'Remember, whatever happens or is said tonight, remember that I love you and soon our baby will be here to love you too.' Nicola rose, and he stood also, gathering her into his arms as much as her stomach allowed. She held him tight and he couldn't get enough of her embrace. It seemed like a very long time since they had held each other properly. Shame washed over him. How had he let his mother come before this magnificent woman who loved him so much? Had he been so desperate for his mother's love, more than he ever realised?

'Come, it is time.'

He hesitated. 'Frances.'

'She knows too. Your mother's acting skills let her down once she is drunk.'

'I cannot believe I was such a fool.' Again, shame filled him.

'No.' She shook her head. 'I will not allow her to make

you suffer anymore. Your mother deserves nothing from you, not your love, your anger, your pity, nothing. Cut her from your heart and mind, Nathaniel, you cannot heal unless you do.'

'I feel nothing for her now.' It was the truth. At this very moment he felt dead inside where his mother was concerned.

'Good.' Nicola's gentle smile soothed his spirit. 'While waiting for your return, I arranged for Mrs Rawlings to secure tickets for your mother and her maid on the first available outbound ship. We are fortunate that there is one leaving at midnight. It only goes as far as India, but that is your mother's worry. Timms can take your mother down to the quay and make sure she boards.'

'Thank you. Though it grieves me to know you've had the trouble of doing this alone.'

She grinned. 'Believe me, it was no trouble. I received an obscene amount of pleasure in doing it.'

Arm in arm they left the room and headed upstairs. Frances met them on the landing. Without knocking they entered Silvana's bedroom. Her maid, Agatha was nowhere to be seen, and Silvana slept soundly on top of the bed. Fran shook her shoulder to waken her and then stepped back to ring the bell by the bed.

'Who dares to wake me?' Silvana snapped, sitting up. She turned, her eyes widening at the sight of them. 'What is it? Has something happened?'

'Yes, Mother, something has.' Nat smiled grimly, just wishing for it to be done with. 'We've rung for your maid, so she can pack your things.'

'Pack? What are you talking about?' She put a hand to her forehead, wincing. 'I've a dreadful headache.'

'That will be the least of your problems, Mother.' Frances picked up a coat laid across a chair. She threw it onto the bed as though the touch of it defiled her. 'Start gathering your things.'

A fleeting look of panic crossed Silvana's face. 'I don't understand.'

'It's easy, Mother.' Nat pulled Nicola in closer to him for support and with his other hand he reached out to take Fran's hand. 'We have finally seen through your charade. There will be no more games. No more lies and false declarations of love. I have dealt with Lombard, who conveniently spilled the information of your treacherous little plan. It is over. Finished.'

'Nat...' She glanced at Fran. 'Frances, dearest...'

He stepped forward and nearly laughed at the frantic desperation in his mother's face. 'You're going back to England, Mother, and you will never contact us again. I will deal directly through Gerald concerning our inheritance. My solicitor in London will be instructed to ensure that none of my money flows into the family coffers. Father left the townhouse in Kensington, where you live, to me. On your return to London you will remove your belongings and leave the house. From now on, you'll have to rely on the money Father left you and what Gerald can do for you. As far as Frances and I are concerned you are now dead to us.'

Silvana jerked to her feet, an ugly grimace marring her features. 'I won't allow it!'

'You have no choice. If you cause problems over my decisions, then I will return to England and publicly denounce you as my mother, and the world will know of the distasteful person that you are.'

She turned to Nicola, her eyes narrowing with loathing. 'This is all your fault!'

'Actually, Madam, it is yours.' Nicola smiled grimly. 'You are unnatural, despicable, and you bring nothing with you but misery wherever you go. I should feel rather sorry for you, but I don't.' Her smile grew wider. 'In fact, I shall be the happiest woman in the country when you leave this house.'

Nat's chest swelled with pride at his darling girl's stance. Unable to tolerate being in his mother's presence another moment, he stalked from the room and the woman who'd done nothing for him but give him life.

Outside the door he stopped and held Frances. 'We'll be just as we were before. I promise.'

'Only better,' she whispered, before releasing him and turning to Nicola. 'I'm going to bed. Will you be all right?'

Nicola kissed her cheek. 'Perfectly fine. I'll see you in the morning. But if you need us in the night, just knock.'

When Frances left them, Mrs Rawlings came up the stairs. 'Mrs West, everything is as you wish it. Timms is waiting downstairs as requested.'

'Thank you, Mrs Rawlings. My husband and I are retiring early. Will you see that Mrs West's belongings are taken down and she is gone from the house within the hour?'

'With pleasure, Madam,' Mrs Rawlings said, with the mere hint of smirk on her lips.

Inside their bedroom, Nat pulled Nicola into his arms and kissed her with a deep yearning. 'I'm so sorry, sweetheart.'

'It is not your fault, Nathaniel. You mustn't let this be a burden you carry. I won't let you.'

'I cannot help feeling as though I have failed you, and Frances, but especially you.'

She grinned. 'Well, I have to say that when I first married you I did think that I might have women problems with you, but I never expected the other troublesome woman to be your mother.'

'It's not a laughing matter, Nicola.'

'Nonsense. We will laugh about this, because she doesn't deserve our tears.' She kissed him softly. 'We survived this.

There was an opportunity for us to flounder and break, for our marriage to be made a mockery by her. But we are the victorious ones, not Silvana.'

'I'm not worthy of you.' He rested his forehead against hers. 'I haven't been much of a husband lately, have I?'

'Shush. Enough of that. I'll hear no more of it.' She placed her finger against his lips. 'From tomorrow, no, from this minute, we begin again.' Taking his hand, she placed it over the bulge of her stomach. She smiled up at him as the baby kicked. 'We have so much to look forward too, my love.'

EPILOGUE

'Nicholas!' Nicola searched the crowd strolling through the gardens and buildings of the Governesses Home. A group of children ran past her and into the schoolroom, but her son wasn't amongst them. 'Where is that boy?'

'Leave him be, my dear.' Mr Belfroy chuckled from his chair under the Norfolk Pine. 'He'll come back when he's ready.'

Smiling, she walked over to stand by his chair. She placed her hand on his shoulder with the familiarity of old friends. 'He's spoilt.'

'Nonsense. He's a good boy.' Belfroy tapped his cane towards the gathering of Sydney's dignitaries. 'And he doesn't want to be bothered with that horde.'

Nicola grinned. 'You'll have to go up and deliver your speech soon.'

He sighed and pulled his hat brim a little lower. 'I don't know why. They don't want to hear the ramblings of an old man. They'd much rather listen to you.'

She groaned, feeling light-headed at the thought of

speaking in front of all those people. Instinctively, she looked for Nathaniel and spotted him talking to Sir Hercules Robinson, the Governor of New South Wales and other gentlemen of politics. Her nerves increased. When Florence first suggested a garden party to celebrate the ten-year anniversary of the Home's opening, Nicola hadn't thought she'd be making a speech, otherwise she'd not agreed to it.

'We've come a long way, Nicola.' Belfroy spoke into the comfortable silence between them.

That he called her by her first name for the first time surprised her more than she could say. 'Yes, we have, Mr Belfroy.' She swept her gaze around the property taking in the orchard and gardens, the orphanage dormitory, the schoolroom and lastly the back of the big house itself. 'Your commitment has brought a lot of happiness and hope to many people.'

'All this was your vision, my dear.' He slowly creaked to his feet. 'Without your ambition to help others and your tireless energy, none of this would be as it is.'

'But your generosity, your inherit kindness started it.' She supported him to stand upright. 'We make a good team, don't we?'

'That we do, my dear.' He tucked her hand through his arm and patted it. 'It was a lucky day when we met.'

'Very true.' Nicola thought back to the windy day when she'd been so hungry and despondent. Mr Belfroy had done more than give her a place to stay, he'd given her the chance to hope that her prospects would take a turn for the better, and they did.

'I'm sorry Hilton couldn't make it.'

She looked at him, pondering his words. Her family had become his, her children loved him like a grandfather, and he was Godfather to them, but was it enough for him? 'How is Mr Warner?'

'He works constantly from what I can gather from his letters. Hilton has amassed a colossal fortune.'

'He is happy?'

Belfroy shrugged as they began walking towards the crowd. 'Who am I to judge?'

'He's never come back to this country.'

'He never will, my dear.' Belfroy gave her a sorrowful look. 'When one's heart gets broken, we cannot keep returning to its source or we'd lose our sanity. No, he has a wife and two small sons and lives for his businesses. That is enough.'

'I didn't realise I'd hurt him so severely all those years ago. I am sorry for that.'

He patted her hand. 'It was an unintentional hurt, my dear. You know, anniversaries can be dreadful things.' Belfroy sighed. 'They make people remember things that are better left alone.' He patted her arm. 'Come, this isn't the occasion for sadness. Smile, my dear, or your husband will have me locked away for upsetting you.'

Grinning at the remark, Nicola covered his hand with hers. 'He wouldn't dare, he knows how much you mean to me.'

'Nicola. Mr Belfroy.' Florence, holding up the skirt of her green gown hurried towards them. 'It's time for the speeches.'

The serious expression she wore made Nicola want to laugh. 'Why are you looking so worried? You won't be talking in front of everyone.'

Florence, a twinkle of mischief in her eyes, dropped her skirt and straightened her shoulders. 'Being second in charge does have its advantages, you know.'

With her free arm, Nicola slipped it through Florence's. Together the three of them walked back up the garden to the paved area where people waited, eating and drinking. She left Florence to help Mr Belfroy get ready and quickly stepped over to Fran, who stood behind one of the refreshment tables. 'What are you doing? We hired staff to serve.'

Fran rolled her eyes. 'I thought I'd just help out for a moment as they got a little busy and well…I couldn't let them struggle for the want of hands.'

Hiding a smile, Nicola gestured for her to come out from behind there. 'You should be staying with your fiancé, the poor man.'

'Oh, he's right enough. He was debating with the mayor about the state of the roads near his shop.' Fran stood on tiptoe seeking out John Lawson, the baker and son of Mrs Lawson, who helped at the soup kitchen. John had courted Fran for eight years and she finally agreed to marry him next spring. The difference in their stations caused gossip at first, but Fran didn't bat an eyelid at that, as Nicola knew she wouldn't.

Nicola searched too, but for a different reason. 'Have you seen the children?'

'The girls were here…' Fran looked around, acknowledging certain guests with a nod of her head and a cheery smile. 'Milly was holding Thea's hand. They might have been looking for you or Bertha.'

'I told Bertha to keep a close watch on them today. There's too many people around and you know how little Thea is, she'll be trampled.'

'That's why Milly was holding her hand, mothering her, but I could tell she was bursting to run off and play.' Fran laughed.

Nicola raised an eyebrow. Her daughters were total opposites. Milly, at six years of age was dark like her father and older brother. Boldly beautiful, she behaved like a boy, which exasperated Nicola and consequently Milly was the apple of her Aunt Fran's eye. Whereas, Thea, only four, was a delicate image of Nicola and adored by her father. Most times, when Thea couldn't be found, one only had to look for Nathaniel and Thea would be close by.

'There they are.' Fran pointed to the area past the tea tables to a group of children sitting on the grass. Miss Barker was handing out macaroons to them. 'They are completely happy, so go and enjoy yourself.'

'Mama.' Nicola twisted around as Nicholas tugged on her sleeve. 'Mama, I've lost my spinning top.'

Before Nicola could reply, Fran took his hand. 'Come, Nicky, I'll help you find it.'

Nicola pushed back his light brown hair tenderly. He was a boy version of his father, complete with his violet eyes that Nicola adored so much. 'You look hot, my love. Go with Aunt Fran and get a drink, then ask the others to help find your top.' She watched them weave through the people and her heart swelled with love and happiness.

She turned as Florence drew the crowd together and announced Mr Belfroy. The people grew quiet and Nicola stepped closer to the house steps where Mr Belfroy stood.

'The poor fellow appears tired,' Nathaniel suddenly whispered in her ear from behind.

'He's old,' she whispered back, sad at the thought.

'He's lasted longer than any of us believed he would.'

She looked up at him from over her shoulder and felt his hands on her waist. He kissed her cheek and then concentrated on listening to Belfroy. Apart from a dusting of grey in his hair and the odd line around his eyes, Nathaniel was still the handsomest man she'd ever seen. Over the years, her love for him had only grown and deepened.

Within minutes, Belfroy was introducing her and indicating for Nicola to go up and join him on the steps. Taking a deep breath, she walked up to stand beside him and faced the crowd, who clapped loudly.

Smiling, she paused, and gathered her thoughts. So many familiar faces looked at her, friends, acquaintances and most importantly, former and current governesses. She took a deep breath. 'Distinguished guests, ladies and gentlemen, family and friends. Thank you all for coming on this special day as we celebrate ten years of Mr Belfroy's Home for Governesses being open.' Another round of clapping started and as she waited for it to ease, Nathaniel winked encouragingly.

Straightening her shoulders, Nicola raised her chin so her voice would carry. 'Early in eighteen sixty-seven, I heard Miss Maria Rye speak at an assembly. This great lady, who works tirelessly for the good of single, educated ladies, inspired me to come to Australia to work as a governess. Little did I know I would be working to help these dedicated women rather than be one. I am proud of what has been achieved here and my part in it.' She paused and stared lovingly at her family. 'But let me begin at the beginning...'

ABOUT THE AUTHOR

Hello,

If you enjoyed my story please leave a review online, it helps an author very much, and we appreciate them more than you know.

Thank you

AnneMarie Brear

Australian born AnneMarie Brear writes historical novels and modern romances and sometimes the odd short story, too. Her passions, apart from writing, are travelling, reading, eating her husband's delicious food, reading, researching, and dragging her husband around historical sites looking for inspiration for her next book.

Say hello to AnneMarie on her social media or join her newsletter please visit her website: **www. annemariebrear.com**

Lightning Source UK Ltd.
Milton Keynes UK
UKHW011836181221
395882UK00001B/169